Julia Alone

Ann Stevens took up writing in her middle years, after working and bringing up her two children. Her writing career took off quickly, with numerous short stories being published and winning competitions. She lives with her solicitor husband in a thatched cottage in a Devon village.

Julia Alone is her third novel, and follows the successful publication of *November Tree* in 1995 and *Finding Maggie* in 1997.

JULIA ALONE

Ann Stevens

HarperCollins*Publishers*

HarperCollins*Publishers*
77–85 Fulham Palace Road,
Hammersmith, London W6 8JB

A Paperback Original 1998
1 3 5 7 9 8 6 4 2

A catalogue record for this book
is available from the British Library

ISBN 0 00 651136 8

Typeset in Meridien by
Palimpsest Book Production Limited,
Polmont, Stirlingshire

Printed in Great Britain by
Caledonian International Book
Manufacturing Ltd, Glasgow

For Penny

PROLOGUE

It was my wedding day, and I was having cream on my cornflakes.

For good measure I scattered on some brown sugar and had just taken the first sinful spoonful when Natalie came into the kitchen.

Stupidly, I felt guilty, tucking in like a child before the rest of the family were up. But it was only half-past seven, and a Saturday. I hadn't reasonably expected to see anyone before nine. Defiantly, I took another spoonful, eyeing my daughter dubiously as I did so. She was wearing a long and baggy tee shirt which, even so, barely reached her knees. Her red hair, fresh from the pillow, was an unruly fuzz, her eyes were heavy with sleep. Her long legs and bony feet were bare.

'Darling, I've told you before. I don't think you should walk around like that. Not with Matt in the house. You're not a child any more.'

She was fourteen, getting daily more delectable. And more truculent. 'Oh – Matt,' she said dismissively, upending the cream jug over her bowl. 'You've taken all the cream,' she pouted.

'My day today, I can have what I want,' I joked. 'And what do you mean, "Oh – Matt"?'

'Well, you'll be married soon. You don't have to worry about him.'

'That's not the point.' I sighed. I knew what I meant, but didn't want to make an issue of it. Not today. Instead I asked anxiously a question that I supposed I should have asked her long ago.

1

'You do like Matt, don't you?'

She shrugged. 'Of course. But what if I didn't? You'd still marry him.'

Would I? When Matt had asked me, after several months of living together, I had unhesitatingly agreed. It hadn't occurred to me to get the children's approval. Now, almost too late, I bravely said, 'No I wouldn't, not if it made you unhappy.'

She gave me a slanting look then lowered her eyes to her bowl. She stirred her spoon as she spoke. 'Perhaps it's having him here at all that makes me unhappy. I can't walk around in my nightclothes.' She gave me a tentative smile so that I didn't know what her words concealed.

Confused, I said, 'Eat your cornflakes, they'll go soggy.'

To set an example, I spooned in my own, but somehow they had lost their glory.

As we finished, Stefan joined us, dressed in a navy tracksuit for his morning run.

'What's the matter, can't you sleep?' he asked. 'Wedding nerves, I expect. I notice Matt isn't sharing them.'

'Matt likes his sleep, as I'm sure you know by now.' My voice was tart, for something told me that my husband-to-be shouldn't be sleeping like a baby as he had given every appearance of doing when I left him. He should be pacing the floor in anxious anticipation. As, metaphorically speaking, I was. It was not going to be so very much of an ordeal: a small register office ceremony in front of my parents and children; Kate, my best friend, and Harry, her husband, and Matt's sister, Claire, and her family. But it was a big step, which I had only taken once before. That had ended in pain and grief. By marrying Matt I was exposing myself again. But it marked the end of years of loneliness. I should be feeling happy. I *was* happy.

So I said to Stefan, 'I'm not nervous, I'm excited. And happy. I hope you are too.'

'Course, Mum.' At seventeen he already topped me – now, standing by my chair, he seemed enormous and I felt overwhelmed that this man, whose voice had broken, who had begun to shave, who could put a reassuring hand on my shoulder as he now did, was my son. I put up my hand to cover his. For an instant the feeling was almost sexual.

'Coffee before you go?' I asked, looking up at him with love.

He shook his head. 'No, never. Back in half an hour.' And he was out of the back door, a navy streak with an expensive haircut – short at the back, long on top – that he assured me was cool. As was the earring I had resisted for so long, before giving in. The truth was that everything he did delighted me. My resistance had not been disapproval, but a rejection of the mutilation of his baby flesh. Now Natalie wanted her ears pierced, and she knew I had lost the battle before it was even engaged.

We sat over the table, my daughter and I, while the coffee brewed in the cafetière between us. I felt content that we should have these moments, as they were few and far between. Lately I had sensed her growing away and more often than not she evaded my eyes when we talked. I supposed it was just her age, but that didn't make it any easier.

'Shall I?' she asked, reaching out to the coffeepot. I nodded. She lowered the plunger slowly, then poured two cups. As she did so I eyed her hair, its auburn mass glinting in the morning sun that now flooded the kitchen.

'I wish you were coming to the hairdresser's with me,' I commented unwisely. 'You know – girls together.'

She patted her hair impatiently. 'They can't do anything with it. That's the worst of curly hair – it's always the same.'

'Even so . . .' My voice trailed off. Nat had hated her hair since a boy at primary school had called her Carrots. I loved

3

it, the way it sprang back from her white brow, making her green eyes stand out startled and aware. Just like David's. When he first died, though she was only three, it had hurt me to look at her, and yet I would clutch her to me and bury my face in her hair just as I used to do with David. It smelled of Johnson's baby shampoo in those days. Now it was Wash and Go, which she used every morning under the shower.

As if reading my mind, she gulped her coffee and stood up. 'Mind if I have the bathroom first? Just in case Matt comes down and *sees* me,' she added with a hint of sarcasm.

I let it pass, and sat on at the table, drinking the coffeepot dry, idly considering my good fortune, letting excitement take hold for the first time. In under four hours I would be a married woman. No longer a widow. No longer alone. It had been a long road, a heavy load, lightened since Matt came into our lives but still tenuous, insecure. I had felt uncertain of my place, doubtful of his love, feeling myself and my children a weight on Matt which he would surely one day set aside.

Instead of which . . . a tremor of anticipatory joy made me stand up and go to the window. The spring garden was bright now, daffodils standing out against the uncut grass. I have always been a notoriously untidy gardener. It would be Stefan, eventually, who got out the mower. But buds were breaking on the apple tree, under which still hung the old swing. The grass beneath had long since healed from the drag of childish feet.

I stood there a long time, savouring the moment. When the door opened behind me I assumed it was Matt, and turned with joy. But it was Natalie, dressed now in sweater and leggings, her malachite pendant round her neck, her feet annihilated by Pooh Bear slippers. She looked puzzled and held out an envelope.

'The post already?' I asked.

'No. Matt gave it to me.'

4

I took the envelope, seeing my name. Of course, a wedding card. How like him. Guilt that I hadn't done the same made me hesitate, then I ripped it open and pulled out a single sheet of paper.

I read, 'Julia – I can't go through with it. I'm sorry. Forgive me. Matthew.'

'Matthew'? Since when had I called him Matthew?

Natalie was staring at me as if she knew what it contained. I tried to speak but my voice had fled the camp.

Natalie spoke instead, hanging onto the door handle as if her life depended on it.

'He's gone, Mum. He just left. He was carrying a bag. He just said, "Sorry".'

Sorry. I gripped the paper as if it would somehow sustain me, stop my legs crumbling beneath me. I was aware that Natalie had crossed the room and taken my arm. She pulled out a chair and pushed me gently onto it.

'Are you are all right?' Her voice was small, her green eyes scared.

'Yes,' I whispered, but I wasn't. I was devastated, destroyed, shocked beyond belief, abandoned and betrayed. I was Julia Leathlean, forty-two years old and on my own again.

PART ONE

ONE

After David's funeral I took his pyjamas from beneath the pillow and sniffed them, burying my head in the soft poplin and gasping in his essence as if my life depended on it. Then, my eyes dry but burning, I sealed the pyjamas into a plastic bag. I kept them beside the bed. Sometimes at night I would open the bag and take the garments into bed with me. Once I even wore them, and lay aching with a helpless longing. Gradually his smell faded. One day, eleven months after his death, I wrenched them from the bag and threw them into the washing machine before I had time to think. I ironed them carefully, my mind a blank. Then I emptied his underwear drawer into a bin liner, added the pyjamas, and left the whole lot out for the dustman.

It was a small step, but one in the right direction.

It was eleven years since David died, but we had eight years together, the sum total of my happiness until I met Matt. It was the essence of that happiness that had supported me through the years between, the sense that gradually permeated my grief that, somewhere, David still loved and looked out for me. It was illogical, but logic doesn't enter into it when you are desperate and despairing. You will clutch at any lifeline.

David was a doctor. Ironic then that he should be snuffed out at thirty-three by a rare infection, picked up months previously on his hospital rounds. He had just gone into general practice, and we expected our lives to be easier.

There is nothing truer than the old maxim that life is what

happens to you while you are making other plans. We had moved house to accommodate what we hoped would be a growing family. Stefan was six, Natalie three. We wanted another baby, both having been only children, and lonely. It wasn't what my parents had planned for me. I was to be a doctor, like my father, but my heart wasn't in it. The human frame and its various ills didn't fascinate me, and I lacked the necessary altruism. I had met David at medical school. I had been grateful to marry him and, when he qualified, start our family. My parents were tangibly disappointed in me. Their grandchildren were a poor substitute for my white coat. They blamed David in some indefinable way. When he died, his culpability was confirmed. He had let me down, left me defenceless and unqualified.

He had not however left me unprovided for. A mortgage protection policy ensured the house was paid for and a prudent life policy enabled us to live. So as a widow, I was considerably more fortunate than most. My children did not go without shoes, nor suffer the humiliation of free school dinners. I did not have to apply to the state, I was not a one-parent-family statistic.

Of course the children suffered, Stefan in particular. But he was old enough to have memories, which Natalie wasn't. As she grew older she would sometimes say, 'I wish I could remember him, you are lucky,' and I would sense Stefan enlarging on his recollection, to impress her and to reassure himself. It was if he were claiming his father as his special territory. Yet David had adored Natalie, and I made sure she knew it.

'You have your daddy's hair,' I told her once, but later, knowing whom to blame, she was to hold this against him.

'He always wanted a little girl,' was another ploy, and Stefan reacted fiercely: 'We used to play football. Girls can't play football.'

So they grew up, missing him as a fact as much as a

person. 'I wish I had a daddy,' wept Natalie, having fallen and grazed her knee, or been teased at school, or subjected to the hundred and one disappointments of childhood. 'I wish Daddy was here,' complained Stefan, as I was watching alone on sports day, and he won his race. 'Everyone else has a father.' This was palpably not true, but it was how it seemed to him. And to me. And I would agree, fighting back my tears.

They never saw me cry. After they had gone to bed, I would sometimes sit on the swing in the garden, the swing which David had put up, and sob my heart out. My hair was longer then, and I would twist it into damp ropes, as I had done as a child, and once I found that I had put my thumb into my mouth. It gave me a shock, this regression to infancy, but where else could I find comfort? When the storm was over, I would push the swing, wildly, soaring up into the apple tree higher and higher as if I could take flight and escape the misery that pursued me night and day.

For I was angry too, fiercely resentful that David had left me alone. The anger clashed with my grief, making me feel guilty and confused. I wanted to beat him with my clenched fists, and at the same time hold him to me, tenderly, just once more.

Throughout all this suffering, my parents watched anxiously. It was years before I recognised that they must have suffered too. One's child's pain is sometimes worse than one's own. Their first reaction was to offer me a home.

'Don't be alone, Julia. We have plenty of room for you all.'

'But I have a home. I could never leave it.' What I meant was that in leaving it I would be leaving David. What's more, I would lose my hard-won independence. I had always been swamped with love. My career had been chosen for me, with luck I had escaped. Nothing on earth would induce me to return to the parental clutches, much as I loved them.

Also, we could never have lived together. I am an untidy person, disorganised and spontaneous. My mother runs her home like a business, weeding out the inessential and the inefficient like a ruthless employer. My father is seldom there, and when he is he retreats to his study. It was inconceivable that I could introduce childish tantrums, a flood of toys and laundry, nightmares, bedwetting and my own inveterate untidiness into their calm domestic domain.

Sometimes, when I lived at home, I used to wonder if it wouldn't have been easier for my mother if we hadn't pursued the normal habits of living, if we had taken breakfast the night before so that she could clear the things away before breakfast time, if we hadn't slept in our beds and creased the sheets. Leaves in autumn were gathered as soon as they touched the lawn, fading plants were ruthlessly pulled out before they had finished blooming. When I returned from my honeymoon, she had rejoiced in telling me that she had found a good home for my wedding dress, it had been sold in answer to a postcard in the newsagent's. Useless to tell her that I wanted to keep it to show my children, to try on in middle age and bemoan the fact that I could no longer fasten it. Souvenirs were regarded as sentimental, postcards and letters destroyed, my school reports eventually relegated to the bin. As a reaction to this, I kept everything, which mounted up in a growing tide around my own home and gave me a sense of reassurance, interspersed with occasional irritation at the muddle.

Counter-reacting similarly, Natalie grew up as tidy and organised as her grandmother. She would tut at the teetering piles of old newspapers on the coffee table, and moan at the dishes in the sink. Her bedroom wasn't the room of a teenager. Books and tapes were neatly lined on shelves, her bed was adorned with just one bear, her shoes stood in pairs in the bottom of the wardrobe and sweaters were kept in plastic bags. Running the Hoover round the clear expanse of her carpet, I felt it as a rebuke, and longed for a touch of scruffiness.

I felt more at home in Stefan's room. Here at least one sensed some adolescent fervour. His computer would be left on for hours on end, discarded cassette boxes surrounded the stereo, his desk was piled with books and handwritten notes. Tee shirts were screwed into half-open drawers. Posters covered the walls, with ardent messages about whales and motorway extensions, love and peace. Stefan, I felt, was a true teenager, and I adored him.

But at the time of David's death these teenage years were a long way ahead, and I had to buckle down and bring the children up. At first, it seemed a daunting task, without David's steady guidance. He had always been so sure, so positive. In the first months of bereavement, anxious not to increase their weight of sorrow, I was lenient and tolerant, letting them have their way. Or maybe it was just the lethargy of grief that let them rage around me like spoiled hoodlums. My mother was appalled at their behaviour.

'You shouldn't let them get away with it, Julia. You're making a rod for your own back.'

'But they've had a hard time, how can I punish them?'

'Well, if you don't do it now, they'll be running your life.'

I turned away, not wanting to hear. But some last vestige of reason told me she was right. After a year, when I first began to laugh again, I took them in hand. I imposed regular bedtimes, chastised rudeness and punished downright naughtiness with a smack. It seemed to me that they responded gratefully. Once more the lines had been drawn. Somebody was in control.

In the many letters of condolence I had received, one message had stood out loud and clear: 'at least you have the children'. Now I perceived what a blessing they were. They were a reason – more, an urgent requirement – for carrying on. They enabled me to drag together my tattered remains, to get up in the morning, to find a reason to go on living.

A tower of strength through all the early days was Kate, my friend from schooldays, who lived a couple of streets away. She it was who would take my desolate phone calls late at night when I couldn't bear to go to bed; who would bundle her twins into the pushchair and come and get my children's tea when I could hardly lift a hand to butter bread. When I cried, she would hug me close and rock me back and forth in a way my mother was unable to do. Kate was my lifeline and my comfort. From her, I learned what it was to be a friend.

On the anniversary of David's death, she arrived unannounced in the car.

'I'm taking you all out. No arguments. We're going to the zoo.'

I stared at her reluctantly. I had planned to take the children to visit David's grave. I had bought flowers, told them we were taking them to Daddy.

'Well, you can do that too. But then we're going to have some fun. It's time to let some light into your life.'

I felt stirrings of resentment, pulling my grief round me like a comfortable coat. I didn't want to open it, for with the light would come the cold draught of reality. Effort would have to be made, appearances kept up, I would have to comb my hair and change my tights and clean my shoes. 'I'm not ready,' I bleated feebly, but Kate would have none of it.

'Stefan and Natalie are ready. Take them to the grave by all means. It's an important rite of passage, I realise that. And then we're going to the zoo.'

So I dressed the children warmly in anoraks and woollen hats, for it was late February and a bright but wintry day. I combed my hair and changed my tights and pulled on leather boots and a quilted jacket. I picked up the flowers I had bought for David, slammed the door on the empty house and we all climbed into the Peugeot.

Stefan was strapped into the back, Natalie I held dangerously on my lap, feeling the fluffy brush of her bright hair beneath my chin.

'Are we going to see Daddy?' she asked, swinging her legs uncomfortably against mine and knocking my shins with her new red shoes.

I said gently, 'Well we won't see him, but he'll know we're there. You can talk to him if you like.'

She twisted round so that I could see the question in her green eyes. 'How will I know what to say?'

'You only need say something if you want to. We'll see.'

Stefan called out from the back, 'I shall tell him I scored a goal in football.'

'He'll like that.' I felt choked, and suddenly grateful that we were not alone, that Kate, and Ben and Dominic, her five-year-old twins strapped silently into the back, were with us. I glanced sideways at her as she turned into the gate of the cemetery. Strong profile, thick swept-back dark hair, white polo neck snugged under her determined chin, she looked a tower of strength. I reached out and touched her arm.

'Thank you,' I murmured as she parked the car.

'Shall we stay here? It's up to you.'

I hesitated. An innate feebleness wanted to drag her along, to cling to her arm and weep. But something else told me this was an act I must do alone. I must demonstrate some strength to the children. And to David, who would want to see that I was coping. So I set Natalie on the ground, unstrapped Stefan and got the flowers out of the boot. Rust chrysanthemums and yellow lilies, they glowed in the winter sunshine like hope. As we set off among the graves, I heard one of the twins say complainingly, 'This doesn't look like the zoo. Where are the elephants?' To my complete astonishment, I felt my mouth curling round a smile.

The grave was a shallow rectangle of gravel in a low kerb. A plain marble stone was engraved with David's name and dates. A simple message read: 'Loved and much missed'. There was a stone vase set in the gravel. I had collected a can of water from the tap by the gate and I filled the vase and kneeled on the gravel to arrange the flowers. The children stood behind me, their eyes wide and thoughtful.

'Is Daddy still there?' Stefan asked as I got up and brushed gravel from my knees. He asked this every time we came, and every time I told him, 'His body is, but his soul has gone to heaven. He can see us from there so why don't you give him a smile?'

Instinctively, he raised his eyes to the bright sky and smiled. I saw the gap in his teeth and my heart wrenched. 'Tell him about your goal,' I urged, but he shook his head, suddenly overcome with shyness.

'I can't, it's silly, he can't really hear me.'

I hugged him. 'Well that's all right. Just think it instead.'

Natalie nudged against me, muscling in between us. 'I want to tell him something,' she said.

'What's that?'

'I want to tell him that I wet the bed last night, and I'm sorry.'

Tears which I had been fighting down welled up and I couldn't speak. I watched her go to the end of the grave and address the gravel. Her little lips moved quietly, as if it was a secret between David and her. When she had finished she stood for a moment, then looked up at me.

'It's all right. He's not cross.'

'Of course not. Now you two go back to the car. I won't be a moment.'

I watched them go along the path, then turned back to the grave. My tears were now flowing unchecked in a tidal wave of relief. Words poured out of me, of anger and pain and loneliness. 'Oh David, I'm doing my best, but I will do better now, I promise,' I concluded, wiping my eyes fiercely. 'Surely, I'm over the worst now? Please help me to go on.'

I stared at the bright flowers, struggling to see their message of hope, of life continuing. Gradually my eyes dried and my focus cleared. And into my mind flowed a sort of peace.

When I got back into the car and pulled Natalie onto my lap she looked at my scrubbed face and gave me a pursed wet kiss on my lips.

From the back Stefan said impatiently, 'Are we going to the zoo now? I'm hungry.'

I blessed Kate for that day, which I could truly say I enjoyed. It was a new experience for the children, and as such was something I had never shared with David. There were therefore no comparisons to be made, though the temptation was strong to wish we were doing it together. I determinedly pushed such maudlin thoughts aside. I ate beefburgers with the children, laughed with Kate when Dominic remarked of the orang-utan that he had a 'horrid orange bottom', took a photograph of Stefan riding on an elephant, held Natalie up to watch the sea lions being fed and complained of the fetid smell in the lion's enclosure. The children ran about, shrieking and laughing and chasing the twins, and I took Kate's arm and said again, 'Thank you. This has done us all so much good.'

'I'm glad. Why not come to supper next weekend? Would your parents baby-sit?'

I was surprised, but supposed they would. It was a year since they had been asked. I realised that I had not left the house alone in all that time. Suddenly, the thought of an evening out seemed infinitely desirable. 'I'll ask them. They could come for the weekend. It would be a good excuse to do some tidying up.'

Kate looked at me approvingly. 'Good girl. Now, is it too cold for ice creams, do you think?'

I laughed. 'I don't think it's ever too cold for ice creams. Though I'd prefer a cup of tea.'

So we went to the cafeteria and bought the children ice creams in glass bowls with fan-shaped wafers, and a pot of tea for two, and two pieces of coffee sponge which I found myself eating with enthusiasm. I asked the children what they had enjoyed most about the outing. Ben chose the penguins, Stefan the lions, Dominic the ice cream and Natalie, after some thought, announced, 'I saw an elephant doing pooey.'

Suddenly I found myself giggling like a schoolgirl. The laughter welled up in me, bursting through my coffee cake, and the tears in my eyes were not tears of sorrow. And Kate said seriously, 'The best bit for me has been hearing you laugh.'

I dressed carefully for my evening with Kate and Harry. Zipping up a rust-coloured jersey dress which I hadn't worn for a year, I was surprised at how much weight I had lost. It suited me. I told myself grimly that every cloud had a silver lining, and added a gold and rust scarf and a cameo brooch David had given me for our first anniversary.

Natalie was sitting on my bed sucking her thumb and watching me.

'Do I look nice?' I asked her, mentally doing a twirl.

She removed her thumb and looked at me consideringly. 'You look different. And I don't want you to go.'

Her face buckled and her mouth fastened on her thumb. I sat down beside her. She was dressed for bed in a Mickey Mouse nightdress and slippers. My mother had wanted her safely tucked up before I went, but Natalie had had other ideas.

'Nana and Granddad are here with you,' I told her reassuringly. 'And I'll be here when you wake up in the morning.'

'But you never go out.'

'I used to. Daddy and I used to. But you've forgotten. There's nothing to worry about. I'm going to tuck you up now and read you a story, just like I always do. And Nana and Granddad will be downstairs if you want anything.'

She said nothing, but put up her arms babyishly to be carried. She smelled sweetly of bathtime and toothpaste, and my insides loosened. I was reluctant to part with her to the opened bed and when I pulled the duvet close around her it was like a hug.

'What story?' I asked.

'"The Princess and the Pea".' This one always amused her. We used to play a game that she could feel a pea under her mattress, which meant she must be a princess. But before I had got to the end, her thumb had slid into place and her eyelids drooped. I felt a huge relief. I had thought there was going to be trouble.

I dropped a kiss on her forehead, tucked teddy in beside her and switched off the light.

Downstairs, my father was playing draughts with Stefan. My mother was watching a medical drama on television, embroidering a cross-stitch sampler at the same time. She was never one to sit idle.

'She's gone out like a light,' I told her, with some satisfaction. I had sensed implied criticism of the children's behaviour since their arrival. To be honest, I had not been pleased with them myself. Natalie had insisted on eating her lunch with her fingers and Stefan had wandered off before I'd served his pudding, despite my insistence that he sit at the table.

'Don't let him have any,' insisted my mother. 'He's got to learn.'

'That won't cut any ice, he doesn't like rice pudding anyway.'

'Well he should be made to eat it,' she said pointedly, with an incongruous switch from treat to threat.

'I just don't want a scene. Not today.'

So Stefan didn't have any rice pudding, and later complained that he was hungry so I gave him an apple which my mother regarded disapprovingly as eating between meals. My father said soothingly, 'An apple won't hurt him, Eleanor,' but she objected obstinately, 'It's giving in. It's no good keeping on giving in.'

Teatime had been somewhat better. I had given them egg sandwiches and buttered buns sitting in front of the television, and had the satisfaction of seeing them eat obligingly well. Meanwhile I offered my parents chocolate cake which my father professed to be 'as good as your mother's', while my mother fussed about the crumbs the children were making on the carpet.

'I'll clear them up before I go,' I promised her, though normally that would not have been my first priority.

When it was time to leave I said to Stefan, 'Last game, then you must go to bed.'

He looked at me mutinously and my heart sank.

'I'm going to stay up until you get back,' he said defiantly.

I heard my mother mutter, 'You'll be lucky,' and looked at my father helplessly. He said, 'That won't do, old chap, you'll be fit for nothing in the morning.'

'Don't care.' With a sudden sweep of his hand, Stefan knocked the draughts off the board and flung himself on the sofa, wailing. I stood paralysed while my mother put down her sewing and said firmly, 'Leave this to me, dear. You just go.'

'But I can't! He's not used to it, don't you see? They're neither of them used to me going out. I can't leave them. I just can't go.'

That said, I slumped down into an armchair, my heart boiling with disappointment.

My father stood up. 'Julia,' he said, 'you're going. We can

cope. After all, we coped with you all those years ago.' He gave a short laugh.

'But it isn't fair, on you or him.'

'And staying home isn't fair on you.'

He pulled me up from the chair. Reluctantly, I picked up my bag. I didn't know what was best. Either way, I seemed to have been beaten. I was a useless mother who couldn't control her children, and I was a feckless mother who deserted them. I looked at my mother.

'Don't be cross with him,' I pleaded. 'He can't help it.'

'I won't be cross. Just firm. As you should have been, months ago.'

Smarting at her criticism, I felt a flash of healthy anger. Very well, I would leave them to it. I bent to kiss Stefan goodbye but he thrashed his arms and buried his head in the cushions. Feeling utterly useless, I left the room and closed the door on the rising crescendo of his cries.

They followed me all the way to Kate's, echoing in my head as I drove. Although it wasn't far, it was raining and I had taken the car. Mentally, I was apologising to David; for deserting our children, for failing to bring them up right, for cravenly giving in to my mother. My mood of anticipation had evaporated. Freedom, it seemed, was bought at too high a price.

But the smell of garlic and wine that greeted me did much to restore my spirits. It was the aroma of an evening out, much as the smell of nail varnish when I was a teenager had signified a party. Harry took my jacket, and the bottle of wine I had remembered to bring.

'It's a Merlot, Australian, I hope that's all right,' I said as Harry unwrapped the green tissue paper.

'Lovely.' He gave me a neighbourly kiss on the cheek. When David was alive Harry used to flirt with me, but one did not flirt with the recently bereaved. One did not touch them for fear they might explode, or disintegrate, or cling on pathetically, and weep. Instead, I was ushered briskly into the sitting room. 'Kate's busy in the kitchen, she'll be with you in a minute. Let me introduce you to Howard, a business colleague of mine.'

I turned startled eyes to a man who was rising from a chair. I had not expected to meet anyone else. An instant deep suspicion seized me. Kate and Harry were match-making! I had had my time of mourning, now I was to find somebody else. Resistance to the idea filled me with an unreasoning dislike of the man who was now stretching out a broad hand to shake mine. He was bulky and heavy-featured, and towered above my five foot seven. But his voice was warm as he said, 'Hello, Julia. I've heard so much about you.'

'Oh, what?' My voice was sharp. No doubt that I was a pathetic widow who badly needed cheering up, that I could do with some sex, that I was his for the taking.

He replied equably, seeming not to notice. 'Oh, you know, that you and Kate have been friends for years. You have two lovely children. And I was so sorry to hear about your husband.'

He sounded so genuine that it was impossible to feel cross. I sat down, stretching my legs to the bright fire. 'Thank you.' In all the months, I had learned how to take people's expressions of regret. 'Don't be' had never seemed quite satisfactory, for it threw their sympathy back in their face. Admission of misery only embarrassed them and made them wish they hadn't spoken.

Harry pressed a glass of wine into my hand and left the room. I was instantly suspicious again and sipped my wine in silence, not wishing to help matters along.

Howard took some coal from a brass scuttle and set it carefully on the fire. 'Bit of a cheek really, fiddling with someone else's fire. I find people are usually very possessive about them. But I don't have one at home, and it's irresistible. What about you?'

'Pardon?' I wasn't sure what he meant.

'Do you have an open fire? I don't think you can beat them for company.'

'Oh yes, I do. And no, you can't.'

I subsided again, feeling awkward. It seemed I had lost the art of small talk. I took another sip of wine, wondering if it was the Merlot. I was irritated that I couldn't tell.

After a prolonged silence, Howard tried again. 'We're in the same boat actually. On our own with children. I have two girls, eleven and nine.'

Courtesy demanded some response. 'Really? Is your wife . . . ? I mean . . .'

'She ran away. Three years ago. With the builder who was doing our loft extension. It would be funny if it wasn't so tragic. Best thing about it was that she didn't want the children. Though how do you explain that to them?'

I didn't know. I had my own problems. 'How do you look after them? You work with Harry, don't you?'

'That's right. Another much-maligned estate agent. I have a housekeeper. She has a child of her own, a teenager, and was glad of a home.'

I couldn't think of any more to say and was glad when Kate came into the room.

'Sorry. It's a stir fry, and everything has to be done at the last minute. Shall we have our starter?'

We followed her into the dining room, where Harry was filling glasses with white wine. Kate was wearing a long black skirt and a swathed rose-pink blouse. Her dark hair was held back with a black velvet bow. With my long loose brown tresses I suddenly felt rather scruffy and made an instant decision to have a haircut. At least my mother would be pleased. She was always commenting on my hair.

The starter was a delicious smoked salmon mousse wrapped in glistening slices of smoked salmon and served with lemon and thin slices of brown bread and butter. I hadn't eaten anything so fancy since I couldn't remember when. Determined to be a good guest I asked Howard if his housekeeper produced food like that.

'Mrs Sullivan? No, bless her, she's very much a meat and two veg lady. But I do sometimes. I like to cook. And I'm teaching Diana.'

'She's the eleven-year-old?' I asked, pleased at remembering her age.

'That's right. The youngest is Deborah. All she wants to do is play her recorder! I can see it will be flute next, then an oboe. You must meet them sometime.'

I bristled. This seemed a bit premature. But maybe he was just proud of them, the way I was of mine.

Kate was smiling at me encouragingly. I felt like a teenager at her first party, not sure how to behave. Surely Kate wasn't expecting me to flirt! Frantically I scoured my mind for something to say, eventually producing, 'I left Stefan in a tantrum, I wonder if he's all right,' which couldn't have been more deadly as a conversational gambit.

To my relief Harry started talking about property. It seemed the market was buoyant. They were in for a good year, prices were rising and properties selling themselves. I listened with half an ear. I was worrying about Stefan, visualising my mother's tight-lipped insistence that he go to bed, and thinking that maybe I shouldn't stay for coffee. I forked over my stir-fry turkey without enthusiasm.

'Salad?' Kate held out a bowl of glistening leaves. I gave her a thin, apologetic smile. I wasn't being much of a guest. I let the men's voices roll over me as I ate the salad, an adventurous mix of coriander and rocket and basil, and various red and green lettuces, curly and crisp.

I was startled when Harry turned to me and said, 'You

24

could sell your house easily, Julia, if you had a mind to. Edwardian semis in Putney are much in demand.'

I gulped down a mouthful of salad. 'Sell? But why should I want to?'

Harry looked discomfited. 'Oh, you know, I thought maybe fresh fields, pastures new.'

'But I love my house. I couldn't leave. It's where David and I . . .'

Kate glared at Harry.

'It's okay,' she said to me, gently. 'We quite understand. Harry, open the dessert wine, would you? I'll fetch the pudding.'

There was an uncomfortable silence when she left the room. To break it I asked Howard where he lived, though not caring very much.

'Wimbledon Common. I sold up after Valerie left. Couldn't bear the associations. Particularly the loft extension! But I can see it's different for you.'

'It's comforting, you see. I feel David's still with me. And I think it's important for the children to have continuity.' I didn't know why I was telling him this and felt the need to lighten the mood. 'So, I'm afraid you won't be having me on your books!'

He grinned obligingly. Our little heart-to-heart was over. I noticed for the first time that his eyes were overbright, his heavy face flushed. He had been making heavy inroads into the wine. 'Ah, pudding,' he now said enthusiastically, as Kate set before him a crème brûlée. He tapped the crisp top with his spoon. 'Perfect. I must try this with Diana.'

'The thing is not to refrigerate them,' Kate told him. 'I find it makes them go soggy.'

We ate in silence. Then Howard asked, 'Has anyone seen *Amadeus*? It's supposed to be marvellous.'

'We went last week. Had to queue, which is unusual these days.'

I felt coldly excluded. It was so long since I had been to the cinema, so long since I had even taken any notice of what was on. I kept silent while Kate and Harry expounded on the delights of the film. As they talked, I noticed Howard watching me consideringly, and felt uneasy. When Kate finally asked, 'Coffee?' I said apologetically that I thought I had better go.

'I'm not sure what's going on at home,' I explained.

She didn't try to dissuade me, but took me to the door.

'Sorry,' I said. 'Not exactly glittering company, I'm afraid. I'm out of practice.'

She murmured something reassuring, about having to start somewhere. Then she said apologetically, 'I'm sorry about Howard. It was Harry's idea. He feels sorry for him.'

I gave a short laugh. It sounded bitter. 'I thought it was me you were setting up. But I could really do without that.'

She sensed my disapproval for she put her hand on my arm.

'Give it time. And Howard's a really nice guy. Don't hold it against him.'

There didn't seem to be anything to say to this, so I kissed her goodbye. It was still raining hard, and I ran to the car, feeling obscurely disappointed in the evening, and worried about returning home.

When I opened the front door, all was quiet. I let myself into the sitting room, to find my father sitting over the dying embers of the fire doing *The Times* crossword. He looked up with a smile and patted the sofa beside him. I sat down.

'Good time?' he asked.

I shrugged. 'Oh well, you know.' I paused. This was my father, I could tell him.

'Well actually,' I burst out, 'it was awful. I felt as if I had lost a limb. So lonely! And I had nothing to say. I've forgotten how to socialise.'

He put down the paper, looking at me with love. 'Poor little Julia.' His voice was a caress.

'Not so little. I'm all grown up now. A mother, a widow. What more is there?' My voice was bitter.

'You'll always be my little Julia. Don't you think it's hurt us, this past year, to see you so miserable?'

Self-absorbed as I had been, the thought had only marginally occurred to me. I felt a guilty pang. It was time to put a braver face on things, for their sakes if not my own. 'Well, I suppose things can only get better,' I told him philosophically. 'How's it been here?'

'Stefan went up about nine. I let him beat me at draughts a couple of times. And he had a banana and some milk, he was hungry again by then.'

'And Mother let him?' I was astonished.

He looked at me patiently. 'She does her best, you know. She just doesn't like to see you making a rod for your own back.'

A flare of rebellion made me say, 'But I want to spoil them. To try and make amends. It's not their fault there's only one of me.'

He shook his head. 'But that isn't necessarily the way. I can understand how you feel, but you've got to show them who's the boss. They'll thank you for it in the end.'

'And I'll thank you, I suppose.' But my voice was tender. I knew he loved me. He nodded, with a smile.

'Well, I'm for my bed. Your mother's gone up already.'

He bent and hugged me. I felt the rough rub of his sweater against my cheek and felt a wild wrench of longing to be held properly by a man. But not any man. Not my father. Certainly not Howard. By David.

TWO

In those days, before Natalie was at school, I had to be careful about money. David's pension only just covered our living expenses and enabled me to run the car. In the week following my visit to Kate's, I found myself thinking about the house.

If I sold it and bought somewhere smaller, it would release some useful capital. We didn't need four bedrooms; my large and homely kitchen was a luxury. My parents had been implying all this for some time. They wanted me to move out to Kingston, to be nearer them.

But every time I contemplated it, I felt something like panic. How could I wrench myself up by the roots and start somewhere new? I had only lived in the house a year or two but it represented all our dreams. Besides that, I loved it. I loved the deep porch with its glowing tiles around the white front door, which was topped with a glass fanlight that stained the carpet with red and blue sunshine; the square hall with its easy-rise staircase, and the large haphazard kitchen we hadn't got round to renovating. There were eccentric sashes which either stuck or slipped, and the bedrooms had pretty Art Deco fireplaces. The tangled garden with its swing and apple tree suggested country living, while around the corner, conveniently, was Putney High Street, and Sainsbury's. I enjoyed walking across Putney Bridge, its twin churches framing it like bookends. I liked living near the river, though as my mother never ceased to tell me, the river ran through Kingston too.

But Harry had said I could sell it easily. I could move onto an estate, with three bedrooms and a postage stamp garden, a built-in kitchen and noisy neighbours. Plenty of people did. It was the sensible thing to do. Only I didn't want to be sensible, I wanted to be happy, if such a thing were possible ever again. I tried to talk it over with David, but I knew that he wanted me to stay. Or maybe I just wanted to be persuaded. I pushed the problem from my mind. Something would turn up. I went to the post office and cashed my Family Allowance and, for a brief while, felt rich.

But could I afford to go to the cinema? I felt a ridiculous longing to see *Amadeus*, to rejoin the land of the living and discuss the latest film with someone. Besides, I loved Mozart; his music could always make me weep.

I was weighing up the pros and cons, the guilt against the need, Stefan's new football boots against the price of a ticket, when, as if directed by fate, Howard rang.

'I hope you don't mind. I got your number from Kate. The thing is, I was wondering if you would like to see *Amadeus*. With me I mean. This Saturday perhaps. Kate says she'll baby-sit for you.'

Does she indeed? I felt an irritated sense of being manoeuvred, as if plans were being made against my will. And yet I wanted to go. It was surely an answer to a prayer.

But did I want to go with Howard? On a date? It had been so long, and there were certain obligations implicit in accepting, or so I believed. All sorts of awkward considerations, like asking someone in for coffee and wondering whether you were going to be kissed, flashed through my mind. I was definitely too old for all that. Yet what was the alternative? To sit alone for the rest of my life, growing old and bitter, and always lonely? To be foolish and dependent and ultimately a nuisance to everyone? In desperation I asked David what to do. 'Go,' came the reply. Maybe that was what I wanted to hear, but because there seemed to be no very good reason to ignore him, I agreed.

When Kate arrived to baby-sit, both the children were ready for bed though it was far too early for Stefan. Fearful of a repeat of the last weekend's performance I had told him firmly that he could stay up until nine o'clock if Kate didn't mind, but that this was on condition that he made no fuss when I went out. To my surprise, I found that firmness worked. He sat on the sofa as if butter wouldn't melt in his mouth, a pile of books on his lap waiting for Kate to read to him. But when I went to tuck Natalie into bed I found her sitting up on the pillows, her thumb in her mouth, crying.

Oh no, I thought, not you this time. I asked her what was the matter.

'I don't want you to go again,' she whimpered pathetically, so that guilt rose hot in my throat.

'But you'll be asleep,' I pleaded with her. 'And I'll be here in the morning, just like last time.'

'I want a story.'

'You shall have one.'

We were heavily involved in Postman Pat when I heard the doorbell ring and Kate opening the door. At the sound of Howard's voice in the hall, Natalie's ears pricked up.

'Who's that down there?'

'He's just a friend, called Howard. He's taking me to the pictures.'

'I want to come to the pictures.'

'You wouldn't like the film.'

'What's it called?'

'It's called *Amadeus*. It's for grown-ups.'

'Is it like *E.T.*?' She had seen this on television, and been frightened of his face.

'No, not like *E.T.*'

She stared at me solemnly, trying to imagine the unimaginable.

'Will you tuck down now?' I asked her fearfully.

She shook her head, but now there was knowing mischief in her eyes. She knew she had me.

I glanced at my watch. 'I tell you what,' I said in desperation. 'I'll get you a video of *Mary Poppins* if you're good.' It was the sort of bribery of which my mother most definitely would not approve. I firmed up my voice, mindful of my new resolution. 'Now lie down like a good girl, I'm going.'

She looked at me woefully, her eyes boring into my soul which cringed apologetically.

'Good night,' I said firmly, bending to kiss her.

'Leave the light on,' she said in a small voice. So I did.

Downstairs Stefan was eyeing Harry suspiciously as he chatted with Kate. His eyes swivelled to me accusingly as I stood in the doorway.

'Hello, Howard,' I said brightly, ignoring my son, which was the worst thing I could have done. He cast his books aside and lunged at me, burying his head in my stomach.

'I want you to read to me, not Kate. And I'm hungry. And I want a drink.'

I dropped my hand on his head, smoothing the blond hair while I looked helplessly at Kate.

'I'll see to him,' she said quickly. 'You just go.'

It all seemed so familiar, and I had failed again. Anxious to reassert myself I said quite crossly, 'I gave you the rules, Stefan. Nine o'clock if you're good. Otherwise it's bed straight away.'

Howard was keeping tactfully silent. I glanced at him. 'Shall we go?' I sounded braver than I felt. Stefan's grip had tightened and I didn't know how I was going to free myself without an undignified tussle. But it seemed that Howard had ideas of his own.

'Let go, Stefan, and I'll tell you something.'

I felt the thin arms loosen, then Stefan turned round to look at Howard.

'What?'

'Well, I've got a motorbike. I'll give you a ride on it one day if you're good. That's if Mummy agrees.'

He looked at me questioningly, but my mind had veered off at a tangent. Surely we weren't going to the cinema on a motorbike? I glanced down at my slim navy skirt and high-heeled shoes. 'Are we . . . ?' I said uncertainly.

Howard laughed. 'Of course not. It's just a hobby. But I'd be glad to give Stefan a ride round the block one day.'

The boy's face had brightened. 'Can I, Mummy?'

'Are you going to be good?'

He nodded.

'Well then, I suppose so. If you don't go too fast.' I looked at Howard as I said this, nervous for my son's safety. But he looked solid and dependable and after all, he was a father.

'So – let's go,' he said, and once more I left the room, leaving my son behind.

When we were in the car I said, 'It's a good job my mother didn't hear that. She's against bribery at all costs.'

He shrugged. 'Well, needs must when the devil drives. Don't forget, I've been through it myself. And it does get better, I promise.'

I felt strangely reassured, both by his words, and by the fact that I was not the only parent who indulged my children.

I loved the film! I had forgotten what it was to be so completely taken out of myself and I left the cinema ablaze with the music.

'What a story! How clever Peter Shaffer is. The irony at the end, where no one believes Salieri, and Mozart goes on for posterity.'

'Do you think he really was such a gross little man?' Howard had his arm under my elbow and I allowed him to turn me into the entrance of a coffee shop. 'It's hard to equate his music with his vulgarity.'

I sat obediently at a table while Howard fetched two cups of coffee, but when he came back I said, 'We'd better not be long. I told Kate eleven.'

'Oh, we won't be too late. I don't think the car will change into a pumpkin.'

Nevertheless I tried to drink quickly, but the coffee was far too hot. Resignedly I asked, 'Tell me about your motorbike? Do you ride it often?'

'No, I haven't the time. It's an indulgence really. I like polishing it! It's a Harley-Davidson, and I go to rallies sometimes. Val hated it. Now at least I am free to do what I like. There are some advantages to a single life.'

I shuddered. 'Well I've yet to find them. People say you can eat biscuits while you're reading in bed. But I don't like biscuits and I can't get used to sleeping alone.'

I found myself blushing, realising the implications of what I was saying. It was true, the bed was wide and cold and I missed David's animal snuffles as he drifted into sleep, the sense of something warm and solid if I woke in the night, which I now did increasingly. But I also missed the sex, and had turgid dreams of trembling pleasure which left me feeling emptier than ever and somehow soiled. I felt that Howard knew all this as he looked at me over his coffee cup, and it was more of an embarrassment than a comfort.

I finished my drink quickly, anxious to be home. 'Do you mind?' I asked, pushing back my chair. 'I feel I must relieve Kate. For all we know she may still be reading *The Hobbit*!'

But she was not. She was slumped in an armchair, watching a chat show. She looked up.

'No Howard?'

'We had coffee on the way home. I hope you don't mind.'

'No. I'm not your mother, suspecting you of snogging on the porch. Did you, by the way?'

'Did I what?'

'Snog on the porch.'

I found myself blushing furiously. 'Kate! Of course not. I shook his hand in the car, and said thank you like a well-brought-up girl.'

'Shook his hand? That's a bit formal, isn't it?'

'Well it's a long time since I did this sort of thing.'

She heaved herself out of the chair and switched off the television. 'Do you like him? Howard?'

I shrugged. 'I've no idea. He's pleasant enough, I suppose.' It suddenly seemed important to put her straight on the matter. 'But I'm not looking for a relationship, Kate, it's far too soon. So please don't try and engineer anything.'

She grinned at me, pushing at her dark hair and pulling on a coat. 'Nothing is further from my thoughts. Anyway, I'm sure Howard can do his own engineering. Are you seeing him again?'

'Well, there's the motorbike ride. He's coming round next weekend.'

Her grin widened. 'I see,' she said knowingly, and I said sharply, 'He promised Stefan. I can't let him down.'

'Well – have fun.' She picked up her bag and opened the front door. 'And let me know if I can help out again. It's all in a good cause – getting Julia back on an even keel.'

I watched her go down the path and into her car. As I closed the door it occurred to me that I hadn't even thought to ask about the children.

'So,' my mother said. I could hear the satisfaction in her voice. 'You're seeing him again.'

'I'm not seeing him at all. He's coming to give Stefan a ride.'

I had not meant to tell her, but Stefan had wanted to speak to her and his excitement had burst out with the news. Mummy had been to the cinema with a man, who had promised him a ride on his motorbike. Because he was such a good boy. I could almost hear my mother tutting at the terms of his obedience. Now she expressed other anxieties to me.

'Are you sure he'll be all right? Harley-Davidsons are enormous. Is this man reliable?'

'He assures me he won't go over twenty miles an hour. And they're only going round the block.'

She had thought of something else. 'Will he wear a helmet?'

'Yes. One of his daughters'.'

'Daughters'? He's got children?'

'Yes, he's divorced.'

I could hear her digesting this. Divorce has always been a dirty word with my mother. I told myself she could hardly have felt better if he had still been married.

To change the subject I asked, 'How's Dad?'

'Oh, overworking as usual. Too many night calls, and often for no good reason. I wish he'd take early retirement.'

'And then what would he do? I can't see him taking to the golf course.'

'Do you know, dear, I sometimes wonder. He can't read and listen to music all day. There's the garden, of course.'

'But you do that.'

'But maybe I could do with a hand. And it would be nice to have him at home.'

But it seemed to me her voice was doubtful and she was reassuring herself rather than me. Having Dad around all day would be considered untidy, and that my mother never could abide.

After the phone call, I decided to make a chocolate cake. The least I could do was offer Howard something after their ride. I was whizzing the food processor when I found to my astonishment that I was humming. I stopped abruptly. It was a long time since I had hummed, though it had always been a habit of mine, one that had irritated my mother and amused

35

David. What did it mean? Tentatively, I probed my feelings. Could it be that, for the moment, I was happy? If so, what about David? Instinctively I clutched at the comforting cloak of sorrow. I knew a panicky sense of loss; could it be that one day I would forget David? Urgently, my heart called out to him. 'Are you there? I'm sorry I wasn't thinking of you. Forgive me!' I switched off the processor, and listened. Sure enough, his presence floated into the silent kitchen. He hadn't gone. It had just been a momentary lapse on my part, an absorption with the task in hand, an anticipation of Stefan's treat. Spooning the mixture into tins I told David about Stefan's ride, hoping he would understand about Howard, for there was nothing really to understand. He was just a friend.

But I was making him a cake.

When the doorbell rang, Stefan ran excitedly to open it. Howard stood there, enormous in a leather jacket, carrying two helmets, black and gleaming like bulbous mushrooms.

'Hello, young man. All set?'

Stefan hopped from foot to foot, looking at me questioningly as if expecting a last-minute curtailment.

'Natalie and I are coming out to watch,' I told Howard, gathering Natalie's hand in mine. She was staring at Howard solemnly. 'This is Howard,' I told her, remembering that they hadn't met. 'And, Howard, this is Natalie.'

He smiled down at her, and we went out into the road. The bike stood there, a shiny red and black monster.

Natalie tugged my hand. 'I don't want to have a ride,' she said nervously.

With a sense of relief I assured her that she didn't have to.

I had dressed Stefan in a thick padded anorak. Howard lowered the helmet onto his head and fastened the straps. It swamped him, beneath it his neck looked impossibly thin and frail. One knock and it would surely snap. I felt a stab of fear. What sort of mother was I, letting him take such a risk? It was not too late to change my mind.

But Howard was lifting him onto the back seat. It was almost too wide for his legs. Then he swung his own leg over and told Stefan to hold tightly round his waist. My heart was in my mouth as the huge engine roared into life.

'Wheeee!' Stefan's face, annihilated by the helmet, broke into a smile of ecstasy.

'Take it slowly,' I said urgently. 'He looks so small, how will he stay on?'

And then they were off, cruising at a stately pace down the quiet street. As they disappeared round the corner it occurred to me to wonder for the first time if it was legal. Taking Natalie's hand I turned and walked the other way, my eyes fixed on the distant corner waiting for them to appear. The sound of the engine faded away and then there was a long silence.

'Where are they?' Natalie asked, tugging my hand. She looked worried.

'It will take a little while,' I reassured us both. 'They're going quite slowly.'

But were they? Once out of sight, would Howard accelerate like a reckless teenager, throwing caution to the winds and my son from the back seat like a cast-off shoe? I strained my ears. A car came slowly round the corner and passed us as we hesitated on the kerb, eyes straining towards the corner.

'Where is he?' Natalie asked again, and I could have shaken her in exasperation for voicing my fears.

I nearly burst into tears at the sound of a distant siren. Then it was overlaid with a low growl, followed in a moment by the blissful sight of the bike taking the corner so slowly that it didn't even lean. Relief made me gather Natalie into my arms, and we followed them back to the front gate. When we arrived, Stefan was standing on the pavement, helmet in his hands. His eyes were shining.

'That was brilliant! We saw Kate with Ben and Dominic and she didn't recognise me until I called out.'

My heart was so full at his pleasure that I could barely speak. Howard must have seen this as he put his hand on my shoulder as we walked up the path. I could smell the leather of his jacket, which creaked as he moved.

'Tea?' I offered as we went inside.

He unzipped his jacket with alacrity.

'And I've made a cake,' I told him, as if this was an unusual achievement. 'I thought we'd sit at the table, it's easier with the children.'

I had laid the pine table in the kitchen, and Natalie climbed onto her chair, reaching for her orange juice.

'We thought you weren't coming,' she said conversationally. 'Mummy was frightened, she was squeezing my hand.'

'Nonsense.' I put the teapot on the table. 'But it did seem rather an age,' I confessed.

'That's because we were going slowly. But it was great, wasn't it, Stefan?'

He nodded, his face glowing. 'Brilliant!' he breathed. 'Can I have some cake?'

I went to pick up the knife, but Howard had got there first. In astonishment, I watched him cut four slices, and pass a piece to each of the children. I sat back in my chair, feeling blissfully redundant, dazzled by the realisation that to have someone else to cut the cake should be such a treat. I couldn't speak for gratitude, and for incredulity that it should be so.

Howard seemed anxious to help me put the children to bed, but here I drew the line. It was an intimacy we didn't require. And for so long I had been a slave to their every need that I was not anxious to relinquish my position. The episode over the cake had accentuated my vulnerability. It would be so easy to clutch at something just because it was convenient.

For the same reason, I hesitated when he asked me out to supper.

'Come on,' he urged me. 'Give yourself some fun.'

'I don't think I'm ready for fun.' What I meant was that I didn't think I was ready for him. 'Can I think about it? I know it seems silly, but there are the children to think of too. I don't feel I can keep leaving them.'

'But they have to learn you have a life.' Suddenly he sounded like my mother and I felt irritated and resentful. He was trying to pressurise me.

'I'll ring you,' I said, using the age-old put-down, knowing that I wouldn't. Howard was two years along the line ahead of me, whereas I was still in mourning. Already I felt I had somehow betrayed David. It was time to call a halt.

He looked a bit put out as he picked up his jacket.

'I can't thank you enough for Stefan's ride,' I said, anxious that I shouldn't appear ungrateful. 'The only problem is he will now probably grow up wanting one of his own and then what shall I do?'

'Let him have one. Motorbikes are only dangerous if they're not treated with respect.'

I wasn't sure, but the problem was still comfortingly far ahead. I watched him roar off into the dark, and returned quite gratefully to the house.

That night, Natalie wet the bed again. She had been getting so much better, I wondered what had upset her.

She was unable to tell me. Thumb in mouth, she shook her head as I gently probed. As I stripped the bed, I was confirmed in my decision that it was far too soon to disrupt the even tenor of their days.

Kate, however, had other ideas. We were shopping together later in the week, and unwisely I had told her of Howard's invitation.

39

'Great. Well, I'll baby-sit of course. It's good to see you getting out a bit.'

We were at the vegetable counter and I loaded a cauliflower and some carrots into my trolley and looked dubiously at the leeks. They were cheaper at the greengrocer's. I decided to leave them.

'But I'm not going,' I said emphatically, grasping my trolley. Kate picked up mangetout peas and two avocados which I looked at enviously. Dropping them into her trolley she looked at me in amazement.

'Why ever not? I thought you liked him.'

'I never said that. Anyway, that's nothing to do with it. I have other considerations.'

She sounded exasperated. 'It's supper, Julia. Hardly a lifetime commitment.'

Obstinately, I said nothing, pushing my trolley towards the pasta. Natalie trailed along, holding the handle. The other three were at school.

'Anyway,' Kate said when she caught up with me at the frozen food cabinet, 'I've got some news for you. I'm going back to work.' She selected chocolate-chip ice cream and butterscotch sauce. Reluctantly I took a small packet of vanilla.

I was not surprised. Kate had been quite a career woman before she had the twins, something to do with marketing. But I was surprised to find I was envious. And not a little put out. How would I manage without her company?

'But how will you manage in the holidays? And after school?'

'We're getting an au pair. Harry's quite excited! He visualises long Scandinavian legs and sexy underwear on the line!'

'Which I should imagine is the last thing you're looking for!'

I unloaded my shopping onto the moving belt, hoping I

40

had enough money to pay for it. Natalie reached for some sweets, but I pushed her hand away.

'Not today, darling,' I told her, feeling mean. Not for the first time it occurred to me that I must, eventually, get a job too. Feeling depressed, I paid the bill and turned to wait for Kate, who was carelessly flourishing her credit card and whose purchases were a teetering pile on the counter. Not for her the exigencies of economy. Not for her the lonely meal on her lap when the children were in bed. To my horror I found tears coursing down my cheeks as I walked to the car, and I brushed them away in case Natalie should notice. I was not even to be permitted the indulgence of self-pity.

At Easter, I went to stay with my parents. It was not something I relished, but it was better than being alone. The children were excited and I realised how restricted our lives had become.

But I couldn't resist urging them, 'You will be good, won't you? Nana isn't used to a mess, and Granddad doesn't like noise.'

I had been trying hard to be firm with them and hoped they wouldn't let me down. I piled the car with books and games and clothes for all eventualities, for although it was April the weather veered from hot to wintry, with slashing showers racing on the wind.

When I turned into the drive, my mother was cutting daffodils. She wore a blue tweed skirt and matching jumper, and had rubber gloves on her thin hands. She laid the daffodils carefully in a wooden trug and bent to remove a daring dandelion which had somehow escaped her trowel. I noticed for the first time how grey she had got. The realisation disturbed me. She was getting old.

The children tumbled from the car.

'Hello, dears,' she said, embracing them coolly. She waited

41

until I had extracted the luggage, then gave me a light kiss on the cheek.

'You're looking thin, dear. But I like your hair, it suits you shorter.'

I felt ridiculously pleased. It was still somehow essential to win her approval.

'Where's Dad?'

'He's on call today, he's been called out. I hope he'll be here for lunch.'

She picked up one of the cases but I objected. 'Leave that to me. You see to your flowers.'

She dropped the case on the gravel drive. 'Well, don't carry them both at once, you'll hurt yourself.' She indicated a floral canvas bag and the children's Wellington boots. 'Children, help your mother, you can carry those.'

Dutifully, they picked them up and followed us silently into the house. I gave them an encouraging smile as I held the door for them, then went back for the second case. I could easily have managed them both but, already, we were all doing what we were told.

After lunch, my mother produced Easter eggs, one for each of us. The children's contained chocolate buttons, mine four milk chocolates.

'Mother,' I said in surprise, 'we usually wait till Easter Sunday.'

She looked hurt and I realised I had been ungracious. 'But it's lovely of you. They can have mine on Sunday.'

'That's what I thought. Now what do you want to do? A walk while it's fine?'

'I think the children would just as soon stay in the garden. And I'm happy just to mooch. Perhaps we can all go to Richmond Park tomorrow.'

'Well maybe we can persuade your father to mooch with you. That's if the telephone leaves him in peace. I'll be in the garden, I'll keep an eye on the children. And,' she added, as if to show how hard she was trying, 'there are hot cross buns for tea.'

The following day it was bright and warm. We set off for the park, taking a picnic lunch. We went in my father's big Volvo, with the children and me in the back. It was a treat to be driven. As we passed through the wrought-iron gates of the park I had a curious feeling of being on holiday, and resolved to enjoy the day.

We parked and walked across the springy grass, following a herd of deer who drifted further away as we approached. Natalie ran after them, waving her arms and shouting, 'Deers! Come here, deers!' and they stampeded away in alarm.

'Hush,' my mother remonstrated. 'You're frightening them.'

Natalie took no notice and skipped ahead, singing to herself. Stefan ran to join her and they stopped beneath an oak with low spreading branches.

'Can we climb it?' Stefan asked when we reached them.

I was dubious. It looked a bit dangerous and I wasn't sure if it was allowed. But my mother's saying, 'I don't think so, Stefan,' spurred me on to agree that it would be a good idea. I looked to my father for support, and with a nod he lifted Natalie onto a lower branch where she sat, looking down.

'I'm the king of the castle,' she chanted. Stefan reached to pull himself up and she kicked at his hand. 'Get down, you dirty rascal.'

'Natalie!' It was my mother again. 'That's unkind.'

Natalie looked sulky and her thumb slid into her mouth.

'I think,' said my father soothingly, 'that this would be a good place for our picnic.'

'Can we have ours in the tree?' Stefan was pulling himself up onto the branch.

'I don't see why not.' My father opened the bag he was

43

carrying and spread a thin rug on the grass. My mother had packed neat foil packages of ham sandwiches, sausage rolls and tomatoes.

'Are there crisps?' asked Stefan.

'Oh, I didn't think of crisps.'

She looked dismayed, and I felt sorry for her; she was trying so hard, and it seemed she couldn't win.

I had been given my old room, with a single bed and rows of books on the shelves – the *Narnia* series, *Watership Down* and hospital romances from the time when I had shared my parents' dream. With widowhood it seemed came reversion to childhood, a loss of dignity and adult status. Meanwhile the children shared the king-size double bed in the spare room, two little bumps beneath the duvet under which, I believed, Natalie had been conceived. We had always been reticent about making love in my parents' house, but that night we couldn't help ourselves, and afterwards David had said, grinning wickedly, 'That's one up on your mother. I bet you'll get pregnant. What *would* she say?' And I had hit him with the pillow and we had stifled our laughter under the duvet.

When we returned from the picnic my father engaged the children in a game of halma, the board dating from my childhood, and I retreated to my room and stared disconsolately at the bookshelves. Surely it was time to clear them. I didn't want any of the books and the children were acquiring plenty of their own. I felt a sudden urgent need to put my childhood behind me. It hurt to be returned so peremptorily to the past, without the dignity of a husband to support me. It seemed imperative to take a stand.

I went down to the kitchen where my mother was making supper. She was chopping onions and she wiped her eyes with an apologetic smile.

'I sometimes wonder,' she said, 'about the first person to

cut an onion. He – or she – must have got something of a shock!'

It was an amusing thought but I had other things on my mind and plunged straight in.

'Can't we get rid of all those old books in my room? It's like a museum in there, it gives me the creeps.'

She looked at me in surprise, her eyes red and wet.

'But I like them there. I go in there sometimes and think about you, about when you were a girl and doing your homework up there. That sort of thing is important as you grow older.'

I was amazed at her sentimentality and said brusquely, 'It sounds more unhealthy to me, brooding on the past.'

She scooped the onions into a pan of sizzling oil, and said nothing.

'It's so unlike you,' I persisted. 'You never keep anything.'

'I keep useful things. Your children can read them when they visit. In fact, your father and I were wondering whether you'd like to leave them here for a few days. It would give you a break, and we'd enjoy it.'

'A break? For what?' The thought of the empty house filled me with horror, as did the thought of the children rampaging through my parents' orderly existence without me to keep control of them. Even as I thought it, I realised that my control was still a transitory thing. Without me, my mother would be able to impose her own rules. But was that fair on the children? 'I don't think they'd want to stay, they're very clingy at present,' I excused them.

She shrugged. 'It would do them good. They have to realise you have a life.'

'A life? My life is them at the moment.'

'Exactly. And that won't do.' She paused while adding cubed steak to the pan. Then she asked diffidently, 'Do you still see that friend of yours? Howard was he called?'

'I never really saw him, as you put it. We went to the cinema once.'

'And he gave Stefan that ride on his bike. The child has never forgotten it. He sounds a nice man. We'd rather hoped –'

I knew what she'd hoped. 'Forget it, Mother,' I said tersely. 'It's too soon.'

She stirred the pan, then turned to look at me. To my surprise her expression was tremulous.

'Darling,' she said. I was startled; she never called me darling. She went on, 'If you only knew how I hate to see you alone. We both do. We love you so much, we only want your happiness.'

I was both touched and uneasy. I was not used to expressions of love, and she seemed clumsy and awkward, busying herself with pots and pans as if regretting revealing herself. Something seemed to be demanded of me, so I put my hand equally awkwardly on her arm.

'Thanks, Mother, I know you do.' I wondered if I ought to kiss her, but decided against it. My mother and I only kissed hello and goodbye. With my father it was different. He hugged me, and I him. Love between us was an easy and natural thing, not buttoned up and restrained as it was with my mother. But I didn't want to cause her unhappiness, so I said, 'I promise you I will try and be happy. Please don't worry about me.'

'That's easier said than done. If only you had a career, something to fall back on, to fill your life.'

I had heard this before, many times. There was no point in explaining that I hadn't wanted to be a doctor, that it wasn't David's fault. I had defended him so often over the years, and it made no difference. However there was some truth in what she said. I was thirty-two years old. What was I going to do with my life?

She transferred the casserole to the oven and turned to the

sink. I picked up a tea towel, and dried while she washed, in silence.

It was into this void that Stefan suddenly burst, crying eagerly, 'Granddad's going to teach me to play chess! Can we stay here while I learn?'

I turned to him with a flash of anger at my father. It was unfair to go behind my back, to wean the children away from their dependence on me; they were all I had, my whole purpose in living. Although one look at my son's bright expectant face told me that it would be selfish to refuse.

But it seemed necessary to warn him. 'I wouldn't be here. Will you be all right on your own?'

I heard my mother give a tut of irritation. 'Of course he will. Anyway, Natalie will be here.'

'I'm not so sure about that,' I snapped. 'Have you asked her too?'

'Well, I did suggest that we made some cakes. She seemed quite keen.'

'I make cakes with her, you know.'

My mother spoke calmly. 'Then you know how she enjoys it.' Then her expression became almost pleading. 'Please let them stay, we'd so enjoy it.'

'But the noise, the muddle.'

'We can cope I'm sure.'

Just then my father came into the kitchen, holding Natalie by the hand. She had chocolate round her face. 'I've finished my Easter egg,' she told me smugly.

'Darling, you won't eat your supper,' I remonstrated gently, before my mother could.

She came to me and put her thin arms round my waist. I stroked the bright bush of hair. 'Do you want to stay on for a day or so with Nana and Granddad? Just you and Stefan?'

She looked up at me doubtfully. 'Not you?'

'Not me. It will be very grown up.'

'I'm four,' she said. 'I'm going to school soon.'

47

'Yes. And this will be practice.'

My mother butted in. 'We can make some gingerbread men. And plant some seeds, then later in the summer you can come and see how they've grown.'

Her eagerness was somehow pathetic. Natalie nodded, and released her hold on me.

Helplessly, I knew that I had lost.

I left on Easter Monday after tea. The four of them stood on the drive watching me go, and I felt as if I were losing a limb. Two limbs. For the past year we had been a unit, tight against the world. Now the world had intervened. As I lost sight of them I was seized with panic. Suppose something happened to them? Suppose I never saw them again? It was all I could do not to turn round and pull them into the car with me.

Instead, struggling for reason, I drove steadily on through the Bank Holiday traffic. It was a fine warm day and the A3 was busy. The first caravans of the year were out, returning from the coast and the country, happy families crowded in cars eating sweets and singing songs as we used to do. As I still did, when the children were with me. Now the car was silent and empty. Like my life.

Like the house when I let myself in, carrying my solitary bag. It closed around me, cold and quiet as the grave.

'David?' I called out urgently. I listened, every tissue strained with the need for comfort. But I couldn't summon him. All I could hear was the ticking clock. I dropped my bag and stood disconsolate in the hall, too miserable even to cry. There were to be three nights and two days of this silence. How would I get through?

I felt as if I had lost everything; all those whom I loved, my status as a wife and mother, as an adult even, relegated to the nursery, my children appropriated by those who knew best, who could better deal with them than I, who clearly thought that I should be getting on with my life and forgetting David.

I went into the kitchen. Natalie's furry slippers were under her chair, we had forgotten to take them. I picked one up and pressed it to my cheek. She seemed very far away. Would she be in bed? Would she perhaps be crying? It suddenly seemed urgent that I ring, but what could I do if she was? It would be too upsetting. I could only say, 'I told you so,' with a sort of vicious delight, and I felt too depressed for anger.

I boiled the kettle, but, too dispirited to make tea, I wandered into the sitting room, switching on lights and drawing the curtains. Used to my mother's manicured spaces, I realised what a mess the room was in. Toys, newspapers, a discarded pullover, sewing things from some mending I had done two weeks ago. Half-heartedly I began to gather things up, thinking that in the two days ahead I could perhaps spring-clean the house. But instead I sat down heavily on the sofa, fiddling with a car of Stefan's. There were some dead daffodils in a vase, their trumpets withered and sour-smelling. The water was brown. They looked like I felt, a shrivelled husk standing in a murk of grief. How could I pull myself out and struggle through to the spring?

I sat awhile, examining an idea. Then I got up and consulted the phone book. With surprising purpose and calm, I picked up the phone, and dialled Howard's number.

THREE

Howard called for me at seven the following evening. I had spent the day doing desultory housework and wondering if I had done the right thing. He had sounded pleased when I said, 'How about that meal you suggested a while back?' but pride had prevented me from giving him a reason other than that I was on my own and wouldn't need a baby-sitter. It would not have been kind to let on that I was desperate, that I was scraping the barrel to find some residue of my self-esteem. Neither would that have done my self-esteem much good. So I kept it light. I tried to feel light as I waited for him to come for me. I tried to explain to David, but I don't think he was listening.

Howard arrived in a taxi, explaining that this would enable him to have a drink. I didn't question it at the time, thinking only that it was sensible. We went to a restaurant overlooking the river in Richmond. The last of the daylight shone on the water, and the first lights made twinkling reflections, disturbed by the odd passing boat. There were pink cloths and linen napkins and real flowers on the table. The menu was far too extensive, making me wonder whether they would do anything really well. However, the novelty of choosing won me over. I selected warm chicken liver salad, followed by pork tenderloin with caramelised apples and a green peppercorn, port and cream sauce. Howard chose lentil soup and venison casserole with a medley of winter vegetables. He ordered red wine and sat back with a self-satisfied smile.

'So – you've dumped the offspring. It's a good feeling, isn't it? I mean, to have a bit of freedom.'

I wasn't so sure, and said so.

'Of course,' he went on, 'I don't really have any problem on that score, with Mrs Sullivan living in.'

'But don't they mind being left?'

'They're used to it. I decided pretty soon after Val left me that it was important for me to make a new life. You can't do that with children hanging round your neck.'

My salad had arrived and I prodded the liver thoughtfully. Was that so? I didn't feel as if my children were so much hanging round me as supporting me. And surely they needed me in their turn?

'Perhaps it's different for your two. After all, they still have a mother.'

He grunted into his soup. 'Not that you'd know it, for all the notice she takes of them.'

I was shocked. 'Doesn't she see them then?'

'When it suits her, which isn't often. She even forgot Deborah's birthday last year. And who is it who has to pick up the pieces? Me. You'll find that out.'

I nodded. I had found it out already. But at least Stefan and Natalie knew it couldn't be helped, their father would have been with them if he could. I wondered at Valerie's ability to so betray her children.

Two bottles of wine arrived and I raised my eyebrows.

'I hope you don't expect me to drink one of those, I'm strictly a two-glass girl.'

He looked at me quizzically as the waiter poured the wine. 'Pity. Still, I expect I shall manage, I don't have to drive.'

I felt a swift distaste, and remembered how flushed and excited he had got at Kate and Harry's. I didn't like men who drank. David had been very abstemious, not drinking at all when he was on call. Despite the salad, which was delicious, lightly dressed in flavoured oil which contrasted well with the warm and cloying liver, the evening began to stretch ahead uncomfortably.

But Howard was a good conversationalist, and it was a change to indulge in adult talk, and eat a meal without stretching out to cut up somebody's meat. He told me about an Easter rally he had been to on his motorbike, and described the people he had met there.

'You get all sorts – doctors, solicitors, house painters, there was even one unemployed computer programmer, though how he affords it I don't know.'

'I expect he earned enough when he was employed – these people do.'

'You sound rather bitter, if I may say so.'

I was startled. I hadn't meant to. 'Maybe I'm just feeling rather hard done by,' I explained apologetically. 'Or perhaps I wish I was one of them. I do feel singularly ill-equipped for the job market, but I feel I must do something when Natalie goes to school.'

He looked at me over his casserole. 'Can you type?'

'Good heavens, no. I can't do anything useful. I was training to be a doctor when I married David.'

'Really?' His expression was respectful. 'So – why don't you go back and finish it?'

'Oh, my heart wasn't in it. I found it too stressful. And too difficult, if I'm honest. I doubt if I would have qualified in the end. I was glad of the excuse to give up. But one good thing, it made me appreciate David's work and his problems. We were able to share that.'

The sadness which always overtook me when I spoke of David made me push away my plate on which pork still lurked in its creamy sauce. 'That was lovely, but rather rich. I'm sorry.'

'No worries.' He was wiping his plate with a piece of bread. I noticed that the first wine bottle was empty, and his face was flushed. I wondered if I could reasonably get away without a pudding, plead a headache or some other excuse, but the waiter had brought the sweet trolley, piled

52

high with profiteroles and gateaux and apple pie, and Howard was pointing to the chocolate cheesecake with a sweaty finger.

'Doesn't that look scrumptious? I'll have that. And some cream. What about you, Julia?'

I chose fruit salad, without cream.

'Surely you're not slimming,' he said in a bantering tone. 'You have a lovely figure, though perhaps rather too thin if anything.'

I bridled. 'I just don't feel like cream,' I told him firmly, as if I were putting down a child. But what he said was true, my dress was hanging off me and my cheeks were getting the sunken look of someone who has been ill for a long time. But then I had – I had been sick at heart. I had every excuse. It was not for him to tell me, nor to express his preference. I decided to eat my pudding quickly and then ask to go home.

Howard, however, was getting into a festive mood and began telling jokes. One or two were funny and I found myself laughing despite myself. He picked up the wine and held it out to me. I shook my head, putting my hand over my glass, and watched nervously as he drained the bottle into his own.

'Have you noticed,' he said, as he finished his cheesecake, 'that women very seldom tell jokes? Why is that, do you suppose?'

I shook my head. 'I don't know about the others, but for my part I've usually forgotten the punch line. But it's interesting how few stand-up comedians are women. Maybe women don't see that as their role in life – making people laugh.'

'Yet a funny woman is really sexy. Val was funny, it was her best feature. I missed laughing, when she had gone. And Kate is funny. Harry's Kate. Don't you find her so?'

'Well, she can certainly cheer me up. Howard, do you

think we could go now? Not wait for coffee? I'm not used to being out late, rather pathetic of me I know . . .'

'Late? It's half-past nine!' He threw back his head and laughed, displaying rather a lot of teeth. I was both discomfited and irritated.

'Well, just let's say I want to go.' I seized on an excuse. 'I said I'd ring my parents, and they go to bed early.'

'On one condition – that you give me some coffee at your house.'

Unwisely, but suddenly desperate to get away, I agreed. He called for the bill and ordered a taxi, and I escaped to the ladies' room. Despite the food and wine, my face was pale and to pass the time I applied lipstick and blusher, and combed my hair. Then it occurred to me that it might seem as if I were trying to look attractive so I rubbed my face with cold water and pushed a hand through my hair. Standing at the hand dryer I wondered what was the matter with me. So, Howard had had a bit too much to drink, but he had been perfectly agreeable. What more had I been expecting? I had had a free meal and some company and I would be home again by ten o'clock; at home in an empty house which had felt like a prison all day but to which I was now straining to return. I wanted a bath, and my own bed. And I wanted to talk to David.

In the taxi I instinctively sat at the end of the seat away from Howard but even so I could smell the drink on his breath. I could hear him chuckling to himself and decided not to enquire. But he wanted me to know.

'I was thinking about female comedians,' he said. 'When they're really funny, they're talking about sex.'

It was impossible to ignore. 'But I don't agree, I find that quite distasteful, especially in a woman. I don't think sex is funny, I think it's a pathetic way to get easy laughs.'

'On the contrary, sex can be very funny. It's only not funny when you're not getting it.'

My face burned and I was glad of the dark. I felt like an old-fashioned prude and was bitterly regretting my agreement to the coffee. But when we arrived, before I could stop him, Howard had leaped out and paid off the driver. If for nothing else, he would have to come in and telephone for another taxi. Cursing my ineptitude, I opened the door and reluctantly let him in.

'We'll have it in the kitchen, it's warmer,' I said, determined not to let him in any further. Amenably, he sat down at the table, which unusually, thanks to the labours of the day, was clear of papers and china, watching me as I filled the coffee machine and switched it on. I felt uneasy with his eyes on me, and sat opposite him, trying to think of something to say. But he spoke first, and his voice was maudlin.

'I get lonely, Julia. Don't you?'

I told myself it was the drink talking, and preferred the ribald good humour of earlier.

'Of course I do,' I said, all calm reasonableness. 'But it doesn't do to dwell on it.'

'But what do you do about it?'

'I put up with it.'

'No, that's not what I mean.' He looked at me acutely, and his meaning was perfectly clear. I flinched and my face blazed again.

'I know what you mean, and it's none of your business.'

Then, suddenly, he was up and standing behind me. 'I could make it my business. You're very attractive . . .'

'You said I was too thin,' I said desperately, trying to keep it light.

His hand was on my shoulder, his winy breath on my cheek.

'Let me kiss you, Julia.'

'No.' I turned my head away, trying to rise from the chair. Somewhere in the distance I heard the coffee bubbling, then he had pulled me up towards him and was pressing himself against me. His hand found my breast – the other was squeezing my buttocks. I could feel his urgency hard against my groin.

I struggled as his lips found mine. Then, suddenly, it was so good to feel a man's hands on me that I felt myself slipping away. Desire bloomed like a hot flower and I let him lift my skirt. My lips opened to take his tongue and my legs parted for him. It was only when he began to push me to the floor that I heard David calling.

Horrified, I pulled away, giving him a sharp push backwards. 'Don't!' I shouted. 'How dare you?'

He reeled back against the draining board, his face flushed and bemused. But his voice was angry as he shouted back, 'But you loved it, try and tell me you didn't. What's the matter with you? Are you a woman, or what?'

He grabbed my arm and wrenched me towards him. With my free hand I swung at his face and gave him a stinging smack. With a gasp, he dropped my arm and put his hand to his cheek. 'So,' he said through gritted teeth. 'That's the way you want to play it, is it? Exciting! I never knew you had it in you.'

I backed away so that the table was between us. 'Now listen,' I said, trying to control the trembling in my voice. 'It was a mistake. You caught me unawares. I don't want you. I don't want anyone.'

He said sneeringly, 'Well you could have fooled me.'

He began to advance round the table. His bulky body, which had once looked reassuring, was now threatening. In a panic, I picked up a chair and held it out, legs towards him.

'Don't come any nearer.' Suddenly I wanted to laugh. Howard had turned into a cliché, and it all seemed so melodramatic. But there was a wild intent in his eyes that warned me not to drop my guard.

'I want you to go,' I said firmly. 'Now, and quietly. And we'll forget it ever happened.'

The fight seemed to go out of him as he eyed the chair. Maybe he knew he was beaten. He shook his head and rubbed at his eyes as if confused. He looked pathetic and disgusting. I edged to the kitchen door and opened it.

'Please go.'

'Can't I call a cab?'

'No.' I didn't want him in my house a moment longer. For all I knew he might rape me.

He looked at me long and hard. 'There's a name for women like you. You rang me – remember? You're a fool. You won't be so proud after three years, I can tell you.'

I didn't answer. He turned and went to the front door.

'Bitch.' He spat out the word as he opened the door. Then he was on the step and I ran at the door and slammed it, fastening the chain and leaning against it, trembling. 'Bitch.' The word rang in my ears. I felt sick, and unclean, frightened and ashamed.

Ashamed most of all, ashamed of my body which had nearly betrayed me.

The night seemed endless. Tormented with thwarted desire and horror at what I had so nearly done, I lay awake till dawn. Several times, hearing a noise outside, I got up and peered through the window into the empty street, fearful that he had come back for me. What did I fear? That he would take me by force, or that I would willingly give him what he wanted? Either option was unthinkable.

Tossing on my pillow I apologised over and over again to David. 'Forgive me, it was only because I miss you so much,' I told him. Eventually, I found a sort of peace and slept like a dead thing until nine. Then I got up, showered, and telephoned my parents.

My mother answered the phone, pre-empting my enquiry. 'Hello, dear, all's well this end, you don't have to worry. And we'll have them back by lunchtime tomorrow.'

57

'Actually,' I said, feeling feeble and pathetic, 'I was wondering if I could come and get them. Today. I'm missing them, you see.'

'Oh dear. We had arranged to take them to a film this afternoon. *The Tales of Beatrix Potter*. They'd love it.'

'Well, perhaps I could come too. And stay the night. I don't want to deprive you.'

I hated myself for my weakness, hanging on for her reply as if my life depended on it. What if she said no? But then how could she refuse? They were my children. And I was hers.

'All right. I won't tell them, it will be a surprise. Come for an early lunch, we have to leave at a quarter to two.'

Relief made me expansive. 'Lovely! It will be nice treat. Thank you. Where are they now, can I talk to them?'

'They've dragged your father off to the park already. He's so enjoying having them, Julia. We both are. We must do it more often.'

I shuddered. At that moment, it was the last thing I wanted. I was too vulnerable, too scared. Too lonely.

'Well, I'll see you at half-past twelve.' I replaced the receiver. Then, having second thoughts, I lifted it and laid it on the shelf. There was nobody likely to ring that I wanted to talk to.

When I arrived at the house, Natalie was on the drive with a skipping-rope. She looked up when she heard the car and her face was a picture of surprise and joy which soothed my ragged soul. I leaped from the car and hugged her to me.

'Nana bought me this, but I can't do it,' she said when I released her. She held out the skipping-rope. 'Stefan can but he says it's sissy for a boy. He won't help me.'

'I don't think anyone can help you skip,' I told her soothingly. 'It's just something that happens. Like riding a bike.'

She looked disappointed and dropped the rope onto the gravel.

'We're going to the pictures. To see dancing. Will you come?'

'Of course, that's why I'm here. I didn't want to miss the treat.'

Holding hands, we went into the house. The Hoover hummed in the sitting room. My mother hardly looked up as we entered.

'Just clearing up after their elevenses,' she explained, as if a full medieval banquet had taken place with bones on the floor and breadcrumbs everywhere. She wore a floral pinafore and her face was flushed.

Despite my irritation I felt moved to say, 'I hope they haven't been too much work. I'm sure they've tried to be good.'

She switched off the cleaner and unplugged the flex. She didn't answer, which made me nervous.

'Where's Stefan?'

'In the study, playing chess. He seems to have quite a grasp of the game.'

'He's a very clever boy.' I felt a bursting pride and longed to see him. Natalie went to help with the lunch and I went along to the study, knocking on the door as I had been taught to do. The two of them were sitting in deep thought, their heads bent over the board. I noticed several of my father's pieces on the table in front of Stefan and he was in the process of moving his knight. His head gleamed blond – my father's grey hair was getting thin. For a poignant moment I imagined David's vibrant fuzz in its place, and felt cheated. But my father looked up and reached out a hand to pull me to him. I dropped a kiss on his head. Then Stefan, his move completed, looked up and saw me.

'Mummy! I didn't know you were coming.'

'Neither did I till this morning. But I couldn't wait any longer to see you.'

My father flashed me a penetrating look, but he couldn't guess. My voice was light, the horrors of the night put firmly behind me. 'Besides, I wanted to come to the cinema with you. Are you pleased to see me?'

He was watching my father hovering over his bishop and answered abstractedly. Dad squeezed my hand comfortingly. 'Of course he is. But this is an important game. We've won one each this morning.'

I smiled. It was so like him to let Stefan win. He had done the same with me when I was a child. But I couldn't resist saying, 'Well don't make it too easy for him, nobody else will. Perhaps he can join the chess club at school, and he'll get no favours there.'

I watched them for a bit, then joined the others in the kitchen. Natalie was arranging lettuce leaves in a bowl, singing to herself. She was clearly happy, they both were. Had I been missed at all?

'They're both obviously enjoying themselves.' I tried not to sound sad.

'I think they've been happy.' Mother dropped her voice to a whisper. 'But she wet the bed last night. Lucky you brought the rubber sheet.'

I was aghast and said so. 'All that washing, I'm so sorry.'

But was I? Surely, instead, I was glad that Natalie had been just the tiniest bit upset.

The film was a huge success. Stefan, who had expressed the view that dancing was 'sissy', was clearly enchanted, and Natalie was so wrapped up in the various stories that she called out a warning when Jemima Puddle-Duck was about to be pushed into the pot. There was a ripple of laughter from the seats around, but she was unabashed, staring with bright eyes at the entrancing animals on the screen. For my part, I relaxed into the charm of the music and the costumes, and felt very glad that I had come. I hoped my presence had not spoiled my parents' treat.

When we came out into the early evening Stefan asked, 'Can we go to McDonald's?'

Mother looked perturbed. McDonald's was not really her scene. But my father said, 'Why not, Eleanor? It would save cooking.'

'My treat,' I said recklessly and persuasively, but Dad wouldn't hear of it.

'The children are our guests, and so are you.'

Mother reluctantly agreed, with a thin, nervous smile, and we crossed the road and walked to the wide, brightly lit entrance and joined the queue. She looked in bewilderment at the array of goods on offer.

'I've never eaten a beefburger in my life,' she said, proudly I thought.

'Well, there's a first time for everything. Have you chosen, children? I'm having a chicken burger, I think. And chips of course!'

Later, seated at a round table, I was amused to watch my parents. My mother nibbled her bun delicately, dabbing mayonnaise from her lips with her paper napkin. She had eschewed the chips. My father bit in hungrily, as if he did it every day, and it occurred to me that he was really enjoying himself. The children ate in an appreciative silence, sucking their milk shakes and making disgusting noises with their straws which caused my mother to remonstrate, and them to giggle. I was glad they were having this treat, it was one that I couldn't often afford. My thoughts flicked back to the meal I had eaten the night before, and I felt a great sense of relief. I knew where I preferred to be.

But, later, when I was lying in my virginal bed, the ache returned. I rolled over, burying my head in the pillows, murmuring David's name. But, for the first time, the longing which was gnawing my loins didn't take the shape of David. It was longing for a man, any man, with probing hands, urgently demanding. Finally, with a little sob of surrender, I put my hand between my legs and touched myself. The pleasure grew and grew until it brought a shattering release. My body relaxed, and I fell asleep, my pillow wet with tears of shame.

Kate acquired an au pair, Ragnhild, a huge dour Norwegian covered in sticking plaster. As summer progressed she adopted heavy denim shorts, and had septic bites on her legs, blisters on her heels and cuts on her fingers. I felt her life must be one long misery.

Any fantasies Harry might have indulged had certainly been thwarted, and Kate pronounced herself well satisfied with the girl's somewhat lugubrious care of the twins. She herself had blossomed out into smart suits and huge earrings, so that I felt dowdy and depressed by comparison. Natalie would be going to school in September, and I began to apply myself to making plans.

I wanted something local so I bought a copy of the *Wandsworth Borough News* and turned to the Situations Vacant pages. At first glance, there was an encouraging amount, but on analysis they either wanted word-processing skills, or offered bar work, waitressing or caring in old people's homes. The last was the only one for which I felt I was remotely suited, but I knew this would require working at night. And would I have the patience?

I supposed that what I would really like would be something to do with medicine. I might not have become a doctor, but David had. I knew the workings of a doctor's surgery, I knew the problems and concerns. On an impulse, I dialled the number of the health centre, and asked if there were likely to be any vacancies.

'Can you type and use a computer?' was the discouraging reply.

'Well, no actually.'

'Then I'm afraid we can't really help.' The woman's voice was kind, as if she was dealing with an elderly patient, but that didn't prevent me feeling foolish and naïve when I rang off.

It was obvious that I would have to get some training. I sat back, feeling depressed. But it was only what I had expected. At thirty-two, how would I compete in the market with bright young things straight from school and, worse still, with graduates? And if I found something, how would I manage with the children? I could not see myself earning enough to afford an au pair, and my parents were out of the question. They were too far away. And they had their own lives to lead. Suddenly, it all seemed hopeless, and I wrapped my arms round my knees, rocking in the chair, wishing the problem would just magically go away.

As I rocked, I let my eyes drift down the columns to Situations Wanted, seeing offers of home typing, book-keeping, and 'anything considered', and felt a deep despair at the huge untapped resource to which I was proposing to add myself. For the first time I felt a twinge of regret that I had not qualified as a doctor. I knew I did not have it in me, but I wouldn't have been in the situation I was in now. I was just hopelessly closing the paper when an advertisement caught my eye. It was boxed, and stood out from the rest. It read, 'Room wanted in return for child-minding. Trained teacher, non-smoker, caring and considerate. Putney area.'

And the idea struck me that the one asset I had was the house, with its empty fourth bedroom now so seldom used. I didn't hesitate, but wrote at once to the box number, describing the room, the children and my situation, and suggesting a meeting. Then I sat back to wait, sublimely confident that my future was taken care of.

*　　*　　*

63

Natalie was summoned to look round her new school, which was Stefan's and to which she had been on several occasions to sports day and summer fêtes. At her age, Stefan had been to nursery school and thus had been well prepared, but I had deemed it wiser to keep Natalie at home in the light of her bereavement. Now I worried that she might be too timid to take her place with the other five-year-olds. Indeed, as we entered the gates, she said anxiously, 'I'm not going to stay here, am I?'

'Not today. At least, I will be with you. But next term you'll be coming like Stefan does. He enjoys it, doesn't he?'

'He fell down in the playground last week. He had to have a plaster,' she reminded me.

'Yes, well you fall down in the garden sometimes. And the nice teacher looked after him. He told me he had a sweet.'

She gave me a little smile, but did not look convinced.

We joined the other parents in the hall, and I could see Natalie summing up the other children. She was ready for friends of her own age, though she and Stefan played well together and most days she amused herself happily enough. I had been teaching her to read and was proud of her progress. I hoped the teacher would approve, but was none the less glad that she would be ahead of her classmates.

The head teacher, who was new and whom I hadn't met, was a startlingly young woman in a smart suit She gave a little welcoming talk, and introduced the reception class teacher, a Miss Kinross, who looked kind in a dreamy sort of way. She took the children along to see the classroom, and we were able to talk to the head. When it was my turn, she asked me if I had any specific worries.

'I lost my husband eighteen months ago. Natalie is still very vulnerable. She's never been to nursery school, and wets the bed sometimes. Will the teacher make allowances?'

'I'll make sure she's aware of the situation. We get lots of children from broken homes, for different reasons. I'm sure Natalie will cope as most of them do.'

She was very courteous, but I felt unaccountably put down, a neurotic worrier, probably a troublemaker into the bargain. To prove myself otherwise I reminded her that I was Stefan's mother.

She nodded. 'Of course. Well, he seems to be very well-adjusted.' She then completely disarmed me by leaning forward and asking kindly, 'And how are you, Mrs Leathlean? I hope you're feeling better.'

I hesitated, taken by surprise.

'Well – I suppose so, yes. One goes on. I'm thinking of getting a job when Natalie's settled. Maybe that will help,' I added vaguely, not really knowing what I meant.

'I'm sure it will. Though you'll have to make proper arrangements for the children – not that you aren't aware of that, I'm sure.'

'Of course I am,' I said defensively.

'It's just that we see so many cases of latchkey children. It breaks my heart.'

'Well that won't apply to mine.'

'No. And just in case you need it, here's an application for free school dinners. Don't worry, we'll look after Natalie. I look forward to having her.'

I took the form, shook her hand, and feeling slightly reassured, went to meet Natalie from the classroom.

The children were sitting in a semi-circle on tiny red chairs, listening to a story. I saw Natalie at once, her hair glowing like a beacon. Her green eyes were wide and fixed on Miss Kinross's face. The classroom was bright and busy, with pictures and posters and jars of flowers. There was a square of green carpet in a corner, with beanbags round a shelf of books. Labelled shelves and drawers held bright, colourful equipment. On the blackboard I saw the name

Natalie in a list. There was a Jade and a Chloe and an Amir. They had obviously all been introduced.

I wondered which of them would be Natalie's friends.

While waiting for a reply from the box number, I had a letter from David's father.

A widower, and retired, he lived in a tiny house in Padstow, where he had spent his life working on the fish market. He was a Cornishman born and bred, and had told me that the name Leathlean was a Cornish name, which had come originally from France. Having grown up in the soulless suburbs, it always gave me pleasure to feel this weight of history and tradition behind me. David had been a source of much pride to his parents. Colin and I had always been very close. He told me I was the daughter he'd never had. When David died, his grief had equalled mine. He had told me he would always look out for me and the children, though I knew that on his small pension there was little he could do financially. However, we had always spent a holiday in Padstow in the summer, and this year was to be no different.

'Stay as long as you like,' his letter read. He had the strange, crabbed hand of one who didn't write very much, but his sentiments were strong. 'I can't wait to see you all again, the children must have grown, and how are you? I think about you so much, and wish there was something I could do to help.'

He didn't have a telephone, so I wrote quickly back suggesting two weeks at the beginning of August. I found I was looking forward to it, though it was not without its pain, to be in the house where David had grown up, to see his childhood photos and treasures still scattered about the house. But it was important for the children. It kept him alive for them, and they adored Colin. They called him Gramps.

'We're off to Gramps' again soon,' I told them at teatime.

'Wheee!' Stefan's face lit up. 'Will he take me fishing?'

'If you want him to.' I was not keen on fishing, preferring to stay on terra firma. Maybe this year Stefan was old enough to go alone with Colin. Natalie and I would stay on the beach and I would help her with her swimming. She was doing well with armbands. Perhaps we could get rid of them by the time she started school. I felt a little surge of excitement, a positive feeling that things would turn out all right, though it was based on nothing more than the prospect of a change of scene.

When a reply to my letter about the room eventually came, I scanned it eagerly for I felt instinctively that it held the key to my future. It was signed Shelley MacDonald, and it seemed she was a newly qualified teacher with a job in a special school for children with learning difficulties. She was twenty-three, and didn't go out much as in her spare time she was trying to write a novel. She would be happy to look after my children after school and in the holidays if I got a job. She offered the name of her local vicar in Gloucestershire, her family doctor and her course supervisor as referees. She would like to move in at the end of August, ready to start teaching in September.

She sounded perfect.

But caution told me that I couldn't take just anybody into my house. I felt ill-equipped to handle the situation and longed for David to help me. The only alternative was to turn to my father, but something told me that this I must do alone. I must take control of my life, and make my own decisions. For a start, I should meet Shelley, and if I liked her I would take up her references. I would not rush it. All the same, I wrote suggesting a meeting before our trip to Cornwall. I couldn't afford to wait too long.

She rang on receipt of my letter. Her voice was warm with a rich Gloucestershire burr. She told me frankly that she had received three replies to her advertisement, but that my house was nearest to the school. I knew the school, bright purpose-built premises that took children from a wide catchment area. I had seen them arriving, by taxi and minibus, some of them in wheelchairs, and felt profoundly grateful that they were not mine. My respect for Shelley grew. She must be dedicated indeed to work with such children. Surely I could trust her with mine. We arranged to meet on the following Saturday.

I explained to the children that somebody was coming to tea and that they must be good and friendly. Together, we made an effort to tidy the house. I paid particular attention to the spare room, which had become a dumping ground for outgrown clothes and unused toys. Our suitcases still stood in the corner from our Easter visit to my parents. I moved them into my room, preparatory to packing for Cornwall. The other things I bundled up for the charity shop. I vacuumed away the cobwebs and forced open the sticky window to air the room. On impulse, I picked up a shabby armchair at a local junk shop, to make it more comfortable. Would she want a television, I wondered? And would she eat her meals with us? What had seemed so simple suddenly seemed fraught with difficulty, and by the time she was due, I was a bundle of nerves.

My first impression when I opened the door was that she was plain. A big, plain girl with a bland face whose composure was eroded by the tight twist of her mouth as she shook my hand. She was obviously nervous too. She was as much on trial as I was. I showed her into the sitting room, where she sat on the sofa looking round the room. I had put fresh flowers on the bookcase and cleared the coffee table in readiness for tea. The children were perched next to each other in an armchair, unnaturally still, gazing at her appraisingly. They were not used to strangers in the house. It suddenly seemed terribly important that they all liked each other.

'So,' I said, attempting to take control of the situation, 'have you come up from Gloucester today?'

She licked her lips as if her voice had dried up, then told me she had caught an early train, but was staying in a bed and breakfast overnight before going home. Then she said, as if in a confessional, 'Actually, I'm visiting another house tomorrow. I hope you don't mind.'

I was amused at her naïvety, and felt it strengthened my position. However, I was not pleased to find myself in competition with some other householder who, no doubt, could offer more in the way of luxury than I could. I felt I must make my position quite clear from the beginning.

'I'm afraid I can't afford to pay you. Not at present, anyway. Are you quite sure that free accommodation is enough recompense? I'm hoping to get a job in September. There'll be a lot of baby-sitting required.'

She was picking at her thumb as I spoke. I noticed the skin was quite ragged. I slotted another piece into the jigsaw. She was a nervous and uncertain girl, not one I needed to be wary of. But I had to know that she understood the position.

I was relieved when she said guilelessly, 'I'm not earning very much to start with. I can't really afford to live away from home, but I wanted to come to London.'

'What about meals? Were you expecting the use of the kitchen, or did you want to eat with us?'

'What do you suggest?'

I realised I didn't know what to suggest. I was singularly unprepared. Shelley went on, 'I'm a vegetarian, so it would probably be best if I got my own meals. But I wouldn't want to eat in my room.'

'No. Well, we've got a big kitchen. Or the dining room, if you'd prefer. I'll show you round.'

'And I'd need a table in my room, for my computer.'

My eyes widened. 'That shouldn't be a problem,' I bluffed. 'I'm afraid there's no television. Would you want one?'

'I have one. And a CD player. Would you mind music?'

'So long as it's not too loud.' Inwardly, I was groaning. There were so many things I hadn't reckoned on. I felt stupidly ineffectual and Shelley, by comparison, seemed to have grown in stature. She had obviously prepared her list of requirements well.

'Would you like to see the house?' I suggested. 'Then we can have tea.'

The children had been sitting like statues all this time, listening intently. As I stood up Stefan pulled my arm. 'Is she coming to live with us?' he asked in a whisper.

I covered his hand with my own. 'I don't know. Perhaps. We have that room standing empty, and Shelley needs somewhere to live.' Belatedly, I realised I should have explained more fully. It seemed I was a failure both as a landlady and as a parent. 'Come on then,' I said, unnecessarily loudly, beckoning Shelley to follow. 'This is the kitchen. Not very smart I'm afraid, but we like it. I could let you have a cupboard, and a shelf in the fridge.' As I said it I wondered what I was letting myself in for. I would hate to have someone else's yoghurt in my fridge, someone else's dishes in my sink. And suppose the children didn't like her? But, I told myself, I had no choice.

I was relieved to hear Natalie say as we made to go upstairs, 'I'll show you my room first. I've got a doll's house, you can play with it if you like.'

I was even more relieved to see Shelley look down at her and pat her frizzy mop of hair. 'You've got lovely hair,' she said, and, for the first time, she smiled.

When I opened the door to the spare room, she glanced round briefly, saying, 'I think there would be room for a table if we moved the dressing table,' then looked at me nervously as if she had said too much. 'Would you mind?' she asked, and I said I wouldn't, while wondering where I would get a table. She could have a chair from the dining room, and fortunately there were plenty of sockets.

'The curtains are pretty,' she said, as if trying to please. 'And there's a lovely view over the garden.' But she didn't commit herself, and I closed the door reluctantly.

She left after tea, during which the children had opened up and Shelley had responded with a quiet confidence which showed that she was used to children. While they talked, I observed her closely. She had thin, straight, mousy hair which seemed insufficient for her broad, plain face. She was slightly overweight, and wore a creased linen jacket over crumpled slacks. She had certainly not dressed to impress, but the effect was strangely reassuring. I couldn't imagine the house being beset by gentleman callers!

When she left, she thanked me and told me she would telephone me the following evening. Trying to regain the upper hand, I told her that I too would think about it, and give my decision when she rang. In reality, I had already decided. In a way, it had all been too simple, but I wasn't going to look a gift horse in the mouth. Closing the door behind her, I realised that I would be bitterly disappointed if she decided not to come.

I spent the next day sorting things to take to Cornwall. The children ran in and out of my room, carrying shorts and tee shirts and plimsolls for the beach. Their buckets and spades and fishing nets were always left in Padstow, along with David's fishing rod and line, which Colin was teaching Stefan to use. To the collection I added warm pullovers and waterproof anoraks and Wellington boots. I selected a variety of skirts and shorts for myself and all the time I was waiting for the evening, when Shelley would ring.

When the phone rang, I leaped at it eagerly, but it was only Kate.

'Just ringing to wish you a good holiday,' she said.

'Thank you. And you.' For Kate and Harry were off to the Virgin Islands, taking the redoubtable Ragnhild with them.

'How can you bear to have her along?' I had asked, and Kate had replied that her presence would be useful in the evenings. 'And there's been an unexpected bonus,' she had told me. 'Compared with Ragnhild, Harry seems to find me ravishingly attractive! It's done wonders for our sex life.'

Lucky you, I had thought, not wishing to know. I had not told her about Shelley, but now I said, 'I must go, I'm expecting a call.'

'Oh? Someone interesting?' I could feel her antennae bristling.

'Not in the way you imagine, no.' Something else I had not told her about was my terrible evening with Howard, and she had given up mentioning him, for which I was thankful. I rang off firmly, before I could be pressed further.

At half-past eight, the phone rang again, and this time it was Shelley. Her voice already sounded familiar, but I was nervous, feeling myself at a disadvantage.

'About the room,' she began, unnecessarily. Then, doubtfully, 'Would you be happy for me to have it?'

'I've given it a lot of thought,' I told her, equally unnecessarily. 'And I'd like you to come, if you want to. Subject to references of course.'

I hoped I sounded reasonably businesslike, and that she didn't guess that while I waited I held my breath.

'I'd like that,' she said at last. 'I think it would suit me very well, and the children are delightful.'

I swelled with pride and relief. We agreed that all being well, she would move in on the first of September, on a three-month trial on both sides. I had decided that I would spend that time learning how to type and operate a word processor. Then, if all was going well, I would try and find a job.

I put down the phone and stared at it with satisfaction.

It seemed that the rest of my life was beginning.

FOUR

Colin's cottage was at the end of the harbour, opposite the long mole from which the ferry and the pleasure boats set out. It was painted white, with blue door and windows, and had two bedrooms and an attic, fitted out like a ship's cabin, where the children slept in bunk beds. The first morning in Cornwall I woke to the sound of tinkling rigging and the call of seagulls. I lay for a while in the room that had been David's. There were two beds, pushed close together, for the room was small. More often than not, David and I used to squeeze into one, giggling and cuddling. Now I had room to stretch and I did so, luxuriously, conscious of a feeling of comfort that there was someone else in the house, that somewhere Colin was probably already up and drinking tea. Gradually, the sound of the children's voices penetrated the room, drifting up from the kitchen. It was a releasing feeling, not to be needed. I turned over and drifted back to sleep.

The weather was fine and when we went out later to buy ice creams, the sun sparkled on the boats in the harbour. At the foot of a ramp, two boys were poking in the mud with sticks, and seagulls wheeled the breeze. On the harbour wall a Punch and Judy show had been set up and Stefan ran to watch. Natalie held back, looking nervous.

I pushed into the crowd of children and grabbed Stefan's hand. 'Hold on to Natalie, there's a good boy.'

Unwillingly, he took her hand. Her eyes were fixed anxiously on the grotesque puppets, but she made no move to run away and I backed off gratefully. There were times when I needed a moment's space.

Colin and I sat on a bench and he looked at me with his shrewd, kindly eyes.

'You're looking thin, girl, we'll have to build you up a bit. Plenty of Cornish pasties for you.'

'Oh, don't worry about me. How about you?' For Colin had aged visibly since the previous year. His bushy white hair, which had once been red like David's, was thinning, and his face was drawn. Maybe, as in my case, it was the sickness of loss. Maybe it was simply age taking its toll. Of maybe it was something else. I had noticed he got breathless carrying my bag upstairs when we arrived, and his pace round the harbour had been measured, while the children raced on ahead. I felt sadly concerned when he didn't answer, but instead commented on one of the boats in the harbour.

'Smart little number. Stranger around here. I saw it come in yesterday, chap wore a white yachting cap, bit showy I thought, for Padstow!'

The children ran up, asking for their ice creams. We wandered round the small town while they ate, reacquainting ourselves with the bookshop, the toyshop with its stand of kites and fishing nets and plastic beachballs, the delicatessen where we bought pasties for lunch. Stefan wanted to go to the aquarium in the fish market and see the conger eels where Natalie recoiled at the sight of the huge lobsters lurking under the rocks. Then we went home and ate our lunch on the little white-walled patio behind the house. In the afternoon we took the ferry across the River Camel to Rock and the children made sandcastles and paddled, while Colin and I sat on the sand and talked about David.

'We were so proud, having a doctor for a son. But we always knew he would do something with his life.'

I had heard it all before, but there was something soothing in the reaffirmation. I drew an abstract picture in the sand with a pebble, then smoothed it with my hand, feeling the cool grittiness on my skin.

He went on, 'And he would have been very proud of you, and of the children. You're a brave lass.'

'Not so brave. I still have to ask for his advice.'

'And do you get it?'

'Usually, yes. But it's a funny thing, he seems to tell me what I want to hear. So maybe I'm imagining it.'   .

He glanced at me, and his look was perceptive. 'Just you cling on to it anyhow,' he said. 'I remember when Enid died. It was just the same.'

I watched Stefan turning out a perfect sandpie on top of the castle, and remembered when David had been crouching there with them. 'The children miss him. It's so unfair.'

'Yes. Life is unfair.'

My eyes misted. David suddenly seemed very close, and yet perversely, in this place where he had been a boy, he seemed further away than ever.

The days fell into an easy pattern. In the mornings, we would drive to one of the nearby beaches – Treyarnon, Constantine, Harlyn Bay – where the children would dig and bathe. Stefan was keen to try David's old surf board in the curling waves, and was soon swooping in on his stomach to land beached on the sand. It was too rough for Natalie to swim, but she splashed vigorously at the water's edge. Colin never came in the water and I had my hands full, watching them both. I seldom had the chance to swim myself.

In the afternoons, Colin would take them out in his boat. It was a rowing boat with an outboard motor and in it they would potter round the estuary while I would walk stretches of the coastal footpath as I had done with David when we were first married. Striding briskly over the tight springy grass, watching the waves hurling themselves at the black rocks far below, I would talk to David and, sometimes, I

76

would sense him near me. Indeed I could almost see him, striding along in his walking boots, binoculars round his neck, hair and eyes bright and expectant. Once, I stopped by a stile where I had long ago sat to have my photograph taken. He had come up to me afterwards and kissed me, long and thoughtfully, while I sat still, my hair whipping in the wind, my skirt flapping restlessly round my legs.

'What's that for?' I'd asked him tremulously and he had answered, 'Because I love you, that's all. Never forget that.'

Now, putting out my hand to touch the rough wood of the stile, I felt tears coursing down my face. I climbed up, and sat as I had done before, and imagined his arms round me, his lips on mine. I heard again my fatuous question, and heard his words, and despite my aching loneliness, it seemed to me that he had known, all that time ago, and that his words had been meant to help me now. I knew it was silly. But it was what I wanted to believe.

When I got back to the cottage, Natalie rushed to meet me.

'I got a fish, Mummy, I got a fish!'

I hugged her. 'A fish! What sort?'

'A mackerel. We're going to have it for supper.'

'Well, it must be a jolly big one.'

She looked doubtful. We went inside. Stefan was in the kitchen watching Colin as he floured the fish, which must have weighed about a pound. He looked sulky.

Colin looked up. 'Didn't she do well? Her first fish.'

I glanced at Stefan. This was the first time that Natalie had been fishing with them. I guessed he felt she had stolen his thunder.

'Stefan?' I said, putting my finger under his chin.

He didn't look at me but said, 'Fishing isn't for girls. That's what Daddy used to say.'

So that was it. He was still jealously guarding his position. I didn't want to contradict his father, whom I was sure hadn't meant it quite like that, but I didn't want him to be huffy either. It wasn't fair on Natalie.

'But it's Natalie's holiday too,' I said at last. 'And I'm sure she'll share her fish with you for supper.'

He shook his head, rubbing his finger through the flour on the table, then knocking some purposely onto the tiled floor. 'Don't want it. I don't like fish anyway.'

I looked helplessly at Colin, who gave me a warning look. Perhaps there was no point in pursuing it.

'Then I shall share it,' I said decisively. 'Come on, Natalie, we'll lay the table.'

We went into the little living room and Natalie spread a cloth on the table.

Smoothing it carefully, she asked, 'Would Daddy have taken me fishing? When I was a big girl?'

'I'm sure he would. If you'd wanted to go. I expect he just said that to Stefan to make him feel special.'

I put the cutlery on the table and watched her set it carefully. She was already a tidy, fastidious little girl and each spoon and fork was set precisely in line, the napkin folded neatly beside the knife. When she had done, she looked at me and to my horror I saw her eyes were swimming with tears.

Very quietly, she said, 'I wish I had a daddy.'

On the last night of our holiday, Colin and I were sitting on the patio after the children had gone to bed. The sun had gone down but warmth still radiated from the white walls, and the geraniums glowed a fiery red in their stone tubs. It had been a good fortnight, and I was grateful. I didn't want to return home, and sensed that Colin wasn't relishing it either.

'Why don't you come and stay with us sometime?' I suggested. But I knew what the answer would be. Colin had always preferred to stay on his own territory. London frightened him. And he missed the sound of the sea.

'There's something you should know,' he said, after his

usual polite refusal. 'I'm not so well as I was. My heart's a bit dicky.'

Somehow, it was no surprise, but it was still a shock to hear him say it. I exclaimed in sympathy and concern, but he brushed it aside.

'I've had a good life,' he said reassuringly. 'I don't say I'm not ready to go. And maybe I can do some good for you that way. There'll be a little money after I'm gone. I've left it all to you. And the house, though it won't make very much.'

I didn't know what to say. It seemed unthinkable, to have him gone. He was my last link with David. Awkwardly, I thanked him. 'But you're not finished yet,' I said hopefully. 'Use your money, I don't want it.'

'And what would I use it for? My wants are few. I don't want to take a world cruise. Truth to tell, I only keep it for emergencies, or you could have it now.'

'I wouldn't dream of it,' I protested. 'I don't need it. David saw to that.'

He gave me a sad little smile and took my hand in his horny one.

'Just so long as you're all right. It's the least I can do for David.'

He released my hand, took a red handkerchief out of his pocket and blew his nose stridently. He looked very frail, and rather pathetic. Portentously, I wondered whether I would ever see him again.

We arrived home with a table strapped to the roof of the car. I had told Colin about Shelley, and he had insisted on giving me the table from David's room.

'It will be yours one day, have it now, when you need it.'

I was full of gratitude and, unloading the table from the car, derived a kind of comfort from having it with me. It was the table at which David had done his homework. I had a sense of its coming home.

The children ran inside, dragging bags and coats. I was pleased that they seemed glad to be home.

'It was a lovely holiday, wasn't it?' I asked them as we unpacked and piled the washing in a heap.

They nodded. 'I love Gramps, I wish we could see him often,' Stefan said.

'I wish we could see him lots,' agreed Natalie.

'Yes, but if he lived in London, then we wouldn't have our lovely holidays at the seaside, would we?' Even as I spoke, I wondered whether there would be any more visits. I trembled at the children's further loss, and prayed it would be long in coming.

Among the pile of post there were replies from Shelley's referees. It sounded as though she would be an exemplary tenant. I wasted no time in writing to her to confirm our arrangements, then began to apply myself to making room for her. I surveyed my disorderly kitchen cupboards and decided to have a clear-out. While I was still thinking rather than doing, my father rang.

'We were wondering what you'd like for your birthday,' he said, after the preliminaries were over.

I was pleased to be asked, as I had already thought about it.

'I've decided to go to evening classes to learn to type and use a word processor. Would you pay for that?'

He hesitated for a moment then said, 'That sounds a splendid idea. It will help you get a job, if you really must.'

'Yes, Dad, I really must.'

I knew he didn't like the idea. He had even offered to make me an allowance, to enable me to stay at home. But apart from being too proud to accept, I realised that a job was what I needed, if I were to keep my sanity when Natalie went to school.

The next thing was to find the classes and I went to the local library to pick up a leaflet. I felt a sense of satisfaction as

I scanned it. With Shelley installed, I would have no worries about a baby-sitter. I felt I had arranged things very sensibly. David would have been pleased with me.

I awoke in the night to hear rain roaring down outside. Thunder rumbled overhead, briefly preceded by lightning. I lay waiting for the children to wake up, trying not to admit my own uneasiness. In the past, I had snuggled into David; secure against his back I told myself no thunderbolt could get me. Now I felt exposed, in the way that I had felt exposed ever since his death. I had an image of myself and the children, huddled in the bottom of a box, from which the lid was missing. The lid had been David, keeping us all safe. Now he was gone, we were prey to all that life could throw at us. Bleakly lonely, I clutched the sheet and waited.

I was almost glad when Natalie came into the room, illuminated by a flash which brought her scurrying under the bedclothes. Pulling her close, I realised that I was now that lid, that I was all the children had, all any of us had, to hold out the world. I spoke to her soothingly, and together we counted the spaces between light and sound as the storm moved away, the rain lessened, and we slept.

But all was not well in the morning. Stefan came running into my room before I was properly awake, and bounced importantly onto the bed.

'My bed's wet,' he announced in thrilled tones. 'And the carpet.'

Bewildered, I looked at him through bleary eyes. Surely he hadn't had an accident? Stefan had never wet the bed.

Impatiently he shook me. 'It's dripping from the ceiling. Come and see!'

Reluctantly, I followed him into his room. My eyes went first to the sagging plaster above the bed, then to the dark and shiny patch on the beige carpet. As I watched, a solitary drip expanded to a gleaming globe, then dropped with a thud onto the duvet. I pulled it aside urgently, but this only exposed the mattress. Helplessly I stared at the bed. It was against the wall and would need moving to the other side of the room. But the floor was covered in toys. They would have to be picked up first. It all seemed too much. I wanted to crawl back into bed and pretend it hadn't happened.

Stefan began stamping in the wet patch with his bare feet, shouting excitedly. 'It's like the beach,' he cried.

Unable to help myself, I grabbed him violently and pulled him to my side. 'Stop it,' I shouted. 'You're making it worse.' Anger made me grip his arm until he squirmed and whined in pain.

Seizing on my anger as a source of energy I snarled, 'Pick up all these toys, I'll have to move the bed. And be quick about it.'

I released his arm. Casting me a fearful glance he went on his knees and began to pile cars into a plastic box. I seized the duvet and began stripping off the cover. Another drip fell dismally onto the bottom sheet, wetting that as well. I gave a little helpless gasp. I was only making matters worse, but I didn't know what to do. I glanced out of the window. The sky was lowering with rain, but it seemed to have stopped for the moment. That meant the worst was over for a while. I would move the bed and put something to catch the drips. I would air the bedding. And I would ring a builder. Thinking calmed me, and I dropped to the floor to help Stefan. He said nothing, keeping himself away from me as we dismantled an elaborate Lego construction and consigned it to its box. When we had enough room, he helped me pull the bed into the dry. I was ashamed at what it revealed; balls of fluff, old comics, two socks, unmatching, that had been missing for ages. There was a conker, its polished skin blurred with dust. I picked everything up, resolving to bring up the vacuum cleaner before I got breakfast. Then something good would have come out of the disaster.

Natalie was standing wide-eyed in the doorway, watching me. Stefan had wisely disappeared, avoiding my anger. But it had dissipated, to be replaced by the lethargy of anxiety. I didn't want to have to deal with the problem. I didn't want to apologise to Stefan, or help Natalie dress, or organise the builder. I wanted to go back to Cornwall, and walk the cliff path with David. If I couldn't do that, I wanted to go alone.

'Go and get dressed,' I said to Natalie, padding downstairs to fetch the Hoover. I was still barefoot, in my nightdress, and felt cold, but nothing would stop me cleaning up the legacy of neglect under Stefan's bed. I pushed the cleaner fiercely into the corners, and rubbed my hand along the skirting board, dislodging fluff. The electronic roar helped to drown out my thoughts, to postpone the next inevitable progress into the day.

I cleaned that carpet until the pile wilted under the onslaught. Then I switched off, and heard the dreadful sound of the rain roaring down outside. I looked instinctively at the ceiling, seeing the drops swell, and multiply until they fell onto my head like tears. I stood for a moment, in surrender, letting them slide down my face and into the neck of my nightdress. What was the point in trying to stop such relentless trouble?

I don't know how long I would have stood there. For ever it seemed, in helpless impotence. But Stefan arrived, pulling urgently at my arm.

'I've brought a bowl, is it big enough?'

I glanced down, saw the washing-up bowl in his hands, and gasped with gratitude.

'It will do for a start.' I stepped aside, feeling my feet cold and wet. 'Put it down here.' I indicated the centre of the patch on the carpet and heard the satisfying smack of the drops on the blue plastic.

He was looking at me anxiously. I gave him a rough hug,

asking his forgiveness, telling him my gratitude. 'Let's get dressed,' I told him. 'It's getting cold.'

He looked round his disrupted room. 'I can't get to my cupboard,' he said in a matter-of-fact voice.

It was true. The bed had effectively blocked both his wardrobe and his chest of drawers. But cast on a chair were the clothes he had worn yesterday. They were due for a wash but would have to do.

'Put those on,' I said, indicating the stained jeans and crumpled tee shirt.

I hurried into the bathroom and ran a hot shower, washing my hair which was wet already, and dressing quickly. In the kitchen, Natalie had put out the cereals and was getting the milk out of the fridge. She had dressed herself in a zany collection of mismatching skirt, top and socks, and her hair stood out in a bush where she had brushed it. I smoothed it affectionately and pulled out a chair for her. She helped herself to Krispies and milk and began to eat noisily. I bit back a remonstration and put on the kettle, desperate suddenly for coffee. The rain coursed relentlessly down the window and I wondered when I would have to empty the bowl. While the kettle boiled and the children ate in silence, I got out the Yellow Pages and turned to the section containing builders.

'Of course it's urgent, I've got rain coming into the house.'

My voice was sharp, abraded by necessity. The voice on the other end of the line was very laid-back and I fought down all the warnings I had heard about cowboy builders. He was the third I had rung, and the other two had no one available to come today.

The voice, that of James O'Leary according to the book, said reluctantly, 'Well, I suppose I could send someone round just to have a look. It's probably just a tile that's slipped.'

'Could you?' My voice melted with gratitude. 'Only it looks as if the rain has set in for the day.'

'First thing after dinner. Everyone's out for now.'

'But couldn't you come yourself? Please?' I was tempted to tell him that I was widow, with two small children, to throw myself on his mercy, but pride intervened. Instead I said, 'There's no one here to get on the roof. And it's my son's bedroom,' I added. 'Where is he going to sleep?'

I heard a faint sigh. 'I'm sorry, I'm working in the office today. VAT returns to do. I'll send someone as soon as I can.'

I had to be content with that. Replacing the phone I marvelled at my incompetence. David would have had someone round at once. But then, David would have gone up onto the roof himself. My vulnerability filled me with horror. Doubtfully, I wondered if I shouldn't have got an estimate, maybe rung round for competitive quotes. But there wasn't time for that. The bowl when I went to check was filling up fast, and it wasn't really big enough; water was still splashing the carpet and I ran anxiously to look at the sitting-room ceiling underneath. Sure enough, a patch of damp was spreading above the sofa and the air smelled of wet plaster. In despair, I ran out into the rain to the garden shed and pulled out a sheet of black plastic under which David had once grown potatoes. It was muddy and full of holes, but I folded it as best I could and spread it over the carpet in Stefan's room, setting the emptied bowl on top. I bundled the duvet into the airing cupboard and put a hot-water bottle on the mattress. Downstairs I could hear the television on. I didn't approve, so early in the morning, but hadn't the energy to object. Instead, I sat on my unmade bed, arms tight about my chest, rocking myself to keep in the pain.

We were sorting the kitchen cupboards when the builder arrived. Rather, I was emptying them and wiping the shelves, the children were busy playing shops with the tins and packets and sticky bottles. Stefan had brought down the

Monopoly money, and basic groceries were changing hands for improbable sums. I was enjoying listening to them, when there was a knock at the back door and I opened it to see a young Adonis in blue overalls. He was better-looking than any man had a right to be, and this and the toolbag in his hand encouraged me to think that all would be well.

I followed him out to his van to fetch his ladder, and followed him back again foolishly, explaining all the while our difficulties, which he already knew. My slippered feet scuffed on the wet path, rain dripped from the guttering but it had stopped falling.

'At least you won't have to go up in the rain,' I said agreeably as he set his ladder against the back wall.

'That's true,' he said, indulging me. I watched as he mounted the ladder then, thinking belatedly that he would not like it I went back into the kitchen.

The children started up guiltily, fixing me with anxious eyes. At their feet was a pool of tomato ketchup and broken glass.

'We dropped it,' said Stefan, loyally presenting a united front.

'Sorry,' Natalie whined. 'We tried to clear it up.'

The dishcloth was in the centre of the mess, and their hands were red. I seized Natalie's, expecting gashes, severed fingers. But it was only tomato sauce.

'Leave it alone,' I snapped, more fiercely than I meant. 'You'll cut yourself. We must pick up the pieces first.'

They hung back as I picked up the sticky fragments of glass, setting them onto a newspaper which I folded bulkily round them before depositing it in the dustbin. I got the floor cloth and filled it with soapy water, smoothing it over the tiled floor until it gleamed.

'Mind you don't walk on it, it's slippery,' I snapped.

They were still watching me warily, waiting for my anger. I wanted to shout, 'You stupid children, why can't you be more careful?' Instead I said resignedly, 'It can't be helped. Can you pass me those tins? I'll put them back into the cupboard, but I'll have to squash them up, to make room for Shelley's things.'

Stefan handed me some baked beans. 'Why is she coming to live here?' he asked, looking worried.

Before I could answer, there was another knock on the door. The young man was standing there.

'All finished?' I asked brightly.

He hesitated. 'Well – it depends what you mean. I've fixed the loose slate, but you've got a lot of trouble up there. You need a new roof as far as I can see, or else this is going to be happening a lot.'

I stared at him in horror. It was true, when we bought the house the surveyor had said the roof would need attention before long. But not now. Please, not now.

'Surely, we could just patch it up? I mean, it's a big roof. It would be expensive.'

The young man shrugged. Suddenly he didn't seem so reassuring and his handsome face looked out of place, an anomaly on such a harbinger of doom.

'Would you like us to give you a quote?'

Now it was me who shrugged, helplessly. 'I suppose I haven't got much choice. At least I'd know what I was up against.'

'Right. I'll just go up again and take some measurements, have another look round. It maybe won't be as bad as I think – but don't bank on it.'

He went back to his ladder, whistling as if he hadn't a care in the world, which he probably hadn't. Horribly depressed, I returned to the cupboard.

'Why, Mummy?' Stefan persisted as I arranged the tins. 'Why is Shelley coming to live with us?'

'Because,' I said wearily, 'I don't think I can manage any longer alone.'

*   *   *

'So,' I said to Kate, who had brought the twins round to play. 'I've had an estimate for five thousand pounds for the roof, and I've got somebody whom I don't even know coming to share my kitchen cupboards. Am I mad or what? She's not even paying rent. Is it any wonder I feel depressed!'

Kate pushed at her hair, sending her silver earrings swaying. She was dressed in an expensive suede jacket over a silk blouse. In my blue dungarees and tee shirt I felt immature and inadequate. A hopeless adolescent with two children and a leaky roof, and a lodger arriving tomorrow.

Kate said decisively, 'You mustn't keep on doubting yourself. You arranged for Shelley to come for sensible reasons. Her being here will enable you to do your course, get a job. She will be somebody else in the house. And that will be good for the children.'

'But suppose they don't like her? She has to bring them home from school, give them tea. I feel as if I am deserting my post.'

'Well, tell yourself you have no choice. You haven't, have you?'

'Well . . .' The truth was, I knew that part of me was acting out of selfish reasons. I needed to get out of the house as much as I needed the money. At least, until now. Until the roof had let me down.

'I need to get the money for the roof from somewhere,' I said, rather defiantly.

Kate glanced at her watch, a slim gold one set on her slim gold wrist. They had not long been back from the Virgin Islands and she was looking like a ripened peach. 'I'll speak to Harry,' she said, smoothing back her suede cuff. 'Perhaps we could give you a loan.'

'Oh no!' The words were out of my mouth before I realised how ungracious they were. 'I mean, that would be wonderful of you, but I couldn't. I don't want to be in debt to you, without knowing when ever I'd repay it. I'll just hang on and hope for the best. Maybe it won't rain for the next few years!' I laughed feebly.

She was looking at me seriously, like the friend she was, reading my distress and really wanting to help.

'Well, just remember us, in an emergency? We're doing all right now I'm working. We'd like to help. Now we'll really have to go. Shall I call the children?'

They had been making a camp in Stefan's bedroom. 'Let's go and see what they're up to,' I suggested. But we were forestalled by Dominic, running down the stairs with a furious expression on his face, barefoot and dishevelled.

'Stefan bit me,' he said, holding out his hand which bore a line of red indentations.

'What!' Incredulous, I raced up the stairs and into the bedroom. Some old curtains were draped from the bed to the chest of drawers, weighted down with books. The bedding had been stripped from the bed and I could hear Natalie inside the tent talking to Ben. But my only interest was Stefan, sitting on the end of the bed and glowering.

I seized his arm. 'What's all this? Why did you bite Dominic?' He had never done such a thing before. I searched his distracted face for the amenable boy I knew.

'Because he wouldn't let me be Daddy. But I'm the eldest.'

'Why wouldn't he?' It was Kate, joining in from the door. She was holding Dominic's bitten hand in hers like a trophy, but her voice was doubtful. Maybe he had deserved it.

Stefan hung his head.

'Dom? Why wouldn't you let Stefan be Daddy?' Kate leaned towards her son, urging a response. He bit his lip, then angrily blurted out, 'Because he hasn't got a daddy. He wouldn't know how.'

I felt as if I had been punched in the chest. My blood all ran inward, then out again in a hot flood towards Stefan. He looked up at me and shouted out, 'It isn't fair. Why haven't I got a daddy?'

Then he flung himself onto the stripped bed and began to cry.

I looked at Kate helplessly and she stared back with wide horrified eyes. Her usual determination seemed to have deserted her.

'I think we'd better go,' she said. 'I'll deal with this at home. It was an unforgivable thing to say.'

'But he's only five,' my own anger allowed me to say reasonably. I wanted to shake Dominic, to smack some repentance into his smooth, fathered body. But he *was* only five.

Kate leaned into the tent. 'Come on, Ben. We're going home.' She turned to Dominic and released his hand. 'Find your shoes, we'll talk about this later.'

I sat on the bed beside Stefan, letting my hand rest on his shoulder. His fingers were making frantic indentations in the mattress. 'I'm sorry, Kate. About Dominic's hand. He shouldn't have done that.'

She shrugged. 'Well – *he's* only seven. I'll see myself out. I hope it all goes well tomorrow. When Shelley's settled, you must come to supper. I'll give you a ring.'

She stooped to tie Dominic's trainers. Her shiny hair and shiny earrings swung, looking inappropriate to the task, and I thought suddenly of Ragnhild.

'How's Ragnhild?'

'Oh, as joyous as ever. She has Saturdays off. She has a boyfriend, a sullen student with rimless glasses who calls her Hilda. They've gone to Kew today. He has a car.'

'Right.' It all seemed very remote from my problems, which for the moment took the shape of my damp and despondent son, huddled against me on the bed. I gathered him into my arms, seeking words of comfort, something beyond my own pain which would show us both the way ahead.

FIVE

Shelley arrived by taxi, out of the back of which she produced four suitcases, a large cardboard box, a collection of carrier bags, and a guitar. She stood on the pavement paying the driver, while I gazed helplessly at her profligacy, and wondered about the capacity of the spare bedroom. Then it occurred to me that it would be courteous and welcoming to offer her assistance. I took the handle of a large black holdall and began to lug it up the path, Stefan following behind with a carrier bag.

When everything was crowded into the hallway I pushed my hair back nervously and said, rather belatedly, 'Hello. Welcome home.' I hoped it sounded as casual, but warm, as I intended. In fact, I was very nervous, already wondering if I had done the right thing.

Shelley looked nervous too, but determined not to show it. She made no apology for her luggage, saying merely, 'The box has got my computer in it, don't touch it.'

Stefan asked eagerly, 'Have you got a computer? Can I use it?'

I silenced him with a frown.

'I think,' I said firmly to Shelley, 'that some coffee is called for before we tackle this lot. Don't you?'

We sat at the kitchen table, the children drinking juice and helping themselves to unaccustomed chocolate biscuits. The silence became awkward so I asked her, 'You said you were writing a novel. How is it going?'

She gave a self-deprecatory shrug. 'Oh well, you know . . .'

'I don't know. I can't imagine how anyone writes a book. Have you done much?'

91

'Two chapters. But I've written them over and over again. I'm a bit of a perfectionist. And with a computer you can do that, of course. Keep on changing things. I wonder if I haven't overdone it. I think perhaps the first draft was the best.'

I didn't know what to say, whether to commiserate or encourage. I took a biscuit, feeling the exquisite melt of the chocolate through the crumbs. It was a rare treat, and one I had no intention of getting used to. But I took another one, searching my mind for conversation. I thought perhaps I had better establish some rules.

'We breakfast at seven-thirty, if you want to join us.' It sounded rather abrupt. 'I've cleared a cupboard for you, and you can have a shelf in the fridge.'

She looked pleased, her impassive face softening. 'I'll do some shopping tomorrow. And I like a bath each morning, is that all right?' The words came out in a rush, as if she had screwed herself up to say them. Even so, I felt it was she not I who was setting the pace.

'Of course. We'll just have to work round each other.'

The implications appalled me. I wasn't used to fitting in with another adult. I was used to doing my own thing. I gave her what I hoped was a friendly smile. 'I'm sure, with a bit of give and take, everything will go swimmingly.'

Now she was looking doubtful. She bit nervously into the biscuit she had been holding in her hand for five minutes. I decided to take the bull by the horns.

'I've arranged with the school that the children can stay up till four-thirty in the after-school club. That should enable you to pick them up. Of course, it won't be necessary until I get a job. I'm doing a typing and word-processing course first. That's two evenings a week, starting next week. So I shall need you to be here on Tuesday and Thursday nights.' I was speaking quickly to forestall objections. But she merely nodded.

'I understood that would be the arrangement. Perhaps I could go up now and start unpacking? Is there a table?'

'Yes. And a chair. I'm not sure about wardrobe space though . . .'

'Oh, I'll manage. I can leave things I'm not using in my case. I thought it best to bring everything. I won't be going home very often, I can't afford it.'

I got up from the table. 'I'll help you get your things upstairs. Then I'll start on lunch. I thought you'd like to join us today. It's pasta, no meat,' I added, seeing her doubtful look. 'I know you don't eat meat.'

Her face cleared. I was getting used to the expressions which crossed the flat planes of her features. Basically, I thought, as I humped cases up the stairs, trying not to knock the paintwork, she was amenable enough, but she had made up her mind what she wanted. Later, as I heard the sound of music, and the unaccustomed thump of feet overhead, I tried to take comfort from another being in the house. Instead, I felt that my space had been invaded. Furthermore, I wondered if David would mind.

By the time the first night of my classes arrived, I felt easy enough in my mind to trust her. But I still worried about leaving the children. Natalie seemed to have taken to Shelley, but Stefan was holding back. When she offered to read to them, he would climb obstinately onto my lap and stare at her with wide appraising eyes, as if he were being asked for something he was not prepared to give. While Natalie leaned confidingly against her, enjoying the pictures, Stefan would reach for my hand as if for reassurance. Changes were harder for him, and Shelley in our house represented change. He was clearly wondering how far things were going to go.

On the afternoon before my class I sat between them on the sofa and said as calmly as I could, 'Tonight I have to go out. Remember, I told you I'm going to learn to use a computer, like Shelley does.' She had given them both a demonstration, and Stefan in particular had been impressed. He was using a computer at school, and indeed I was wondering how soon it would be before he asked for one of his own. Now he asked, 'Are you going to write a book too?'

I laughed. 'No, darling, but I'm hoping to get a job.'

He looked anxious. 'Who will look after us if you do?'

'Well, you'll be at school most of the time. And Shelley will be here. That's why I asked her to live with us.'

He looked mutinous. My heart shrank with thoughts of the evening ahead. 'You like Shelley, don't you? And she's used to children, she's a teacher.'

'I don't want her to look after me. I can look after myself.'

I realised with relief that he had given me the loophole I needed.

'Maybe. But Natalie can't. Shelley will stay with you tonight, while I'm at my class. She will put Natalie to bed. But you can see to yourself. You're a big boy now.'

He still looked doubtful. 'Will you be back in the morning?'

I hugged him. 'Of course. And I'll come and see you when I get home, though you'll be fast asleep.'

Natalie had said nothing. I turned to her, pulling her into my arms. 'You understand, Nat? I'm going out tonight, but Shelley will be here to put you to bed. That's all right, isn't it?'

'Will she read to me?'

I stroked her shock of hair, thinking suddenly of David's. 'Of course.' But I was abstracted. David's presence was vivid in the room. 'I'm sorry,' I told him silently. 'But you see, it just has to be done.'

The evening class consisted of twelve women and two men.

Some of us, me included, had mastered two-finger typing, but it was obvious that to get the most from a word processor, touch typing was essential. One evening a week was therefore devoted to learning to type, the other to operating the word-processing package. I had already set our old portable on the end of the kitchen table. Armed with a book of exercises, I returned home full of enthusiasm, prepared to do an hour's practice before bed. But to my alarm, Stefan was sitting at the table, drinking hot milk. Shelley was with him, gathering playing cards into a pile.

She looked at me defensively. 'I'm sorry, but he wouldn't go up until you were home. We've been playing snap.'

'And I won nearly every time,' Stefan told me triumphantly.

I looked at him wearily. 'Well, finish your milk and get up to bed. It's half-past nine.'

He slid from his chair, holding out his hand. 'Now you can tuck me up,' he said with satisfaction. He had got what he wanted. But it wouldn't do. I told him as I pulled the duvet round his chin, 'I won't be cross, just this once. But I'm going out again on Thursday, and I will be cross if it happens again. Do you understand?'

He nodded earnestly. 'I just wanted to see what time you came home. Now I know.' His eyes slid away from mine and up to the ceiling. 'You were going to paint my ceiling. Where the water came through.'

I glanced up at the brown patch on the plaster, and sighed. 'Yes, I know. I will do it, I promise. If you're a good boy on Thursday,' I added unfairly. As a bargaining point, it was feeble, but I felt I needed all the help I could get.

The following week, the school term started. Up till then, our arrangements in the morning had been pretty relaxed, but now, with everyone having to get out at once, the bathroom routine became strained. To enable Shelley to have her bath, I had to rise and wash myself and the children punctually at seven o'clock. I have never been good in the mornings. The discipline of punctuality made me irritable. Then, while we were eating our cereal, Shelley would come in to the kitchen and start chopping fruit into yoghurt and making herbal tea, the smell of which turned my stomach. She would take her meal into her bedroom, which was something of a relief. I told myself that if this was the sum total of my annoyance it was a small price to pay. The children were getting used to her presence, and when – I told myself positively – when I got a job, I would need her to be around.

I had worried about Natalie's first day at school. When Stefan started, David had been alive. Stefan had been a happy, well-adjusted little boy, and we had taken him together, seeing him pass through the school gate, vulnerable none the less, his neck fragile below freshly cut hair. Natalie was more clinging, the child of a one-parent family, her little world turned upside down.

She set off happily enough, skipping beside me along the road. She had on the uniform green pullover and skirt which looked good with her red hair and green eyes. I proudly thought she would be the prettiest in the class. Stefan was striding ahead, bossily telling her she must hurry or she would be late and get into trouble. I crossly told him to be quiet. We were in plenty of time, and there was no call to go worrying her like that. But still I quickened my step, pulling her along behind me.

At the playground gate, Stefan ran off with barely a backward glance. Natalie gripped my hand, looking bewildered by the crowds of children who were running round the playground, or gathered in noisy, exclusive groups. I was reluctant to let her go, alone, into the mêlée. Then with relief I saw Miss Kinross standing by the doorway surrounded by tiny children. The reception class, all safely assembling under her wing.

'There's your teacher. Remember Miss Kinross? She's waiting for you.'

Natalie looked up at me tremulously but didn't say anything. We crossed the playground and I handed her over.

'Natalie Leathlean,' I told Miss Kinross as I released her hand. Miss Kinross ticked her name on a list and leaned down to her.

'Hello, Natalie. I remember your lovely hair.'

I saw Natalie's lips break into a tentative smile.

'She'll be fine,' the teacher told me. 'It's better to just leave.'

I pulled myself together. 'Of course. 'Bye, Nat, I'll be here to meet you.'

She turned to me with a look of panic but I just raised my hand with a bright smile. 'Have a nice day,' I told her, and turned away quickly. Recrossing the playground, I told myself that surely I wasn't the only one to leave with tears in her eyes. At the gate, a mother and father stood helplessly with a tiny boy clutching his mother's legs, sobbing. I met the mother's eyes in sympathy. It was what I had dreaded. I saw the man stoop down and extricate the child. He picked him up, and together the couple walked through the gate, the child still crying. I did not envy them that, but I did envy them for being together.

Every day, while they were at school, I practised my typing, and began to achieve fluency. Meanwhile, the classes were beginning to instil into me the rudiments of word processing. I found that I enjoyed technology, and one evening I asked Shelley if she would demonstrate her computer to me. It was fascinating. I couldn't possibly afford one, but now I began to want one for myself.

I had never really worried about money since David died, as we had enough for our daily requirements. But the scare over the roof had made me realise how vulnerable we were.

There was simply no capital for emergencies. Despite myself, I began to think of Colin.

He had told me he had some money put away. Certainly, it was for his emergencies, but might he not think our roof had some priority? With winter coming on, I was feeling increasingly worried. How desperate would I have to be to ask for his help? Meanwhile, I painted over the patches in the ceilings and told myself it wouldn't happen again.

October drifted into November, and I finished my course. Meanwhile the leaves skittered round the garden and drifted outside the back door in damp golden bundles. I let them lie; it was Shelley who suggested we sweep them up and have a bonfire. We cut back the borders and piled the fire high. The acrid smoke drifted up into the still, damp air and clung to our clothes and hair. I took some comfort from working with her in the garden, and the children enjoyed it, gathering leaves and stalks from the bare beds with muddy hands. We went indoors and sat round the fire together, and in some strange way it felt like a family.

At the end of the month, I took my typing and word-processing examinations, but while I was waiting to hear the result, something happened that put all thoughts of it out of my head.

Natalie was very quiet when I picked the children up from school. Unusually, she wasn't carrying a picture or a model for my inspection and praise, and she didn't answer when I asked her about her day. She seemed dispirited and I put it down to tiredness. Stefan as usual was full of news.

'Miss Patience read out my composition again.' But he sounded anxious. 'I wish she wouldn't. It's embarrassing every time. The others will think I'm too clever.'

'Do they say that?'

'No. But they might think it.'

'Well, you're not clever at everything. You don't come out top in maths.'

He seemed relieved. 'I got six wrong today. I had to do them again.' It seemed a funny thing to be pleased about, but I understood. At his age, acceptance by one's peer group was everything. Thinking about him, I forgot Natalie, and hardly noticed when she disappeared to her bedroom before tea instead of watching television.

While I cooked, Shelley stood at the sink washing her salad and trying, I guess, to ignore the sizzling meat. She was telling me about an autistic child in her class who had attacked a classroom assistant with a pair of scissors.

'It's an ongoing problem, I'm afraid, violence in the class-room. People don't realise what risk we're at, in schools like ours.'

I nodded sympathetically, shaking the chips. 'Don't you get frightened?' I asked. 'I mean, surely it's asking too much, to expose you to risks like that?'

She shrugged. 'Par for the course. And it's worth it. To make progress, however small, is so rewarding.'

I turned the chips onto heated plates and added beef-burgers.

'I'm glad to hear it. I must go and call the children.' I went into the hall. Stefan was watching *Neighbours* and came away reluctantly. There was no response from Natalie when I called up the stairs so I went up to her room and opened the door.

A ghastly sight met my eyes, for on the duvet, in a gleam-ing tangled pile, was Natalie's hair. And Natalie herself, shorn like a convict, was staring at me with frightened eyes, huge without the framework of her curls, her head small and bony on a fragile neck.

I gasped, 'What have you done?' Then I held out my arms. She ran to me with a curdling sob and I felt the rough tufts of her remaining hair under my chin.

'I hate my hair,' she sobbed against my chest. 'Duncan called me Carrots. And he said I looked like a Brillo Pad.'

Anguished pain smote me so that I could hardly breathe. 'Oh darling.' I rocked her fiercely to and fro. I could think of no words of comfort. Impotent fury at Duncan rose sourly in my mouth. Natalie's need of me froze me into inadequacy. 'I understand,' was all I could think of to say, while my eyes fixed grieving on the pile of hair on the bed and my mind ranged over the impossibility of getting her presentable for school next day.

We sat for quite a time, rocking and crying, for I found myself weeping with her in helpless pain. Then I remembered the food.

'Your chips will be cold,' I told her, gently releasing her, trying for normality. 'Come down and eat them, and we'll think what to do about your hair.'

I wiped her eyes, and mine. I took her hand and led her downstairs, bracing myself for Stefan's reaction. He was seated at the table, eating, with Shelley at the other end assembling some vegetarian rice dish. Before he could look up I said warningly, 'Don't say anything please, I'll explain later.'

Shelley gave us a startled look, but said nothing except, 'I've put your plates in the oven.'

'Thank you.' I helped Natalie onto her chair and got the food. Stefan had stopped eating, and was staring at his sister, bursting with comment which he had the sense to keep to himself. Natalie picked at her chips and I myself tried to eat, with little appetite. All the time I was railing at Shelley's presence, at her silent witness to our distress. Yet when the children had at last finished, and left the room, with Stefan saying to Natalie, 'What have you *done*, you goof?' I found myself turning to Shelley and saying desperately, 'One of the boys teased her about her hair and she's cut it off. What am I going to do?'

With a calm practicality, Shelley said, 'Well I think the first thing is to get her to a hairdresser. They can tidy up what's left. As to the teasing, you can speak to her teacher, but there's not really a lot she can do. She can reprimand the culprit, but he might take it out on Natalie.'

I gave a deep sigh of despair. I had the sense that this was a problem that wouldn't go away. Natalie had her hair for the rest of her life. It was something she would have to learn to live with. Fleetingly, I wondered if David had ever suffered the same persecution. I couldn't ask him, and the pain of loss was as sharp as ever as I sat considering how hurt he would have been that this inherited trait could cause her such misery. Her rejection of her father's badge seemed a disloyalty that was too much for me to take. I put my head in my hands and began to howl.

To my surprise, I felt Shelley's hand on my shoulder.

'She'll get over it. Children are resilient. Remember, I see far worse problems than this. And I see parents suffering agonies, of guilt and recrimination and fear of the future. Natalie will survive. And so will you.'

Her words penetrated gradually through my tears and I felt calmer. I sat up, blew my nose and wiped my eyes. The debris of the meal lay about me on the table, in Natalie's case only half-eaten. They had had no pudding. I would have to call them back. But first, there was something I had to do.

I went reluctantly up the stairs to Natalie's bedroom. I had to brace myself to look at the shiny discarded hair on the bed, then I gathered it into my arms tenderly, like a corpse. I bent my head and kissed it. It smelled of shampoo. It seemed too beautiful, too personal, too precious to throw away. But in the end I stuffed it into a carrier bag and carried it out to the dustbin. Replacing the lid I felt scoured and tested, and hoped I would not fail.

The next morning I telephoned the school and asked to speak to Miss Kinross. The secretary said she was in class, could I wait till playtime? I asked her to say that Natalie wouldn't be in till later. Then I rang my hairdresser and made an appointment for eleven o'clock. Natalie was reluctant to leave the house but I pulled a woollen hat over her tufts and piled her into the car. At the hairdresser's I pulled off her hat in front of Jennie's astonished eyes and asked her if she could do anything with it.

'What happened?' she asked, looking at me incredulously.

'Natalie decided to give herself a haircut.'

'So I see. Well, she hasn't left a lot to work on, but I can even it up a bit. And,' she said encouragingly to Natalie, who was looking truculent, 'it will soon grow again. You'll soon have those lovely curls back.'

Natalie met my eyes in the mirror. Her expression was agonised. I watched as Jennie snipped and shaped, feeling a physical pain as more of the precious hair fell to the floor. But the effect was miraculous. From looking unevenly scalped, a hairstyle of a sort emerged. Beneath the shallow halo, Natalie's face looked peaky and sharp, her green eyes huge. But it was, just, possible to imagine that we had chosen it.

She was looking at herself uncertainly in the mirror. 'At least I don't look like a Brillo Pad,' was all she said.

'No.' I agreed. Jennie brushed her down and removed the pink smock that had covered her clothes. I had every intention of her going to school, but when we reached the car she hung back.

'I don't want to go to school. I look funny.'

'No, you don't. You just look different. You can tell everyone I decided to have your hair cut short.'

'They'll laugh. Duncan will laugh.' What she meant was that Duncan would know he'd won. Sympathy moved me to say, 'Well, perhaps just today, you can stay at home. But tomorrow you've got to go. Promise me you won't make a fuss?'

She nodded, relief making her smile.

102

'I tell you what,' I said as I strapped her in. 'Let's go down to see Nana and Granddad. Give them a surprise.'

Her face lit up, but she asked nervously, 'Will they like my hair?'

'I'm sure they will. We'll tell them that we like it.'

I started the car. Common sense dictated that I telephone them first, but I wanted to be on my way. I turned towards Putney Bridge, then out along the Richmond Road. As I drove, I heard Natalie singing in the back seat and glanced at her in the mirror. She was staring out of the window. Seen in profile, her white nose looked sharp, her skull bony and fragile. But she was absorbed in what seemed to be happier thoughts. How easy it was to be a child, I reflected. How simply diverted were one's troubles.

As I drove up the drive, my father was backing his car out of the garage. I stopped, and he stopped, and got out to greet me.

'Were we expecting you? It's my day off, we thought we'd go out to lunch.'

'Oh. Oh dear. No, it was just an impulse. Natalie's not at school today, we thought we'd have a treat.'

He had already seen Natalie in the back of the car. 'Is she ill?'

'No. I'll explain later.'

'Well, come inside. Your mother will be pleased to see you.'

'But your lunch . . .'

'That will keep.' He opened the back door and Natalie slid out into his arms. He kissed her. He didn't seem to notice her hair. 'Come inside, young lady, it's cold out here.'

Mother was in the hall, fiddling with her hair in front of the mirror. She was all dressed up in a camel coat and skirt with a Jacqmar scarf at her neck. I felt terribly guilty. I should have rung.

103

But Dad said, 'Look who's here, Eleanor. Isn't that a lovely surprise?'

She looked round, pleasure pushed from her face by a stunned amazement when her eyes rested on Natalie.

'Your hair!' she exclaimed. 'What have you done to your hair?'

'We felt like a change,' I said defiantly. 'And we've come to lunch, as Natalie has a day off. I didn't realise you were going out. I should have rung.'

'Yes, you should.' She stared at herself in the mirror once more, adjusting her scarf. Then, reluctantly I thought, she pulled it off and folded it carefully. She unbuttoned her coat and hung it up.

'No,' I said belatedly, feeling awkward. 'You go out, have your lunch, you don't often get the chance.'

Dad intervened. 'And we don't often get the chance to have you. Do we, Eleanor?'

She didn't look at him. 'I don't know what we've got to eat,' she said, bustling through to the kitchen.

Dad said, 'I'll put the car away.'

Natalie and I followed Mother in silence.

'Will spaghetti do?' she asked, opening the larder.

'That's my favourite,' Natalie told her. But it was tinned spaghetti that was being taken from the shelf. Pasta as we knew it wasn't in my mother's repertoire. At her instruction I made and buttered toast, while she heated the lurid contents of two tins and ladled it out. Natalie had set the table and Dad joined us.

'Isn't this nice?' he said as he sat down, beaming with pleasure. I blessed him silently, and watched Natalie as she struggled with the slippery strands. 'Perhaps she could have a spoon,' I asked, getting up to fetch one. Natalie smiled at me gratefully, her cheeks smeared with sauce. I ate my own food, remembering how I had hated it as a child. Worse, then, my mother had sometimes added a fried egg, and the yolk and tomato sauce had blended into a cloying orange mix which stuck in my throat. Thankfully, today, we hadn't been offered eggs.

'There's some fruit for afters. Would you like a banana, Natalie? And I have some yoghurt in the fridge.' She handed the bowl to Natalie who took a banana and began to mash it into a dish.

'So,' asked my father, 'how were the exams?'

I cut into an apple. 'I'd rather not say. Tempting providence to say I expect I did all right!'

'So now you have to think about finding a job. We don't like it, you know that.'

'But, Dad, I need to do something with my life, apart from the money.'

My mother's mouth was thin with disapproval. 'The children are your life. They need you there.'

'I will be there. And that's what Shelley's for. The children like her. Don't you, Natalie?'

To my relief, she nodded, her mouth full of banana.

'And she's very good with them. She is a teacher, after all.'

Dad leaned towards me, giving me one of his caring looks. 'It's just that we worry about you. We don't like to feel that life is hard. It's not what we wanted.'

'But plenty of women work. If I'd been a doctor, I'd have worked.'

Mother said sharply, 'Being a doctor is rather different. That's a profession.'

Dad looked at her warningly. 'Well, I'm sure Julia will find something worthwhile. I just hope she's not disappointed.' He turned to me. 'I don't expect it will be easy, finding something suitable.'

'I know, but I'm trying to feel positive and optimistic.'

He smiled. 'Good girl. Now, Natalie, how about we go and have a game, and leave the ladies to natter.'

It was the last thing I wanted, but I was glad to see her go off happily, talking about Snakes and Ladders.

'That child looks ill,' said Mother. 'I can't think what you were thinking of, cutting off her hair.'

I opened my mouth to tell her the truth, but she looked so stern, so off-putting that I closed it again. I would not get much comfort there.

I passed my exams, though not, I was told, with flying colours. Nevertheless, I had my precious certificates, my passport to a job. I was deemed to be a proficient typist and word-processor operator. I had the faintest glimmerings of computer literacy, enough to make me want to go further. I felt confident and optimistic. I was on my way.

I decided to enrol at a recruitment agency. After dropping the children off at school, and wearing my one good suit, I entered the gleaming portals of an office in Putney High Street that offered 'Highest Salaries for Qualified Secretaries'. A large rubber plant with glistening leaves stood inside the door. The carpet was deep red. There were several desks at which sat gleaming young women in red suits and red and navy scarves, like air hostesses. At that early hour, all the chairs facing them were vacant. How, I wondered, did one get a job like theirs?

They all looked up expectantly and I took the nearest chair, smoothing my skirt and pushing at my hair. I felt unexpectedly nervous. It was a long time since I had come up for assessment. I thought of the certificates nestling in my handbag, but they seemed poor comfort in the face of the efficiency opposite me. If this was what was required, I had a long way to go.

The young woman, whose badge told me she was called Alison, gave me a shiny smile and asked my name and age.

'Julia Leathlean. I'm thirty-three.'

She wrote this at the top of a long form on a thick pad.

'I see. And you're returning to work after the children, I expect?'

'Well no, not exactly. I'm a widow. And I need to work. I haven't worked before. At least, not as a secretary.'

She put down her pen and clasped her hands loosely on the desk. Her nails were red and glossy. I clenched my own hands in my lap, feeling as if we had already struck a problem.

'Do you have a degree?' she asked hopefully.

'I'm afraid not. I was in medical school. I'm not stupid, I've got word-processing and typing certificates. I'm confident that with my experience . . .'

'Experience?'

'Well – of life.' It sounded pretty pathetic.

'I'm afraid at your age, with no office experience . . . maybe a typing position, what speed have you?'

'Sixty words a minute.'

'Um.' She picked up her pen and entered a large 60 in the appropriate space.

'Would you like to see my certificates?'

She glanced at them and handed them back. She tapped her pen on the desk. 'Do you have children?'

'Two. They're both at school.'

'And in the holidays? What arrangements have you made?'

'I have live-in help.' It sounded grand, I thought.

'That must be very expensive.'

'No –' I began. Then, feeling that it was none of her business, 'Look, do you think you can help me?'

She had began tapping at her computer thoughtfully. 'There's a typist's job in Wandsworth. But I don't think your speed is high enough.'

'It will get better.'

'Do you want to go along? They're only paying six thousand.'

107

I swallowed hard. Six thousand sounded good to me. 'I'll give it a whirl. Anything else?'

She was still tapping and waiting. At last she said, 'Here's one, not far from you. Office junior in a firm of solicitors. Not quite what you had in mind, but you could perhaps work your way up.'

I thought of the hours I had spent practising my typing. 'No thank you.'

'You're right. They're really looking for a school leaver.'

She tapped away some more, then sat back. 'I'm afraid that's all. The secretarial posts are all asking for experience. Shall I make you an appointment for the typing job?'

I sighed. I supposed I had better start somewhere. 'Yes please.'

She picked up the phone and pressed buttons which beeped tunefully. I watched her jewelled nails hypnotically and noticed that another jewel shone on the fourth finger. I imagined her husband-to-be working somewhere in the city. I imagined their future home, stylish and well-equipped, with money coming in and the rain kept out. When she handed me a card with an appointment, I felt as though I were being given the crumbs from her table. It was hard to smile as I thanked her, and walked out into a drizzly rain. I had no umbrella and I had not brought the car. My suit would get wet. Depression settled down like a blanket and when I got home I stripped off my wet clothes, lay on my bed, and cried.

But after a while I felt resolve coiling up from the flaccid depths of my despair. After all, I had an interview. I had a chance. I was as good as anybody else. I had been David's wife and that must count for something. I sat up, and dragged a comb through my damp hair.

'Sorry for being such a wimp,' I told David, staring at his photograph. 'I'll show them . . . just you wait and see.'

SIX

I rang Kate, reporting the little progress I had made. I had been looking for sympathy; instead she said crisply, 'What you need is an outing. I'll take you to lunch. Next Saturday. No argument. Leave the children with Shelley and meet me at La Rosina's in Lower Richmond Road at one. Okay?'

I agreed helplessly. I wasn't in the mood, but it was ages since I'd been out to lunch. Recklessly, I bought myself a new blouse. Positive I had decided to be, so positive I would appear. Kate was waiting outside when I arrived, and the first thing she said as we sat down was, 'Nice blouse, you don't often wear stripes. Very businesslike.'

'My new image,' I said brightly. 'Off with the old, and all that.'

She looked pleased. 'Good,' she said, patting my hand. 'That's what I like to hear.'

We ordered garlic bread, which we ate while we consulted the menu, and in due course a bottle of Chianti arrived, with huge plates of pasta. Greedily, I picked out all the clams first. Kate was rummaging through our joint side salad. She looked up and we both smiled together, my lips greasy with sauce.

'This is really lovely,' I told her. 'Thank you so much.'

She put down her fork. 'Well, actually it wasn't entirely altruistic. I felt like getting out of the house too.'

'You? But you're out of the house all week. I thought Saturdays were precious.'

She paused thoughtfully for a moment, then said, 'It's a funny thing, I feel more relaxed at work now than I do at home. Isn't that odd? The thing is, there I seem to be in control. Home seems to be chaotic. Ragnhild's all very well when I'm not there, but really she's just another person to consider when I am. And the boys are so bloody noisy! And I hate this time of year, with winter closing in. Sometimes, Monday mornings can't come soon enough.'

I felt distressed. 'Have you told Harry?'

'Not in so many words. But I think he feels the same. Sick, isn't it? We wanted children so desperately; now, sometimes, they're just frankly in the way! It seems to be a symptom of the times we live in.'

I was worried. 'Do you think I'll feel like that? If I get a job? Because I can't afford to. The children are all I've got. And I'm all they've got, for heaven's sake.'

Kate looked aghast. 'Oh, you know me. Sweeping generalisations and all that. There's no reason at all why you should feel the same. You're a more balanced person than me. And a lot will depend on the job. How much satisfaction you get out of it. Perhaps I was really meant to be a career woman, whereas you . . .'

I smiled ruefully. 'I'm just a mum! And I can't see me getting much satisfaction from the job I'm going for. Just a typist. I shall be only too relieved to get home.'

She sucked in the last of her spaghetti and wiped her mouth on a checked napkin. 'But it's a start. Who knows where it will lead?'

'Well, I won't be getting the key to the executive lavatory, that I do know.' I began to giggle, and helped myself to more wine. Kate did the same, and we clinked glasses solemnly.

'A toast,' she said. 'To the executive lavatory!'

'The executive lavatory,' I repeated, rather too loudly. Some people at the next table turned round and we burst out laughing, shamelessly.

'Seriously,' Kate said when we had calmed down. 'I'm sure you'll get the job, and it will lead to great things.'

She leaned towards me, setting her elbows on the table and gazing at me intently. 'You must think positive.'

'Oh I am,' I told her merrily. 'And I want a pudding, although I'm full to bursting. Will you join me?'

'You bet. Anything's better than the twins' tantrums and Harry getting irritable with them.'

'Thanks,' I said lightly. 'I'm flattered.'

I thought of my own house as we waited for the menu. It seemed a peaceful refuge, with Shelley and the children going about their business, waiting for me to come back. I didn't resent them. Not yet. I hoped I never would. Kate's dissatisfaction, when she had a husband to share things with, was difficult to grasp. But then, familiarity bred contempt. People took things for granted, and always wanted more. I vowed never to get like that. The menu arrived.

'Chocolate cheesecake,' I said firmly. 'With cream. I feel in the mood to celebrate!'

I took the bus to Wandsworth for my interview, not wanting to worry about parking. It was a fine day. I was able to wear my suit again, and my new striped blouse against which I hung a silver chain. I took my best black leather handbag. Subconsciously, I was not wanting to look as if I needed the job. But I knew that I had to look as though I wanted it. Motivation was everything. Actually, I didn't want the job, but I knew I would take it if it were offered. And I very much wanted it to be offered.

There were two other girls in the waiting room, one in her twenties, the other barely out of school. She had several silver rings in her left ear. She wore a leather jacket over a tee shirt which was inadequate both for her breasts and the time of year. Her skirt was tight and short; thick black tights led to scruffy shoes. She appeared to be chewing gum. The older girl said hello as I sat down, and asked me what time my appointment was.

111

'Eleven,' I said, looking at my watch. It was ten to.

'They're running late. Mine was for half-past ten.'

The younger girl blew a lazy bubble. 'They must have had loads of applicants. It was in the paper.'

My heart sank. Coming through the agency, I had foolishly imagined I was to be the only one.

We sat in a sort of resigned silence. I had the idea that they had done this many times before and the feeling was growing in me that it was something that I would get used to as well. At five past eleven, the half-past ten girl was called in. Nobody had come out.

'They seem to let them out another way,' the schoolgirl enlightened me. 'Tactful, eh?' She blew another bubble. I wondered if she would take the gum out of her mouth for the interview.

'Is this your first job?'

'Nah. I work at the checkout in Safeway. But me dad says I must try and better meself. I did typing at school. So I'm giving it a go.'

I mentally discounted her as opposition. But the other girl had looked smart and efficient. No doubt she also had years of experience. Then there were all the rest, unseen but still to be reckoned with. I felt a deep despondency settling on my new-found confidence. What, after all, did I have to offer?

After twenty minutes, the girl was called in, and I was left alone. There were some pamphlets on a table about the firm. It seemed this was the head office of a company making lifts somewhere near Sheffield. There were photographs of heavy machinery with smiling men in overalls, and a long shot of a post-modernist factory building with a fountain outside. I read details of turnover and output, trying to commit them to memory, thinking it might be useful to show I had a grasp. Then I was called in.

The interviewer was a grey-haired woman, neatly dressed, with matching lipstick. She introduced herself as Mrs Maitland.

'I'm the Personnel Manager. For a job at this level, I make the decision. Now, tell me about yourself.'

I told her. I produced my certificates. I explained that there would be no problem over the children. I impressed on her my enthusiasm for joining the world of work, and my interest in lifts. She made notes as I talked, then asked me to move to a desk in the corner. It contained a word processor with which I was unfamiliar.

'Perhaps you would type out this specification for me. You have ten minutes.'

The machine was already switched on. With damp fingers, I began to type. The language was technical, peppered with figures, and symbols I had to search for on the keyboard. I felt the time slipping away. At the end of ten minutes I hadn't finished. Humbly I told her so.

'Just print out what you've done.'

I looked helplessly at the machine. 'I'm afraid I'm not familiar with this model.'

'That's all right. You'd soon pick it up, I'm sure.' She came across and pressed a sequence of buttons. The printer leaped into operation and I saw my words imprinting on the paper. I quickly noticed several errors. There hadn't been time to check it. I looked at her in despair as she took the paper and put it with my notes.

'Thank you, Mrs Leathlean. We'll drop you a line.'

She held out her hand and I shook it with a thin smile. She opened a door behind her desk. 'Just go down the stairs and you'll find yourself back at the entrance. Thank you for coming.'

As I descended the stairs I found my legs were shaking. I told myself I would have to get used to it, for I was certain I had not got the job. Outside the gates I turned left towards the bus stop. The wind was cold despite the sunshine. Litter blew along the pavement and the crowds of shoppers moved about their business, unaware of my distress. Passing a coffee house advertising Kenco coffee, I turned impulsively into its warmth and comfort, and there, sitting at a table, was the older girl from the interview.

I was unaccountably pleased to see her. I did not feel like drinking alone. 'Can I join you?' I asked, as she looked up and recognised me.

'Please do. I'll have another cup.'

'I'll get it.' I went to the counter and ordered two cappuccinos and a large iced bun.

'How did you get on?' she asked as I sat down.

'Oh, I blew it. Didn't even finish the typing and it was full of mistakes.'

'I hate typing,' she said, fiddling with her scarf. 'But it's all I can do and I have to work.'

I glanced at her hands. She wasn't wearing a wedding ring. She followed my eyes. 'Divorced,' she said. 'Last year. Now he's playing up over maintenance, and I've got a little boy. He's three.'

'What do you do with him in the day?'

'My mother has him. Good of her, she's given up a lot. It will be easier when he goes to school.'

The coffee arrived. I bit hungrily into my bun. Stress always gives me a ravenous appetite.

'How about you? You're married, I see. By the way, my name's Claire.'

'Julia. And I'm a widow.' I still hated saying it, couldn't believe it described me. 'Two children, both at school. I manage, but I thought it would be easier if I got a job. Besides that, I have to do something with my time.'

'Still – nice to have a choice.' The sides of her mouth pulled down and I sensed a quiet desperation beneath her pleasant exterior. Suddenly I found myself hoping that she had got the job. I thought of her mother, maybe giving up her weekly bridge and her regular appointment at the hairdresser's. I wondered if my own mother would have done the same. Somehow, I doubted it.

We talked a bit, after that, about our children, about where we lived, about what it was like to be alone.

'The worst part is not being accepted by couples,' said Claire. 'I don't mean old friends – though in our case some of them have taken sides. I mean new people one meets. I've been working with a great girl, married, we always have our lunch together, but she never asks me home to supper. When I was with Don we were always being asked out. You seem to need a partner as a sort of passport into society. Don't you feel that?'

I considered. I hadn't met anyone new since David had died, so it hadn't really arisen.

'It will. You'll find you have joined another club, the one where single women go. It makes me very bitter.'

'I don't feel bitter. Only sad.'

'Well, of course it's different for you. You haven't been kicked in the teeth, you don't have to feel betrayed.'

She looked so unhappy that my heart warmed to her. It seemed my loss was maybe not the worst, my grief not the only one.

'Did he meet someone else?' I asked her, since she seemed willing to talk.

'He went off with my best friend. So I've lost them both.'

I thought about it, in terms of Kate, and David. Since his death, Kate had been my lifeline. 'I'm so sorry,' I said. It sounded inadequate.

'And he took half the furniture. I have the house, and in theory he pays the mortgage. But he insisted that he needed a bed, and chairs and tables. It's not as if we had much to start with.'

I thought gratefully of my own cluttered rooms, my own unsullied memories. At least, David had been mine. I hadn't had to share.

'Do you have a car?' I asked her, thinking that I knew the answer.

'I wish! That went with Don too. Anyway, I couldn't afford to run one.'

I was beginning to feel blessed. It was a curious sensation, that of feeling more fortunate that someone else. I felt comforted, the débâcle of the interview slipping behind me. And I liked Claire, for her honesty and for the sense of gratitude bequeathed me by her pain.

I was pleased when she said, 'Perhaps you'd like to come round one Saturday. Bring the children to tea, and meet Josh.'

I didn't hesitate. 'I'd like that. Tell me, are you working now? Why do you want this job?'

'I've been made redundant. Last in, first out, that's the way it goes. You'll find out, once you get going. Nothing is certain in this life it seems.'

'Well, I hope you get the job. I'm quite sure the girl with the bubble gum hasn't a chance!'

It was the first time I had seen Claire laugh. 'If she has, I'll eat my hat! I'm not so sure about you, though.'

'I told you, my typing was abysmal. I'll have to go home and practise.'

'What will you do?'

'Just keep on trying, I suppose. Now, when shall I come? The children would enjoy it, they don't get out enough.'

We fixed a date and exchanged telephone numbers. Outside the coffee shop we parted, each to go our own way. The wind was still brisk, but somehow it seemed less cold, insulated as I was by an unaccustomed sense of my own good fortune in having my husband die.

The letter arrived next day. It obviously hadn't been a difficult decision. 'Sorry to have to disappoint you on this occasion, but I wish you better luck next time.'

Next time! There would have to be a next time. Somehow, holding the letter in my hands, staring at its logo and a picture of a lift, I doubted my stamina. Despondently, I bought the papers and scanned their pages. There were the usual openings for care assistants and bar workers. I really couldn't see myself doing that. There was one for a personal assistant for a managing director, and one for a typist in a travel agent's in Putney High Street. This appealed to me, particularly as it said 'experience not required'. I circled it emphatically in red, and rang for an appointment.

The girl on the other end had a clear, cool voice, and asked my age before she asked my name. When I told her, she said, 'Oh I'm sorry, we're looking for a school leaver.'

I felt a surge of irritation as well as disappointment. 'Well, why didn't you say so in your advertisement? It would have saved me a phone call.' I banged down the receiver. After all, I had nothing to lose. For a moment, it made me feel better, but it didn't alter the situation. Miserably I went into the kitchen to start to prepare the supper.

Shelley was there with the children. They were chattering away happily and for a brief moment I felt outside their little circle, redundant and useless, unwanted by everyone. Shelley was showing them how to make flowers out of tomatoes. She always took tremendous trouble over her food, and I admired her. Left alone, I felt I would degenerate into eating poached eggs, and baked beans out of the tin. As it was, I had to force myself to give the children a wide choice of foods, to educate their palates. David had loved his food and together we had experimented with Italian, Chinese and Thai cooking. I missed him, chopping and stirring and sampling beside me. He was exuberant and generous with the flavourings; then he would stick in a finger, lick it, and shout a triumphant 'Yes!' when he got it right. Cooking wasn't fun any more, but I was determined not to be reduced to casseroles and sausages. Tonight we were having stir-fried chicken. It was expensive, but the children loved the cashew nuts and the spring onions. But my heart wasn't in it as I cut the chicken breasts into strips, and heated oil.

Shelley must have noticed, for she said, 'No luck?'

'No. I'm too old. I feel that's going to be the story of my life.'

'I wonder,' she said thoughtfully. 'Perhaps the best thing to do would be to temp for a while.'

I looked at her with gratitude. I hadn't thought of that. I seemed to be singularly unresourceful, like a rabbit caught in headlights. But here was a new way ahead. When we sat down I found myself eating with enjoyment, full of renewed hope for the morrow.

The next morning I rang the agency, but they weren't very encouraging.

'I'm afraid we don't have so much call for temps these days. Firms prefer to try and manage without. Our books are already full, I can't place everyone as it is.'

I heard myself pleading. 'Well, couldn't you just add my name to your list?'

'I'm afraid it wouldn't do much good.'

'Please . . .'

'Mrs Leathlean, I'm sorry. I can tell you are pretty desperate, but so is everyone these days. It's no good making you promises I can't fulfil. But why not ring me again after Christmas? There's a lot of absenteeism in the New Year, maybe I'd have something to offer you then.'

I rang off and reached for the Yellow Pages. There were several agencies specialising in temps, but they all told me the same. It was the recession. They had too many people on their books already. They were very sorry.

I had to accept, as graciously as I could. I took my certificates from my bag and looked at them sorrowfully. They had seemed to offer such promise, but now they didn't seem to be worth the paper they were written on.

It was less than three weeks to Christmas, and I determined to put the matter out of my mind until afterwards. I had shopping to do, and decorations to think about. Shelley would be going home to her family and I felt strangely reluctant to let her go, although on Christmas Eve we were supposed to be going to my parents. But as the time approached, I began to feel it would be nicer for the children if we stayed at home. Perhaps Mother and Dad would come to us? I asked Shelley if she minded if they used her room and she said she didn't.

I spoke to my father on the phone, and I knew if it were up to him they'd come like a shot. 'But I'm not so sure about your mother. She's made plans. You know how organised she likes to be.'

'Couldn't you persuade her? I really feel the children should be at home this year. I need to establish that we can manage without David.'

'I do understand. I'll speak to her. But she's already ordered a goose. Perhaps we could bring it with us?'

'I'm sure I could cope with that.' Actually, I was grateful. Christmas was so expensive. To my amazement, as if reading my mind, Dad said, 'We thought we'd give Stefan a computer. Would you have any objection?'

I was nearly speechless with delight. 'He'll be thrilled, absolutely thrilled. But would you know what to choose?'

'We've already looked into it. I've a fairly good idea, since we installed them at the surgery. I expect it will come complete with computer games. You've no objection?'

'Well, I expect I'll have to ration him. But he'll be delighted to be like his friends. Thank you, Dad – that's very generous.'

'We'd do more, you know that. But you never ask.'

I thought of the roof, but pride kept me silent. 'Just come for Christmas, that's what I want most of all.'

Certain that they would agree, I bought the ingredients

for a cake and pudding. The children helped me stir and I told them to make a wish.

'I know my wish won't come true,' Stefan said. 'But I wished it just the same.'

I knew he was thinking of David. 'So did I,' I told him. 'We can't help wishing, can we?'

His eyes were very bright as he spooned the mixture into the cake tin. I wondered then, not for the first time, just how long we would have to live with the pain, and guessed that it would be for ever.

Claire's house was in a small terrace with a concreted front garden which had obviously once held a car. There was a stone tub by the front door with the skeletal remains of summer planting, and the tiles of the porch were chipped and cracked. But the door was painted a cheerful red and when she opened it we were met by the smell of baking.

'Josh and I have been making cakes.'

Natalie held out to her the pot plant we had brought as a gift. Stefan was staring round the small empty hall. His expression said it compared unfavourably with our own. Embarrassed, I introduced them both and Claire showed us into the living room. It was nicely carpeted in rose pink and the curtains at the windows were lined chintz. Two rooms had been knocked into one so that it ran from the front to the back of the house. There were two armchairs and a low coffee table. A small television bore a large photograph of Josh. Josh himself was kneeling at the coffee table scribbling in a colouring book. He looked up and gave an impish grin. My heart warmed to him at once. He was sturdy and cheerful, a far cry from the plaintive and pathetic child I had been imagining.

At the back of the room a kitchen table stood bleakly. There were books, hundreds of them, overflowing the one

120

small bookcase onto shelves made of wood resting on bricks and boxes. Claire followed my gaze.

'He took the bookshelves. Petty, since all the books were mine.'

Natalie had squatted beside Josh. 'Colour her hair with brown, not blue,' I heard her say bossily. She picked up a felt-tipped pen and began to help him. Stefan was sitting sideways on the edge of one of the armchairs looking aimless. I realised I should have brought some of his toys. Josh was too young to have anything to interest him.

But Claire said, 'I thought we'd have tea straight away. It always settles them down. Then perhaps we could play a board game. Josh can manage Snakes and Ladders.'

I turned to Stefan. 'Hear that, Stefan? You like Snakes and Ladders.'

But he seemed not to hear. He was staring dreamily into space with a look I knew well to be boredom.

'Come and help us get the tea,' I suggested.

'He can lay the table. It will be nice to have someone old enough to do it properly.'

We followed Claire into the kitchen and she gave Stefan a cloth and some paper serviettes. Seeing the food she had prepared, I said, 'It's quite a party. By the way, did you get the job?'

She shook her head. ''Fraid not. So we're soldiering on on benefit. It will be a lean Christmas for us.'

'But you'll go to your mother's?'

'Oh yes. She's just round the corner.'

'My parents are coming to me this year.' I was still pleased to be able to say this. Mother had agreed, and was bringing the goose and the crackers. It would not be like the Christmases I remembered, but I was going to do my best. I had even tried to persuade Colin to join us, but as usual he had refused. I had invited Kate and Harry for a drink on Christmas Eve. Impulsively I now invited Claire to join us.

'Do come. Would your mother mind you leaving Josh?'

'I shouldn't think so. But I'm not sure. I'm not used to socialising. I don't feel I have very much to offer.'

I understood, but only, it seemed, up to a point, for she went on, 'When someone treats you like shit, you get to thinking you deserve it. My self-esteem is pretty low at present.'

She sounded so bitter that I reflected once more on the difference in our circumstances. My own grief had been a purer thing, untainted with resentment, save at a cruel fate. Through all the storms of angry tears, I had salvaged my sense of worth. I certainly did not feel I had got my just deserts. David had been mine to the end – he had loved me, I had not been betrayed, my self-esteem remained intact. I suddenly left an immense gratitude.

It seemed imperative to reassure her. 'You mustn't think like that. You've got to come up fighting. And the only way is to make a new life for yourself. Come and have a drink, meet some new people. You were complaining that no one ever asks you.'

She didn't answer, arranging cups and saucers on a tray. Then she took a deep breath and looked up. 'Okay, yes – I'd like to come. Something civilised and grown up for a change. Thank you very much.'

I smiled. It was nice feeling that I had something to offer for once. I was as grateful to her for that as she was to me.

While she made the tea, and poured glasses of squash, I looked round the kitchen, which was small and compact and equipped with modern units with white fronts. It was tidy and sterile compared with mine. Two stools stood up to the small breakfast bar under which stood a twin-tub washing machine. There was no microwave, no freezer. But the shiny saucepans on a rack were matching stainless steel and the cooker was modern. I saw Claire look at me and realised I was staring rudely, appraising her circumstances. Given her need, I was stricken that I had not brought anything for tea. But I wouldn't have wanted to embarrass her, or undermine her independence. I knew how dearly we women alone held on to that.

'Call the children,' she said when the tea was ready. She picked up one of the stools and added it to the four plastic kitchen chairs ranged round the table. Setting it down, she said bitterly, 'We used to have teak, to match the sideboard.'

I glanced at the sideboard, on which she had stood the begonia we had brought. There was an empty fruit bowl and a pile of letters. The bleakness of her life made me ashamed. On her instruction, I lifted Josh onto the stool. His body was warm and solid and his dark wavy hair glistened. I wondered if Don ever saw his son. I wondered if Josh missed his father, if he wet the bed and had nightmares and cried like my children had done. Most of all, I wondered how Claire coped.

Handing me my tea, she said perceptively, 'It's not so bad, you know, one gets used to it. As you must surely know.'

I nodded. 'But as you say, I don't blame anyone. Except fate, and that's futile.'

I sensed she would have liked to talk, but the children made it impossible. We fed them their tea: egg sandwiches, fairy cakes topped with hundreds and thousands, chocolate finger biscuits. I was touched to see Natalie helping Josh. She was quite the little mother. Anxious to draw Stefan in I told Claire, 'Stefan is playing Joseph in his school nativity play. I'm very proud.'

'Well done, Stefan. What are you going to wear?'

'Mum's made me a robe out of an old blanket. It's a brown one that Dad used to take camping. And I'm wearing a tea towel on my head. I think that's rather stupid. I shall look like one of the shepherds.'

123

'And Nat's an angel,' I put in quickly. 'With tinsel on her head.'

And David won't be there to see them, my heart cried out. At least, if you were divorced, the father sometimes came along. But there was no chance of that for us. David was gone for ever.

I asked my parents if they would come to the play, but it was the bridge club Christmas dinner. I resigned myself to once more going to the school alone, but to my surprise Shelley asked if she could come with me.

'Surely it will be a bit of a busman's holiday for you?' I said. I knew she had been busy with her own school production.

'No, actually it will be a change. I'd like to see Stefan and Natalie, naturally, but I'd also like to see the standard. What normal children can achieve. We tend to forget. Our expectations are always high, but they are seldom lived up to.'

'Then let's hope you're not disappointed. Stefan doesn't seem very sure of his words.'

'He'll be fine on the night. It's surprising what dressing up can do. I was in several plays while I was at college, and it was amazing how people turned up trumps in the end. The rehearsals were always dreadful, we never thought we'd be ready. But on the night – fantastic!'

'Well, I certainly hope so. He's so full of himself.'

We arrived early at the school, the children sitting excitedly in the back of the car, fully costumed, Natalie's tinsel gleaming on the new curls which were covering her head. The scoured look had gone. I had resolved to keep her hair short for the time being. I don't know what I was trying to achieve, as it was still red, and frizzy. But at least she could have less of it.

The children went backstage and we took our places near the front. Watching the couples arrive, I was grateful to have Shelley to talk to. Now and then, someone would arrive alone, usually a woman, but there was a man, the father of a boy in Stefan's class, whose wife was a kleptomaniac, in prison for shoplifting. Stefan had told me this, and I had seen the man meeting his son from school. He was apparently an artist, and worked from home. I had spoken to him once or twice, thinking that he must be deeply embarrassed at his position, but to my surprise neither he nor the boy seemed to be too uncomfortable. His wife was receiving psychiatric help, he told me. I nodded and smiled as he passed my seat, and he gave me a casual smile of response, but didn't join us. He seemed self-contained in his aloneness and I envied him.

I envied the couples, too, and I envied the children who had the support of both parents, and grandparents, and uncles and aunts. By the time the play started I was at a low ebb, and when Stefan approached the innkeeper and asked for a room in a loud, proud voice, I felt proud too, and sick at heart that Shelley was the only person to share it.

Shelley's parents were in London, and they called to take her home for Christmas.

I liked them immediately, especially for the pride they showed in Shelley. She sometimes seemed to me to be rather a pathetic person, staying in each evening and working on her computer, with very little social life. We seemed to be united in our aloneness – two solitary women coping as well as we could. I was grateful for her company, and when her mother said to me while Shelley fetched her bags, 'I do so miss her. She's my only child,' I felt almost guilty.

'She's good company,' I agreed. 'Sometimes I don't know what I'd do without her.'

Mrs MacDonald looked at me anxiously. 'Do you think she's happy? We worry she doesn't get out enough. I know she has to baby-sit for you but, even so . . .'

I felt even more guilty.

'I'm not out that much. Shelley is quite free . . . but I think she just enjoys her writing.'

I didn't say that in some ways I was glad of this. Part of me, the selfish part, didn't want her racketing around every night, bringing home men, underlining my own situation.

Mrs MacDonald didn't look convinced, but her face cleared as Shelley came into the room.

'Ready, darling?'

Her father took her case, and I followed them to the car, an ageing Renault. As it drove away, I felt bereft. Now there was just us – and Christmas. A rite of passage for us all.

The previous Christmas we had not had a tree. I had neither the strength nor the will to drag the decorations down from the loft. I did not wish to remember the last time we had hung the gaudy baubles, draped the tinsel, set the fairy on the top.

This year was to be different. We were going to pretend we were a family still, that the gaping hole above us was boarded up, however shakily. Opening the box of decorations on the sitting-room floor, the gusts of nostalgia were dissolved by the children's enthusiasm. I had recklessly bought a six-foot tree. Shelley had helped me pot it and carry it indoors. Then she had retired to her room, tactfully leaving us alone.

The children handed me the fragile baubles, the papier-mâché apples and pears, the garish foil and tinsel stars, the strings of beads. I hung them on the branches, and draped tinsel round the flex of the lights.

'Can I?' panted Stefan, his hand on the switch.

'Just a minute, let's turn out the light.'

It had always been a ritual, that first switching on of the fairy lights. We would sit in the darkened room in the multi-coloured glow, admiring the metallic reflection of the bulbs, smelling the scent of the branches. And David would tell a story. It was always the same story, about a fairy flying home late one Christmas Eve, when she chanced on the house of a poor family who could not afford decorations for their tree. And she flew indoors to rest in the warm, and alighted on the top of the tree, and the joy of the children of the house when they saw her on Christmas morning knew no bounds.

So we sat in the darkened room, and I took a deep breath, and told the story again, just as David would have done, though it cost me dear. The children lay against me on the sofa, their eyes on the lights. When I had finished Stefan snuggled close and gave me a wet kiss. I felt he understood.

Natalie slid down and went to the tree. 'And there she is,' she said with satisfaction, pointing up, entranced. I felt warm and rewarded, that I had been able once again to create the magic. Christmas had begun, and I knew that we would survive.

My parents arrived at lunchtime on Christmas Eve. We had been making mince pies, me rolling, Natalie cutting and Stefan spooning in the mincemeat. The kitchen smelled warm and homely, and I was humming with a sort of contentment.

It was cold outside, with a frosty breath to the air. When I opened the front door the sky was yellow.

'Perhaps it will be a white Christmas,' I said quite gaily, kissing them both and taking bags and packages from their hands. The children hovered expectantly, sensing surprises. There was a huge parcel which I guessed to be the computer. I set it beside the tree, with exhortations not to touch.

Stefan hopped from foot to foot. 'I've got the biggest present of all!'

Noticing Natalie's face I said quickly, 'Size isn't everything. Look, Nat, this squashy one's for you.'

But she wasn't to be placated. Uneasily I wondered if my parents had treated them fairly. A computer would be hard to equal. Children were acquisitive creatures. Even as

I thought it, I remembered a time, before David died, when Stefan had swum a width of the swimming pool and my parents had given him a present. He was bursting with pride, when they produced a gift for Natalie too, 'in case she felt left out'. And I had been angry. It had seemed to me that they were denying Stefan his triumph. Children had to learn that life didn't always seem fair; that others must be allowed to succeed. I had bitten back my objections, only complaining later to David, who had agreed but had tried to calm me by saying they were only doing what they thought best. Now, this Christmas, I hoped perversely that they had treated them equally. It was with relief and joy that I followed Dad to the car and saw, in the back under a rug, a small red bicycle, inadequately disguised with shiny paper.

'I thought we'd leave this here,' he said, looking pleased with himself. He replaced the rug. 'I hope she'll like it.'

'She'll love it. She's only got Stefan's old castoff. Thank you, Dad.' I hugged him and he kissed the top of my head. 'What would I do without you?' I asked him as we went up the path carrying the goose. 'I shall need you tonight, to play Father Christmas. David always used to dress up, just in case they woke.'

'Sounds good to me. Doesn't seem five minutes since I was doing that for you.'

Back in the kitchen, the timer pinged and I took out a batch of mince pies. My mother looked at the racks of pies already cooling.

'Are you feeding an army?' she asked curiously.

'I've asked people in for a drink tonight. Kate and Howard, and someone you don't know, Claire, she's divorced, you'll like her.'

'Well, I've brought plenty of nibbles.' She produced them all from her tartan shopping bag like a conjuror producing rabbits. Nuts, raisins, crystallised fruits, Belgian chocolates. She looked pleased with herself and I exclaimed in gratitude.

'I did manage crisps and garlic croutons. I thought we'd make cheese straws after lunch, and vol-au-vents.'

'I'd have bought wine had I known,' said Dad.

'Dad, it's all right. I've got wine.' The wine rack in the dining room was full; I hadn't used any since David died. I was feeling quite excited. It was a long time since I had entertained. Impulsively, I went up to my mother and hugged her. She looked quite surprised, but pleased, and her cheeks flushed an unaccustomed pink.

We set the food out on the dining-room table on a special festive tablecloth my mother had given me on a previous Christmas. I did not care for it very much, preferring my own white linen for special occasions. But it seemed politic to use it. I had made a cursory arrangement of greenery and tartan ribbon with a red candle stuck in the centre. The printed swathes of holly and ivy on the cloth circled the brimming plates, and the silver gleamed. I left Dad to select the wine from the rack and dust down the neglected whisky and gin. I had bought cans of beer; he arranged these with the glasses and bottles on the sideboard, fetched the corkscrew, generally busied himself as barman. I realised how much I needed him. It hadn't occurred to me how I was going to manage the drinks.

The children ran excitedly from room to room. I had promised them they could stay up in their pyjamas to meet everyone, if they then went to bed like little angels. They nodded earnestly, but I wondered just how angelic they would be.

'Benjamin and Dominic aren't coming, neither is Josh. They'll all be tucked up in bed.'

'But I'm older,' argued Stefan indisputably. 'I should stay up later than Natalie.'

To my surprise my father took his side. 'I think that's right, Julia. Give him half an hour longer. He can pass the nuts.'

Stefan gave a whoop of joy but Natalie looked mutinous. 'I want to pass the nuts.'

But she had reckoned without her grandmother.

'Personally, I think they should be in bed before anyone comes. They must learn that you have a life, Julia.'

'Oh, but it's exciting for them. We seldom have visitors.'

Mother pursed her lips. 'Well, be it on your own head. You'll never get them to bed once people arrive, and you don't want a scene.'

I felt anxious and uncertain and looked to Dad for help. As usual he came to the rescue.

'I'll see them into bed when the time comes. There'll be no scene. Will there, children?'

He winked at them in complicity. I felt both grateful and helpless, as if matters had been taken from my hands, as if I had no control. Endeavouring to regain it I sent them up to undress, and followed them up to get myself ready for the evening. I had already decided to wear a long black skirt and a black silk blouse that David had always loved. I talked to him as I changed and dabbed on some makeup at the mirror. 'I wish you were here,' I told him. 'This is a big evening for me – my first without you. Hang about, I may need you.'

I picked up his photograph from the dressing table and stared into his eyes. Sometimes, still, I could feel an immense sense of incredulity that he had actually gone, that he wasn't waiting somewhere downstairs, in the garden, or working at the surgery. Then the truth would break through, as annihilating as it had been at the start. This happened now, as I held the photograph, all dressed up, with nowhere to go. A bolt of pain shot straight to my heart as I thought of the evening ahead. What audacity, to think that I could entertain our friends without him. What was I going to talk about? Why would they want to come and see me? My confidence evaporated; I drew no strength from his gaze and put the photograph down with trembling hands. I didn't want to go downstairs. What I really wanted to do was to lie on my bed and cry. I wanted Christmas to go away, to leave me in peace with my grief. Instead, I had to turn brightly to Natalie as she came running into the room in her dressing gown, saying, 'You look nice. You look different.'

I brushed the frazzle of her hair and hugged her. 'You will be good, won't you? We don't want Nana getting cross.'

She stood back and looked at me seriously. 'Nana is often cross, isn't she?'

I was saddened. 'She doesn't mean it, it's just her way. Nana likes things to be organised, and I'm afraid we're not very good at that.'

Kate and Harry arrived on a gust of gritty snow.

'The twins are beside themselves with excitement. Father Christmas – and now snow! I don't know how Ragnhild will get them to bed.'

I took Kate's wrap, an expensive purple cape, and shook off the snowflakes. 'She's still with you then? I thought she would be going home for Christmas.'

Kate pulled a face. 'So did we, but she said she wanted to experience an English Christmas. I could hardly throw her out. And she has her uses. She's promised to build a snowman tomorrow. Sooner her than me.'

She was looking gorgeous as usual. Her hair was tied back with a chiffon scarf. Several bangles clanked at her wrist.

'How's work?' I asked, enviously.

'Oh, never enough time, but I love it. I don't know how I ever survived at home.'

I remembered her confession in the restaurant, but still I longed to be like her – smart, busy, coping. For the first time, I felt we had no point of contact. 'Come and have a drink,' I said, swallowing my envy.

Dad gave her a gin and tonic and we assembled round the fire in the sitting room. Stefan proffered nuts and crisps. I saw Natalie sneak a chocolate, and hoped Mother hadn't noticed. I was wondering how I would get her to bed when Dad suggested that he took her up for a story.

She shook her head, lips clamped juicily over the sweet. 'I want to wait for Claire,' she mumbled.

I said quickly, 'That's all right, Dad, I said she could,' which was a lie. But I wanted to establish that I was in charge.

Kate sat on the sofa beside my mother. 'How are you?' I heard her ask. 'It's a long time since we've met.'

Actually, it had been at the funeral. It seemed a tactless remark, but Mother didn't seem to notice. She asked about the twins, and I turned away, grateful that her attention was diverted from the children, who were kneeling on the floor by the Christmas tree poking at the parcels and devouring crisps. I felt superfluous and wandered into the kitchen, fiddling with coffee cups on the tray, putting mince pies into the oven ready to warm. I was glad when the bell announced Claire's arrival.

It was snowing quite hard now and she was holding an umbrella.

'How did you get here?' I gasped in sudden compunction. There was no bus, and she could surely not afford a taxi.

'I walked. Don't worry, I'm used to it.'

'But I could have come to fetch you. I never thought. I'm so sorry.'

'No problem.' She flapped her umbrella in the porch, and stood it down. She stamped her boots on the mat. 'I've brought shoes.' She balanced on one foot, then the other, changing into black high heels. I took her coat.

'Am I the last?' She looked nervously towards the sitting-room door.

'There's only five of us.' I took her arm and squeezed it. 'Don't worry,' I told her. My own confidence grew in response to her diffidence. She seemed to have that effect

132

on me. Gratefully, I ushered her into the room. The others turned and I introduced her.

'This is Claire. We met at a job interview. Which neither of us got, needless to say!'

They all nodded and smiled. Dad offered her a drink and she asked for wine.

'Come and stand by the fire,' said Harry gamely. He moved to one side. 'How's the weather, still snowing?'

'Yes. Quite hard.'

Stefan came up with a bowl of crisps. He was taking his duties seriously. Natalie sidled up to Claire.

'How's Josh?' she asked.

'Oh, playing up. He's so excited about Father Christmas.'

'I don't expect he knows Father Christmas isn't real,' said Natalie solemnly.

'But don't you get excited, still, about all those presents?'

She considered. 'Yes, but I try to go to sleep, otherwise he might not come.'

'Which reminds me,' I told her firmly, 'it's time you went up now.'

'Just a bit longer,' she wheedled, sliding her eyes towards my father. But he was not to be won over.

'Come up now, and have a story.' He reached out a hand and to my relief she took it.

'Then it's your turn,' I told Stefan.

'I want to see the snow.' He went to the window and pulled aside the curtain. 'Whee! It's settling on the grass. It looks like a proper Christmas.'

'I can't remember our last white Christmas,' remarked Mother from the sofa. 'Julia must have been quite small, we went tobogganing in Richmond Park.'

'Can we go tobogganing?'

I laughed. 'We could, if we had a toboggan.'

'You can come with us, if the snow lasts,' Harry told him.

133

'Whee!' Stefan danced round the room, sending crisps flying from the bowl.

'Careful,' warned my mother. 'You're getting overexcited.'

'Mother,' I said gently, 'it is Christmas.' I wondered at myself for daring to speak up. I caught Claire's eye and it seemed she understood. She was looking more relaxed, and I guessed it was because Harry was talking to her. I went to join them.

'You're looking very well,' he said, giving me a brotherly kiss. 'I tell you who was asking after you the other day. Howard.'

It was the last thing I wanted to hear. Flustered, I answered shortly, 'I can't think why. I hardly knew him.'

'That's not the impression I got.'

Appalled, I wondered what Howard had told him.

'We were rather hoping you two would be friends,' Harry went on.

'Yes, well you can't arrange these things.' I didn't care what he thought. Reminding me of Howard reminded me of horror and shame, it trampled on my pleasure in the evening, my little triumph in playing host. I was relieved when Dad came back into the room saying, 'Good as gold, I told you so.'

He refilled everyone's glass. I heard Harry ask Claire if she'd had a holiday this year, heard her say, 'I wish. I'm afraid holidays don't figure very high on my list of priorities at present.'

'Tough. Everyone needs a holiday. Kate and I took the children to the Virgin Islands. Brilliant. Most relaxing holiday I've ever had.'

He glanced at Kate and a look passed between them suggesting intimacy. Poor Claire, I thought, he's really rubbing her nose in it, it's not very tactful.

I excused myself, to check the mince pies. Stefan followed me.

'Can I have a pie? I'm starving.'

'After all those crisps? Of course you can. Then go on up to bed, there's a good boy. You've been a great help. And don't forget to hang up your stocking.'

'I already have.' He stuffed the mince pie into his mouth, showering crumbs. I was glad Mother wasn't there to see. She would have been getting out the dustpan and brush. I ruffled his hair affectionately.

'Happy Christmas,' I said. Hoping that it would be.

After Christmas dinner we went for a walk beside the river. Stefan would have preferred to stay and set up his computer. He was beside himself with excitement, but I insisted that some fresh air and exercise would do us all good. It was what we had always done, when David was alive.

The snow had melted during the night, much to the children's disappointment. The ground was wet and dirty, a damp wind blowing up the river. Typical Christmas weather. Natalie was on her new bicycle, singing to herself as she rode. 'We wish you a merry Christmas, we wish you a merry Christmas, and a Happy New Year.' Over and over again. I felt a lift of the heart as we strode along the path, watching the river sliding by like burnished steel in the fading light. There were one or two skiffs, manned by hardy souls for whom Christmas meant a day off on the water, not huddled round the fire overeating. Lights were appearing on the opposite bank, and a little traffic crossed the bridge; people coming and going to friends and relations, full of turkey, ready for Christmas cake, bearing presents and bonhomie. Christmas Day had always seemed a strange day to me, out of time and place, when normal life stood still. I am not religious, the nativity means nothing to me. But the day still held magic. A sort of cessation, a cease-fire in the battle of life. Today was no exception. From the children's first awakening, when they had climbed onto my bed with

135

their stockings, to the blue burning brandy on the Christmas pudding, to Natalie's contented singing as she pedalled her bike, I had managed to hold at bay the press of longing for things to be different. I laughed and joked, wore my paper hat, took pride in the fact that I had decorated the tree, remembered the prune and apple stuffing, and put out the mince pie and sherry for Father Christmas. All in all, I thought I was doing pretty well.

When we reached Harrods' depository, Mother said she was getting cold. 'And it's nearly dark. Let's go back and cut the cake.'

I felt too full for cake, but it was what one did. Turning back, I saw Mother take Stefan's hand to hurry him along. Natalie was way ahead, ringing her bell. Dad and I fell behind.

'So,' he asked, 'what's the position on the job front?'

'Oh, I don't want to think about it. It's not going to be easy. I'm either too old, or too inexperienced. I can't win.'

He looked at me sadly but his voice was encouraging. 'Don't lose heart, something will turn up.'

'I thought I'd try some temping. But the agency weren't very hopeful. They said to get in touch after the New Year. I've even been noticing cards in shop windows asking for assistants. But surely I can do better than that.'

He took my hand and tucked it under his arm. 'Of course you can. I hope it will be a good year for you. You're doing very well. Putting up a brave front. Your mother and I were saying so last night. We do worry about you, you know.'

'I know.' Suddenly, tears were trembling. 'It still hurts, Dad,' I blurted out. 'Sometimes, I don't know how I can go on.'

'Don't.' His own voice was husky as he offered me a handkerchief. 'I'm sorry,' he apologised. 'I didn't mean that. You have every right to break down. It's just that it hurts me so much, to see you.'

'I know. I do try to be brave.'

'But if you can't tell me, who can you tell?'

We turned onto the road, leaving the windy river behind. The streets were deserted except for a man walking his dog. Christmas trees shone from lit windows and we could see flickering televisions and family groups clustered round. Our own tree greeted us as we went up the path, a bright beacon, as if someone were there. But they were not.

'Christmas cake,' cried Stefan as I unlocked the door. 'I helped to decorate it, Nana. I put the snowman on, and Natalie put the church.'

'And it's got a red ribbon round it,' added Natalie, leaning her bike against the wall.

'Put it in the shed,' I told her. 'You've got to take care of it.'

'I'll do it,' said Dad, wheeling it away.

'Really, he spoils that child. You both do.' It was my mother, emanating disapproval. I sighed, and followed her inside.

The house was warm, redolent still with the smell of goose and candles. David? I asked silently, as I shed my coat and gloves. But, as so often happened now, there was no answer.

SEVEN

The snow came in with the New Year, this time with a vengeance so that we woke to a blanketed garden with soft mounds where the plants used to be. After breakfast the children went outside, with boots and gloves and woolly hats, to play snowballs. I put plastic bags over their hands with rubber bands, to keep them dry. Otherwise, I knew they would soon be inside, whining with cold.

Meanwhile, I cleared the path and the pavement outside our gate, taking pleasure in the task, working up an appetite for lunch. As I dug and scraped, the traffic slowly began to move past, churning the pristine white into a brown sludge. It was the worst part of living in a town. I always hated to see the sullying of the smoothness, the short-lived nature of the purity. The back garden, too, was trampled and rough where the children had run and scooped. But they were pink-cheeked and bright-eyed, and they wanted to make a snowman.

I helped them gather a pile for his body, then roll a ball for his head.

'Get a carrot,' cried Stefan. 'Dad always used a carrot for his nose.'

So he did. I went and got a carrot, glad that Stefan had his memories, glad that, today, he seemed happy with them. I too remembered a previous occasion, when David and I had gathered the snow together and David had lifted the head and it had fallen, collapsing into powder at his feet as he collapsed with laughter. Stefan had jumped excitedly into the pile, scuffling his boots. 'Hey you,' David had admonished. 'A bit of help would be nice,' and together they had rolled a new head and set it firmly on the body while I stood watching, holding Natalie's mittened hand in mine, both of us happy and secure. I had a photograph of the three of them, with Natalie aged two, plump in a blue zip-up suit, Stefan grinning gappily, David's hair fiery against the snow. Between them, a snowman wearing an old tweed hat of David's, and his college scarf. The hat and scarf were laid down now, tenderly, in a chest in my bedroom. I couldn't bring myself to disturb them. Instead, I took a hat and scarf of my own from the hall, and fetched my camera.

The children dressed the snowman, then posed, beaming, for their picture. This time it was Natalie who was gappy. She was conscious of her gaps, holding her mouth closed when she smiled. It was a characteristic I knew I would remember when I looked at the photograph in future years. So the moment was frozen in time, a time when, unbelievably, they once more seemed to be happy.

During lunch, Kate rang.

'Harry's taking the twins tobogganing. Would your two like to come?'

There was no need to ask them. It was arranged that I would take them over as soon as possible, and we would all stay to supper. Kate and I would have a cosy afternoon by the fire. It sounded wonderful to me. I missed Kate now that she was working. It would give us time to catch up.

We walked round over slippery pavements, the children's gloved hands in mine. Despite the traffic swishing through the slush, there was a muted air to the streets. Front gardens, tatty in their winter hibernation, were beautified by the snow; laden porches spoke of cosiness inside. When we arrived at Kate's, Harry was outside digging out the car. The toboggan, red with shiny, oiled runners, stood beside it ready. Stefan ran to it and stared down admiringly.

'I wish we had one like that.' He looked at me wistfully

but I hardened my heart. Tobogganing was not something I intended to do, and they were too young to go alone.

Kate came to the door. Her face was flushed from the heat that gusted out.

'Come in, do. The twins are ready and waiting, they'll be off in a minute. Then we can settle down.'

We went into the sitting room where a bright fire was burning, adding its heat to the pulsing radiators. I shed my coat and the old cardigan which I had put over a checked wool shirt. I slipped out of my boots and Kate took them into the hall. I sank down onto the sofa, with a great feeling of peace and release. It was a long time since I had had an afternoon off.

When Harry and the children had left, Kate produced a bottle of wine.

'I think wine is called for, don't you? It's not often we get a chance for a good natter.'

She handed me a glass, red and warm.

'Ragnhild's been playing snowballs all morning, she told me.'

I couldn't imagine her playing snowballs, and said so.

'Well, it's all taken very seriously. Not a lot of laughter. But the twins enjoyed themselves. Their main aim was to get snow down her neck, but she was too wrapped up for that! She's not a bundle of laughs, but she's reliable.'

I sipped my wine, feeling envious. Kate had it all worked out.

'You're looking glum,' she said after a while, as if reading my thoughts. 'Life still hard?'

Her familiar sympathy was like balm and I felt myself loosening weakly.

'I'm lonely.' It came out baldly, just like that, surprising myself.

Her face clouded. 'Oh, my dear. It doesn't get any easier?'

'No.' I felt ridiculously near to tears. The words came out

in a rush as if to force down the sobs. 'I feel so alone with the children. I don't know how to cope with all their problems. I've no one to turn to.'

'What problems? They seem happy enough to me.'

I told her about Natalie's hair.

'But it's grown again. It suits her short. Has there been any more trouble?'

'I don't think so. Or if there has, she's coping with it herself.'

'Well then.'

My glass was empty and I held it out for a refill. 'I feel like getting drunk,' I stated dramatically, though I didn't mean it. What I meant was I felt like forgetting, letting go. Giving up. 'Actually,' I elaborated, 'I feel like giving up. Nothing seems to work out as I planned.'

'Shelley's a success, isn't she?'

'Yes, up to a point. But I can't rely on her like you can on Ragnhild. I'm not paying her.'

'Heavens, she pays no rent. I thought everything was understood.'

'And then I can't get a job,' I went on, relentlessly pursuing my failure. 'I need to get out of the house. I need company. God knows, I need money!'

'I thought you managed.'

'I do. But I've nothing in hand for emergencies. I feel so vulnerable.'

Kate pulled her feet up under her and tucked her skirt round them. Her nails were bright, her hair shiny. She looked like everything I longed to be – safe, smart, pampered, secure. Any comfort she offered was eclipsed by envy, and I hated myself for it. She looked thoughtful, then said unexpectedly, 'If you don't mind my saying so, what you need is a good fuck!'

I blushed because it was so true. My hunger for sex had not abated. It had got beyond merely missing David.

It was a real and desperate need, which I was reluctant to admit.

However, Kate was offering me the chance to talk, and the words came tumbling out. 'You're right. I do miss sex. It's such a comfort. Such a release.' I leaned forward, spreading my hands helplessly. 'And I feel deprived. I feel I am missing out on what everyone else has, which is ridiculous, of course, because everyone doesn't, but I look at myself in the mirror sometimes and think, God, I'm growing old, and unloved, and sort of wasted.'

It was a relief to say it. Even so I stared down at my hands, unwilling to meet her eye, waiting for her to speak.

When she did it was to say, 'Nonsense. You've got years ahead of you. There'll be other men. Why don't you try and meet some?'

'Fat chance, stuck at home all day. Anyway, I don't think I'm ready for another man.' I thought briefly of Howard, and shuddered. 'I would feel I was betraying David.'

She made a sympathetic face. 'Well, when you are ready, there are plenty of men out there. You could try a dating agency.'

I recoiled in horror. 'And meet all sorts of weirdos? Not to mention sounding like one myself! Pray God I never get that desperate.'

'But lot's of people do it. It's considered quite trendy nowadays.'

'Maybe. But I'm not trendy.'

'Oh Julia.' She sounded exasperated. 'What am I going to do with you? You're always running yourself down. You don't see what a splendid job you're doing. I'm full of admiration. And things will get better, I'm certain of it. You've only got to hang on in there.'

I sighed. 'Well, it seems like a life sentence to me.' I held out my glass. 'Is there any more wine?'

She took my glass and put it out of reach. 'No more,' she

said firmly. 'I don't want you getting maudlin on me. How about a piece of Christmas cake? Ragnhild made it and it's a bit heavy, though I don't like to tell her!'

I followed her into the kitchen, admiring its wide uncluttered spaces, the ethnic pottery and matching storage jars. It was tasteful and orderly, like Kate's life. My kitchen was shabby and untidy, like mine. Yet perversely I wanted to get back to its familiar comforts, and wished we weren't staying to supper.

But Kate was my friend, and she always spoke good sense. I valued this, and I tried to take comfort from her words as I picked the icing from my Christmas cake like a child.

The snow lasted a week, long enough for us to get tired of it. Then one morning I woke, late, to the knowledge that, in the night, it had gone. The cold glare of the daylight had muted to a gloomy January morning. I lay and stared at the ceiling above my head, and I couldn't believe what I saw.

Spreading outwards from the window was a large, brown, shiny stain.

I leaped up, onto the bed, reaching up to touch it. It was damp. More than damp, it was sodden. There was a sour smell of wet plaster. It wasn't actually dripping, but I was sure that the ceiling sagged.

I sank back onto the bed, hugging my knees and shivering. A hopeless despair fogged my brain. What was I to do? Our home, our one sanctuary, was violated, breached, threatened. And it was beyond my means to put it right, to secure us against a hostile world. Necessity, they say, is the mother of invention. And desperate plights call for desperate measures. I decided to write to Colin.

After breakfast, I told the children it was time they wrote to him to thank him for their Christmas presents. I settled them, protesting, at the kitchen table, and brought my own pen and paper to join them.

'See,' I said. 'I'm writing mine.'

I started easily enough, thanking him for the book token he had sent. Then I paused, wondering how to lead up to the subject of the roof. Five thousand pounds was a lot of money. Was it fair to ask him to so reduce his own resources? But he had said he would be happy to help me. I really didn't want to ask my father, who had done so much already.

I decided not to beat about the bush. 'I have a big problem, and much as I hate asking you, I am wondering if you may be able to help. The thing is, the roof needs replacing, and it's going to cost five thousand pounds. We have had two leaks already, so it obviously can't be put off much longer.

'Forgive me for asking you and please say no if you can't spare it, but it would be such a load off my mind if you could.'

I paused again, chewing my pen. I looked at the children. Natalie was sprawled over her paper, tongue protruding with concentration as she formed the letters.

'How do you spell "present"?' she asked. 'I've put, "Dear Gramps, Thank you for my . . ." I want to put "present" because doll's hairdressing set is too long.'

I wrote the word for her to copy.

Stefan was writing strenuously, listing all the things he had been given. I saw the word 'computer' underlined thickly; it obviously took precedence over everything else, including the simple camera I had given him. Colin had sent him a novelty watch, a cheap gadget that I guessed wouldn't last long, but it adorned his wrist now and seemed to be telling the time. 'Do you know how to spell "watch"?' I asked him now.

He looked at me witheringly. 'Of course I do. But I'm not sure about tobogganing.'

I smiled. It was obviously going to be a newsy letter. I wrote the word down for him, and turned back to my own page. If I wanted it to be more than just a begging letter, I had better tell him some news too.

We walked down to the post box and put the envelope containing the three letters in the post. It was Saturday, the sixth of January. Shelley was arriving back that evening. On Monday, school started. On Monday, I had to start the weary business of job hunting. The interregnum was over. I felt dreary and frightened, drained of all energy. As we approached the house I looked nervously at the roof, wondering just how long it would have to wait.

And then, on Monday, came the letter.

It was from a firm of solicitors in Wadebridge and it regretted to inform me that Mr Colin Leathlean had died. It went on to say that I was the sole beneficiary under his will. It explained that the funeral had already taken place, a cremation with no guests, at Mr Leathlean's request. It commiserated with me on my loss. I would be hearing again in the very near future. Yours faithfully.

I sat at the breakfast table, the letter in my hands. The children were squabbling in the bathroom as they cleaned their teeth. It was the first day of term, Shelley had already left, the room was silent except for the roar of the central heating boiler. I tried to absorb the words, and what they meant to me. Colin, my friend, David's father, was gone. He had never got our letters. I had been spared the humiliation of asking him for money. The money was mine. With luck, the roof could be mended. With more luck, we would have money in the bank. I fought down the tidal wave of relief which threatened to overwhelm the grief that I must surely be feeling too. And then came the thought that I would have to tell the children. But not now, not before they went to school. It would have to wait until the evening.

When they had gone, I telephoned a neighbour of Colin's, a kindly woman who had always kept an eye on him, and she told me what had happened. She had invited him in for a cup of tea and a piece of Christmas cake. 'Lasts for ever if you don't eat it up,' she said discursively, while I waited impatiently for news. When he didn't turn up, she went round and found him in the kitchen, slumped over a bowl of soup, quite dead. It had been a heart attack. He wouldn't have suffered. 'But what do they know, doctors? I don't like to think of him going like that, all alone. It was tomato soup. It was all in his hair.'

I didn't like to think of it either and after I had rung off I had a good, cleansing cry. He had been a good man, a dear man, I had loved him because of David and because of himself. Now he was gone, I was even more alone.

I told the children very gently, holding both their hands in mine.

'I had a letter this morning, from Cornwall. Gramps is dead. I'm so sorry.'

Stefan's face distorted into an ugly howl. 'No! He can't be. Not Gramps too.'

I held him to me. 'This is different, darling. Gramps was old. His heart was wearing out. He told me when we were there last summer.'

'But where will we go for our holidays?'

I had thought about that. 'Well, the house is ours now, we could still go and stay there. Or I could sell it, and we could spend the money on other holidays. We'll see.'

'But who will take me fishing?' he wailed.

'You'll soon be old enough to go fishing by yourself.'

He gave a tremulous sigh. 'I hate people dying,' he said wearily. He slid from my grasp and left the room. I heard the door of his bedroom close sharply behind him, and guessed he had gone to cry.

Natalie had said nothing. She sat with her thumb in her mouth, her eyes very wide.

'Are you all right, Nat? Do you understand?'

146

She nodded. Her thumb slid from her mouth, wet and slippery.

'I expect,' she said solemnly, 'that Gramps is with Daddy in heaven. And that's good, isn't it?'

I told her that I thought it was. It was a soothing thought, if one believed in heaven. I didn't, though I had needed to believe that David was still there, somewhere. Otherwise, why did I talk to him, why did I think sometimes, still, that he was near? Was it merely wishful thinking, dreamed up by the desperate to provide solace and consolation? But wasn't that what religion was, after all? Something to hang on to when all else failed? I had always been sceptical, unable to have blind faith in something my rational mind told me wasn't possible. If there was a God, why had he let David die? And yet Colin's death, while sad, would prove the solution to my problems. Perhaps there was a plan, and the plan was simply that sometimes you won, and sometimes you didn't. I pulled Natalie onto my lap and rocked her mindlessly.

After a while she began to fidget and whimper.

'What's up? Ready for bed?'

'My head hurts.'

I touched her forehead. It felt hot. I noticed then that her face was flushed, her eyes overbright.

'Bed for you, I think.' I carried her upstairs, for the first time for ages. She was very heavy, a dead weight in my arms. I felt a skittering of panic. I had had little experience of childhood ailments. When I pulled off her sweater and vest I saw the spots, red and weepy, scattered over her chest.

'Well,' I said cheerfully, though I didn't feel it. 'It looks as if you've got chicken pox.'

She looked worried. 'Will I die too?' she asked in a small voice.

'Good heavens no, you'll just itch. And I expect Stefan will get it too, so there'll be no school for a week or so.'

147

As I said it my heart sank. The next day I had an appointment with the temping agency. They had agreed to give me a test, and possibly put me on their books. I obviously couldn't go.

I gave Natalie a Calpol to help her headache. I tucked her up in bed with a story, and left her to sleep. Then I knocked gently at Stefan's door.

To my surprise he was already in bed, surrounded by stuffed toys.

'You haven't had all your bears in bed for ages,' I told him. 'There's hardly room for you.'

'I wanted them tonight.' He looked composed, though his face was tear-stained.

I bent to kiss him good night. His arm went round my neck. He felt warm and his pyjamas smelled of washing powder. I wondered if I should examine him for spots, but decided not to disturb him.

His voice was muffled when he said, 'Gramps never got my letter. I should have written sooner, to tell him I loved my watch.'

'But maybe he knows that now. If he's in heaven.'

He pulled back and looked at me sceptically. 'I'm not sure I believe in heaven.'

It wasn't in me to try to persuade him; besides, he went off on a different tack.

'Can I have a photograph of Dad in my room?'

I was startled. 'Of course, if you want one. But why have you thought of that now?'

He looked inexpressibly sad. 'Because I'm starting to forget him, what he looked like. And I don't want to do that.'

His words smote me, both for his sake, and David's.

'You might forget his face, just a little bit, but you'll never forget him as a person. That's what counts. So don't worry about it.'

'But can I have a picture? And one of Gramps too?'

'Of course you can. Now settle down and go to sleep.'

He slid down under the bedclothes until I could only see the top of his blond hair among the toys. I reached out and touched it.

'Good night, Stefan. And don't worry.'

There was a muffled grunt. I turned out the light. Shelley was on the landing as I turned to the stairs.

'Come down and join me,' I said. It was an order rather than an invitation. I didn't want to be alone. 'I feel badly in need of a drink.'

I rang the temping agency and told them of my predicament.

The woman sounded stern. 'I should have thought you would have made arrangements for such emergencies. How do you expect to hold down a job?'

I felt foolish and inefficient. It was not something I had planned for.

'I think we must postpone a further appointment until you've arranged for proper childcare,' the woman went on.

Chastened, I rang off. She was so obviously right that I wondered I hadn't thought of it myself, hadn't envisioned such an eventuality. The cover I had thought I had arranged seemed suddenly dubious and shaky. I poured myself the dregs of the previous night's wine, although it was only ninethirty in the morning. As I steadied myself, I came to the realisation that to get a job had only been a pipe dream. Obviously, it was not intended that I should. With Colin's money, things would be easier. I would stay at home, and look after the children myself.

The thought followed that maybe, therefore, I should get rid of Shelley. But I found myself baulking at the idea. I had got used to having someone else in the house. I liked her quiet determined ways, and what's more, the children liked her. In a curious sense, when we were all in the untidy kitchen together we felt like some sort of a family.

I looked round the kitchen now, taking in the shabby cupboards and drab walls. Maybe I could refurbish it as David and I had always planned to do, with country pine units and dark green walls and spotlights and plants which didn't wilt and die. For a moment thoughts of tidying up the house filled me with excitement, buoyed me up. But after a while I sank down again onto the rock bottom of reality. For I knew I would be bored, and lonely. I was already bored and lonely. I had been looking forward to getting a job, to having something worthwhile to do, to getting out of the house, to meeting people. To being a person in my own right. Instead of Julia Leathlean, widow, and mother of two.

As if to reinforce the final dismal thought, Natalie came trailing into the room. I had let her get up and she had been watching television from the sofa. Now she was rubbing miserably at her chest.

'I tickle,' she said.

I looked at her. The spots had spread to her face, some perilously close to her eyes.

'Camomile lotion, that's what we need. But I haven't got any. I wonder if it's all right to take you out?'

She stared at me abjectly, awaiting some adult decision.

I pulled myself together. 'I'll wrap you up and leave you in the back of the car,' I told her. I got my purse and our coats, and bundled her into a rug in the back seat. I left the car in the car park and her inside with the doors locked, praying she would be all right. I raced round the supermarket, getting as much as I could while I had the chance, trying to think of little treats. Fizzy lemonade, jelly, grapes, ice cream, chocolate buttons. A new book to read. Camomile lotion and a large pack of cotton wool. And food for several meals.

I hurried the laden trolley back to the car, expecting to find

150

it gone, or burned, or broken into, instead of which Natalie was sound asleep in her blanket, her thumb in her mouth. Relief cancelled the guilt as I packed the shopping into the boot and drove her safely home to bed. Maybe I wasn't that much of a mother, I told myself, but I was doing my best.

That night when the children were in bed, I rang my parents.

'Natalie's got chicken pox,' I told my mother. 'I've had the doctor. Nat's feeling pretty miserable. And Stefan will surely get it too.'

Mother commiserated, and asked if there was anything she could do.

'Well, maybe come and see us when they're over the worst. I wouldn't want you to catch it.'

'Oh, I caught it from you, don't you remember?'

I did, but I thought I had heard something somewhere about shingles.

After that I told her about Colin, and she commiserated again.

'He was a nice man, I know you were fond of him.'

'More than that, he was part of David. But he's left me some money, and the house. Wasn't that sweet of him?'

'I wouldn't have expected anything else. You were his family.'

'Still – it will be a help. I've decided not to get a job for the moment. The children obviously need me too much.'

There was a pause. Then Mother said, 'That's a pity, because I think your father's come up with something.'

'Something? What sort of something?'

'A colleague of his. A gynaecologist in Harley Street. He wants a receptionist. Dad was going to ring you later. It sounds perfect for you.'

I was astonished, already looking for the problems. 'But Harley Street? That's miles away. And anyway, what do I do if the children are ill? That's something I just hadn't planned for.'

'Julia.' Her voice remonstrated. 'What are grandparents for if not to help out in an emergency?'

I was even more astonished. 'You? You'd look after the children if they were ill? But I couldn't ask you.'

'Why not?' She sounded hurt.

I couldn't say that I would never have expected her to agree, that I wouldn't have dreamed of interrupting the organisation of her life. I mumbled something about it being an imposition.

'Nonsense. Now what do you think about the job? Dad's gone to the trouble of speaking up for you, and Mr Seligman wants to see you. I can come up at any time and look after Natalie.'

I gave a hollow laugh. 'It's ironic, all day I've been telling myself I don't really want a job, and now this. I need to have a rethink.'

'Well, it's up to you. You know we don't want you going out to work, but you seemed so set on it. This does seem to be a good opportunity . . .'

'Yes. Yes, I'll take it. The opportunity I mean, not the job. He may not like me. There will be other applicants.'

'Apparently not. He's agreed not to advertise until he's seen you.'

Gratitude to my father overwhelmed me. It was to him that I owed such a favour; to the esteem in which Mr Seligman obviously held him. I could not disappoint him.

'What do I do?' I asked, feeling a growing swell of excitement.

'I'll give you his number. You're to ring for an appointment.'

I wrote down the number.

'Let me know when it is, and I'll come over and take care of Natalie.'

152

'Thanks, Mother. Thanks to both of you.' I felt a great rush of love, uncomplicated by the usual restraint. But she didn't answer. She had rung off.

The doctor's consulting rooms were on the first floor of a discreet house in Harley Street, and I spoke into the voice box on the wall to have the front door released from above. I climbed the blue carpeted stairs, admiring the watercolours on the walls, the muted wall-lights, the air of quiet opulence that would surely reassure any patient. At the top of the stairs was a wide reception area, with a palm tree in a Chinese pot and, seated beneath it at a pale wooden desk, a receptionist who, despite her elegance, was very obviously pregnant.

She smiled at me. 'Mrs Leathlean? I'm pleased to see you.'

She held out a hand and I shook it.

'Mr Seligman won't keep you a moment. He's been delayed at the clinic. Do take a seat.'

I sat down on a soft sofa, upholstered in grey velvet. A spread of glossy magazines covered a low glass table. There was an apricot begonia in a white bowl, and a notice, 'Thank you for not smoking.' The girl typed for a few minutes at a computer, then looked up and asked me if I had come far.

'Putney. It took about three-quarters of an hour on the underground.'

'Oh, the underground. I shall be glad to have done with all that.'

She seemed so friendly that I said, 'I can see why you're leaving!'

She smiled, and touched her swollen belly. 'I'd hoped to stay on a few more weeks, but I've got blood pressure. I have to leave this week.'

I wasn't sure what to say to that. Instead I took in her quiet good looks, smart despite her maternity dress, realising that I too would be required to grace the elegance of the surroundings. Was I up to it? Waiting, I began to feel nervous. I was relieved when I heard the front door open and close, and a short, tubby, balding man came up the stairs at a run.

Beady eyes met mine through thick glasses. 'Mrs Leathlean, I'm so sorry to have kept you. I won't be a moment, just let me get my breath.'

He disappeared through a grey door with a gleaming brass handle. I felt immediately more relaxed. He seemed an approachable little man, not too impressive as I had feared. Besides, I reminded myself, he was a friend of my father's. There must be likeable aspects to him. For something to do, I opened my handbag, got out a mirror, patted my hair. Then a buzzer went on the receptionist's desk and she got up and opened the grey door.

'Do go in now,' she said, giving me an encouraging smile. I guessed she wanted me to get the job, as then she could leave in peace.

'So,' he said as I sat down. 'Charles has told me all about you. You could be just what I'm looking for, someone mature and sensible and discreet, who can start at once.'

I thought of Natalie and her chicken pox, remembered my mother's offer and decided to say nothing.

'You can use a computer, I presume?'

'I can use a word processor. Would that be sufficient?'

'It's mainly typing. An hour or two with Vanessa should be enough to put you straight.' He leaned back in his chair. I guessed that his short legs hardly reached the ground. 'It goes without saying that all the work is confidential.'

'Of course.' I cleared my throat. 'Can I just ask about the hours? Only it takes quite a while to get here, and there's the children to see to . . .'

'My consulting hours are from ten till four. The rest of the time I'm at the clinic. I operate on Tuesdays but I would need you to be here to man the phone. Vanessa comes in at nine forty-five and usually leaves at about four-thirty. I can pay you seven thousand a year. Are you interested?'

I swallowed hard. It had all been so quick. 'Are you offering me the job?'

'If you want it. You look presentable, you speak well, you can type, you can start at once. But we'll call it a month's trial if you like. On both sides.'

I found myself smiling widely. 'Then yes, thank you, I'd like to come.'

'On Monday?'

I crossed my fingers. 'On Monday.'

His little eyes sparkled at me as he held out his hand. It hardly reached across his broad desk and I had to stand to grasp it.

'I take it I can call you Julia?'

'Of course.'

'I suggest you spend some time with Vanessa before you go, she'll fill you in on everything. Give my regards to Charles.'

I was dismissed. I had to admire his brevity and wondered if he dealt similarly with his patients. One of them was sitting outside as I left the room, a middle-aged woman in a fur coat with a Pekinese on her lap. The buzzer went immediately, and Vanessa showed her in. I crossed to her desk and stared down at the computer screen. There was a list of appointments, my own name first at ten o'clock, then a Mrs Frobisher at ten past ten. So, he had not allowed much time for me. He was obviously a man of decision. In any event, it had worked in my favour. He had liked what he saw, and given me the job. I touched the computer, possessively. On Monday it would be mine.

Meanwhile, I had to plumb its secrets. Vanessa was a good teacher, and gave me a pad to take notes. She showed me how to access the diary and the patients' notes, and how to type letters and reports. She took me through into a smart kitchenette and told me how Mr Seligman liked his coffee. She told me about watering the palm tree, and the other plants in his office. She gave me the office routine and showed me her list of telephone numbers. Lastly, she gave me her own, for emergencies.

'Don't be afraid to call, this has all been a bit of a rush.'

'I won't.'

In between times, she had been greeting patients with a quiet and reassuring charm which I knew I must learn to emulate. She introduced me, and I felt a growing pride that soon they would be my responsibility. It was an awesome feeling. I resolved to make them welcome, to try to ease their fears. Walking back down Harley Street, I mentally hugged myself. I had a job! I was on my way!

PART TWO

EIGHT

It could be said that that year, two years after David died, was a sort of watershed. Certainly, it was the beginning of my recovery. With less time to think, I stopped scratching at the scab of my sadness and it began to heal. But I still told David all about the job, and I sensed he was pleased for me. I also told him that Colin had died. I wasn't sure that he would already know that; I didn't have Natalie's faith that they would be skipping in Elysian fields together. I told him that he had left me all his money, which turned out to be just less than twenty thousand pounds but which seemed like riches to me. I knew David would have been pleased that his father had been able to help us. I felt sorry that David hadn't lived to enjoy the little nest egg himself. He would have liked to have the house. I decided to keep it for the time being and let it. It could only go up in value, and besides I was not yet emotionally ready to dispose of it. It was still too personally imbued with David.

I had my roof repaired, and a new kitchen – fairly modest, and with dark blue tiles – nothing like David and I had planned, which I regarded as a sign of progress. The rest of the money I put aside for another rainy day. With a regular income, for a while I felt rich and blessed. The children had new clothes, I had new clothes, for I badly needed them for work. We had chocolate sauce with our ice cream, and I no longer envied Kate, except perhaps for having Harry.

I quickly fell into the new routine. I had time to take the children to school before walking to Putney Bridge station and catching the tube to Oxford Circus. They stayed at the

159

after-school club until Shelley fetched them and I was back in time to prepare the supper. In the holidays, Shelley took over, with occasional help from my mother. I congratulated myself that I had it all worked out. I was not so complacent that I didn't cross my fingers sometimes, and pray, in my nonbelieving way, that nothing would go wrong. When there didn't seem to be anything to worry about, I worried about that. That's the way I am.

Housework, never my strong point, dwindled further under the pressures on my time. By the time she was ten, Natalie was fussily clearing up after me, washing dishes and pushing the Hoover round. She kept her own room immaculate, and tried to do the same with mine. Clothes I had left lying around would find their way into the washing basket; shoes would be lined neatly in the bottom of the wardrobe. One day she exclaimed crossly, 'Why are some of Daddy's clothes still hanging up?'

I looked at the two suits and the tweed sports jacket as if I had never seen them before. The truth was I hardly saw them any more, never went and hugged them or sniffed for his long-faded smell.

'You're right,' I said briskly. 'Fetch me a bin liner, they can go to the charity shop.' I pulled them out and laid them on the bed. Lingering sentiment tugged momentarily but I told myself firmly that, after seven years, the time had come to let go. I watched gratefully as Natalie folded them neatly and put them into the bag, feeling as if I were the child, and she the mother.

I continued to see Claire, who had eventually got a job with Marks and Spencer, at the checkout counter. This gave her a useful discount on purchases, which she professed to find worth the change of direction. We had regular tea-parties with the children, and sometimes in the summer I took her and Josh out in the car. We went along the river, onto the common and out into the countryside with picnics. Once, in a mood of bravado, as we sipped wine beneath a tree while the children sailed stick boats on a pond, she said gaily, 'Who needs men?' and I found myself agreeing with her, then immediately apologising to David. But I spoke to him less now. And I didn't think he'd mind.

But then Claire found another man, and decided she did need him after all. I found myself peculiarly bereft, left out on a limb while she swarmed up the main trunk of the tree, embracing life. It set her apart from me. And it underlined my loneliness, my own failure to find a man.

Not that I had been looking. The only man I saw regularly was my employer. Everyone else to do with the job was by definition female. I had quickly got to know his regular patients, and was familiar with their problems. They were all either rich, or well-insured, but they were human beings and as such deserved my sympathy. Those that I felt for most were the young ones, desperate to have children but for some reason thwarted by nature. The older ones, menopausal and malcontent, seemed pathetic and, sometimes, spoiled. But I wondered how I would cope, when my time came. The more serious cases, with cancer and ovarian cysts and endometriosis, preyed on my mind, and I was especially nice to them. In between greeting them, listening to them, processing their appointments, I typed notes and diagnoses, arranged the operating schedule and dealt with drug suppliers and the clinic. I fed the palm tree, which had reached the ceiling, and arranged flowers. It was a charmed existence and I was happy.

But when Claire married Ian, it was the beginning of my discontent.

I had been feeling proud and fulfilled, settled in my life as sole provider and support for my children. I was busy, and sometimes, when I stopped to think, I would cautiously acknowledge myself to be happy. Now, I suddenly realised that I was still, for all my rushing about, essentially on my own. I began to feel sorry for myself. Further, and more importantly, I began to feel an unwanted failure, cut off from the society that couples enjoyed. I still saw Kate and Harry, but other couples seldom invited me out. I had come to rely on Claire; now she had moved on without me. She didn't abandon me, but I felt abandoned. Desperation found me, one day, glancing down the personal columns of the local paper, at all those other desperate ones, and feeling that I was not alone, and furthermore that I had no need to be alone, the solution was in my hands, if I only dared to grasp it.

Why, I wondered, as I scanned the entries, were all these slim, humorous, interesting, loving people on their own? Why were they not enjoying their country walks, theatre visits and ethnic foods together? What, really, was wrong with them? But then, what was wrong with me? Nothing, that I could see. Loneliness had simply been forced upon me by circumstances. The same circumstances that had stranded all these other people, so that they were obliged to advertise for friendship, for love, for sex.

If they could do it, so could I.

Feeling obscurely ashamed, I sat in my bedroom and carefully worded an entry of my own. 'Widow of thirty-eight with two children, slim and medium height, seeks companionship on country walks, meals and theatre visits. Good sense of humour – shared laughter would be appreciated.' As I wrote that I realised how much I missed the laughter that David and I had enjoyed. It had been the linchpin of our enjoyment of one another. Reading through the words I felt a tightening of embarrassment, as if someone were reading over my shoulder. I felt as though I were putting myself up for purchase, offering myself to the highest bidder. Beneath the shame, and augmenting it, was the knowledge that what we were all probably after, after the walks and the meals and the theatre visits, was sex. It was pathetic and humiliating. I was not sure that I could enter the lists with such an implied need written large upon the page. Perhaps, instead, it would be safer to answer one of the advertisements, rather than advertise myself like reject goods in a sale.

I took the newspaper up to bed that night and, with a red pen, ringed those entries which interested me most. I ignored all those who were under thirty-five and over forty-five. Apart from that, everyone sounded personable and attractive, but then of course, they would. I have no particular hobbies or interests; I realised that made me rather a boring prospect, but it enabled me to avoid birdwatchers and sailors and motor-racing enthusiasts. Those with children I also avoided. True, it would make them more tolerant of mine, but my mind was leaping uncontrollably ahead. Would I want to take on another man's children? I realised with a shock that my hopes and expectations were racing far beyond the simple companionship I purported to require, and with a trembling hand I put away the pen and pushed the newspaper under the bed.

Where it lay for several days, until a dream of such vivid ecstasy drove me to action. I dreamed that I met a man outside a shop. We were both gazing into the window, then we turned and our glances met and held, and the next moment we were mysteriously transported to the back of a car where he made love to me roughly and utterly to my satisfaction, so that I woke on the last throb of pleasure and lay, still and sated but in a deep hollow of aloneness. It had not only been the physical union but also a very real feeling of closeness with this unknown, almost unseen, man, that left me now gasping with loneliness. I yearned more than I could say to feel that togetherness again. I ached with self-pity and rolled into my pillow to cry, but the tears would not come. It was as if I were frozen by my misery. In desperation, I reached down and pulled the newspaper from under the bed. In the morning, I would write some letters.

I got up early, before the children awoke, and, again

163

sitting secretly in my bedroom, I wrote brief letters to the two box numbers which seemed most appropriate. One of them asked for a photograph, but I had none that I wanted to send, nothing recent and nothing alone. I did not feel inclined to expose the children. So I apologised and jokingly said that I had nothing to hide. Having written that, I looked at myself appraisingly in the dressing-table mirror. I was still slim, and my brown hair hung to my shoulders in a simple ageless bob. There were signs of strain round my mouth and eyes but when I smiled they disappeared. I smiled now, as if I were greeting this unknown stranger. The effect was not displeasing. I resolved to go into a photo-booth and have some pictures taken for future use. Despite my broken night I felt fired with energy. I was taking matters into my own hands instead of letting myself drift on the uncertain current of fate. It felt good.

I didn't give my address, only my telephone number. I posted the letters on my way to work, then tried not to think about them again.

I got a telephone call a week later, from someone called Joe Brandon. He said I sounded really nice and he wanted to meet me. Just like that.

It was so easy that I was suspicious. When the phone rang, I had been helping Stefan with some homework. I felt we should talk, but now was not convenient. I asked Joe for his number and said I would ring him back later. Now it was he who sounded suspicious, as if I were trying to put him off. I reassured him, though I already had my doubts. His voice didn't please me, having the flattened vowels of South London. But it would be unfair to dismiss him on the strength of that alone. I wanted to know more about him. I promised I would ring him at half-past nine, and put the receiver down.

When we did talk, it turned out that Joe had a sorry tale to tell. His wife had left him and taken his child. He didn't know where they were. He didn't want a divorce; it was clear that he wanted them back. But he was also clearly lonely, panic-stricken and depressed. He went on at length about his miserable circumstances, but my pity soon turned to irritation.

He wanted sympathy, and the reassurance that he could still be attractive to a woman. I was not prepared to be that woman, but I couldn't let him down too abruptly. I let him tell me about his motorbike, though it reminded me uneasily of Howard. I listened while he expounded on the wonders of his child, a little boy of six. I sympathised when he told me he had been made redundant when the garage he worked at closed down. I noticed that he didn't ask me anything about myself, and was glad. I had nothing to offer him, nothing at all. When he suggested that we meet in a local pub the following evening, I braced myself and said that I thought not, I didn't really want to be just a substitute for a wife he wanted back. I was sorry for his situation, but didn't think that meeting other women would help.

He was upset, and began to plead. I was tempted to slam down the phone, but common humanity made me hear him out. At the end, I said simply, 'I'm sorry, Joe, but anyway I don't think we have much in common.' I thanked him for ringing, and said goodbye. When I put the phone down I felt great waves of relief, yet also still curiously exposed. He had my number, he knew my name. Would he leave me alone?

And what on earth did I think I was doing?

It was several days before I heard from the other one, the one who had wanted a photograph. He was well spoken and introduced himself as Hugh Sutcliffe. He apologised for the delay but said he had been away on business, which sounded hopeful. A nicely spoken businessman, I told myself, could be ideal.

I apologised for the lack of photograph. 'That's all right,' he said. 'I can hear from your voice that you're my sort of

165

woman.' I flinched, but then wasn't I making just the same judgements?

'What do you do?' I asked, deciding to get the ball into my court.

'I'm a pharmaceutical salesman.'

'You mean drugs and medicines?' I asked with interest.

He laughed. 'No. More in the way of cotton wool and bandages. And tampons,' he added, and laughed again.

I felt myself flush. It was an undignified profession, and inexcusably intimate to disclose it so soon, and make a joke of it. My interest flagged. I could not imagine cosy diners *à deux*, nor intellectual visits to the theatre, with such a man. But I told myself I was once again being a snob. He was at least showing an interest in me, asking the names of the children whom I had told him were ten and thirteen. We talked about my job, and he told me his wife had been a nurse who had run off with a doctor. He said he didn't have much time for doctors, which I thought was tactless since I had told him about David in my letter.

'I was training to be one myself when I married,' I told him somewhat tartly.

He simply laughed it off. 'When shall we meet?' he asked, assuming that we would.

This was the difficult bit which I simply hadn't reckoned with. But I knew it would be no use. It would be better to be honest from the start.

'I don't think I really want to,' I said, despite myself sounding apologetic. 'I'm sorry.'

There was a silence. Then he said rather irritably, 'That's a pity. I thought you said you wanted a laugh. I think you'd find me quite amusing.'

'Maybe. But I'd rather not.' I said again that I was sorry, wondering how I was going to get off the phone. But it was not a problem, for I heard his receiver go down without another word. It was like a slap in the face, and even if I had deserved it, it left me shaken. I sat looking at the phone for a long time before putting it down, gently, on its rest.

Once again, I felt ragged and exposed. I wondered if I could stand any more, but having come this far I had the bit between my teeth. I would, instead, insert an advertisement of my own. Any replies I had would give me more information to go on, and I could choose myself who to contact.

Nevertheless I waited a few days before sending in my carefully constructed entry to the newspaper. It was as if I were cowering in the trenches before finally going over the top. I did not know what kind of barrage awaited me.

While I was waiting for a response Claire phoned me to tell me she was pregnant. I felt an unexpected surge of envy, not for the baby for I was past such broodiness, but for the confirmation of her bond with Ian. Any wish I might have had to confide in her about the advertisement faded. Instead I felt shamefaced. In the light of her settled existence, my efforts seemed foolish and humiliating. Instead, I tried to enthuse, to share her excitement.

'Actually,' she confessed, 'it's a bit of a mistake. Josh is nearly nine. It's quite a gap.'

'But he'll be thrilled, won't he?'

'I'm not so sure. He thinks babies are soppy. And he's had me to himself for so long. He was even jealous of Ian at first.'

I remembered that. I wondered, briefly, how Stefan and Natalie would react to a man in my life. But it was too late for doubts, for the following day the letters started to arrive.

It was exciting, at first, to realise just how many men there were out there, looking for a partner. But it was also alarming, this evidence of need and loneliness. During the course of three days, the newspaper sent me twenty-five letters. I had been picking up the post as soon as it came, and was able to divert the thick brown envelopes before the children

167

or Shelley saw them. The last thing I wanted was questions about what I was up to. I hid them under my duvet, and read them in the evenings in the privacy of my bedroom. Overwhelmed by such profligacy, at first I didn't know which to choose. But many were barely articulate, or written in indecipherable hand, or, worse, typed, which seemed impersonal. Some said too much; others not enough. Careful consideration soon rendered them down to only three.

The first was a geography teacher. He was thirty-nine and had been divorced for ten years. His wife had taken his two children abroad and he never saw them. He said he missed children in his life and would be interested to meet mine. His hobby, his passion rather, was photography. He lived in Richmond, in a little house which he had renovated himself. He gave his phone number and said he looked forward to hearing from me. His name was Geoff.

The second one was older, forty-six, but he was a widower, an accountant with his own practice and a large apartment overlooking the river in Fulham. He had two children, one at university, one working in the city. He enjoyed the theatre and the opera, and cooking Indian food. He sounded civilised. His name was Samuel.

The third was an airline pilot called Jeremy. He explained that he was not often in London, but that when he was he was lonely, and wanted someone to come back to. He had no time for hobbies, but enjoyed eating out. He had never married. He was forty-two.

I spread the three letters on my bed and looked at them with a foolish excitement. I had already endowed the writers with looks and charm and told myself that it was going to be impossible to choose between them. The possibility of their not choosing me didn't enter my head. After all, they had written, hadn't they? My own previous disappointments were forgotten as I noted their numbers, and waited for the children to go to bed so that I could make the calls in peace.

Stefan, however, had other ideas. There was a programme he wanted to stay up and see, about plate tectonics and earthquakes. He was becoming increasingly interested in geology.

'I've got this essay to write, Mum, it will help me if I see it.'

'But it's late. We could video it.'

'I've got to write the essay tomorrow. Please. Watch it with me.'

Already, as he grew into a man, he could charm me. And I felt inordinately proud of his new enthusiasm, hoping it would lead to a degree and a career. It was not in me to stop him. So instead of me making my phone calls, we sat together and watched the programme. Stefan seemed to know all about the movement of the earth's crust; tectonic plates, ocean trenches, and the creation of the Himalayas. I marvelled at this, and I marvelled that this lanky embryonic man with bright blond hair and eyes which were beginning to be knowing could be my son, and, moreover, could still want to have me by his side. We drank hot chocolate, and I hugged him good night, and went to bed happy.

The following day, I had a shock. The local paper arrived as usual and on the second page there was an account of a suicide. A young man had driven his motorbike into a wall. Friends said he had been depressed since the breakdown of his marriage, and the loss of his job. And his name was Joe Brandon.

Joe. Poor, depressed Joe, who had tried so hard to win my sympathy and my time. I was appalled, smitten with guilt and responsibility. Maybe I could have saved him, convinced him that life was still worth living. But common sense told me that I had had nothing to offer him. And I could retrieve neither his wife nor his job. Even so, I felt raw and vulnerable at this brutal contact with a stranger's life. Once again, I asked myself just what I thought I was doing in so exposing myself. The telephone numbers remained, unused, on my pad for several days as I hugged my privacy to myself, preserving my anonymity.

We were having supper one night when Natalie, whose best friend was called Chloe, suddenly announced that Chloe's mother was getting married.

I knew she had been divorced for several years, and had suspected that it was their fatherless state which had drawn the girls together.

'That's nice,' I commented, feeling the accustomed envy at someone else's happiness.

'She met him through a marriage bureau,' Natalie explained. 'Why don't you do that?'

I stared at her. Was my need so obvious? 'Why do you say that?' I asked.

She shrugged, looking down at her food. She took a forkful of rice and ate it slowly. She looked discomfited.

'Natalie,' I said gently, 'would you like me to do that?'

She put down her fork and looked up. Her face was flushed as she said, 'It would be nice to have a daddy again.'

'Nat!' It was Stefan, interrupting angrily.

'No, it's all right,' I told him.

'Well, don't you think so?' Natalie challenged her brother. 'You said it would.'

'Shut up.' Now Stefan was flushed.

I looked from one to another. How little I really knew them. How little I understood what they might be feeling, what they might talk about together. I had thought they had got over David, that our family, for them at least, was complete. Suddenly I saw that I was wrong. They wanted what other children had. I was not enough for them. The thought saddened me, yet seemed entirely right.

I thought of the telephone numbers on my pad, and was on the verge of telling them. But something stopped me; pride, and a fear of raising their expectations.

'Listen,' I told them. 'I'm sorry you haven't got a father. I'm sorry if you think I've failed you. I just haven't felt ready. Or not, perhaps, until now.'

'Now?' Natalie looked hopeful.

'I'm not promising anything. I'm just saying that, now, I might be able to move on in my life. And it helps to know that you are behind me, that you wouldn't mind.'

'We want you to be happy, Mum.' It was Stefan, looking self-concious and adolescent, yet obviously speaking from the heart.

I smiled. 'I am happy. I've got two wonderful children. Now finish your risotto, I've actually made a pudding.'

After we had washed up, with the usual arguments about who should do what, I helped them with their homework, then Natalie went to bed and Stefan went up to work on his computer.

And, without giving myself time to hesitate, I picked up the telephone and dialled the number of Jeremy, the airline pilot.

I got his answerphone. A cultured voice said that he was out of town, but please leave my name and number. I hesitated. Did I want him to ring me back, possibly when it was not convenient? I decided against it and rang off without leaving a message.

I found that I was trembling. It would have been easy to give up. But the other numbers were now burning a hole in my pad. I tossed up between Geoff the teacher, and Samuel the accountant. Finally I closed my eyes and stabbed a pen down onto the pad. It hit Geoff's number. I punched in the numbers and waited nervously. The phone rang and rang. Good, I thought, and was preparing to drop the receiver when a breathless voice answered.

'Sorry, I was in the shower. Who am I talking to?'

I swallowed hard. 'This is Julia Leathlean. You wrote to me, at the box number.'

He seemed quite unperturbed. 'Oh yes. The doctor's

widow, two children. You were the only one I wrote to this time.'

'This time? Have you been looking long?'

'Let's say it's not easy to find the right one.'

'Oh.' For some reason I felt disappointed, though common sense told me that it was only to be expected.

'I find the best way is to meet, and get it over with. No amount of talking over the phone can equal a face-to-face meeting.'

I quailed at such a businesslike approach.

'But don't you want to know any more about me? Not that there is much, I'm quite ordinary . . .'

'There, you see, you're already spoiling it. I'll decide whether you're ordinary or not. Let's meet. I presume you'd like to, or you wouldn't have rung.'

I felt confused and rushed, but didn't know what to do about it. There was after all some sense in what he was saying. And it was time to take the bull by the horns.

'All right. Let's meet. Where?'

He named a pub on Wimbledon Common. 'Tomorrow night, eight o'clock?' I'll wait outside the door of the lounge bar.'

I wondered how many other women he had waited for, outside the lounge bar, but there was no help for it, I had to go. I had come too far now.

And, I reminded myself, the children wanted a father. If this was what I had to do, then so be it.

I decided to leave Samuel in abeyance. I didn't think I could face another phone call. Feeling unaccountably depressed, I ran a bath and poured in perfumed oil. I needed soothing. I knew already that Geoff wouldn't be the one. How complicated people were, and how different they were from what they seemed on paper.

There was a tall man in a black polo neck leaning against the

172

wall when I arrived. He was not unattractive and my heart lifted a little. He eased himself from the wall as I approached.

'Julia?'

'Geoff.' I held out my hand and he took it firmly.

'It's a lovely evening. Shall we sit outside?'

It was June, and the sun was still shining. For this reason I agreed, and also because it felt less intimate to be sitting outside in the small garden.

'What would you like to drink?'

'A glass of white wine, please.'

I found a bench and sat looking at a bed of peonies and lupins, trying not to think about what I was doing. I had on a flowered skirt and top with a light jacket thrown round my shoulders. I had washed my hair and applied careful, light makeup. Even so, I felt that I was unequal to his appraisal when Geoff came back with the drinks and sat opposite me. He, however, seemed quite unconcerned.

He had brown hair and intense brown eyes and a thin face with a trace of five-o'clock shadow. His fingers as he held his glass were long and slim and his nails were bitten.

'So,' he said, taking a sip of his beer. 'No problems with the children?'

'No. I have somebody living in, so I've usually got a baby-sitter.'

'And where did you say you were going?'

'Oh – out. I do go out sometimes!'

Actually, I had feebly said I was going to Claire's.

'And have you done this before?' He made it sound as if our meeting were somewhat suspect.

'No. You're the first one I've met.' I took a swallow of wine. 'Actually,' I blurted out, 'I'm finding it rather nerve-racking.'

He smiled. It was a nice smile but it didn't reach his eyes. 'No need. Tell me more about yourself.'

'Well – I work for a gynaecologist in Harley Street. I've been there for some years. It's interesting and the hours suit me. Before that – years ago – I was training to be a doctor. But I got married instead.'

'Do you regret that? Giving up medicine?' His gaze was penetrating.

'Sometimes, if I'm honest. But I don't think I would have made it. I didn't have the dedication.'

'And the children? Tell me about them.'

'Natalie's ten. She's quite musical, but a bit of a plodder. Stefan's the bright one. I think he might be a geologist, but it's early days. He's only thirteen.'

He made no comment. We both drank in silence. Feeling uncomfortable, I asked him about his work.

'Oh, the usual stresses and strains of teaching. Too much paperwork, not enough money. Best part is the field work. I take the sixth-formers away in the holidays. It helps to fill the time.'

'And do you ever see your children?'

'No,' he answered shortly, staring into his glass.

'Where are they?' I persisted.

'In South Africa. My wife came from Durban, and she decided to go back.'

'I'm sorry. But surely –'

'She got custody. And I can't afford to keep going out there. I decided a complete break would be less painful, for us all.'

I sensed his desolation. 'And is it?'

He looked at me, and his thin face seemed to be indented with feeling. 'Frankly no, not for me. That's why I'm looking for a new family to fill my life. I make no bones about it.'

'I see. That's very brave, to be so honest.'

Brave maybe, but it put me in a quandary. Much as my children wanted a father, I didn't want to feel that they were part of the deal, possibly as up for inspection as I was.

His glass was empty and I finished my wine. 'May I buy you another?' I offered.

He pushed his glass towards me. 'Thank you.' He named a

beer and I went towards the bar, glad for the moment to be away. There was a sudden temptation to run. I didn't know what I was doing there, listening to a stranger's problems. Did I want to tell him my own? Certainly, I did not. And yet he was presentable, it was nice to sit in a summer garden drinking wine with a man, surely that was partly what I wanted? I might as well enjoy the evening. It was better than sitting at home.

When I returned with the drinks he was smoking a cigarette.

'I hope you don't mind. Stress – it's the price of the job.'

I didn't like smoking but as we were outside, I could hardly object.

'Go ahead.'

'What I need is a holiday, but it's no fun on my own. Do you get away at all?'

'Up to this year we've always been to Cornwall. I have a house down there.'

He looked interested, and in case he should get the wrong impression I said, 'It was left to me. But it seemed an indulgence to keep it just for a few visits a year, so I've let it. A nice young couple, with a baby.'

He nodded, stubbing out his cigarette in the cheap tin ashtray.

'So – what will you do this year?'

'I'd like to take the children abroad. Brittany maybe. But I don't know if I can afford it. And I think I'd be nervous driving on the right.'

'You get used to it. I drove down to Spain one year, mainly to take photographs. It's my hobby, I think I told you. Last holiday I had actually. Lonely, despite the photography. Nobody to show them to when I got back. But it's the photography that keeps me sane.'

I tried to take an intelligent interest, asking what sort of photographs he took, whether he had a darkroom, whether he belonged to a club, which he did. He liked to photograph people, he said. The best pictures he had ever taken were of his children when they were small.

'So natural and unselfconscious. And so beautiful. I won a prize once in a competition for one of Jack on the swing.'

We talked then of our children, as the evening grew cooler. Suddenly I shivered.

'You're cold. Do you want to go inside?'

I considered, but there seemed little point. It was a good moment to end the evening. I wondered what happened now. Did he ask to see me again, or was it up to me? Awkwardly, I stood up. 'I think maybe I'll get back now. It's been very nice, I've enjoyed it.'

'Me too.' He stood up. He held out his hand and I took it. It felt rough and dry. I wondered if he would clasp mine warmly but he gave it a brief, businesslike shake and let go. We walked together to the car park. The silence between us was pregnant, but I could not speak. Anyway, I didn't know what I wanted, except that it would be nice to be wanted.

Geoff however seemed coolly unperturbed. He saw me into my car and said simply, 'Goodbye, Julia. It was nice to meet you.' Then he turned away, a shadowy figure in the dusk. I knew I wouldn't see him again, and didn't care very much except that I felt that I had failed, and, obscurely, that my children had failed as well as me.

Far from letting it get me down, a kind of bravado drove me on. I wanted to know if the system worked. I wanted to explore the fascinating divergence between expectation and reality. Geoff had obviously been disappointed in me. Why? What magic ingredient did it take to make people want to be together? Would I find it in Jeremy, or Samuel? Would they find it in me? A compelling intellectual curiosity drove me on to expose myself further to rejection. I rang Jeremy again, and once more got his answerphone. His very elusiveness was beginning to make him attractive. Once again I rang off. Samuel, the accountant, however, answered immediately, as if he were waiting for the phone to ring, though I told myself this was unlikely. I introduced myself, and explained which one I was, in case he had written several letters. I was right.

'Just let me have a look, I've got the paper here. Oh yes, you have two children. And you've got a good sense of humour. But don't we all say that?'

I was a bit nonplussed. His voice was dry and scholarly, he didn't sound very amusing, but how could one tell?

I swallowed hard and began to talk. I asked him about his children and he told me that one was studying law at Warwick, the other was already making a killing in the city.

'I can't believe how much he's earning at twenty-three, it seems obscene. But he'll be burned out at thirty if he's not careful.'

'Where does he live?'

'He's got a flat in Docklands. Great bleak place. It wouldn't suit me at all.'

'Nor me. I'm not a very organised person I'm afraid. I live in rather a muddle, my daughter's always tidying up after me and she's only ten.'

'Do you work?'

I told him briefly about my job.

'And how do you manage with the children?'

'I've had someone living in for years. A teacher. She lives rent-free in return for looking after them. Not that they'll need it much longer I suppose. I'm lucky to have had her this long, but she doesn't seem to have boyfriends. She sits in her room all evening typing novels which never sell! It doesn't seem much of a life.'

'And do you have much of a life? Do you go out much?'

'I go to the cinema, visit friends, and my parents. My father's a doctor, works much too hard. He retires next year.'

'Do you like opera?'

'I've never been. But I'd love to try.'

'It's a passion of mine. And the theatre. But it's not much fun going alone.'

'No.'

There was a silence. I had his letter before me and was studying his neat, spidery writing which seemed to match his voice. I wondered what he looked like, if he, too, was neat and precise. He dealt with figures all day. He must have a neat and precise mind. Unlike mine. What would he make of my ramshackle accounts, scribbled in a notebook with bills stuffed loosely into a drawer of my desk? What, indeed, did we have in common? He wouldn't be interested in my children, not now, with his own grown up. I supposed he was trying to find a way of ringing off, but instead heard him suggesting that we meet.

'Oh – yes, if you like.' I was flustered now, not knowing whether I wanted to go or not. But there seemed no good reason for refusing. A night at the opera would be very attractive.

'I could cook you a meal,' he was saying. 'Do you like Indian?'

'Well . . .' My hesitation was not with regard to the food, it was at the wisdom of going to his house. It seemed risky, when I had never met him.

'I think,' I said boldly, 'I'd rather go to a restaurant. Neutral territory, you know what I mean?'

I was afraid he would be offended but he accepted the suggestion smoothly, naming an Indian restaurant in Putney. We arranged to meet in three days' time, and I rang off feeling strangely excited. I had a date! And with a man. It was what other people did, trendy, swinging people in the mainstream. I had flushed myself from the backwater of life. I was surging along on the current again. With a swell of anticipation, I decided to buy myself a new dress.

NINE

I told the children I was going out with someone I had met at work. They had no understanding of the unlikelihood of this, merely expressing excitement when I admitted it was man.

Shelley was more percipient. 'How did you meet this man?' she asked when we were alone together in the kitchen.

'Oh, through someone else,' I said vaguely. I was not ready to divulge my secret.

'And is he nice?'

'I don't know.' I had spoken too quickly. Realising my mistake I added, 'It's early days. It will make a change anyway.'

She gave me a knowing look. Her flat face was already broadening prematurely into middle age. She didn't get out much herself, and seemed to rely on us as much as we relied on her. She adored Stefan and Natalie, saying that after dealing with such difficult ones all day, it was nice to be with normal children.

'How's the novel going?' I asked, swooping the iron over one of Stefan's shirts. It was her fourth attempt. None of the others had seen the light of day. She had tried several publishers but been rejected by them all. I had suggested she try and find an agent but she had dismissed this, saying they were as hard to find as publishers.

'It's going quite well,' she replied. 'I think actually it's the best I've done. I've taken your advice and written to some agents with a synopsis. No luck so far, but I'll keep trying.'

'You do that.' I folded the shirt and reached for a pair of jeans. They were Natalie's and she was very fussy. She liked a knife-edge crease down the front, unlike Stefan, who didn't like his ironed at all. They were too dry and I set the iron to steam, hearing it hiss as I pressed down onto the bulky fabric. Shelley sat herself at the table with a bowl of carefully chopped salad and ricotta cheese. The pungent smell of garlic mingled with the damp steam. Our own meal was still in the oven. Shelley was eating early as it was her night out at her creative writing class.

After supper I decided to ring Kate. The twins were eleven now, away at a minor public school, and she had dispensed with Ragnhild and her successors. We sometimes went to the cinema together, and I was interested in seeing a new film, *Howards End*, which was on that weekend. But Kate had other plans.

'We're going to Paris. On a dirty weekend!'

'What – you and Harry?'

'Yes. It's his idea. To try and recapture our youth! He's booked us in as Mr Smith and Miss Murgatroyd. He wants me to pretend to be his secretary.'

'That's really weird!' I didn't know whether to feel envious or disapproving. 'And you're going along with it?'

'Sounds all right to me. Sex gets pretty mundane after fourteen years.'

'I wouldn't know.' I was aware of sounding bitter.

Kate's voice was full of compunction. 'I say, I'm sorry. No news on that front I suppose?'

I hesitated, tempted to tell her about Samuel. But there would be questions that I was unprepared to answer. So I said simply, 'No news. But I'll be agog to hear about your weekend. Will you take a notebook and pencil, and make notes perhaps?'

She began to giggle, and soon, despite myself, I was giggling too, dreaming up ridiculous scenarios. Finally I suggested that I should perhaps ring them up and play the aggrieved wife. 'That would really get the switchboard talking,' I pointed out. But for some reason Kate didn't think this a good idea. I hadn't thought it a very good idea myself; I was only trying to join in the fun.

It seemed I would have to go to the cinema by myself. Unless, of course, I went with Samuel. I felt a frisson of excitement at the possibility, tenuous maybe, but still a possibility.

I arrived early at the restaurant, which was a bad mistake. It meant I had to stand in the foyer watching the door, in a painful mix of dread and expectation every time someone entered. Mostly they were couples, but, at exactly the appointed hour, a tall distinguished grey-haired man pushed through the door and glanced round the foyer. My heart leaped. The manager, an oily Indian in a white tuxedo, came forward and greeted him. I felt even more excited. He was obviously known and respected. Then I heard the man say, 'Has my wife arrived?' and the manager nodded, and showed him through to a table, leaving me limp with disappointment. It boded ill. There would hardly be two such attractive men in the restaurant in one evening.

Five minutes went by. I began to feel irritated. Then the door burst open and in came another man, and this time I knew, with a feeling of fatality, that this was certainly Samuel.

For he was short, about five foot four, and plump. Not plump, fat. He was also almost bald, though he sported a small moustache above a tiny mouth, lost in folds of flesh. Without hesitation, he held out a small fleshy hand, saying, 'Julia. I'm so sorry I'm late, the traffic was terrible, and then I couldn't park.'

I almost recoiled, almost denied that I was Julia, but I found myself taking his damp hand and shaking it. I was

181

ashamed at the disappointment I felt, for he was well spoken and his manner was charming enough; but as we walked to our table I felt myself towering above him, and I noticed as he sat opposite me that his waistcoat was straining at the buttons and his collar was cutting into his neck. He looked hot and uncomfortable. I felt a curl of displeasure. I have never liked fat men; an excess of flesh disgusts me. The thought of touching Samuel, of being touched by him, made me flinch. And yet, I scolded myself as the dark-skinned waiter handed me a menu, I was surely jumping the gun. Samuel was not asking me to touch him, he was offering me a meal. The least I could do was to be gracious.

'I'm afraid you'll have to guide me,' I said, with an ingratiating smile. 'I'm not familiar with Indian food.'

'Well in that case perhaps you'll allow me to choose.'

'Nothing too hot,' I warned him.

He ordered lamb korma for me, with sweet rice, and for himself a chicken phall. 'I like mine very hot', he explained, and then sat back in his chair with his plump hands folded on the pink cloth in front of him.

'So,' he said, seeming to look at me for the first time, 'you're Julia.'

I flinched under his gaze, feeling myself up for inspection just as he was. I fidgeted with the neck of my new black dress, touched the silver pendant at my throat.

'Have you done this before?' he asked abruptly, taking me off guard.

'Once.'

'No success?'

'No.'

He smiled, his little mouth pushing at his cheeks. 'It's not easy, is it? I've written to several over the past few weeks, but you're the first I've met. And now I really don't know what to say.'

'Nor me.' I fiddled with my napkin. The waiter came and

poured wine into Samuel's glass and I watched as he sipped it, and signalled for the waiter to fill my glass. He seemed very sure of himself, totally unaware that I felt poised for flight, sitting on the edge of my seat and trembling.

'So,' I said, when the waiter had gone. 'Tell me more about yourself.' Anything, I thought, to get through the evening.

'Well, I'm an accountant, as you know. I have my own practice, with two junior partners. We deal mainly with corporate work – not too many private tax returns.'

'And your wife?' I asked tentatively, wondering when she had died.

'She died five years ago. Leukaemia. It took two years. I was fairly drained afterwards. It's only recently I've felt ready to . . . well, you know.'

'Look around? I know what you mean. I've been a widow for seven years. At first, it seems disloyal, somehow, doesn't it?'

He nodded. A plate of poppadums had appeared, together with a compartmented black dish of dips. He took a poppadum and dipped it, nibbling delicately and nodding for me to do the same. I did so, tasting spiced yoghurt and cucumber which was fairly innocuous. Daringly I ventured into something red, taking a tiny dollop and tentatively trying it with my tongue. It was hot, but there was nothing to be done but take a bite and swallow it quickly, washing it down with water. Samuel looked amused.

'It's an acquired taste. Helen was the same as you at first, but in the end nothing was too fierce for her. Even when she was so ill, I could often tempt her with a curry.'

He himself was eating quickly. His little hands were deft, his movements precise, his chewing delicate for all its enthusiasm. Now and then he dabbed his moustache with a pink napkin. I realised suddenly that I was staring at him rudely, as if hypnotised. He too was pink – a plump pink rabbit. How could I ever have thought . . . but I stopped

183

myself, for once again I was letting my thoughts race ahead. And I was being unfair, and also conceited. For all I knew, he might be as appalled as I was, struggling to keep the evening going while longing to get away.

I put the rest of my poppadum down on my plate. 'Better save myself for the main course,' I said by way of explanation, but apologetically.

'Right.' He wiped his hands carefully and took a delicate sip of wine. 'That's good,' he said appreciatively. 'I hope you like it. A lot of people drink beer with Indian food but if you choose carefully, wine is far better.'

'I'm afraid I don't know a lot about wine either. David always chose it. Now I don't really buy any, and if I do I just go round the supermarket.'

'I belong to a wine club. I get it by the case.'

I was suitably impressed, and wondered when he drank it, whether he drank alone every evening, thinking that there was something brave about it if he did.

I asked him if he cooked for himself and he said that he did usually, but that sometimes he ate out, either with friends or alone. He and Helen had enjoyed entertaining, but he found if difficult on his own. He didn't think anyone would want to come. I sympathised with the feeling.

'There's something about not being a couple, isn't there? You feel left out of the mainstream.'

'That's why I'm trying to do something about it,' he said.

'And it's little things,' I went on, now pursuing my own train of thought. 'David always used to carve so beautifully, but I've never learned properly. It always seems to me to be a man's job. I do so miss him when we have a joint.'

He laughed, a tight, restrained little sound. 'I feel exactly the same about making gravy and dishing up the vegetables. That was Helen's job. Isn't it sad that our great loss gets reduced to such inconsequentialities?'

'Not so inconsequential,' I said thoughtfully. 'I think they

184

simply serve to underline how great, and how continuous, the loss is.'

The main course now arrived, and Samuel rubbed his hands in anticipation, as if anxious to throw aside maudlin thoughts. 'This looks very good, you're going to enjoy it. At least, I hope you are.'

And I did. Under the influence of the spicy food and the mellow wine, I began to relax, to stop questioning, to take things as they came. Samuel began to talk about opera, which he described as his other great enthusiasm. Once again, I had to confess my ignorance, feeling as I did so that he must find me very boring company, especially when he told me that he had flown to New York to see Pavarotti in *Turandot* at the Met, and had seen Wagner's *Ring* at Bayreuth.

'But isn't that tremendously long?'

'Fourteen hours. But over four days, of course. It's the absolute apogee of operagoing as far as I'm concerned. Rather like running a marathon!'

He laughed again, his little, dry laugh.

'Would you like to try sometime?' he asked unexpectedly.

I was startled. 'What – the *Ring* Cycle?'

He looked amused. 'No. Something simple and accessible, like *Bohème*. It's coming up soon at Covent Garden.'

I played for time, desperately wondering what I wanted to do.

'But surely they'll be all sold out. I thought tickets for Covent Garden were like gold dust.'

'I'm usually lucky. If I'm prepared to pay, that is.'

'And you're asking me to come with you?' I couldn't believe that he wanted it, that he was 'prepared to pay' for my company. Despite my doubts, I was flattered. This time, I hadn't failed the test.

'Would you like to?'

I noticed that his little hands were clenched on the table

as if a lot were hanging on my reply. 'Your tiny hand is frozen' drifted unbidden into my mind – one of the only pieces of opera that I knew. It would be nice to hear it properly, in context. It would be thrilling to go to Covent Garden. It would not, I persuaded myself, be so bad to go with Samuel.

'Yes, please,' I said.

He arranged to telephone me when he had got the tickets. It was raining when we left the restaurant and, after a long wait during which I sheltered inside, he got us a taxi and dropped me off at the corner of my road. Some inner caution persuaded me not to let him know, yet, where I lived. When the taxi had stopped, I turned to thank him and was met with a moist and hasty kiss on my cheek. Something inside me shrank back but I stammered out my thanks and slid out quickly into the rain. I breathed in the damp air thankfully, watching the taxi pull away before turning towards my house. I didn't think as I walked. I didn't want to explore the evening, its disappointments or its possibilities. I was not proud of my response. I was nervous of what lay ahead. I felt sorry for Samuel, but I felt sorry for myself too. We were two pathetic people, clutching at straws, he as surely as I was. So I tried not to think, making my mind a blank as I walked the wet street and put my key into the lock. The children were in bed, Shelley was up in her room. I could hear music playing. I had a sudden longing for her undemanding company. I went up, and knocked on the door.

'Coffee?' I invited, when she opened it.

She looked with surprise at my wet hair. 'Do you want to talk?' she asked.

'Not really. Just fancied some company before bed.'

'Okay. I'll come down.'

I changed out of my wet shoes and towelled my hair. I filled the coffee machine and opened a packet of biscuits.

Despite my meal, the heavy rice, the spices, the strange fragrant green ice cream which had followed it, nervous tension made me want to eat. I needed the reassurance of a chocolate digestive, thick and sweet and familiar against my tongue. Funnily enough, what I really wanted was my mother. Not the mother I knew now, but the one of my childhood, before I had realised her limitations; who administered aspirin and hot milk and rubbed my feet when I was ill. But if I had her, what would I say? That I had just spent an evening with a man, and was desolate because I was sure I could never go to bed with him?

'So what?' she would surely reply – if she could bring herself to talk about the subject at all. 'Bed isn't everything. In some contexts, it isn't even important.'

But I knew that it was.

The next day, I rang Jeremy again.

This time, he was in. I felt a curious clench of excitement as I heard the receiver lift and a voice say, 'Jeremy Dixon, who am I speaking to?' It was a very English voice but there was something mid-Atlantic about his words, a mix of laid-back and abrupt. I heard my own voice breathless as I answered, 'This is Julia Leathlean, you wrote to me, at a box number.'

There was a fractional hesitation. I imagined him, gathering his thoughts, possibly as tense as I was.

'It was a nice letter,' I heard myself saying. 'I'd like to meet you.'

It was out before I realised it. Shocked at my audacity, I demurred at once. 'If you'd like to, of course. Maybe you'd like to talk first . . .'

'No. I'd like to meet. I'm in London for two days, how about tea tomorrow?'

'I'm sorry, I'm at work.'

'Well, Saturday then. At Harrods. I'll meet you outside the Georgian Restaurant at four.'

I'd planned to take the children swimming on Saturday but recklessly cast them aside. 'Fine. I'll look forward to it.'

I was excited. I liked his swift decisiveness, I appreciated the glamour of the venue, found the suggestion of tea instead of dinner attractive and original. They say that hope springs eternal; undeterred by past experience, I was as optimistic as a child with a Christmas stocking. This one, I was sure, was going to be a success.

I went into the kitchen. Natalie was practising the recorder, the music on a stand in front of her. I watched her for a while. She was quite oblivious of me, fingering the instrument deftly, her nails like oval pearls on her pale fingers. She was preparing for an end-of-term concert. She was to play two solos: 'The Raggle-Taggle Gypsies' and a gavotte by Handel. To my ears, she was perfect. My heart swelled as I watched the concentration on her face, the sink and swell of her cheeks as she blew, the curve of her lips round the mouthpiece. I wasn't very fond of recorders, but I was mighty proud of her performance. When she had finished I clapped, and dropped a kiss on her curls.

Voicing a thought which I had been pondering, I asked her, 'How would you like a clarinet when you go to the big school next term?'

She was unscrewing the recorder, shaking out drops of condensation.

'What I'd really like,' she replied, looking at me with her bright green eyes, 'is a piano.'

'A piano? I'd never thought of that. Would you really like one? Would you practise?'

Her face lit up. 'Yes, Mum, I'd love it.'

'A piano would be expensive.' Now her face fell. 'But we could manage it. There's Gramps' money. He would be pleased for you to have a piano if you really want one.'

She dropped the recorder on the table and came to me in

a rush. She put her arms round my waist and hugged me. 'Thanks, Mum. That's brill.'

Stefan came into the kitchen and she told him excitedly, 'Mum's going to buy me a piano.'

'What for?'

'To play, stupid.'

'Oh, how naff. Anything to eat, Mum? It's ages to supper.'

'Half an hour. Can't you wait?'

'No way. We had football this afternoon.'

I let him cut a wedge of bread and gave him margarine out of the fridge. As he spread it he asked, 'Well, how was your evening out? Did you have curry?'

'Not exactly. But it was interesting.'

He stuffed bread into his mouth, talking as he did so. 'What, the food, or the rest of it?'

'Don't talk with your mouth full. Both, I suppose. It made a change.'

Natalie was looking at me expectantly. 'Are you going to see him again? What's his name? Are you going out with him?'

'Not in the way you mean. But we may be going to the opera, if he can get tickets. And his name's Samuel.'

'The opera. How naff!'

'Stefan! I can do without your opinion, thank you.'

'Is he coming here?' asked Natalie. There was something pathetic about her curiosity but I had to tell her that no, he wasn't coming home. The last thing I wanted was for them to meet him, to cast their appraising eyes, to assess him as a replacement for David and to find him wanting. Worse still, to like him, and have to be disappointed.

She shrugged, picked up her recorder, and began to play.

'Not that *again*,' groaned Stefan. 'Can't you play anything else?'

189

'She's got to practise,' I told him crossly. 'Take yourself off if you can't say anything nice.'

He sloped out of the room, snatching an apple from the bowl as he passed.

This time, I made sure that it was I who was late. When I arrived in the anteroom to the restaurant, there were several people there, sitting on maroon sofas or standing around aimlessly. There was only one man alone, a tall and almost ugly man with heavy, sensuous features and wavy sandy hair. But he was slim and smartly dressed, and he had an air of confidence and authority. He would not be embarrassing to be with. Consequently, I hurried across the room quite eagerly.

'Jeremy?' I asked, coming to a halt beside him.

He turned, looked me up and down, and gave a slow smile.

'Even if I wasn't, I'd say yes.' It was the same voice, smooth and pleasing.

I felt a ridiculous spurt of pleasure. He was flirting with me; it was a long time since that had happened.

He held out a large, bony hand. 'And you're Julia. I'm delighted to meet you.'

We shook hands, smiling at each other.

'Are you ready for tea?'

'Oh yes. I love tea.'

'So do I. It's my favourite meal. We don't eat it often enough. And in my line of business, of course, I seldom get the chance. Or if I do it's the middle of the night!'

He put his hand behind me, ushering me through the door. The restaurant was crowded with shoppers and tourists, one of whom was taking photographs of a smiling group of Japanese with the Harrods logo in the background.

'I don't think there's a table,' I was saying doubtfully, when he took my hand and pulled me hurriedly towards a couple of women who were getting up, and assembling their green and gold carrier bags. He smiled at them disarmingly and we waited while they gathered their things, then he pulled out a chair for me and I settled myself. The table was laden with tea things and I felt it would have been better to wait for an empty one. But Jeremy summoned a passing waitress and in no time the crockery and half-eaten cakes were loaded onto a tray, and the white cloth swept clean.

'They obviously ordered far too much,' I said, referring to the food left on the plates.

'It's a set price, so people are greedy. They're determined to get their money's worth. It's rather disgusting, isn't it? I mean, I'm as greedy as the rest of them, but at least I eat it all!'

I laughed delightedly, liking him already.

The waitress returned and he ordered tea. 'Earl Grey all right for you?' he asked me, but I would have drunk anything he chose. 'We help ourselves to food,' he told me, getting up and leading me to a long table spread with sandwiches, scones and cakes. 'Feel free.' He gave an expansive gesture.

But I felt too excited to eat much, and also self-conscious, despite the fact that he was loading a large plate with something of everything. Seated back at the table, I toyed with a smoked salmon sandwich while he devoured two or three. His large hand swamped the tiny triangles of crustless bread, and his fleshy lips seemed to swallow them whole. There were deep grooves running from the side of flaring nostrils to the side of his mouth. Though he was not immediately attractive, at the same time he was. It was more a question of his manner than his appearance. He had a natural confidence in himself that reassured doubts and put me at my ease.

He didn't speak for a while, then he said, 'I'm sorry, I was hungry. You're not eating much. Yet I can't believe you have to watch your weight.'

I shook my head. 'No, I'm lucky that way. When I was a child, I was told I must have hollow legs!'

He gave a burst of laughter. 'Well, they look very nice to me,' he said, though they were hidden from view under the table. The tea arrived. Without hesitation he took the pot and poured two cups, then offered me the milk. To my relief, there was no question about 'me being mother'. It was simply not his style.

Between forkfuls of chocolate cake, I asked him about his work. How often was he home, was he on long or short haul, where had he just been, where was he going next? What airline did he work for? He told me British Airways, and that he had just finished a run of transatlantic flights and was off to Australia in the morning. His time at home varied. Partly for that reason, he had never married. He had never seemed to have the time. Though there had been a girl once, a stewardess. But she had married a chief steward and now had three children.

He spread a scone with cream and downed it in one go. There was something animal and voracious about his appetite, but it was not offensive. His hands, though large, were agile and beautifully kept. I pondered them touching me and thought that I wouldn't mind. There was also something exciting in the realisation that in those hands lay the safety of hundreds of people every day. I wondered what he would look like in uniform. I imagined his pleasing voice coming over the intercom, welcoming the passengers, wishing them a comfortable flight. He would have my confidence, any day.

'Julia?'

I jerked to, focusing to meet his eyes.

'I'm sorry, I'd gone off into a daydream.' I realised I was blushing, and applied myself to my cake.

'A nice one, I hope,' he persisted.

'Very nice,' I told him. I looked steadily into his eyes, and they held my gaze until something clenched in my stomach and I looked away.

'Now tell me about your job.'

So I told him about Mr Seligman and his patients, and the palm tree, and then about my parents, and how my father was looking forward to retiring. He told me his parents were dead, but that he had a sister, younger than he was, with a family.

'You're lucky. I always wanted a brother or sister. But then, I expect you would have liked children?'

I made it a question, aware that I might be treading on sensitive ground. But he said, 'Not really. I've never felt the lack.'

'I wouldn't be without mine. Especially when David died. I suppose, looking back, they kept me sane.'

He asked how old they were, but that seemed to be the extent of his interest. I saw him glance at his watch.

'Do you have to go?' I felt ridiculously disappointed.

'I'm afraid so.' He didn't explain or elaborate. I wondered if he was meeting another applicant, and felt wildly jealous.

He caught the eye of the waitress, and as before she came at once. I guessed that when Jeremy called, people ran. He asked for the bill, then asked me for my telephone number. Trying to disguise my delight I wrote it on a page of a notebook and tore it out.

'I'll give you a ring when I get back.' There was no question of whether I would like this. But maybe I had already given myself away.

'Any idea when?' I tried to sound casual.

'Oh, a week or so.'

It sounded like for ever. He paid the bill and pushed back his chair. We walked together to the door and went down in the lift.

'Do you shop at Harrods?' I asked him.

'Sometimes. But I get a lot of my clothes abroad.'

I nodded. It followed. We walked out through the cosmetics department with its gleaming showcases and smell of luxury, and into Knightsbridge where the sun was shining.

'How do you get home?' he asked.

'I'll take the underground.'

'Well, I'll say goodbye. Thank you for coming, I've enjoyed it.'

'So have I.' I took his proffered hand enthusiastically. He didn't shake mine, rather squeezed it as he gave his long slow smile, straight into my eyes.

'You're the best so far,' he said, then turned to a taxi which had just disgorged a passenger. He slid his long form inside and gave me a wave. I stood watching him as the taxi drove away, his words tumbling in my brain to interpret as I chose.

And so I settled down to wait. I got up and fed the children and saw them off to school, then tidied up and walked to Putney Bridge station and got the tube and walked to the office. I soothed and charmed the patients, serviced Mr Seligman, ate my lunch, went home, cooked supper and helped the children with their homework. And all the time I was waiting, and wondering where he was, and imagining him in the cockpit, managing those incredible dials and levers as calmly as if he were driving a family car. And I was jealous; jealous of the stewardesses, of the passengers in his care, of the owners of the other box numbers who might, even now, be attracting his attention. 'You're the best so far,' implied a thorough and lengthy search. Who knew what treasures he might unearth? Who knew if I would ever see him again?

I scolded myself for a fool for minding so much. We had barely spent an hour together. He wasn't even particularly good-looking. But he had touched something in me; he had excited me; and with every passing day I wanted to have more of him. The silent telephone only served to exacerbate that want.

Then, after two and half weeks, it rang. It could have been my mother, or Kate, or Claire, or someone for the children, but, like all the other times, I told myself that, this time, it was him. I picked the phone up with a thumping heart, swallowing on a lump in my throat. It was a man. But it was Samuel.

'Remember me?' he asked.

I did indeed.

'I'm sorry I've taken so long to get back to you. I had difficulty getting tickets for *La Bohème*, but I've got some cancellations for this Saturday. Can you make it at such short notice?'

It wouldn't be true to say I had forgotten about him. I had been simply hoping he hadn't happened. Now I hated him for not being Jeremy. I wanted to scream at him to get off the line, in case Jeremy was phoning at just this moment. Instead, I remembered, pityingly, his hands as they had been clenched on the table, waiting for my answer. I found myself telling him that I was sure I could manage it, but I'd just have to check with Shelley. I put the phone down and went and knocked on her door. She called for me to come in. She was reading sheets of paper as they disgorged from her printer, red pen in one hand, a mug of coffee in the other. She didn't look up as I asked her if she would be in on Saturday night.

'Yes, as far as I know. I've all this to print out and correct.'

'Good. Thanks.' I shut the door quietly and went back to the phone. I considered lying, saying that Shelley was going out, but I knew Kate would stand in if necessary. I knew that I would move heaven and earth if it were Jeremy on the line. I couldn't lie.

'That's fine,' I said into the receiver.

It was impossible to tell if he was pleased or not. His voice was as dry as ever as we made arrangements to meet in the foyer. I forestalled any suggestion that he might pick me up. I was still preserving my line of escape.

For the rest of the evening, I tried to feel pleased. It was the first time for a very long time that a man had sought my company. What's more, he had been prepared to spend a good deal to give me what was undoubtedly going to be a treat. I was determined to enjoy it.

A bird in the hand was worth two in the bush. I made up my mind to forget about Jeremy.

This time, I was prepared, but even so it didn't prevent me cringing with embarrassment when he walked towards me, barely reaching my shoulders as he shook my hand. Once again I felt enormous. There wasn't time for a drink so we went straight to our seats. The orchestra was tuning up, surely the most anticipatory noise in the world. We were in the stalls, about halfway back.

'Good seats,' I remarked. 'We were lucky.'

'I prefer the circle myself.' He passed me the programme. 'I should read up a bit on the story if I were you.'

I had time to read the first act before the lights went down. I settled myself in my seat, preparing to enjoy myself. In the darkness, I couldn't see Samuel. And neither could anyone else.

The music soon had me in its thrall and it didn't matter that I couldn't understand the words, I understood it all perfectly. The reckless young men, celebrating their youth despite the cold, Rodolfo burning his manuscript in the empty stove to give them a moment's heat, the departure of his friends leaving Rodolfo alone, and the touching arrival of Mimi, her candle extinguished, coughing from her climb up the stairs. I was completely absorbed, and when the lights went up for the interval I had to shake myself. I was almost surprised to see Samuel sitting beside me.

We made our way to the crowded bar and he fought his way through to get us drinks. Waiting for him, I glanced round. Operagoers were a mixed bunch, I decided. Some were in evening dress, others in jeans and anoraks. Seeing my appraising glance, a man in a nearby group smiled at me uncertainly. He was tall and dark, and a small woman in pearls was hanging onto his arm. Suddenly, I envied her. I found myself wishing desperately that I was that woman. Or, instead, that it was Jeremy who was at that moment pushing towards me, holding aloft two glasses. I wanted to turn away, to disown Samuel, who looked small and fat and annoyed.

'I thought I'd never get any service.' He handed me my glass of wine. He had a tall red glass of Campari and soda. I thought, I bet Jeremy would have been served at once, and drank my wine in silence, feeling unfairly resentful. I hoped no one was looking at us. I felt we made a ridiculous pair. I felt that I was at the wrong party, with the wrong person. If it wasn't for my intense enjoyment of the opera, I think I would have made an excuse and run away.

Instead, I followed him back to our seats, and I looked quickly at the programme, taking in the intricacies of the plot. Then the lights went down and I gave myself up once more. The music was sublime, the unfolding story both sad and beautiful. At the end, when Musetta had redeemed herself by pawning her earrings to buy medicine and a fur muff, but all to no avail, and Mimi died, I felt tears running down my cheeks. When Rodolfo, belatedly, realised that she was dead, and sank in despair beside her bed, I pressed my handkerchief to my mouth, stifling a sob.

And then I felt it. Samuel's hand, hot and grasping, on my arm.

I was jerked back to reality, conscious once more of our ludicrous pairing. My flesh recoiled, lurching back from his touch. I didn't think, I simply rose in my seat and began to push my way along the row, stumbling blindly while the audience erupted into cheers and clapping. I was conscious of complaints and irritation, but pressed on until I had struggled into the gangway. I prayed that Samuel wasn't following me. I ran to the red velvet curtain that hid the door and pulled it back. An attendant hurriedly opened the door and I fled outside, through the bar and into the foyer. Only then did I look back.

There was nobody following. I was alone except for a startled doorman who was just opening the doors. Then I was in the street. The air struck cool on my wet cheeks. I realised I was sobbing and I stopped for a moment to collect my thoughts. It only took a moment for shame to flood hotly through me. What on earth had I been thinking of? The fact was that I had not been thinking at all. I had overreacted to what, in all probability, had been merely a gesture of sympathy and comfort.

There was a rank of taxis awaiting the crowds. I climbed into the first one and wearily gave my address. I sat rigid and stunned, staring out at the streets of Covent Garden, still thronged with people. I knew that I had burned my boats. What I had done had been unforgivable. But I knew that it demonstrated something fundamental about my feelings about Samuel. It was unfair and unkind, but I could not find him attractive, and thus I could not feel comfortable with him. Maybe I had cut off my nose to spite my face, but there was no help for it. There would be no more opera. I felt deeply saddened, and cheated. For I had not even allowed myself time to clap.

It was only as we were crossing Putney Bridge that I leaned back wearily into the seat and gave a deep and tremulous sigh. What a wasted exercise. There was no Samuel, and no Jeremy.

I had come a long way, and was right back where I had started.

TEN

I decided to take the children to France. Term ended in two weeks; we would get away then. I had had enough of trying to persuade fate to play it my way. Chastened, I was in a mood to submit.

I went into a travel agent's and after much tapping and staring at a computer screen, a pimply young man managed to get me a tent on a camp site not far from Cherbourg. We could travel the day after the children broke up, and that night, I told them.

'It's about time I went abroad,' was Stefan's initial response. 'I'm the only one who never has.'

'Oh Stefan, surely not.'

'Well, in our gang. Most of them have been to Disney World.'

I felt humbled at the extent of my omission. I had thought they enjoyed Cornwall every summer, but of course, it wasn't enough. Children wanted to be like their peers.

'I'm sorry,' I said, feeling my pleasure in my plans evaporate.

He looked at me sharply and, with a wisdom beyond his years, said, 'But camping will be great. Will we have a barbecue?'

'I don't know. But we can take one with us. I'll buy a portable.'

'We can cook frogs' legs,' he said gleefully. 'And snails!' He looked sideways at Natalie as he spoke, and got precisely the reaction he expected.

'Do we have to?' Her eyes were wide with distaste.

'Of course not,' I soothed. 'You and I can have chicken, leave the frogs and snails to Stefan.'

He looked a bit dubious.

'And you'll be able to try out your French,' I told him. 'There's a shop on the site, you can do the shopping.'

He shrugged. 'Maybe. Is there a pool?'

'Yes. And a games room. And a lovely beach nearby.' I showed them the brochure. It was full of photographs of smiling nuclear families outside palatial red and blue tents, toddlers splashing in a paddling pool, and a pair of lovers entwined against the sea with the sun going down into the horizon. I thought, none of that applies to us exactly. I felt a tremor of apprehension. How was I going to cope? Would the children enjoy themselves? I longed for Padstow and its familiar pleasures, but I knew I had to change and grow, we all had to, and I began to make my preparations.

We arrived in pouring rain, after a tense but mercifully short drive from the ferry during which I had every moment expected to find myself on the wrong side of the road. It had been a rough crossing from Portsmouth and Natalie had been sick. Now they were both ravenously hungry, and we were faced with unpacking in the rain and getting to grips with a Calor Gas stove and unfamiliar utensils.

'I tell you what,' I said, turning to their disconsolate faces in the back of the car. 'Let's leave everything and have something to eat in the café.'

They nodded, without too much enthusiasm. Thinking that they were imagining frogs and snails, I said encouragingly, 'I'm sure they'll have chips.'

'And ketchup?' asked Natalie, climbing out of the car.

'Probably not. But we haven't come to France for ketchup.'

I locked the car, and took a look at the tent to which we had been directed. It stood at the end of a row, under a dripping acacia tree. The grass in front was pale and worn, with a plastic table and four chairs set neatly under an awning. I longed to look inside, but thought that food was our first priority. We had passed a colourful complex beside the entrance. The rest of the site seemed to be deserted. In this weather, I guessed they would all be inside, and I was right.

We passed the swimming pool, rain bouncing on its blue surface. Yellow loungers were drawn up round it, and on one was a sodden abandoned towel. We passed through swing doors into what reminded me of a motorway service station, though rather smaller in scale. To the right, there was a small shop, selling beach goods, newspapers and paperbacks, sweets and groceries. Straight ahead was a games room with couples energetically hitting ping pong balls, there was an amusement arcade heaving with teen-agers and, on the left, a self-service cafeteria. The queue stretched out into the hallway.

There was nothing for it but to join the end.

'I'm hungry,' Natalie whined, leaning hard against me.

I was not surprised, since she had brought up all her lunch.

'It won't take long.' I felt far from sure of that, and was already worrying about how I would manage at the till. I had tried to familiarise myself with the money, but it was a long time since I had been abroad. David and I had been to Tuscany for our honeymoon, and Sweden the year after that. Then, he had managed the money; I had remained blissfully unaware. Feebly, I craved now for his support. I felt cast adrift in a strange land, and was relieved to hear an English voice behind me. Another family had joined the queue.

'You can stop that nonsense for a start. I've had enough of your whining.'

It was the father speaking, in a flat Midlands accent.

I gave him a sympathetic smile.

'The weather's awful, isn't it?' I commiserated. 'I expect it's getting everyone down.'

But he just looked at me without speaking. Chastened, I turned away. I grabbed a tray, which was swimming in a greasy liquid. I took the one beneath, and left that one for the unfriendly man behind me.

We ate ham and egg and chips – familiar comfort food, though there was no ketchup. For pudding I chose French apple tart, with the apple slices laid with geometric precision under their caramelised topping. It was surprisingly good. Stefan had two doughnuts, Natalie, ice cream. They cheered up considerably as they ate, though the rain was still teeming down outside and I felt an enormous reluctance to move. I sat on at the red plastic table, letting my coffee get cold, while the children fidgeted impatiently.

Finally Stefan said, 'We ought to go, Mum. And unpack before it gets dark.'

I looked at my watch. 'It's only half-past seven. It won't get dark for ages.'

'Well, can we go on the slot machines?'

That was the last thing I wanted. Anyway, I had very little change. I used that as an excuse, downing the dregs of my coffee and getting up.

'Come on then,' I said, in an attempt at heartiness. 'Put your anoraks on, let's go and see what's what.'

What we found, having dragged our cases and bags from the car, was a surprisingly commodious living area, off which were two bedrooms each containing two camp beds topped with royal-blue sleeping bags. There was a metal frame supporting a Calor Gas stove with two rings, on which stood a kettle. There were canvas chairs and a round blue table, and a cupboard containing china, cutlery and cooking utensils. There was even a small fridge. I unpacked the teabags and sugar and the few supplies we had brought with us, and set them on the shelves. I gave the kettle to Stefan.

'Go and find a tap, we'll have a cup of tea.'

'But we've just had supper.'

'Don't argue. Tea will make us feel at home. Besides, it's cold.'

It was chilly, and I felt cold inside too, trying to be enthusiastic in the strange canvas space which was to be our home. Natalie was sitting on one of the beds, looking glum. I felt a flash of impatience. This was supposed to be a holiday, for God's sake, a treat. I hadn't brought them all this way to be met with gloomy faces. Doggedly, I dumped her bag in front of her, unzipping it and pulling at the contents.

'Unpack,' I told her shortly.

I went into the other room and opened my own case, pulling out tee shirts and shorts, looking for a warm sweater. From the other room I heard Natalie call out,

'Mummy? What are we going to do if it doesn't stop raining?'

But she needn't have worried.

After a long and miserable night, during which I lay in the narrow bed listening to the rain beating on the tent and longing to be safely home in London, I drifted off at dawn and woke to the red glow of sunshine burning through the canvas. My heart lifted. I looked at my watch. I had slept till after eight. Where were the children? Surely not in bed.

I looked into their room. The beds were empty, Natalie's sleeping bag neatly spread, Stefan's left just as he had got out of it. His pyjamas lay on the canvas floor. Automatically, I picked them up, and folded them under his pillow.

I poked my head outside. There were two mugs and a carton of orange juice on the table, which was pooled with water. But two of the chairs had been dried, a towel hung over one. The children were nowhere in sight.

The family next door were having their breakfast in the sun.

I asked, 'Did you see my children?' but they looked at me uncomprehendingly.

I felt a rush of panic but told myself not to be absurd, it was surely a good thing that they were up and off, exploring and enjoying themselves. I could see a tap fixed to a post, and decided to fill the kettle. They would surely be back soon. The water ran clear and fresh, the rain was steaming off the trees and birds were singing. Returning to our tent, I smelled my neighbour's bacon and felt hungry. I only had bread and cereals. Shopping was an urgent priority. Lighting the gas, I felt cautiously optimistic. I had got us here. The sun was shining. We were going to have a lovely holiday.

And I suppose, generally speaking, we did. For a start, the sun shone unremittingly. The children swam every morning before breakfast, while I sat under the awning sipping tea and reading. They quickly made friends, and I would see them tearing past, en route to the games room or the pool, with a mixed crowd of French, German, Dutch and English children. They would come back to lunch – reluctantly I sometimes thought – and in the afternoons we would go out, to the beach, or a nearby town to explore. I felt that they came on sufferance. They really preferred it on the site. But I wanted them to see something of France. Also, there was a limit to my capacity for sitting reading. And I wanted somebody to talk to.

We visited a local château, and shopped for local cheese and *pain au chocolat* in the market at St-Pierre Église. There were strawberries and cherries, beautifully displayed on beds of leaves and bracken, but Natalie was reduced to tears when she saw live chickens in baskets, and tiny cages full of songbirds. 'They'll probably eat them too,' said Stefan ghoulishly, so that she wailed still harder. We went to Barfleur and wandered round an antiques market and had mussels for supper in a restaurant. I felt my rusty French returning. I enjoyed myself on our excursions, and I think the children did too.

We were there for ten days. After a week, when I wandered to the pool to have a swim, I noticed Stefan, sitting apart from the others on the edge of the pool, his brown legs dangling in the water. He was talking to a little blonde girl with a piquant face and long cloudy hair. They made an attractive picture, the two blond heads together, their smooth brown limbs and quiet, eager faces. With sudden clarity, I understood that Stefan was growing up. He was thirteen. The girl looked about the same. There was something exclusive about their absorption in each other. Even so, I felt compelled to dive in, and swim across to them, surfacing at their feet.

'Hi,' I said brightly to Stefan.

I thought he looked a bit annoyed. I knew myself to be an intrusion but couldn't stop myself.

'Have you oiled yourself? The sun's very fierce.'

He sighed. 'Yes, Mum.'

I looked pointedly at the girl.

'This is Karin,' he said. 'She's Dutch.'

Karin smiled. Her eyes were very blue. She didn't say anything. I felt dismissed. 'Yes, well, don't get burned,' I told him, and swam away. I felt terribly lonely. My son was growing up, he was in all probability in love. One day, he would leave me, they both would, and I would still be alone. I swam fiercely, slashing savagely at the water. Later, waiting for the children to come to lunch, I found myself longing desperately for David. He should be with me during Stefan's rite of passage. We should be able to laugh tenderly, and watch quietly from the sidelines without feeling hurt or threatened. When Stefan finally arrived, late and sheepishly apologetic, his eyes were defensive. Karin's parents were going to Utah beach that afternoon. They had invited him along. And they were going to have supper out. Was that all right? I felt a little hurt. I had suggested a visit to the landing beaches, but they had shown little enthusiasm. But I hadn't the heart to refuse, though Natalie whined, 'What am I going to do?' and poked moodily at her fish.

'We'll go to the beach and have a pedalo,' I told her. Bracing myself to grasp the nettle, I suggested that the next night we have a barbecue, and that perhaps Karin and her family would like to join us.

'Maybe.'

'You'll ask them? This afternoon?'

'All right.' He didn't look very pleased. I gave a little sigh. I had done my best. I hardly felt up to entertaining a family of foreigners, but I supposed it would be better than sitting alone, watching other couples sharing the evening, rejoicing that their offspring were off amusing themselves. I had done too much of that. My mind would wander from my book to dwell on the lunacy of the past few weeks; my futile attempts to control my life, to wrench out some happiness for myself.

To find someone to love.

Now, it seemed that Stefan had done just that. And it made me feel lonelier than ever.

When the time came to leave, I found myself packing up with some reluctance. Despite everything, I had enjoyed our temporary home. It seemed a shame to empty the fridge and stow away the cooking utensils.

Natalie helped me, folding and packing deftly and neatly. Stefan was nowhere to be seen.

'I expect he's with Karin,' Natalie said, stuffing dirty washing into a carrier bag. Then, with a surprising generosity, 'I'll do his packing.'

I looked at her with admiration. She had missed her brother during the past few days, but she had never complained. It was as if she intuitively understood that there

206

was nothing we could do. He was being pulled by inevitable forces, whose power she would someday feel too.

Thinking that, I looked at her appraisingly. She was going to be a striking girl. Her colouring, which she hated, would make her stand out. The sun hadn't tanned her but had brought out a crop of freckles. Her figure was still boyish, her limbs smooth and firm. I found myself looking forward to her transformation into a woman. She might not be a beauty, but she would be interesting.

When the bags were packed and the car loaded, I began to get impatient. I had told Stefan we had to leave at ten.

'Run and get him, won't you?' I asked Natalie.

'But where will he be?'

'Try their tent.' I didn't think I had better go myself.

She was just running off, when Stefan himself appeared. My heart sank. He was slouching along with stooped shoulders. When he arrived he didn't look at me, simply stood in front of me so that I could see that he was crying.

'Oh Stefan.' I held out my arms.

'Oh Mum.' He came into them and I held him, feeling him strong and male and incredibly dear. My heart wrenched with his pain.

'You can write to each other,' I comforted him. 'And maybe next year . . .'

He shook his head. 'That's not the same,' he mumbled.

We stood there awhile, and then I said reluctantly, 'I'm afraid we've got to go, love.'

He pulled back, wiping his face with the back of his hand.

'Get in the car.'

We all got in, and I reversed, then pulled away. The tent looked garish in the sunshine, but sadly deserted. Natalie waved to a group of children as we passed the pool. At the gate, a little figure was standing alone. It was Karin. Her face was streaked with tears, and she and Stefan stared at each other yearningly as we passed. I had never felt more helpless. When he was little, I had cuddled and patted and soothed the tears away. Now, there was nothing, absolutely nothing, I could do.

When we got home, the house was empty. Shelley had gone home for a holiday. On the kitchen table, along with the mail, there was a list of messages. I dumped the box of food on top of it, anxious to get sorted out before I looked at them. The children were heaving their bags upstairs. The house had a close and musty feel and I went round throwing windows open. I sat on my bed for a moment, feeling the soft springiness. It would be luxury after the camp bed. I longed unreasonably to crawl into it, to leave all the sorting out till tomorrow. But there was supper to be cooked. It would have to be fish and chips out of the freezer. We had never had our frogs' legs, I reflected with a rueful smile. I caught my smile in the mirror. I looked well, I thought, brown and relaxed, despite the journey. The sun had bleached my hair. David used to tease me that he had always wanted a blonde. Well, now I nearly was one.

Oh David!

I sat motionless, in a sort of desperate silent communion. After all this time, he could still call to me so strongly that it took my breath away. He would have loved the holiday, been so proud to see his children growing up. It was cruel that he had been denied, that we had all been denied.

Suspecting that I was going to cry, I got up quickly and went downstairs. Stefan had unpacked the food box and put it by the door. He had a piece of paper in his hand.

He held it out.

'There's been a phone call, Mum. Somebody called Jeremy. He wants you to call him back.'

Of course, they wanted to know who he was.

I told them he was a friend of a friend, whom I had met

at somebody's house. I lied because I was still ashamed of what I had done. I couldn't admit to anyone that I had felt such desperation that I had had to advertise for a man. For that was what it amounted to. But that didn't stop the singing excitement that made me beam into the chips as I turned them, that made me want to dance around the kitchen with joyous anticipation. I shovelled out the food and could hardly wait for the children to finish and go to bed.

'Well, are you going to ring this Jeremy?' Stefan asked as he dried the dishes.

'Later.' I poured off the cooled oil and scoured the chip pan. My hands felt trembly. Stefan looked at me slyly.

'Don't you want us to hear?' he asked, speaking from his new, grown-up knowledge of love.

'Of course I don't mind. I just want to sort out here.'

Even so, I waited until they had gone to their rooms. Then I shut the sitting-room door and dialled the number Jeremy had left. I took a few deep, steadying breaths. There was no date on the message. Perhaps he had already gone away again. I was bracing myself for disappointment, when suddenly, there he was.

'Jeremy? It's Julia. I just got your message.'

'Julia!' I thought he sounded pleased. 'I had given you up for lost.'

'And I you. We've been in France, we just got back this evening.'

'And I've been in hospital. In Kuala Lumpur, of all places. Got laid low by some fiendish tropical bug. I'm signed off for a week or so at home. Can I see you?'

I found myself beaming hugely. So simple an explanation. I almost forgot to commiserate. Then I remembered that Shelley was away. It would not be that easy to make arrangements. I had a few days' more holiday, then the children were going to my parents when I went back to work. But I didn't want to wait until then. I would have to ask Kate. All these thoughts flew around my head as I said how sorry I was about his illness, asked him if he felt better, all the usual conventional things.

'I'm not up to going out,' he told me. 'But I wondered if you'd like to come here. I could cook us dinner.'

I forgot all caution. 'I'd love to. When?'

'Tomorrow night?'

'I'll need to get a baby-sitter. Shelley's away. Can I ring you in the morning?'

'Sure. But I hope you can make it. If not tomorrow, another night. I'm home for ten more days.'

It sounded like a lifetime, yet pathetically little.

'Did you have a good holiday?'

'Yes, it was great.' Already, I was foolishly projecting ahead. But I couldn't see Jeremy in a tent. A villa perhaps, in the Italian Lakes? I tried to be sensible, but when I went to bed, I found I couldn't sleep. I lay staring at the slash of light from the streetlamp on the ceiling, wondering if Jeremy was lying awake too, thinking of me. My thoughts wandered to Stefan and Karin. I hoped Stefan wasn't crying himself to sleep. It was a funny thought – that we both might be in love.

I rang Kate next morning and she asked us round.

'I've got some time off, let's get together while we've got the chance.'

So I put all the holiday washing in the machine and we walked round to Kate's house. The front gardens looked parched and dusty; it seemed that England was enjoying summer too. Dominic answered the door, though I didn't know it was Dominic – the twins were ridiculously similar. They were both tall and thin, with thick wavy hair like their father's and beaky noses. They were both very clever, but I comforted myself with the knowledge that Stefan was better-looking. He went off at once with Dominic to use his computer, leaving Natalie stranded with me. However, Kate suggested she might like to watch television in the den, and she gratefully agreed. I was glad, because I had to ask Kate about baby-sitting that night, and I suspected that there might be questions.

'So, who is it? You look all excited?'

'Oh, it's just a man I met.'

'How met?'

'Does that matter?'

'No. Just curious. But I'm thrilled for you. It will do you good. Harry's in tonight, so I'll come round about six. Can you feed me?'

'You can eat with the children. I'll make a casserole.'

I wondered what I'd be eating, and hugged my excitement to myself. Kate was looking at me thoughtfully. Despite myself I found I was beaming at her like an imbecile. She nodded, with a knowing expression on her face.

'I think,' she said, 'I'd better be prepared for a late night.'

'Oh Kate!' I shook my head, laughing.

'Why not? You're looking beautiful. And it's been a long time. It's about time you found a man. Just make sure you enjoy yourself.'

I looked at her gratefully, for that was just what I intended to do.

'I hope you don't mind my going out so soon after we get back.' It was a belated attempt to placate the children, as we walked back for lunch. 'Only Jeremy isn't home very often, he's an airline pilot.'

'Whee! Does he fly jumbos?'

'I suppose so.'

'I wish I could go in a jumbo.'

'You will. Did you tell Dominic about Karin?'

'No. He wouldn't understand. He's only eleven.'

211

I laughed gently. 'And you're all grown up I suppose.'

He looked at me seriously. 'I feel grown up. Karin and I are going to write to each other for ever.'

'Yes, well it seems that way now. But don't be too unhappy about it. There'll be other girls, nearer home.'

'I don't want other girls,' he told me, with all the conviction of first love.

I rang Jeremy as soon as we got back and said I would be with him at seven o'clock. He gave me an address in Chiswick and said to look for the tomato-red front door. He said he would go out and buy us a feast fit for kings. For my part, I needed shopping myself, so after lunch I went to Sainsbury's and loaded up. Then I washed my hair and went through my wardrobe for something to wear. I chose a silk dress in rose pink that I had bought for Claire's wedding. When I slipped into it later, I felt I looked my best, with my bleached hair shining against my tan. My eyes were shining too. I felt young, and reckless, and for the first time for years, glad that I was me.

It was only when I was on my way that caution overtook me. Was this really wise? No one in the world knew where I was going, who I was going to be with. I knew nothing at all about this man, yet I was voluntarily going to his house alone. I paused at a traffic light, wondering whether to turn back. But I knew I wouldn't. Madness it might be, but there was no stopping me now.

The red front door stood out like a beacon in a row of neat Georgian houses near the river. The front garden had been paved and there were two tubs of geraniums, as bright as the door. The ground-floor window was barred with Venetian blinds. I pulled a brass bell pull, thinking inconsequentially of Eeyore's tail hanging outside Owl's house in *Winnie-the-Pooh*. I was smiling to myself when Jeremy opened the door, and the smile broadened when I saw him, so great was my pleasure. I had not been mistaken. He was as I had remembered; he still had the power to stir me, and more than anything, I wanted to be stirred.

He stepped back to let me enter. We were in what had been a narrow hallway, but it had been knocked through into the living area, and the banisters removed so that the stairs, close-carpeted in gold to match the rest of the room, ran rather perilously up the wall. There was a low black leather sofa and a high-backed brown leather swivel chair beside a table neatly stacked with books and magazines. I guessed that was where he sat. The fireplace had been removed and was merely an alcove in the middle of built-in bookshelves, in which sat an expensive hand-thrown pot. The tops of the bookshelves were bare except for a collection of stones and shells. There were no plants, no photographs, not even a clock. Above them hung a single, modern, abstract painting in garish colours. The books on the shelves were neatly lined, a huge television angled against the shelves. An oriental wood carving stood on top. The room was masculine and minimal, and couldn't have been less like my own.

'Oh, it's so tidy!' I exclaimed. 'You should see my living room.'

'Yes, well I don't have children. And I like to keep things simple. It's easier to leave.'

'And easier to clean.' I laughed up at him. 'Not that I do clean a lot.'

'I have a woman in. Now how about a drink? I've some white wine cooling.'

'That would be lovely.'

I sat down on the sofa, feeling the leather squeak beneath me. It smelled new. I ran my hand over the soft cushions and leaned back luxuriously. I felt wildly, unreasonably happy, already drunk. When he handed me the wine, his pale eyes smiled into mine, disarming me further.

213

'You're looking very lovely,' he said. 'Your holiday obviously agreed with you.'

I sipped my wine, telling myself that he was just being polite.

'It was good to get away,' I said finally. 'And the children enjoyed it. Though Stefan is suffering the pangs of first love.'

If I expected sympathy for my son I got none. I told myself that of course, Jeremy knew nothing of the painful claims of parenthood. So I asked instead about his illness, and heard how he had collapsed on a flight to Kuala Lumpur and his co-pilot had had to take over. Jeremy had been carted off to hospital where he had lain for over three weeks.

'I didn't know much about anything the first week. I'm told it was touch and go.'

I shuddered. I could have lost him, and I would never have known.

'When I came out I booked into a beach chalet to recuperate. It was a glorious place, surrounded with tropical flowers, with its own private beach. The sort of place where one shouldn't be alone.'

I wondered if there was hidden meaning in his words and his smile suggested as much. Then, as if discomfited, he stared down into his glass, gently swivelling his chair back and forth. I allowed my gaze to rest on him unseen. He was wearing a denim shirt, open at the neck, and denim jeans, crisply laundered. I wondered if that was something else his woman did for him. An expensive-looking gold watch enclosed his bony wrist. He suddenly looked up, caught my eye, and smiled.

'It's good to have you here. I'm sorry if I'm not very talkative, I'm not feeling very lively yet. But I've managed to cook us a good meal. I hope you like lobster.'

'You shouldn't have gone to so much trouble. Anything would have done. I'm just pleased to be here too.'

And we sat there, just smiling at each other, while my heart raced and thumped and the hand on my glass grew damp.

Then he suggested we go through to the kitchen.

'I don't like food in the living room, so my guests always eat out here,' he explained, pulling out a chair for me. There was not much room, the kitchen was small with only room to seat four round the glass-topped table. There wasn't much evidence of cooking; he had obviously cleared up after himself. He set before me a plate of steaming linguini in a cream sauce with strips of smoked salmon and offered me a piece of Parmesan cheese and a grater. He poured more wine and sat down opposite me.

'I'm pleased to say I've got my appetite back. I lost quite a lot of weight.'

He tucked in in the way I had remembered, deftly winding the pasta round his fork and thrusting it into his mouth. I tried to do the same but have never been so adept. I laughed apologetically as I sucked it in.

'This reminds me of before I was married,' I told him between mouthfuls. 'The only food we could afford was Italian. We went to a little place in Greek Street. And we only had one course.'

'Of course!'

I laughed immoderately at his joke. I was in a mood to be delighted by him.

'What food do you like now? If you can choose?'

'Oh, I don't know. I still love pasta. I like fish – I'd really like to try sushi.' Remembering eating Indian with Samuel, I drew a swift comparison between the two occasions, my discomfiture then, my delight now. Any guilt I felt at how I had treated him evaporated when Jeremy said, 'I'll introduce you to sushi when I'm feeling better.'

Suppressing my excitement I asked, 'I suppose you've eaten all over the world?'

'Yes, well that sounds marvellous, but you have to remember I also eat a lot of airline meals.'

'That sounds marvellous to me. I've not done much travelling, life has been very quiet since David died. We used to go out quite a lot – the theatre, meals – but we never went far on holiday once the children were born. They liked it in Cornwall. David's parents lived there, we used to visit every year.'

He took my empty plate. 'But now you've been to France. Maybe that's just a beginning.'

'Maybe.'

I watched him as he carried over a beautifully dressed lobster and a black bowl of salad. He opened the oven and took out a dish of tiny new potatoes covered in butter and parsley.

He invited me to help myself and when we were served he said, 'As you will have noticed I'm a great reader. Do you read much?'

'Yes. I've always got a book on the go, sometimes two or three. I like travel, and autobiography, if it's someone I'm interested in. And modern women authors. How about you?'

'Biography mainly. And books about flying. It's such an incredible history, in so comparatively short a time.'

'Do you watch much television?' I was thinking of the enormous set.

'Not much. The news, current affairs. And some of the American sit-coms. I prefer to listen to music. I've got a new Mahler, I'll play it to you after supper.'

After that, we ate in silence. Every so often, our eyes would catch and hold. The food, though delicious, began to seem irrelevant. When he brought a lemon sorbet, and told me the recipe had been given to him by his sister, I began to babble like an idiot, telling him I was an only child and had always wanted a brother; that I had wanted a large family but it was not to be. Then he told me that his parents had both died, far too young, of cancer. We seemed to be talking for the sake of talking, our minds weren't attending. Finally, he offered me cheese, which I refused, then made coffee which I carried into the living room while he followed carrying a bottle of brandy. He put the Mahler on and this time, he sat beside me on the sofa.

'Shall I pour?' I asked him, remembering how he had poured the tea.

'Please do.' He smiled, slowly and unnecessarily, into my eyes.

I gave him a cup, feeling his fingers briefly against mine. I was terribly aware of him beside me. I felt twitchy with desire: at the same time, a huge languor pressed me back into the leather cushions. He had leaned back too, his coffee held on his lap. He had his eyes closed, listening to the music. I tried to listen too, but could only think of him. I drank my coffee, trying not to chink my cup and disturb him. I poured myself another cup, hoping to sober myself up. I wondered what would happen now. It was half-past nine. Maybe I shouldn't outstay my welcome. He was convalescent after all. He probably wanted to get to bed. I looked at him over my cup. Perhaps he had fallen asleep. Gingerly I reached out to take his coffee, but he opened his eyes and pulled it away.

'It's all right, I'm not asleep.'

I was contrite. 'Sorry. I didn't mean to disturb you.'

He leaned forward and put the cup, undrunk, on the tray. Then he reached out and took my hand.

His voice was very deep when he said, 'But you do disturb me, Julia. Very much. As a matter of fact I wasn't listening to the music at all. I was wondering what to do.'

I stared at him, breathless, my mouth parted, afraid to move.

Then he leaned forward and kissed me, very gently, brushing my tongue with his own.

I sat there, motionless, letting sweetness drown me.

He stayed close, impaling me with his eyes.

'Did I do the right thing?' he asked.

'Yes,' I whispered.

He was still holding my hand. Gently, he pulled me up and led me towards the precipitous stairs. I followed him up, on legs that would barely hold me. We crossed the landing into a cool, white room with a king-size bed. The duvet and pillows were black and grey, and the sheet when he pulled the duvet back was crisp and white and freshly ironed. I had time to register that he had surely changed the bed especially before he was pulling me down beside him, his hands fumbling with my clothes. There wasn't time to undress. After a breathless struggle, we merged together with an untidy urgency, and a pleasure that left me crying with gratitude.

ELEVEN

'So, you look like the cat's that had the cream. Are you going to tell me about it?'

Kate slid her legs off the sofa and leaned towards me, her eyes sparkling with curiosity. So of course, I told her. I had been longing to, longing to share my happiness.

'And was it good?' she asked bluntly.

'Like food to a starving man.' But I blushed as I said it. I wasn't used to discussing my sex life. I wasn't used to having a sex life to discuss.

'So – when are we going to meet him? And what's his name?'

'Jeremy.' It felt good to say it. 'But I don't know about meeting him. He's a pilot, he's away a lot.'

'RAF?'

'No – British Airways.' I thought she looked disappointed.

'Don't worry – he still wears a uniform. Not that I've seen him in it, but he'd look good.'

'Is he handsome?'

'Not conventionally, no. But he has an air about him. Wavy hair, hazel eyes, tall and slim. Thin, in fact. He's been ill.'

She nodded. 'And when are you seeing him again? Do you want me to baby-sit?'

I shook my head. I had to resist saying tomorrow, and the next day, and the next. 'The children are going to my parents at the weekend. That will give us a week. Then he's off to South America.'

She got up, pulling on a cardigan. 'Well, I'll leave you to

your dreams.' She hugged me. 'I can't tell you how glad I am. You deserve some happiness.' At the door, she turned. 'Forgive me, Julia, but I am your oldest friend. You did take care, didn't you? I mean, are you on the pill?'

I shook my head. 'But there's no need to worry. Jeremy did the gentlemanly thing.'

'So – he was well prepared. Safe sex, and all that.'

It hadn't occurred to me, but I supposed that she was right.

When she had gone, I undressed and looked at my body in the long mirror on the wardrobe. I was wearing pretty well for thirty-eight, I thought. And now for the first time I felt it was to some purpose. I felt fulfilled and used, no longer wasted, my womanhood squandered. I was both aroused and relaxed, and fell into my bed naked and wanton, not washing, not wishing to relinquish the intimacy we had enjoyed. I dropped deep into a dreamless sleep, hugging the memory to myself.

Before we went to France, I had been looking into the question of Natalie's piano. I had been appalled at the price: over two thousand pounds for something that might well be a five-minute wonder. Common sense suggested that we bought second-hand, but I wasn't sure how Natalie would take that.

The subject hadn't been mentioned again, and I wondered if she had forgotten. However I didn't think it fair to let the matter lie. In the car on the way to my parents' house, I asked, 'Do you still want a piano, Nat?'

She leaned forward and gripped the back of my seat.

'You bet.'

'Only I've been looking around. They're terribly expensive. I don't think I can afford a new one.'

She was silent.

'But perhaps we could find a second-hand one. Would

you mind? I'm sure it would still sound the same. And that's what counts.'

'I suppose so.' She sounded crestfallen.

'I'd make sure it looked nice,' I assured her.

She made no comment, but after a moment she said quietly, 'I hate being poor.'

'Natalie! We're not poor. We have everything we want. And we've just had a lovely holiday.'

'We didn't go in an aeroplane. Chloe's going to India. And Helen's father's got a boat. *And* she goes horse-riding.'

I was gripped with despair. 'You could go horse-riding if you wanted to,' I told her recklessly. 'But I'm not sure I'd want to go to India.'

'You would if Daddy was alive.'

I heard Stefan remonstrate with her quietly. I searched my mind for a suitable response, for here after all was the crux of the matter. I wished I could look into her face; speaking with my eyes fixed on the road seemed painfully impersonal. And yet in some ways it made it easier.

Eventually I said, 'I'm sorry, Natalie, that you haven't got a daddy. But if he'd been alive, he wouldn't have spoiled you, you know.'

'But I could have had a new piano. One of my very own.' She sounded so miserable that I could have cried. But it was no use both of us giving in. Bracing myself, I told her, 'It will be your very own. You won't even notice the difference. And let's face it, you haven't even tried yet. You may not be so keen when it comes to doing all the practice.'

'Mummy, I *am* keen.'

'Shut up, Nat.' It was Stefan, speaking crossly. 'Mum's quite right about your stupid piano.'

She turned on him. 'It's not stupid. What do you know about it?'

'I know Mum's got to spend a lot of money on you, and you're not even grateful.'

221

'I *am* grateful.'

'Well,' I said firmly. 'I'll look in the local paper while you're away, see what I can come up with.'

She sat back in her seat, defeated. After a silence, Stefan asked, 'Will you be seeing this Jeremy while we're away?'

I met his eyes in the mirror. 'Yes. Do you mind?'

'I suppose not. No – of course not.'

Natalie asked, 'Is he nice? Can we meet him?'

'One day, I expect.'

In the mirror I saw Stefan glance at her, and he gave her a nudge. I sensed complicity, and was glad that their quarrel was over. But something made me say, 'I don't think we'll mention him to Nana and Granddad. It's our secret, yes?'

'All right.' I wondered, then, if that had been wise. It was encouraging deceitfulness. But I wasn't ready for my mother's probing questions, her ill-concealed delight. I wanted to hug the secret to myself a little longer. I felt tightly bound to the children, and reliant on them for their silence. I felt especially close to Stefan when he said, 'You will ring me, won't you, if a letter comes from Karin?' I knew I would be waiting for the post as anxiously as him, dreading his disappointment, sharing in his delight. I wondered how I was going to bear it.

I spent the night in Kingston, then hurried back to Putney early on Sunday for I was meeting Jeremy for lunch. We were going to walk on Hampstead Heath, and have supper in a riverside pub. Beyond that, I tried not to imagine, though my body had ideas of its own. I had been to the doctor and got a prescription for the pill. If I was going to embrace a life of reckless debauchery, I had better be prepared.

We ate at an Italian restaurant in Highgate. Sharing a plate of garlic bread while we waited for our pasta, I told him that I was looking for a piano. I described a little of Natalie's disappointment, and waited for him to comfort me. But all he said was, 'I can see that you're a worrier.'

'What mother isn't?' I asked him.

He shrugged. 'Fortunately, I wouldn't know.'

I was struck by that word 'fortunately', but at that moment he reached out and took my hand, all greasy from the garlic bread. My body slipped and lurched. 'Forget your worries today,' he said. 'Let's be purely selfish. Let's just think about us.'

And that's what we did. We ate a huge lunch, then walked it off on the Heath. I had difficulty matching my stride to his long legs, and found conversation impossible. On reaching the top of a long incline, he leaned against a tree and held out his arm. I went into it, gratefully. I hoped he might kiss me, but he didn't. We stood looking out over the trees towards the distant gleaming towers of the city. They looked unreal – a painted backdrop against the bright sky.

Then he said, 'It's nice the way you don't talk all the time. I hate silly, chattering women.'

'So, what do you like to talk about?'

'Oh, sensible things. Politics perhaps.'

'Well, let's talk about politics. I'm a socialist, for what it's worth. My parents are staunch Tories, but David taught me to think a bit more about it. Though socialism's not what it was. I think Labour have lost their way.'

'Life's changed. There isn't the need now.'

I pulled away. 'There's always need,' I told him vehemently. 'Maybe you can't see it, flying rich people about the world all the time.'

He looked amused. 'Well, don't let's argue. We can agree to differ.'

So much for sensible discussion, I thought. We walked on, up to Kenwood House. I would have liked to go in but Jeremy said he wasn't keen on old houses. Anyway, he had seen it before. I felt saddened. David and I had loved to go round stately homes. It occurred to me fleetingly that Jeremy was not the sort of man to make concessions. But, I told myself defiantly, that was what I had liked about him from the first; his decisiveness, his certainty. Walking back to the car, I led him on to talk about his work.

'Do you enjoy it? I mean, don't you get fed up with travelling all the time?'

'No, it suits me. Mainly, I suppose, the actual flying is incredibly boring. There's not a lot to do at thirty-five thousand feet.'

'Have you ever had any near misses? Or any other potential disaster?'

'We had an engine go down once, going over the Pole. We had to come down in Greenland.'

'Do you ever get frightened?'

He looked down at me with a tolerant expression. I felt that maybe I was chattering, but it was too late. 'If I was frightened, I wouldn't do it,' he said. 'And I like visiting foreign parts. I like staying in hotels, strange as it may seem. And working with different colleagues every week or so. I'm not a very settled sort of person.'

Part of me noted this remark, but he had launched into a story about a stopover in Buenos Aires and, for the rest of the evening he entertained me with anecdotes of places I had no hope of seeing. After a couple of glasses of wine with our supper, our eyes began to catch, kindling a promise. He drove me back to his house to collect my car, but I knew that wouldn't be all. I followed him unquestioningly into the house, and once inside the door he kissed me, deep and long. It was almost the first time that day that he had touched me; we had not behaved like lovers. Yet now we did, removing each other's clothes with a concentrated intensity before falling onto the big bed and losing ourselves in pleasure. This time I had time to enjoy the smooth angularity of his lean body, the spicy smell of his hair. This time, I didn't cry, but took the pleasure as my due. I lay, sleepy and relaxed, reluctant to move, wondering whether he would suggest I stayed the night, wondering what I would say if he did. But after a moment he sat up, looking perfectly composed, brushing back his hair.

'I'll make you a coffee before you go,' he said. His tone was matter of fact and I felt dismissed, and even rather foolish. I waited till he had gone before sitting up. Suddenly, I was ashamed to let him see me naked.

And so it went on all week. I met him each evening after work, for the theatre or a film or a meal, and ended back at his house in bed. I didn't question my feelings, and began to settle into being part of a couple. It was a comfortable feeling, despite the fact that we only had until Sunday before he went away. The children were coming home on Saturday, and I suggested he came to supper that night. I wanted him to meet them. I wanted him to see my home. In a silly, precipitate way, I wanted to try us out as a family.

But to my surprise, he refused.

'I don't think so really. I don't relate very well to children.'

We were in a taxi, travelling back from the West End. I turned on the broad seat, startled and disappointed.

'But you'll have to meet them one day,' I blurted out, unwisely.

'Will I? Why do you say that?'

'Well.' I knew exactly what I felt, but how to say it? 'Well, if we're to have any future, I suppose.'

'And why can't we just go on as we are? It suits me very well. You've enjoyed this week, haven't you? I know I have.'

'Yes. You know I have. But it doesn't represent my real life. I have the children, we're a family, I can't cut them out, pretend they don't exist.'

'I can.' I could only see his face in the flash of passing lights, but I could hear his voice. It was firm, and final. I felt a wave of panic, of confusion. And then, the first glimmers of anger.

'But you knew I had children, when you wrote. Why did you bother?'

'Let's just say I hadn't had much luck. Beggars can't be choosers.'

I was insulted, and very, very angry. I drew away to my end of the seat, clasping my arms round myself as a barrier.

'So, you've just been making do. I'm sorry. I'm sorry I've been such a disappointment.'

He reached out his hand, but I ignored it. 'You haven't been a disappointment. You've been great. But I'm not looking for any commitment. I don't want all that family stuff. I said in my letter that I wanted someone to come home to. I still do. I thought that, like everybody else, what you were really looking for was sex. Well, I gave you that. Can't you just be satisfied?'

I shook my head in bewilderment. 'No, I can't. The sex was great, I can't deny it. But I'm looking for something more. I want to rebuild my life. I want the children to have a father. And I have to put them first.'

There was a long pause. 'So – what you're saying is, you don't want to see me again. It seems a pity.'

It did seem a pity. But I knew with a shattering clarity that it had to be. 'I'm sorry, Jeremy. But I don't want to be just a sex object, someone to pick up when you return, then forget about when you're away. I want closeness, belonging, sharing – with all that that entails.'

The taxi had stopped outside his house. We sat staring at each other across the dark space between us. 'So,' he said at last. 'That's it. It's a pity. You were the best of the bunch.'

'Well – you'll just have to keep looking,' I flared bitterly, irritated beyond endurance. I opened the door and got out

226

into the quiet road. I left him to pay the driver and got into my own car. I didn't look at the tomato-coloured door. I knew I would never knock on it again. I started the engine and drove away without looking back. But, once round the corner, I parked by the kerb and leaned my head on the wheel, for I couldn't see through the tears of disappointment.

I wondered whether he would ring me, but he didn't. I was both hurt, and relieved. There was nothing more to say. We were after different things. It was a relief to realise that I hadn't loved him. My heart, if not my pride, was intact.

When, after three weeks, Shelley told me that he had rung and asked me to ring back, I thought about it, but did nothing. After all, there didn't seem to be much point.

That was the end of my search for love. I felt scarred and bruised, foolish and angry, unwilling to expose myself again. There were too many pitfalls, too many misunderstandings and discrepancies. I retreated to the safety of my widowed state, sadder and wiser. I didn't tell Kate the truth. I was too proud. I simply said he hadn't suited. Which was, of course, true in its way. I didn't tell Claire either. She had not known about Jeremy; now I was pleased about that. The fewer explanations needed, the better, as far as I was concerned.

I had told the children in the car on the way home from my parents'. I wanted them to know at once, in case they had been building up their hopes.

'It was nothing important,' I said. 'We had a few nice outings, now he's gone away.'

'Pity,' said Stefan. 'I wanted to meet an airline pilot. I might be one myself.'

I made no comment. He was always coming up with ideas of what he wanted to do. Instead, I said to Natalie, 'There's a piano advertised in the paper. I've arranged to go and see it tomorrow.'

227

She didn't say anything.

'Well,' I urged, 'isn't that good?'

'Actually,' she said – she sounded embarrassed – 'there's no need. Granddad's going to buy me one.'

'Natalie! You didn't ask him?'

'Yes, she did,' said Stefan. 'I told her she shouldn't.'

'Why not?' she retorted. 'He buys you things.'

'Yes, but not for thousands of pounds.'

I sighed. It was a solution, certainly, but I was not sure that I wanted it. I didn't like being indebted to my parents. I hadn't seen Dad when I collected the children, he had been out on a house call. Mother hadn't said anything. Perhaps she didn't approve. I didn't want her disapproval, but then I hadn't asked myself. It was surely between my father and Natalie. Later that night, I telephoned him, but it was my mother who answered.

'He's out, I'm afraid. An emergency call.'

'I wanted to thank him for the piano. It's very generous of you both.'

'It's too generous. It wasn't my idea, but he will spoil them. I think she could have done perfectly well with a second-hand one. Suppose she doesn't take to it?'

'I've told her, if she doesn't practise, we get rid of it. But she shouldn't have asked, I know that.'

'I don't suppose she did, directly. But she knows how to wind your father round her little finger. Tell me, what's the matter with Stefan? He seemed very quiet.'

'Didn't he tell you? He's in love. He met a girl in France, and now he's waiting for her to write to him.'

'He's a bit young, isn't he?' She sounded disapproving.

'I don't know about that. It's happened anyway. They were really very sweet together.'

Now she sounded terse. 'Well, I hope you've told him what's what. You don't want him getting into trouble.'

228

'You mean have I talked to him about sex? Well, I haven't really. It's a bit difficult, without David.'

'You could ask your father. I'm sure he would be happy to have a chat.'

It was very tempting. I didn't relish raising the subject with Stefan, but I thought it was something I ought to do. 'No, thanks,' I said. 'I can cope.'

But can I? I asked myself when I had rung off. Stefan needed a father. But there was absolutely no prospect of that.

A letter from Karin arrived, a fat pink envelope covered in continental writing. Stefan seized it from my hand and ran up to his room. I felt relieved, and curiously jealous, and then ashamed and humiliated as well. When he came down to breakfast, his face was glowing.

'So, she still loves you then?' I said teasingly.

'Mum.' He looked embarrassed.

'Well, I'm glad she's written. Now perhaps we can all relax.'

He gobbled down a few cornflakes and a cup of tea. 'Can I go now? I want to write back.'

I let him go. Natalie had already gone into the dining room, and I could hear her picking out scales on the piano, which had arrived the day before. It was a Yamaha, pale teak and gleaming, with a music stool to match. My father had done her proud. Now she was desperate for lessons. A woman was advertising in the local paper and I planned to ring her that evening.

Shelley was back from Gloucestershire, and term was starting next day. Natalie was going up to the comprehensive and had a new uniform, a maroon pullover and skirt which clashed with her hair. Stefan was upstairs, writing a love letter. They were growing up.

And I was growing older. My life was rushing past, and

getting nowhere. My recent foolish hopes had made me feel restless. I wanted a change. I wanted something to happen.

More than anything, I wanted to feel in control of my destiny.

The first thing that did happen, happened at the start of the Christmas holidays.

Shelley told me she was leaving.

She had been with me for six years. The children were old enough for us to manage without her, but it was a shock none the less. I had become used to her inconspicuous presence. The sound of her music, or her clattering printer, had become part of our lives. She had not sold her novel, and seemed, finally, to have lost heart. Now, she wrote articles on special needs children for teaching magazines, and seemed to have more success. She was twenty-nine, and thought it time she had a home of her own. I quite agreed with her. She went to her parents for Christmas, and didn't come back. I cleaned her room, and wondered what to do with it.

We settled down, of course. I quickly spread back into the vacated kitchen cupboards, and got used to her absence while I was cooking. The children were quite able to look after themselves until I got home, and they seemed to grow in maturity, peeling potatoes for me, and clearing the breakfast dishes from the drainer. About this time, Stefan began to excel at cross-country running. Before long, he was running for the school, and began to train every morning before breakfast, and in the evenings. He was still writing to Karin, but I noticed that her letters were becoming more infrequent. Then, during the summer holidays, he started hanging around with a girl from his class, swimming and going to the pictures, and the letters stopped completely. I congratulated myself that it had been a pretty painless initiation. But the need to talk to him became more urgent. He and Carole would spend long hours in his room, ostensibly working on the computer. She was a pretty little thing, well-developed and, I thought, sexually aware. Stefan was now fourteen. One evening, after she had gone, I braced myself and told him I thought we should have a talk.

'What's it about, Mum?' he asked me. He was sitting forward on the sofa, his arms dangling between his legs. He had a new haircut, and was browned by the sun. I thought he looked devastingly attractive, and dangerous. I couldn't blame Carole if she was tempted.

'Well,' I started hesitantly. 'It's about you and Carole. I've given you a lot of freedom this summer. I just hope you're not abusing it.'

'You mean, you hope we're not having sex,' he said bluntly.

I was embarrassed. 'I've never talked to you about it. It's something your father would have done. I should have told you everything, long ago. I hope it's not too late.'

'We were taught everything at school. Ages ago.'

It would have been easy to give up at that point, but I soldiered on resolutely.

'What they probably didn't teach you was the immense power of the sex drive. It's the most basic human instinct. It needs to be, if the human race is to survive. But that doesn't mean we should give in to it. You're both very young. You could ruin your lives with one mistake.'

'I'm not going to make a mistake, Mum.' He looked very cool, and in control, but I still felt there was more to say.

'You're growing up in a dangerous world, Stefan. We never had to worry about Aids when I was young. There's more to safe sex than just not getting pregnant.'

He nodded. 'I know all about that. Don't worry.' He gave me a disarming smile. 'Can I go now?'

I let him go, but I realised he had still not told me what I needed to know, and probably never would. Whatever he and Carole were getting up to was his secret. I could only stand on the sidelines, and hope for the best.

The following winter I was forty years old.

I tried not to let it get me down, but it did. When Kate was forty, Harry threw her a surprise party. We all hid in a darkened room, with balloons and streamers and champagne cooling, and when Harry led her in we jumped up, crying, 'Surprise, surprise!' and showering her with cards and gifts. Kate clasped her hands in delight. She looked proud and gleaming and beloved, at ease with herself and her advancing years. The twins came in carrying an enormous cake, ablaze with candles, and we all drank too much champagne.

On my birthday, the children and I went to dinner with my parents, a far more decorous occasion.

My father had retired, and was looking very well, but Mother was getting arthritic and looked every one of her sixty-three years. It hurt me to see her limping about, easing herself so painfully in and out of chairs. It hurt me, too, to hear her so sour and critical with Dad. She seemed to be engaged in an ongoing campaign to have him clear out his study.

'I've told him,' she said, 'now he's retired, he doesn't need all those medical books. There's no use in hanging on to clutter.'

Dad looked at her resignedly. I guessed they'd covered this ground before. She was trying to enlist me on her side.

'It's not clutter, Eleanor,' he said mildly. 'It represents my life. I may have retired, but I'm still a doctor. It's what I am.'

'But we'd have so much more room if you got rid of them.'

'Room for what?'

She dismissed the question. 'And they're so hard to dust.'

232

'Well, don't dust them. I don't mind.'

I decided to intervene, though I knew it was dangerous. 'Dad's right. The study's always been his room. Let him have it how he wants.'

She turned on me, her mouth a tight line. 'I might have known you'd take his side. He's always spoiled you.'

'No he hasn't.' My voice was tight and angry.

Natalie slid off her chair and wound her arm round Mother's neck.

'Don't be cross, Nana. It's Mummy's birthday party.'

It sounded so poignant that I could have wept.

'Quite right, Natalie.' It was Dad, looking determinedly cheerful. He raised his glass. 'Let's drink a toast to Mummy.'

They all raised their glasses. Dad had persuaded Mother to let the children have some wine. I watched with amusement as Natalie sipped hers and screwed up her face with distaste. Stefan, however, took a large mouthful, staring at me challengingly. But I wasn't going to protest. I smiled round at them as Dad said, 'Well, here's to you, Julia. They say life begins at forty. Let's hope, for you, it does.'

I did not feel so optimistic.

Shortly after that, an advertisement appeared in the paper for a receptionist at the local medical centre.

I stared at it thoughtfully. I had been with Mr Seligman for a long time. Maybe it was time for a change. After all, it had been what I wanted. The centre was just around the corner, I could walk there. And there would be more variety. I was becoming just a little tired of gynaecological problems. I was tired of spending all day in a world of women, of working alone with nobody to talk to.

I knew the centre, of course, having visited it as a patient. It was bright and new, with red armchairs arranged on a patterned carpet, tables piled with magazines, a children's playroom, an aquarium full of soothing fish. There were three receptionists and eight doctors. There was a nurses' treatment room and everything was computerised. The more I thought about it, the more excited I became. I obtained an application form and filled it in carefully, sent it in and settled down to wait.

I didn't have to wait long for I was called to an interview the following week. Two of the doctors saw me. They told me the hours, which would include one evening a week from five to seven, and one Saturday a month. I told them I could manage that. I told them that I started training as a doctor myself, as if that could make any difference, and that I had been married to a doctor. They were more interested in my present job, which I felt stood me in good stead. They both shook hands and thanked me for coming. I walked out past the waiting patients feeling hopeful, and desperately keen.

And for once luck was with me, for I got the job.

So, in a way, a new life did begin for me at forty. From the start, I enjoyed the job, the bustle of people coming and going, the contact with the doctors, the feeling of being involved. I made friends with the other receptionists, mastered the computer, dealt with the patients with an ease born of long practice. Cautiously, I admitted to myself that I was happy.

And then I met Matt.

PART THREE

TWELVE

Claire had invited us to a bonfire party on Guy Fawkes night. Stefan said he didn't want to go. He and Carole had arranged to go to a big public display on Wimbledon Common with a crowd of school friends.

'Do you want to come, Nat?' I asked.

She shrugged, pulling at the green malachite pendant Stefan had bought her from the Natural History Museum. She put it in her mouth and sucked on it, a habit which irritated me intensely, though it was wiser not to comment. Puberty had settled on her like a fog, making her difficult and moody. It was hard, sometimes, to tell what she wanted. She would spend hours at the piano, working out her feelings, or so I supposed, in long and complicated pieces set by her teacher. She had taken three exams in swift succession. Usually, said her teacher, she reckoned on a year per grade, but already she was working for Grade Four: a Haydn sonata, Fantaisie No. 12 by Telemann. My father's investment had paid off. But I wished she would get out more. For a girl her age, she didn't seem to have much fun.

So now I urged her, 'Do come, Josh will be there. And Zoe.' Zoe was Claire's new baby, her 'afterthought' as she called her, an appealing two-year-old with a stammer. 'You love Zoe,' I told Natalie persuasively. 'Perhaps you can look after her.'

She released the stone, which dropped to her chest, gleaming wetly.

'Okay.' She sounded so dispirited that I was moved to ask her if there was anything wrong.

'No.' She looked quite affronted, as if I had no right to ask. I suppressed a sigh of irritation. Where was my open little girl, whose emotions I had been able to read on her face? Now she had a shuttered look, keeping me out of her secrets.

Claire and Ian had recently moved into a modern three-storey town house, with a small patch of garden approached through the utility room. It was a characterless place, but they liked it. When I thought back to the sparse surroundings in which I had first met her, I had to admit that she had done well. Ian was a small, intense man who worked with computers. Josh had just started at the same school as Natalie and Stefan. He was still a good-looking boy, with his dark hair and eyes. Zoe was blonde with blue eyes which she used to good effect, winning friends and influencing people. Her stammer was causing Claire a lot of anxiety, but she had been told she would grow out of it. I hoped so. It was difficult to talk to the child, for the temptation was to finish her sentences for her, but Claire had been told not to do that.

Natalie was very good with her. When we arrived, the little girl came running up to us, bundled up in a scarlet anorak and padded trousers. 'We've made a b-b-b-bonfire,' she burst out excitedly.

Natalie took her hand. 'You show me,' she said, leading her out into the garden.

Claire was looking pretty and animated, with a pink bobble cap and scarf.

'Come upstairs and have a drink before we start.'

I followed her up narrow carpeted stairs and into the L-shaped living room. It was dominated by the computer equipment ranged along one end, and Ian and Josh were standing at the keyboard, tapping in a desultory way. There was a lurid game on the screen, but they didn't seem to be taking it very seriously.

Sprawled in an armchair, nursing a glass of beer, was

a man of about thirty, with short curly dark brown hair like Josh's, and heavy-rimmed glasses. He uncrossed his legs and stood up. He had an amiable expression and was very tanned, and I liked him immediately, even before he spoke.

'This is my brother, Matthew,' Claire explained. 'He's just back from Saudi Arabia.'

'Call me Matt.' He had a warm grip as we shook hands.

'And this is Julia.'

'Hello, Julia.' He gave me a friendly smile and I smiled back.

We sat down and Claire brought me a beer.

'What do you do in Saudi?' I asked Matt.

'I'm – or I was – a chemical engineer with an oil company. But I came to the end of my contract and thought perhaps I'd had enough of sun and sand. I can't tell you how green England looks when you've been in the Middle East. So now I'm looking for something here.'

'I see.'

'Meanwhile, I'm enjoying getting to know my niece and nephew. I love kids.'

Claire perched on the arm of his chair. She had removed her hat and scarf and held them loosely in one hand. In the other she held her glass.

'Matt's staying with us for a while,' she said. 'The children think it's great, having an uncle. He spoils them rotten.'

I liked him even more.

'I've got two of my own,' I told him. 'Though I suppose you'd hardly call them children any more. They're teenagers – with all that that implies!'

He nodded. 'Untidy rooms and loud music. I remember it well.'

'Well actually, that doesn't really describe my daughter. She plays the piano, and keeps her room immaculate. Stefan's more typical. He's nearly sixteen, and seems to like to live in a tip. Not that I'm very tidy myself,' I added. 'So I can't really complain.'

He was listening to me with a smile. I felt that I could go on talking to him, but Natalie and Zoe came into the room demanding that we light the bonfire and start the firework display. Claire put on her scarf and hat and Ian and Josh vacated the computer, switching it off reluctantly, I thought. We trooped downstairs and out onto the small patch of soggy grass. I wished I had thought to wear Wellington boots.

I was aware of Matt standing behind me as Ian put a match to the bonfire. As the flames roared up, helped by a paraffin-soaked rag, I turned to him. His face was lit by the ruddy glow and his eyes behind his glasses were shining like a child's.

'Magic, isn't it?' I said.

'You wait for the fireworks. We've bought some huge rockets. And Catherine wheels. I spent all afternoon nailing the damn things to posts!'

The first of the rockets went up with a bang and a whoosh. I saw Zoe put her hands over her ears and look up at Natalie for reassurance. Natalie herself was gazing upwards at the tumbling stars. On her face was an expression of pure and honest wonder such as I hadn't seen for a long time. It made me happy to see it.

Matt said, 'Aren't we supposed to go "Aaahh"? Say it with me – aaahh.'

I joined in, as the next rocket drove upwards into the smoky air. As the dots of light – red, then blue, then yellow – faded and fell to the earth, I felt his hand on my shoulder. It felt warm and friendly.

It felt good.

When the fireworks were over, we stood round the dying fire into which Ian had put jacket potatoes, wrapped in foil. As the heat faded, we instinctively drew nearer. I felt my cheeks glowing, though my feet were cold. Natalie was sitting on a garden bench, her arm round Zoe, who looked nearly asleep. Josh was poking at the fire with a stick. Claire was in the kitchen, cooking sausages. Matt and I stood in a companionable silence, hypnotised by the glowing heart of the fire, the slowly subsiding ash, our eyes stinging from the smoke which blew intermittently towards us. Suddenly, Ian cried, 'The sparklers. I forgot the sparklers! Run and get them, Matt.'

Matt went into the house and came out with a paper packet. He slid out the sparklers and bent to the fire. There was a glittering conflagration, and he turned triumphantly like a phoenix rising from the ashes. He gave one to Natalie, who waved it gently in front of Zoe, whose sleepy eyes watched its shining arc. Josh took two and raced about the garden, whooping.

'And one for you?' asked Matthew, offering me one. 'Or are you too grown up?'

'Never!' I took one, and stood awkwardly, trying to feel spontaneous. He divided the rest into both hands, and wove them in and out in swooping arcs, a look of concentration on his face. Tentatively, I joined in, so that our hands were weaving in the dark, trailing fire. He caught my eye, and laughed.

I laughed back. 'Stupid, isn't it?' I said. 'What are we doing?'

'Just enjoying ourselves,' he told me. And it was true. I was enjoying myself; I felt like a child again, with laughter bubbling under the surface.

And so, apparently, did Matt. 'I feel like a kid,' he confessed. 'But then, I often do. I don't take life too seriously.'

The sparklers had fizzled out. We threw the burned-out sticks into the fire, and he leaned to poke the potatoes. 'These are done. Where are those sausages? I could murder some grub.'

'Me too.' It was true, I was starving. Just then, Claire

called us in, and Ian gathered the ashy packages onto a tray and we trooped indoors. Natalie was trying to carry Zoe, and Matt, noticing, swooped the little girl up into his arms, planting a kiss on her bright hair. We processed upstairs. The table was set with plates and cans of beer. Ian unwrapped the potatoes and we dolloped on huge lumps of butter. We sat round eating the hot food, our faces red from the fire and the night air. There was a jolly atmosphere around the table. Matt seemed to be teasing Natalie about something. I saw her fingers go to her pendant, and held my breath. But then she laughed, her green eyes flashing. It was good to see her so relaxed. I heard Matt ask her about school. Usually, when I did this, she would clam up, but to my amazement I heard her telling him that she enjoyed French and music and didn't care for games. He asked her if she played an instrument, and she told him about her piano. I turned to Claire and said with pleasure, 'He's nice, your brother. Let's hope he stays around.'

'Yes, we hope so. Though not here for too long. We don't really have the room.'

'Well, he'll find somewhere of his own soon surely. He must have been earning quite a bit.'

'Yes, you'd think so. But I'm afraid Matt isn't the most sensible person on this earth. He's blown most of his capital on a Porsche. Says it's always been his ambition to own one. But he's nearly thirty-four. We told him to put his money down on a house, but he wouldn't listen. He's always been like that. I mean, knowing his contract was coming to an end, you'd think he'd have done something about getting another job. But he just expects that something will turn up. And knowing Matt, it probably will.'

I looked at him, with Zoe now on his lap, tickling her and making her laugh. I didn't want to think ill of him. 'Still, he's very good with children. They must enjoy him.'

Claire looked at him fondly. 'Yes. But he's spoiling them.

And he's the only one who can beat Josh at his computer games. But . . .' And now she looked serious. 'I don't think it's a good thing for him to stay too long. He overexcites Zoe, as you can see. I'll never get her to sleep now, though she's obviously exhausted. And Ian, though he never complains, wants us to have the place to ourselves again. For a start, Matt's brought so much stuff with him. And we've had to have Zoe in our room, which isn't ideal.'

To my surprise, she blushed as she said this, and cast a glance at Ian, who was opening a can of beer. I caught a brief glimpse of their intimacy, and nodded understandingly.

And then I heard myself saying, 'He could always rent my spare room. If that would help.'

I hadn't given it a moment's thought, it just slipped out. I was preparing to retract, when I saw that Claire's face had a sort of hopeful look.

'Could he really? I wonder whether he would . . . but I wouldn't want it to look as if I was throwing him out.'

I had a curious sense of burning boats. Well, I thought, in for a penny, in for a pound. 'I could suggest it, if you like. Then you wouldn't be involved.'

'Would you? Well, if you're sure. I mean, do you want a stranger in the house again?'

'I could use the money. And it probably wouldn't be for long. Until he gets a job. After all, he could be working anywhere. And he won't want to stay when he's earning.'

Claire was looking dubious now. 'Well, don't be too hasty. Sleep on it. Then if you're sure, give him a ring. But don't feel you have to do it, because of what I was saying. We can manage for a bit longer. Don't put yourself out for us.'

I laughed. 'I'm not that altruistic,' I assured her.

Besides, I told myself, having Matt around might be fun.

I didn't exactly sleep on it, I lay awake, wondering what I had done.

Claire had been right in asking if I really wanted a stranger in the house. It wasn't something I had planned on, though the room was clearly wasted. The only people who stayed in it were my parents, and now my mother was reluctant to leave her own bed. But it would be very easy to tell Claire that I had changed my mind, that I had spoken without thinking, which I had. But something – not altruism but a certain self-interest – was telling me otherwise. I had liked Matt. Natalie seemed to like him. What had I to lose? It would be a useful extra income, which I could use to decorate the living room. I had been putting that off for years. I needed new curtains, new loose covers, possibly even a carpet. The more I thought about it, the more my impetuous suggestion took on the guise of a sensible idea. Somewhere in the small hours, I decided to pursue it, and then I fell asleep.

The next day was a Saturday. Stefan was running in a cross-country race, and it was raining. I said I would take him to school to catch the coach. That way, he would start off dry. He seemed rather quiet in the car, and I asked him why.

He looked down at his hands when he answered, and his voice sounded muffled and strange. 'I finished with Carole last night. Or rather, she finished with me. She wants to go out with Simon Reynolds.'

'Oh Stefan!' I reached out and gripped his hand. 'I'm sorry.'

'I feel a complete fool. Everyone will be talking about it.'

'No they won't.'

He sniffed, and wiped the back of his hand across his face. 'I just wish I could hate her, but I can't.'

I nodded. 'You'd feel better if you could feel angry. But then, anger is hard to live with. And it's very destructive.' I pulled into the kerb outside the school gates and turned to him. He looked at me abjectly. 'You'll miss her, I know. But

244

you will get over it. Remember Karin? I expect you hardly can, now.'

'But I'll see Carole every day. And Simon.' His eyes were full of a beseeching misery. 'How am I going to bear it, Mum?'

I wanted to hug him, but there were several boys hanging about by the gates and I didn't think he'd thank me. 'You will,' was all I could say. 'And good luck in the race.'

I smiled encouragingly as he got out of the car. As he walked away, his bag hanging heavily in his hand, all the cares of the world on his shoulders, I felt his pain as if it were my own, and the more so, because it was his.

I had shopping to do. Sainsbury's was packed, and the lines at the tills were long. I was standing resignedly with my trolley when I was interrupted by one of those coincidences one only reads about in books.

It was Matt, standing behind me with a trolley piled mainly with cans of beer. He had a bundle of newspapers under his arm.

I returned his greeting, looking at his trolley with a smile.

'Iron rations?' I asked lightly.

'I picked up some bargains too. Doughnuts – two packets for the price of one. Did you see them?'

'Don't tempt me. I'm starting to put on weight. Middle-age spread setting in.'

'Nonsense. You look all of thirty.'

I laughed. 'And another ten,' I told him.

'Well, I'd never have guessed it,' he said, and I willingly believed him.

He patted the newspapers under his arm. 'Job hunting,' he said. 'Needs must, though I'm enjoying being unemployed. If it wasn't for the money, I'd never work again.'

He reached out and helped himself to some chocolate bars.

'Go on,' he said. 'Spoil yourself.'

'I shouldn't.'

'What's life all about if not for enjoying ourselves? I'll treat you.'

'No!' I laughed, and put out a restraining hand.

'Claire complains that I spoil the children. But I like to buy them things.'

I made no comment, but asked instead, 'Do you like living there? How long has it been?'

'About a month. It's all right, though I don't want to outstay my welcome. But I don't really want to find anywhere else until I get a job. That could be anywhere, though I'm hoping to stay in London.'

Now seemed the moment to speak, so I grasped the nettle. 'I have a spare room. You could rent that, if you like. Until you get settled.'

He stared at me, his eyes questioning. 'Are you serious?'

'Yes. It's standing empty, and I could do with the money. It's quite a big room,' I went on persuasively. 'I could put a little cooker in if you didn't want to share the kitchen.'

'Oh, I was hoping you were offering me food as well.' He spoke jokingly, but I sensed that he meant it.

'Well, I could, but it would cost more obviously.'

'But easier. For me anyway. I'm a lazy git. And I'm not used to fending for myself. We single men lived in quarters in Saudi. Everything was taken care of.'

'Didn't that get monotonous?'

'A bit. But I'm afraid now I'm rather spoiled.'

He smiled disarmingly, as an indulged child wins round a parent, and I found myself won over, offering board and lodging for what seemed a princely sum, which he accepted with alacrity. We arranged that he would move in in a week. He released his trolley and held out his hand across the cans of beer.

'Here's to us,' he said as I took it. 'And may I say, I couldn't have wished for a nicer landlady.'

246

Turning to unload my shopping, I reflected that I didn't much care for the title, but that I couldn't have wished for a better lodger.

The following Saturday, the Porsche arrived outside before we had finished breakfast. Stefan answered the door, and Matt followed him into the kitchen, carrying a large cardboard box and grinning in his disarming way.

'Sorry to be a bit early. Only it's going to take a number of trips. There's not much room in the back.'

Stefan however was full of admiration. 'It's a great car. Really cool.'

'That's it. That's why I had to have it.'

I pushed back my chair.

'I'll take you up to your room.'

He hadn't wanted to see it in advance. Now, going upstairs, I felt nervous. Suppose he didn't like it? Suppose there wasn't room for all the stuff Claire said he had? I opened the door tentatively, but he pushed it wide with the box, and dumped it on the table. Then he looked around.

'It's great. I knew it would be. And sunny. I like the sun. In England, it isn't something you hide from, it's something you welcome. And it makes all the difference to a room.'

'Yes, it's lovely in here in the morning. Then it moves round to the front.'

He went to the window and looked down over the garden. It was damp and dishevelled, the borders still untidy with summer growth and silted with dead leaves.

'It looks as if you could do with some help in the garden. I used to like gardening, as a kid.'

'I loathe it. And there never seems to be much time. Stefan helps, sometimes. He cuts the grass in summer.'

'He's a good-looking lad.'

'Yes.' I glowed gratefully. 'He runs for his school,' I couldn't resist saying.

He turned and smiled. 'Well, I'll fetch the rest of my things, and then go back for some more. It will take a couple of runs, I expect. Do you think Stefan would like to come and help?'

'He'd love a ride in the car. Let's go and ask him.'

I knocked at Stefan's bedroom door and gave him Matt's invitation. His face lit up.

'Cool. I'll be right down.'

I opened the front door. The Porsche was parked by the kerb, shiny red in the sun. It was not as long and low as I had imagined, but it had a potent crouch.

'You'd better leave it on the drive,' I told Matt. 'It will be safer.'

He was looking at the car fondly, as if at a child.

'It's a 911,' he said, as if I would understand. 'Two years old. It will do 130 miles an hour.'

'Oh? And when can you do that round here?'

He grinned down at me. 'Never mind, it's the thought that counts. And it makes for good acceleration. I like to be first away at the lights.'

'And how many miles does it do to the gallon?' I asked, sounding like his mother.

He shrugged. 'About twenty-five.'

He took a suitcase off the back seat together with some carrier bags. 'Not much room for passengers I'm afraid. But it's not as if I have a family.'

While he took the bags inside, Stefan came out.

He ran his hand down the gently sloping back. 'The engine's in the rear,' he said. There was longing in his voice.

'Well, get in, I should. Matt won't be long.'

He opened the passenger door and eased himself into the front seat. Matt came back, got in and started the engine. It made a satisfactory growl. I watched as they drove away, then turned back to the house. Natalie was standing at the front door, zipping her pendant back and forth along its chain.

'Can I go next time?' she asked.

'I suppose so. But you'll have to help Matt carry things.'

'I can do that.' She put her arm through mine. It was an unexpected gesture of friendliness. 'He's nice, isn't he? Matt? I think it will be good, having him here.'

'I hope so. But I don't expect it will be for long. Just until he gets a job.' I realised I was warning her. Don't get attached. This isn't the daddy you've been hoping for. Though, watching her wander off towards the piano, I wondered whether that hope had been extinguished long ago. She was not a little girl any more. I felt saddened, but also relieved that the obligation to replace David had somehow evaporated without my noticing it. I went into the kitchen to clear the breakfast and think about lunch. It was to be Matt's first meal, and I was planning something special.

There was a meeting at the school about drugs. Both the children brought home notes about it, and I filled in one of the replies to say that I was coming. Not that I thought I had anything to worry about, but I felt it was best to be informed.

'Not that either of you would, would you?' I asked them. 'I mean I've always brought you up to realise how foolish it is.'

'No, Mum,' Stefan said patiently. 'You can't run, and take drugs.'

'Lots of athletes do,' put in Natalie. 'Then they get banned.'

'That's a different sort of drugs, silly.'

Natalie looked petulant, and sucked on her pendant.

'Has anyone ever tried to sell you any?' I asked Stefan. I had heard of dealers hanging around school gates, even infiltrating the playgrounds.

He shook his head. 'We've been told all about it. Never to

touch discarded needles, the difference between stimulants and hallucinogens, the dangers of adulterated drugs.'

Then Matt said unexpectedly, 'I tried pot, when I was at college. It didn't do me any harm.'

I looked at him in exasperation. 'Matt. What sort of example is that?'

'Sorry. I didn't realise I was supposed to be setting an example.'

No, I thought, but you are grown up. Or are supposed to be. But then it was hardly fair to criticise. He was only the lodger, after all, not a role model for my children.

When I returned from the meeting, armed with leaflets and full of warnings about mood swings, glazed eyes, sore lips from glue sniffing and thefts of money and valuables, Matt was in the kitchen, sitting at the table reading his latest copy of *The Automobile*. I unwound my scarf and took off my gloves. It was a February night, and cold, but it was warm in the kitchen, the more so because there was somebody there waiting for me.

'I thought I'd make you a hot drink,' he said. 'Coffee – or chocolate?'

'Chocolate would be nice. But why? It's not particularly late.'

He measured milk into a pan. 'Because I wanted to apologise. For letting you down this evening. Over the cannabis. I guess I'm not used to teenagers. Or parental responsibilities. I realise now that it could have made things difficult for you.'

I looked at him. His face was unusually serious, his eyes grave behind his glasses. Instantly, I forgave him, but I felt compelled to agree that it certainly hadn't helped, but that I wasn't expecting him to bring up my children. Just perhaps to think before he spoke next time.

'Yes, ma'am,' he said, setting down a cup of chocolate. 'A biscuit with that?'

I patted my stomach, hating its soft roundness where once

all had been hard and flat. 'Don't tempt me. You have one by all means.'

He opened the tin, taking two custard creams. 'What's the harm of a little biscuit? You take life too seriously.'

'Well, perhaps you don't take it seriously enough. Doesn't it worry you that you haven't got a job yet?'

He pushed in the final half-biscuit and crunched. 'Actually,' he said when he had finished, 'I have. It's not quite what I was looking for but it will do for the time being. I'm starting work in Putney Garden Centre next week. I told you I used to like gardening. I should be able to pick up some things for you cheaply. Seeds, compost . . .'

'I'm not really into seeds and compost,' I said ungraciously.

'Well, I'll do it for you. Spring's on the way.'

'How much are they paying?'

'Enough to cover the rent, if that's what's worrying you. And some left over for petrol.'

'Oh Matt!' I laughed indulgently. 'You and that car.'

'Well you like riding in it too.'

It was true. I had only been in it twice; once at his insistence, when he had driven me through Richmond Park. The second time he had taken me shopping on a rainy day when my car wouldn't start. He had also cleaned my plugs, saving me a garage bill. I had been impressed, and grateful. And now he was offering help with the garden. There was a lot to be said for having a man about the house.

Now I said, matching his tone, 'Oh yes, I love it. It makes a change, feeling like one of the beautiful people.'

'You are one of the beautiful people.'

I felt my breath catch in my throat, but surely he was only teasing? He was smiling at me over his cup. There was no reason on earth to take him seriously. Why, then, did I feel so discomfited, my cheeks flushing like a teenager's. And why did I find myself wishing that he was speaking the truth?

*   *   *

We spent Easter in the garden, hacking and burning, weeding and pruning, giving the lawn a cut and trimming the edges. The daffodils were fading under the apple tree but the wallflowers were out and the perennials, freed of their dead superstructure, were pushing up juicily out of freshly turned earth. It was all most satisfactory, and what's more I had enjoyed it.

I told Matt so, as we cleared up on the Monday afternoon. 'It makes all the difference, to have someone to do things with.'

'Of course. That's what life's all about.'

'Then why . . . ?' I stopped. It was none of my business, but it did seem strange to me that someone so friendly, so disarming, so warm and funny, was still on his own. Matt was quite often out, but he had never mentioned a girl, never brought anyone back, though I had tried to indicate that this would not be a problem. I was if nothing else a broad-minded landlady, though I couldn't deny that it would be disturbing if he had a woman in his room. Why this should be so, I didn't analyse.

'Why what?' He looked at me quizzically, shading his eyes from the sinking sun.

I poked my fork into the lawn. Without looking at him I said, 'I sometimes wonder why you've never married. You don't seem the kind to be a loner.'

'Well, I was in Saudi for seven years. Not much chance of meeting girls there.'

'But you didn't have to be.'

He took the fork gently from my hands. 'Let's put these away,' he said, going to the garden shed and stacking the tools inside. He shut the door and leaned against it, his arms folded. 'You could say I was running away. From a broken heart.'

'Oh.' Now that he had revealed himself, I felt sorry. 'You don't have to tell me. I didn't mean to pry.'

He shrugged. 'It was a long time ago. Anyway, I don't think I was ready to settle down. She knew that. So she married someone else.'

'I'm sorry.' I felt a sudden urge to hug him, and had to hold my hands tightly to my sides.

'Don't be. As I said, it was a long time ago.' He rubbed a muddy hand through his curls. 'Let's go in, and have some tea.'

'It's a bath for me first. I'm going to be stiff.'

'Then I'll massage you,' he said. 'I'm rather good at that.'

I wondered how he knew, whom he had practised on, but had to admit the idea appealed to me. The kitchen was warm after the darkening garden. We dropped our boots on the mat and Matt washed his hands at the sink and filled the kettle. 'Quick bath,' he said, 'then call the children. I'll light the fire and we'll toast crumpets. And,' he put his hands on my shoulders, making me feel both warm and dominated, 'I shall insist that you eat one, with plenty of butter.'

Later, when we were all watching television in a half-hearted way, he patted the floor at his feet. 'Come and sit here, and I'll rub your shoulders.'

I hesitated. Natalie looked at me questioningly, then nodded. 'Go on, Mum, you're always saying they ache.'

I slid to the floor at Matt's feet. His hands were strong and warm, and they kneaded the muscles in my shoulders as if he were making bread. I felt like a piece of dough, soft and warm and springy, bending to the pressure of his fingers, my eyes drooping with relaxation. Gradually, my head slid against his knee, and I fell asleep.

When I awoke, the children had gone. Matthew was sitting very still, one hand still on my shoulder. I shifted with embarrassment, turning my head to apologise.

'No matter. I'm very flattered. Mind you, maybe I shouldn't be. It doesn't say much for me if when I touch a girl, she simply falls asleep.'

I couldn't interpret what he was saying, couldn't read his eyes.

But I could read his lips when he leaned forward, and kissed me.

He apologised at once.

'I'd no right,' he said. 'Only you looked so sweet and sort of muzzy.'

I couldn't understand his contrition. After all, I hadn't repelled him, I had simply sat there, feeling a warm sweetness seep through me, driving away the last vestiges of sleep. But I had been too stunned to respond, and maybe he had taken that as rejection.

'It's all right,' I reassured him. 'We're both grown-ups. I'm not going to hold you to anything!'

'That's not what I meant.' He looked confused, and pushed at his glasses like a little boy. 'But it won't happen again.'

'Oh. Well, if that's how you want it.' I scrambled awkwardly to my feet. 'I must get supper.'

'I'll help.'

'No!' I spoke sharply because I wanted to be on my own. I wanted to think.

'Okay,' he said. I thought he sounded hurt. 'Well, I'll be in my room.'

And after that, nothing more was said. I had decided that if he didn't raise it, I wouldn't. Why imbue a simple, friendly act with importance by discussing it? Things were going well. Why complicate the issue? But that night, sleepless in bed, my body told me that if he were to kiss me again, I wouldn't say no.

But he didn't. Spring melted into summer, and with the application of cut-price seeds and compost, administered by Matt, the garden burgeoned into colour. He also brought boxes of bedding plants, which I planted out at the end of May, and hanging baskets which I hung outside the doors. He was enjoying his job at the garden centre – pricking out, potting on, propagating. He could do it, he explained, without thinking. It seemed a waste to me. He was a skilled man, a graduate. But he seemed not to see that he was wasting himself. It wasn't up to me to nag. For my part, I had recently had a rise at the health centre. With Matt's rent, I had more money than I had ever had before, and I began to think about a holiday. But Stefan forestalled me. He wanted to go to Sweden to camp with the school. And Natalie had the chance of a visit to Paris, also with the school. That left me rather out on a limb. I decided, instead, to redecorate the living room, as soon as they went away in August.

Matt came upon me one day with fabric and wallpaper samples spread about me on the living-room floor.

'That's nice,' he said, picking up a swatch of blue.

'Too cold, I think, for a living room.'

'Well – I stand corrected,' he said, with mock humility.

'I was rather favouring the apricot paper for the walls, and tan for the curtains and the loose covers. That way, I could get away with the same carpet.'

'Why not go the whole hog?'

'Too expensive, I think.'

'Oh, live dangerously for once.'

'Matt! You're a bad influence.'

But I flicked longingly at a bundle of carpet samples. There was a luscious cream, which now the children were grown up . . . I had lived with the green for so long . . . Matt was looking at me with a teasing smile, as if he knew exactly what I was thinking.

'Oh, what the hell!' I threw down the samples. 'It can't hurt to get a quote.'

'That's my girl. You can't take it with you.'

I gathered up the samples and piled them untidily on the coffee table.

'It's a long time since I did any decorating, and then I was only the mate,' I told him. 'David was marvellous at papering.'

'Well so am I. I expect.' He laughed, pushing at his glasses. 'I'll help you anyway. I can't have you wearing yourself to a frazzle.'

I liked that, but I replied lightly, 'You'll be expecting a rent rebate next!'

'Not at all. It will be a pleasure. When do we start?'

'In a couple of weeks. When the children are away. Then we can put some of this stuff in their rooms.' I glanced round. The accumulation of books and papers seemed to have grown inexorably over the years. One of the armchairs was permanently occupied with books I intended to read. 'What I really need is another bookcase,' I said experimentally. 'I don't suppose you're a carpenter as well as everything else?'

He shook his head. 'Count me out on that one. My one effort at school was a coffee table with wobbly legs. If I remember, my report said, "His silly attitude doesn't help." Or maybe that was for something else!'

I laughed. I seemed to do a lot of laughing when Matt was around. It was refreshing. It was also undeniably rather sexy. I remembered how David and I used to laugh. We even laughed when we were making love. It made it warm, convivial, intimate in a way that transcended mere passion.

I scrambled to my feet, and Matt put out a hand to steady me. It did quite the opposite; it sent my senses reeling so that I almost clutched on to him. Instead, I managed to thank him brusquely and offer him coffee. He accepted, leaving his hand on my arm, I was sure, for a moment longer than necessary. Behind his glasses, his brown eyes were very serious for a change. I could not fathom their depths.

*　　*　　*

The children were both due to leave on the same day, Stefan from the school by coach, Natalie from Waterloo by train. The problem of how to get them there was solved by Matt offering to drive Stefan to the school.

'I'd rather you took Natalie. I hate driving into town.'

'Okay. Natalie it is.'

Stefan looked rather put out when we told him. 'I'd have liked the other boys to see the Porsche,' he confided in me later.

'Well, I don't think that's a very good reason. After all, it isn't ours.'

'No.' He seemed to be thinking about something. I waited, folding washing quietly, not looking at him. Eventually, he said, 'Will you be all right while we're away? I mean – on your own with Matt.'

I answered carefully, 'Of course I will. It won't make any difference.'

He didn't seem satisfied. 'It seems funny, leaving you with him.'

'Darling, he's a lodger. And I shall be busy decorating.' I didn't tell him of Matt's offer to help. I wondered what was going on in his sixteen-year-old head, and was curiously touched. I wanted to put his mind at rest.

'Don't you think about me at all. Go off and have a good time at camp. It will seem strange to me too, you know. It's the first time you've been away alone. For the first time, you will be somewhere that I can't imagine. You will send me a card?'

'Of course.' Then he grinned at me. 'Thanks for letting me go. I'm sorry we're not having a holiday all together.'

'Well, you're growing up. That's what happens. Soon, you'll be off to university. I've got to get used to it.'

Suddenly, he came up to me and put his arms round me.

'You're a good mum,' he said. I had to look up to meet

his eyes; he was taller than me. I felt strangely humble, and tremendously touched.

'And you're a good son. Now go off and get on with your packing. And don't have the music too loud!' I couldn't resist as a parting shot, in case he should see how moved I was.

The house seemed very quiet without them. No tinkling sonatas from the piano, no heavy rock from Stefan's room, no thundering feet on the stairs. No squabbling, or meaningful sighs from Natalie.

Instead, there was Matt.

He had taken a week's holiday, as I had, and after a quick lunch on the day the children left, we started to clear the sitting room. Books, papers, ornaments and pictures went into Stefan's room, and as much furniture as would fit upstairs. Matt lifted the carpet and we bundled it outside to be taken to the tip. I had succumbed to temptation and was spending some of Colin's money on the new cream replacement that I yearned for. The suite we pushed into the middle of the room and covered with dustsheets, though new covers had been ordered – thanks to Matt's rent. Watching him heave the heavy sofa into position I reflected that I had a lot to thank Matt for. I was actually quite looking forward to the coming task. His was the moral support I needed. And, with him, it would be fun.

Next day, I dressed in a sweatshirt and old dungarees I hadn't worn for years. When Matt saw me he said, with what I thought was admiration, 'You look about sixteen.' I pulled in my stomach, and smiled.

'Well, what should I do?' I asked him. 'You're the boss.'

'Me? I'm afraid it's a case of the blind leading the blind. But I suppose we have to rub down the woodwork, and strip the wallpaper. Which would you prefer?'

I considered. Both sounded tedious. I opted for the wallpaper. We had bought a packet of stripper and I mixed it in a bucket and began to slosh it about. Matt meanwhile started on the windowframes. He hummed cheerfully while he worked. After a while I began to tear the paper from the walls. It came away in satisfying strips and I started to enjoy myself. It was only when I was halfway round the room that it hit me like a punch in the stomach; the memory of putting that same paper on, with David. It felt as if I were burying him all over again; scrumpling him up in a damp and sticky heap on the floor, to be carried out with the rubbish. I stood very still, all satisfaction seeping away. I wanted to cry, but Matt was there, he would think me foolish. I watched him dully, sanding away with his back to me, black cord jeans covered in dust, his wavy hair shining, one brown hand braced on the windowledge. What was he doing there, rubbing off the paint that David and I had applied? Destroying my memories, intruding on my privacy so that I couldn't even cry?

Suddenly, he stopped rubbing and turned round.

'What's up?'

He crossed the room, looking concerned. I stood, my arms hanging, the epitome of dejection among the piles of paper. I hardly had the energy to answer him, yet knew I must explain.

'Memories,' I said. 'When David and I did this room, we were so full of hopes and plans.'

'I know.'

And suddenly, it seemed that he did. He held out his arms, and I went into them, putting my head on his chest and letting weak tears fall onto his sweater. He stroked my hair. It felt good, and I let myself stand there for a while, my sticky hands holding on to his sleeves. I wondered if he would kiss me, but he didn't. Finally, it was he who pulled away. He took a tissue from his jeans and wiped my eyes. His fingers were dusty. 'Blow,' he said, as if I were a child. Obediently, I blew my nose, and he dropped the tissue onto the floor.

259

'All over now?' he asked bracingly. 'Shall we get on?'

I nodded. I felt comforted, enabled, my grief acknowledged and permitted and excused. I had paid my dues to David. Now I could move on.

Two days later, we were painting the ceiling. Matt had rigged up a plank between two stepladders, and we each stood at one end, covering the ceiling with rollers. I had suggested that we try and paper it, but he hadn't been keen.

'I remember my parents doing that once,' he said. 'They nearly came to blows. Dad was up the ladder trying to stick one end, Mum was holding the other end on a broom. As fast as they stuck one end, the other one came down on their heads! I think we'll just stick to emulsion.'

I laughed at the picture he had drawn.

'How old were you? Were you helping?'

'About ten. I suspect I was just getting in the way. But I didn't like it because they were getting irritable with each other. It wasn't like them. It worried me.'

I imagined him at ten, looking rather like Josh did now with his head of gorgeous hair, his brown eyes looking worriedly at his parents.

'My mother gets impatient with my father these days,' I told him. 'I don't like it either. But I suspect it's because she's in pain. She has arthritis.'

He had nodded, as if he understood.

Now, painting the ceiling, we chatted companionably, about his time in Saudi, about Claire's children, whom he had visited recently, about Natalie and Stefan, whom, I had to confess, I wasn't missing as badly as I had feared. Then it was time to move the plank. We each climbed down our respective steps and I put my tray of paint on the floor. I laid the roller on top and flexed my shoulders to ease the ache.

'Want a rub?' Matt asked.

'That would be bliss.'

He sat down on the dustsheeted sofa, pulling me down between his knees. I gave up my aching shoulders to his strong and pummelling hands, letting my mind go into freefall. Squeeze and rub, squeeze and rub; the ache melted away, to be replaced gradually by another ache, more compelling, more difficult to ignore, so that finally I pulled away and turned to face him.

He was looking very serious. Then his face broke into a grin. 'You've got paint on your nose. Here – I'll rub it off.'

He touched my nose lightly, his eyes holding mine. Then, very slowly, he lowered his hand and brushed my lips. Without thinking, I kissed his fingers. We sat frozen for a long, pulsing moment. And then I was crushed in his arms, our mouths searching hungrily, drinking in each other's juices as if dying of thirst. His hands began to roam my body, leaving trails of desire. After a measureless time, he pulled back and smiled down at me.

'Your room, or mine?' he asked. His voice was breathy. He pushed at his glasses, as if suddenly uncertain. In answer, I took them firmly off and laid them on the sofa. Then I pulled him down towards me. We didn't make either room, but did it there and then, on the bare and dusty floor. And afterwards we rolled in the dustsheets, clinging on with joy, and we laughed and laughed.

THIRTEEN

I expected to wake up next morning with Matt beside me, but the bed was empty, with just a dent in the pillow where he had lain. On the blue flowery pillowcase there was one dark, curling hair. I touched it, gently, with my fingertips, and smiled.

Then the door opened and Matt came in, carrying a tray of coffee and toast. There was a pink rose in an eggcup, and a card from Stefan with a picture of a Swedish lake. Matt settled the tray on my knees, and climbed back into bed.

'No croissants, I'm afraid. If we were in France, I'd have gone out to buy you some.'

'Like that?' I giggled, for he was wearing only boxer shorts.

'If madam had so desired!' He kissed me on the nose, reminding me of what madam had so desired, the night before, and was in danger of wanting again.

'Steady,' I told him. 'You'll upset the coffee.'

I poured two cups and stood the pot on the bedside table. Then I picked up Stefan's card. It didn't say much, they had only just arrived at the camp site, he was getting the card off early so that it reached me before he did. The weather was hot, and there were mosquitoes.

'And he sends you best wishes,' I told Matt.

As I said it, I felt uneasy. What would Stefan think if he could see us now? I felt vaguely guilty. Our privacy had been invaded, and I felt sad that my pleasure at getting news of my son should have been blurred by other emotions.

I put the card down on the tray. 'Of course, this can't go on,' I said firmly. 'Not when the children get back.'

'Oh?' He made a disappointed face and my heart sank. Surely he wasn't going to be difficult?

But he said, 'I do understand. It would be a bit of a shock for them, particularly Natalie. But . . .' He slid his hand under the bedclothes and stroked my thigh, 'I presume I can still have visiting rights? When they're safely tucked up in bed?'

I looked into his brown eyes. They, and his roving hand, were irresistible.

'I'm sure something can be arranged. Now – how about this breakfast? Since you've gone to so much trouble.'

He withdrew his hand with an exaggerated sigh. 'Women,' he complained. 'They've got no sense of priorities.'

'Oh yes, they have,' I said teasingly. 'And when you've finished your toast, I'll show you.'

But now it was he who said firmly, 'No, we've got wallpaper to put up. We can't be dallying in bed all morning.'

'Who says?' Now it was my hand that wandered.

He gripped my wrist. 'I do. And I'm the boss.' And gratefully I allowed it to be so.

When Stefan came home, he stood in the doorway of the sitting room and stared at the expanse of cream carpet.

'That's cool. Do I need to take my shoes off?' He looked down at his grubby Reeboks and I shook my head.

'Just remember to wipe your feet. And keep them off the new loose covers.'

When Natalie arrived, she exclaimed, 'It's ace, Mum. And so tidy! Let's try and keep it this way.'

I caught Matt's eye and smiled. Natalie never gave up trying to organise me.

'And have you both had a good time?' I asked them, to be told by Stefan that camp was great, they had done abseiling

263

and canoeing and white-water rafting. But the food had been awful. 'We were starving most of the time,' he said, piling into my steak and kidney pie.

'We had brilliant food,' said Natalie.

'Well, so you should, in Paris.'

'But we were only staying in a school. We slept in dormitories. And Helen snored! I don't know how people stand it, at boarding school.'

'Did you go up the Eiffel Tower?' asked Matt. 'I remember doing that on a school trip. As a matter of fact, it's the only thing I do remember. Except the revolting lavatories.'

We all laughed, and Natalie told us about the Sacré-Coeur and Montmartre, Les Invalides, the Louvre and Versailles. And I marvelled at her, at them both, for having all these experiences without me, but it didn't hurt, not as much as I had expected, for all the while Matt's eyes were on me, and I knew that I had been having experiences of my own.

The children went back to school, and Matthew and I returned to work. I didn't mind; I enjoyed the surgery and the feeling of usefulness and importance it gave me. A new doctor had joined the team. His name was Henry Millbank and word had got round that he had just lost his wife to a brain tumour. We were thus disposed to both like and pity him, but he was very stiff and tight-lipped, buttoned up on his grief. It seemed an impertinence to commiserate, so I decided to play it his way and offer only courtesy and respect. I was in charge of his appointments, so it was important that I strike the right note from the beginning.

'Sooner you than me,' said Betty Marker. She was one of the practice nurses, a big, motherly woman who lived on her own but looked as if she should be looking after somebody. 'He looks a dry old fish.'

'Hardly old,' I corrected her. 'About fifty.'

'Well, he behaves old. And he never smiles.'

'He's bereaved! It seemed to be years before I smiled, after David died.'

'I forgot. You would understand, of course. But I still don't take to him greatly.'

'You're just put out that you can't mother him.'

She looked suddenly quite cross. 'Nonsense,' she snapped. 'He'd be the very last –'

But we were interrupted by the telephone, and I never did hear what she was going to say.

A week or so later, I received a letter from Padstow. My tenants were leaving the house, having at last decided to buy something in Wadebridge.

'I'll have to go down and look at the house when they've gone. See what sort of state it's in. Shall we all go? Make a weekend of it?'

Stefan looked doubtful. 'I'm running every weekend up to half-term.'

'Nat?'

'Not Padstow,' she said witheringly.

'But you always loved Padstow.'

'When I was a kid, maybe.'

I looked at Matt, and raised an eyebrow helplessly.

He said firmly, 'Well – I'd like to go to Padstow. I'll drive your mother. If it's just the two of us, we can go in my car.'

Stefan looked envious. 'Can we stay on our own?' he asked.

'Oh I don't know about that. Perhaps Kate can have you.'

'Oh Mum. We're not babies.'

'That's your trouble,' Natalie complained mutinously. 'You'll never let us grow up.'

'That's not true. But I'm responsible for you, and there's only me. Maybe, because of that, I take it more seriously. What do you think, Matt? Am I being unreasonable?'

He pushed at his glasses uncertainly. 'I think,' he said

eventually, 'that there's some truth in what they say. They can't come to much harm for one night. But if you'd be happier sending them to Kate's, then that's what you must do.'

I was both pleased that he had supported me, and sorry that he had supported them. But he had done his best.

'Very well, I'll ring her this evening,' I told them. 'And I don't want to hear another word about it.'

We set off on a vibrant October morning, with frost still white in the shade and the leaves burning cider-gold on the trees. I was wearing a new red padded jacket. Matt said I looked like one of the plastic tomatoes they used to have in Wimpy bars, but I didn't mind. I was happy.

Natalie had gone resignedly to Kate's, and Stefan would be returning there after his run. He was no problem; he and Dominic would undoubtedly play computer games. Kate said she'd do some baking with Natalie.

'I doubt that will go down very well. If she wants to sulk, I'd just let her.'

'Oh dear. I'm not used to mutinous girls.'

I felt guiltly, lumbering Kate with my problem child. 'Perhaps she'd like to listen to some music,' I said helpfully. 'Offer her the run of your CD player.'

'Okay. And perhaps this afternoon, some shopping.'

I looked at her dubiously. Natalie's idea of shopping was hanging round the jeans shops with her friends. But it was Kate's problem, I suddenly decided, so I said nothing. Now, bowling down the A3 with Matt, they already seemed far away. Out of sight, out of mind.

'There never was a truer saying than that,' I said.

He turned his head slightly. 'Than what?'

'Out of sight, out of mind. I thought I would be worrying about the children, but I'm not.'

He laughed. 'We've only been gone ten minutes. If I know you, they'll be on your mind all day.'

266

'No.' I looked at him with a slow smile. 'I'm going to enjoy myself. It's not often I go away for a dirty weekend.'

He took his hand from the wheel and enclosed mine. 'It's worked out rather well, hasn't it? Nice double room – no creeping about in the small hours!'

'Lovely!' I squeezed his hand and settled back contentedly. It was going to be a long ride, but the Porsche purred along, eating up the miles. Soon we were on the motorway, and the needle crept round to 90.

'You're breaking the limit,' I said warningly.

'I'll keep an eye out for the police.'

I was uneasy, though we did not seem to be the only ones. Volvos and BMWs were rocketing along in the outside lane, and a big Mercedes flashed to get past. Letting him go, Matt pulled over into the left-hand lane.

'Services coming up. Some coffee, I think. And a bun!'

'Already? We've a long way to go.'

'I'm starving. And it's still early.'

He nosed into a parking space and we got out. There was a Renault estate parked next door, piled with children and luggage. A woman was in the driver's seat, and she looked at the Porsche and then at me, and then back at the car. I read envy in her look. I remembered a pop song, once, about a woman thinking she would never, now, drive through Paris with the wind in her hair. Well, a service station on the M3 wasn't Paris. My hair hadn't been streaming behind me in the breeze, but I felt carefree enough, slamming the gleaming red door and swinging my bag onto my shoulder. I gave the woman a smile. She smiled back, and gave a little shrug of resignation as she started her engine. The children in the back had already begun to fight. I watched her go, feeling more than happy with my lot.

The sun was low in the sky when I opened the door of my little house in Padstow. It slanted across the harbour, gilding

267

the masts of the boats, but the house was in shadow. I had asked to come to the house alone, and now I stepped into the hall, bracing myself for painful recollection. But the bare boards and empty walls presented themselves as just that. I crossed into the little living room and switched on the light. Empty white-painted bookshelves round the little fireplace, darker patches on the wallpaper where pictures had hung, and a can of fly spray abandoned on the windowledge. There was nothing, here, of Colin, or David. It was an empty house where other people had dwelled.

I roamed through the house, opening cupboards, inspecting paintwork and trying switches and taps. It was shabby; the tenants certainly hadn't bothered much about interior decoration, though I had had the outside painted twice. But it was clean, and everything seemed to be in order.

I went back into the sitting room and sat on the windowseat, looking out over the harbour. Lights had come on across the water and there were not many people about. I was cold, but I didn't want to leave. For I had known as soon as I opened the front door that I had come to say goodbye.

The house had stood me in good stead. The rent had been a useful addition to my income, and I had been happy just to know it was there. But it was a responsibility too. And, in a sense, I knew that it was holding me to the past. Now, I felt strong enough to make the break. More than that, I felt an obligation to move on. I had decided to sell, but I just needed a moment with my memories. I needed to explain.

So I sat there, letting my mind rove over the past, conscious of tears sliding down my cheeks as I thought back down the long years, to the day David had first brought me to the house and his mother had kissed me and said, 'We're so happy that David has found a nice girl at last.' She was a little woman, busy and capable, who always wore an overall in the mornings, and washed and changed when she had finished her chores. I grew to love her, and Colin.

I remembered coming to them after our honeymoon, smug and sated and brown, bearing the wedding photographs, and snaps of us outside our Tuscan villa. And, later, bringing Stefan, then Natalie, to be admired and worshipped.

I imagined David, coming home from school to that little house, going up to his room where, later, he and I had squashed into a single bed, laughing and loving. He had worked at the table which, now, held Matt's CD player; which Colin had given me on that last holiday we spent together. And he had become a doctor, filling his parents with so much pride.

I remembered our walks on the cliffs, the children in the boat with Colin, his mother flouring the mackerel they caught and serving them up for supper, the chink of rigging on a breezy morning. And I knew it was over, all of it, and would never come again. But I knew, too, that I was ready. I wiped my wet cheeks with my hand and got up stiffly. I touched the seat gently. It was warm from my body, but would soon be cold, like the rest of the house. There was nothing left any more.

'Goodbye,' I called foolishly into its dark spaces, as I stood at the front door.

Then I slammed it shut, and went back to Matt.

We were staying at the Seafood Restaurant, opposite the fish market where the chef bought the fish which had given him his reputation. We had a room overlooking the river, prettily furnished with floral prints and pink shaded lamps. Matt was waiting for me, sitting in a pink velvet armchair watching the television news.

He pressed the remote control, darkening the screen.

'Okay?' He looked at me carefully and I gave him a brave smile.

'Okay. It needs a lot doing to it, if I wanted to let again. But I've decided to sell. I'll ring the agents on Monday.'

'Good. A clean break. I was hoping you'd say that.'

I looked at him in surprise. I hadn't realised he had given the matter any thought.

'What difference does it make to you?'

He reached out and pulled me down onto his lap. 'It doesn't. But it makes a difference to you. It means you're not hanging on to the past.'

'I wasn't hanging on. It was an investment, a source of income.'

But I knew he was speaking the truth. I put my arm round his shoulders, not wishing to seem argumentative. 'Anyway, that's all over now. I'll invest the money somewhere else. I'll really feel quite rich! And to celebrate, this trip's on me. The room, the dinner. Everything.'

'Right.' He reached out and patted the bed. It was covered with a pink sprigged spread, and piled with cushions. It looked inviting. Matthew, smiling so close, looked inviting. 'What about another celebration?' he suggested. 'Before dinner.'

'Well,' I said teasingly. 'I suppose it will warm me up.' And I slid off his lap and onto the bed, opening up my arms.

Later, we sat in the bright and airy restaurant, with its plants and posters, and looked into each other's eyes and laughed a lot and I thought, Padstow will have other memories for me now, and it felt good.

Winter came early after a golden October, bringing November fogs and frosts and a dull, drizzling damp. Nobody went to look at the house in Cornwall.

'It's the wrong time of year,' the agents said reassuringly. 'Give it until next spring, when the holidaymakers arrive. Someone will decide they want to live here. Or they'll want a holiday home. It's reasonably priced. You'll sell eventually.'

And with that I had to be content, though I didn't like the

thought of the house standing alone and unloved, cold and damp, all through the winter months.

My consolation was Matt, who came to my bed each night, and left in the small hours for his own room. It was an unsatisfactory arrangement, and one which I daily expected him to rebel against. But in his usual cheerful manner he seemed to accept the constraints of our relationship. Until one dreadful night at the beginning of December, when we were woken at two o'clock by the door to my room opening, and the light from the landing flooding in.

I turned over to face the light, and to my horror Natalie was standing in the doorway.

'I've got awful period pains,' she whined. 'Will you get me a hot-water bottle?'

I scrambled out of bed, eager to hustle her out of the room. But she reached out and switched on the light. I heard her gasp, and her hand flew to her mouth.

'Mum?' There was query in her eyes, and a momentary panic.

'Natalie. I'm sorry . . .' I didn't know what I was sorry about. That Matt was in my bed, that she had had to find out like this?

She didn't say anything, simply staring in bewilderment at Matt's untidy head raised from the pillows. He reached out for his glasses and jammed them on, but he didn't say anything. After all, what was there to say?

I pushed her gently out of the door and closed it behind us.

'Go back to bed, I'll bring you a bottle,' I said. 'Do you want a hot drink?'

She shook her head. 'No. I feel sick.'

I stared at her, feeling accused. 'Get back to bed,' I said again, ineffectually. 'I'll bring the bottle, and we'll talk.'

I was trembling as I filled the kettle. She had looked so shocked, so young. What had I done to her? Feeling ashamed, I leaned against the draining board listening to the kettle's rising hum. I filled a bottle in a red furry jacket, and hugged it close for comfort. I took paracetamol from the cupboard, and a glass of water, and, reluctantly, made my way up to Natalie's bedroom.

She was curled in a ball under the duvet, staring with stricken eyes which met mine with a huge question, then slid away. I handed her the bottle and she pressed it against her stomach with a little moan. I sympathised, remembering the pain of my own teenage years, before I had had my babies. Useless to tell her that it would be so much better after that. My mother had tried that approach, to be met by the claim that I was never, ever, going to submit myself to labour pains. I passed her two tablets and the glass of water, which she drank leaning up on one elbow. Then I sat on the end of the bed, and rubbed her feet in the soothing way she had always loved.

'I'm sorry if you've had a shock. I didn't want you to find out that way.'

'So – when were you going to tell us? How long has it been going on?'

'A few weeks.' Somehow, that sounded better than months.

'Do you love him?'

I hesitated. It was something that I had asked myself, many times. More importantly, I needed to tell her something that she could understand. Belatedly, I realised that I needed to set her some sort of example.

I began, 'Sometimes, darling, when you're older, you don't actually have to love someone. I like Matt. I'm fond of him, and he's very good to me. To all of us. And I was tired of being alone. Can you understand that?'

'Are you going to marry him?'

'Would you like that?' I digressed.

She shrugged, her shoulders thin above the duvet. 'I'd

never thought about it. Matt doesn't seem like a father exactly.'

'Well, we've never talked about marriage. But we enjoy being together. I enjoy us all being together. Don't you?'

'Yes. But you don't have to go to bed with him.' I could see her mind chasing round the implications. 'You've always told me that it's important to love somebody. Not to go with just anybody.' Her eyes were confused, and accusing, and I quailed inside.

'Matt isn't just anybody. Believe me, I do try and practise what I preach. But it's different for me. You're just starting out. The rules are different, I guess, when you're young. I know it's hard for you to understand that. But please try.'

She turned over, stretching out flat and closing her eyes.

'I think I want to go to sleep now.'

I reached out and put a hand on her shoulder. 'Please understand, Natalie. It's no threat to you, or Stefan. Just be glad that it makes me happy. Please?'

Her eyes remained shut, and she made no reply.

'Forgive me,' I said desperately, squeezing her shoulder.

Her eyes flew open, and they were filled with tears.

'Oh Mum!'

She sat up, pushing back the duvet and opening her arms. Thankfully, I pulled her close to me, pressing my face into her fuzzy hair. We rocked together for a long moment, the closeness a soothing balm. When she pulled away, her eyes were dry, but very bright.

'I do want you to be happy,' she said.

'Thank you.'

She slid down into the bed, arranging the hot-water bottle. As I let myself out of the room, she said clearly, 'Are you going to tell Stefan – or am I?'

When I got to my own room I was frozen, and longing for the comfort of Matt in the bed. But he had gone. If ever there was a case of shutting the stable door, this was it. I felt hurt. I needed his reassurance. I needed to tell him what Natalie had said. What's more, I needed to know what we were going to do now. I contemplated going to his room to talk, but reasoned that if he had wanted to face it, he would have stayed. Miserably, I hunched under the covers, drawing up my cold feet and wishing I had a hot-water bottle too, but lacking the energy to go and make up one.

At breakfast, Natalie was pale but calm, greeting Matt as if nothing had happened and favouring me with a thin, nervous smile. Stefan was out running. When he came in, she gave me a challenging look before going upstairs to get ready for school.

Stefan unzipped his tracksuit jacket and sprawled at the table, breathing fast. 'Beat my own best time today,' he said, with a huge grin.

'Well done.' It was Matt, being bracing and cheerful. We needed to talk, but there would be no chance before the evening. I poured Matt a cup of coffee and tried not to meet his eye. For the first time, I felt embarrassed with him. It was as if we were complicit in some shameful crime. And I felt that I alone had had to take the blame. I wanted him to acknowledge some responsibility, to take some share in its resolution. But there was nothing to be done now. Stefan was chattering away, blissfully unaware. But he was nearly seventeen. He had had girlfriends. Surely, he would understand?

When I arrived at the surgery, I felt fretful and tired, and it obviously showed, for Betty, the nurse, said, with concern in her voice, 'You look all in. Aren't you well?'

'I had a broken night. Natalie was upset about something.'

'Oh. Poor kid. Boyfriend trouble?'

'Something like that.'

'I'll make you a coffee.'

I looked at her gratefully. She was a caring soul, warm and soothing. I guessed her patients must love her. For the briefest moment I felt I could confide in her, but now wasn't the moment. Phones were ringing and patients were already arriving for appointments. Now wasn't the moment for coffee either.

'I'll wait for my break, thanks all the same,' I told her, and picked up the telephone almost eagerly, ready to absorb myself in someone else's problems rather than my own.

It was nearly nine o'clock that evening before Matt and I could talk. Stefan had been watching television; now he departed to his room to do his homework. I sat at one end of the sofa, Matt at the other. Somehow, it seemed imperative to keep space between us, to let the light of reason in.

'Why didn't you wait for me?' I pitched in, sounding aggrieved, which I was.

'Panic, I suppose. And it did occur to me that Nat might want to come into bed with you for a bit of reassurance.'

'Hardly. I think my bed has become a den of iniquity.'

He looked at me worriedly, pushing at his glasses.

'Did she take it badly?'

'She didn't say much. It was how she looked. So shocked. Betrayed. I felt I had let her down. After all the bracing little talks we've had, about self-control, and saving herself.'

He folded his arms, then unfolded them again, and smoothed the pile of his corduroy jeans. 'What did you tell her?'

'I told her it was different for me. That I was lonely, and it was good to find someone to . . . love.' I said the last word experimentally, with an upward lift to my voice. I waited, nervously.

His eyes met mine with a startled impact. Then a crooked, awkward smile pulled at his mouth. 'I'm glad you said that,' he said quietly. 'Because I think we do, don't you? Love each other?'

I nodded. It was so easy, really. And so comfortable, so safe.

We were still sitting apart, but he reached out a hand, and I took it. 'So, I think I should move into your room, don't you? No more shillyshallying about?'

I nodded again, powerless to make any decision of my own. Then I remembered Stefan.

'Will you tell Stefan? Sort of man to man?'

He didn't look very keen. 'Don't you think it would be better coming from you? You're his mother.'

I pushed down a flicker of disappointment. I had thought we were going to be a partnership. But I told myself I was asking too much. Matt wasn't their father. The responsibility still lay with me. I withdrew my hand and stood up.

'Well, no point in putting it off,' I said, making for the stairs. I knocked at Stefan's door.

'Who is it?'

'Me. Mum.'

'Come in.'

He was seated at his desk, books piled around him. He was working for his A levels, and taking them very seriously. I apologised for interrupting him.

'No hassle. Sit down.'

I sat on the bed, in a tiny space between his school bag, various CDs and a pile of computer magazines. I opened my mouth to complain at the state of his room, and shut it again. After all, I wanted him on my side.

I spoke out quickly. 'I wanted to tell you about me and Matt. We've decided to live together.'

He leaned back against his desk, long legs stretched in front of him, his hands clasped on his chest. It was like sitting opposite a doctor, and for a moment I thought of David, wondering what he would have made of the situation. Would he have understood? If he was still there somewhere, did he forgive me? I had to believe that he would. For the moment, Stefan's approval was more important.

'I know,' he said, surprising me.

'How do you know?' I stammered. 'We've only just decided.'

'Natalie told me. On the way home from school. Well, she said you were sleeping together, which is the same thing, isn't it?'

'You know perfectly well that it isn't.'

'So, okay, you're going to live together. What does that mean?'

I was confused. 'I suppose it means that we have some commitment. And that Matt will be moving into my room, and we'll be a sort of . . . family, I suppose.' It didn't sound very convincing.

I was shocked when he said, 'I hope you don't want me to think of Matt as my father.'

'No. But why not, if you don't mind my asking?'

'Because he's not the fatherly sort. He doesn't treat me like a son. And I wouldn't want him to. He's too young, for a start.'

His words went home, reminding me of something which I always tried to forget. The seven-year difference in our ages.

'He's not too young for me,' I told him defensively.

'Fair enough. If he makes you happy. I'll be gone soon anyway, you must do what you think's best.'

I felt bleak, dismissed and redundant, but I suspected I should be grateful that he had made it so easy. I wanted to thank him, but felt that that would be undignified. So I stood up with a smile, said something foolish about him getting on with his work and not staying up too late, went out, and closed the door.

Matt was on the landing, between my room and his.

'Just taking a few things across,' he said, with a cheerful

smile that convinced me that, after all, everything was all right.

There were to be ten of us for Christmas that year; my parents, the children and me and Matt, and Claire, Ian and their children.

I wanted it to be really special, and Matt entered into the spirit of the thing like the child he was at heart. He bought from the garden centre a tree so tall that it had to be delivered, and we had to cut the top off to get it into the sitting room.

'What a waste,' cried Natalie, eyeing the mini tree that was lying on the ground. 'Can I have that one in my room?'

'We'll need more decorations,' I said when we had brought it indoors. 'We've never had such a big tree.'

'No worries,' said Matt, producing two bulging carrier bags. 'Baubles, tinsel, ribbons, even more lights. I think we can spare some for Natalie.'

She dived into one of the bags, pulling out shiny, gleaming, twinkling glories and spreading them on the floor. 'Can I have all the pink ones?' she asked. 'I fancy a tasteful tree, like you see in shop windows.'

For my part, I preferred the red and gold and silver ones, so I agreed happily. Matt potted up the little tree and carried it to her room, where she started at once to decorate it. Downstairs, Stefan and Matt draped the lights round the branches, winding tinsel round the flex. I had dragged our old decorations out of the loft and opened the box with its usual sentimental memories of Christmas past. There were gaudy glass birds with silky tails, strings of silver beads, delicate glass icicles – things my mother had thrown out as being tawdry. There were glossy red apples and pears that David had bought, and little packets wrapped in gold paper and tied with red ribbon, made by the children long ago one wet December afternoon. The three of us loaded the branches with every last one of the goodies, while Handel's *Messiah* played on the record player and a cold wind got up outside, making the fire smoke. When we had finished, we stood back and Matt slipped his hand round my waist and kissed me. I kissed him back, eyeing Stefan over his shoulder. But he took no notice. It was good to be able to be so open, so relaxed together. I reached out my hand to Stefan and pulled him against me.

'It's going to be a good Christmas,' I said. 'Isn't it?'

I very much wanted his agreement, his complicity in our new togetherness, but all he said was, 'Yes, Mum, if you say so. Can I go round to Simon's now? He's got a new CD I want to hear.'

I let him go. After all I still had Matt. And Natalie, who had come downstairs, and was playing 'Silent Night' on the piano, so beautifully that it brought foolish tears to my eyes.

I cooked an enormous turkey. Helping me ease it from the oven to the serving plate, Matt said, 'I hope you're not going to ask me to carve.'

'No, I thought I'd ask Dad. He always has.'

The plate was heavy and I let him carry it in, following with potatoes and vegetables, sausages and bacon and cranberry sauce. My big new family were already seated and I felt a glow of satisfaction. Zoe, perched on cushions and wearing a red velvet dress, was sitting between Claire and Ian. Josh was talking computers with Stefan. My father, at the head of the table, was sharpening the carving knife. Mother, watchfully, followed Matt with her eyes as he went round the table pouring wine.

'Pinny, Mum,' whispered Natalie, who was sitting next to me.

I whipped off my apron apologetically and sat down. Little Zoe was staring excitedly at the turkey.

'A b-b-b-big ch-ch-icken!' she managed to exclaim.

'No, darling, it's a turkey.' Claire tied a napkin round the child's neck and, meeting my eyes, smiled.

Dad began to carve, and the festive meal proceeded. When everyone was served, Dad raised his glass of wine and said, 'A toast to the cook!' and everyone drank, and I beamed happily at them all, catching Matt's eye as I did so, and he winked. He was sitting opposite my mother. When I turned my head, she was looking at him appraisingly. She hadn't seen Matt since the summer, and I knew she was no fool. I also knew there would be questions.

They came as she helped me with the washing up.

She was at the sink, rubber gloves that she had brought with her on her hands, rinsing glasses under the hot tap.

'Tell me, Julia,' she began. 'Is there something going on between you and Matthew?'

'Matt, Mother. No one calls him Matthew.'

She pursed her lips. 'I don't like abbreviations. I hate it when you call Natalie "Nat".'

'But it's his choice.'

She put the last glass on the drainer, and tipped a load of cutlery into the bowl. 'You haven't answered my question,' she persisted.

I polished a glass for an unnecessarily long time while I considered my reply.

'It depends what you mean by "going on",' I tried at last.

'You know what I mean. Are you having a relationship?'

'You mean am I sleeping with him?'

She gave a little impatient tut, careful not to look at me. 'Of course you would put it like that. I'm more interested in what's behind it. Do you care for him? Does he care for you?'

'Yes, Mother, we care for each other.' She made no answer, but stood knives carefully in the drainer. 'That's good, isn't it?' I asked her. 'I mean, aren't you pleased?'

'It depends. I don't think it's a very good example to the children, if you are sleeping with him. And I'm not so sure about Matt. He seems very young.'

'He's thirty-five.'

Now she turned and looked at me. 'Well, just let's say he doesn't always behave like it.'

I felt a spurt of irritation. What did she know about it?

'He's fun, Mother. He keeps me young. He makes me laugh, and he makes me happy. And the children have no problem with it, no problem at all. So please don't interfere.'

She turned again, her pink gloved hands gripping the edge of the sink. Her face was flushed. 'I don't call it interfering, I call it concern for your happiness.'

'Well,' I snapped, 'I am happy, so just be pleased for me.'

We were staring crossly at each other, speechless and, for my part, upset that our lovely Christmas should have come to this, when Dad came into the kitchen carrying the remains of the Christmas pudding.

'Lovely pudding, Julia. Where shall I put it?'

I gestured vaguely to the cluttered table. 'Find a space somewhere,' I said abstractedly.

He moved a pile of vegetable dishes, put the pudding down, then eyed us curiously. My mother was still holding the sink, looking upset. 'What's up?' he said.

'Julia thinks I'm interfering. But I'm only concerned about her. And the children. She has to think of them.'

He turned his gaze on me. 'So, what's all this about?'

I sighed. 'It's about me and Matt. Mother doesn't approve.'

'Of what?'

My mother said, 'They're what I believe is called in today's parlance "an item".'

Dad looked surprised, and then delighted. 'Well,' he said, 'I should have guessed. You look better than you've looked for years. You've put on weight. It suits you.'

'Don't tell me!'

'Nonsense. It must be contentment.' He came across and gave me a hug. 'Well I'm delighted for you anyway. I've always hoped you'd find someone else. It's been a long time.'

I silently blessed him. As for my mother, there was nothing I could do. She would come round, in time, or she wouldn't. She began to wash the plates in silence, and in silence, I dried them, while laughter emanated from the sitting room and I felt that Christmas was going on without me.

Shortly into the New Year, Stefan announced that he wanted to have his ear pierced.

I shouldn't have been surprised; I knew it was the fashion. But I had always congratulated myself that Stefan stood out against the crowd; that with his interest in sport, in keeping fit, he would not have been tempted by something which I privately thought effete. Without thinking, I reacted more violently than I should. And, for the first time, I found myself at loggerheads with my son.

'No way,' was my immediate reaction. 'You're not punching holes in any part of your body.'

He looked taken aback, startled by the fury of my response.

'Okay. There's no need to go ballistic. And I'm not going to punch the hole, I'd have it done properly, at the jeweller's.'

'And how much does that cost?'

'Five ninety-five. And that includes a gold stud. I've got the money.'

'Well, you can keep the money. You're not having it done.'

He looked obstinate, doggedly pressing on. 'Why not? Give me one good reason.'

'I don't like the sort of boys who wear earrings. They're

dropouts – layabouts. I don't want you to be one of them.'

'But, Mum, all my friends have them. You like Simon. And Ben and Dominic have them, and they're younger than me.'

'The twins?' So Kate had been prevailed upon. But apparently not.

'They did their own, with a safety pin.'

'What?' I was horrified. 'Is that safe? I hope you're not thinking of doing that.'

'No. I told you.'

All this time, Matt and Natalie had been listening in silence. Now Matt shocked me by saying, 'I can't see what you've got against it. All the boys do it, it's trendy. If I were younger, I'd do it myself.'

I couldn't believe what I was hearing. I had been counting on his support, and now he was siding with Stefan. If that was what he felt, at least he could have had the sense to keep quiet.

Then Natalie joined in. 'Let him, Mum. It's no big deal.'

I turned on her with an anger which was meant for Matt. 'Don't interfere, Natalie. I'm not going to be persuaded. I don't want Stefan tampering with his body, and that's final.'

There was a mutinous silence round the table. I picked at my food without enthusiasm, feeling their united censure. Finally I picked up my plate and went to the sink. Running water furiously into the bowl, I wondered just what it was that made me oppose my son. Usually, I was happy to give him everything he wanted. I trusted his judgement. I respected him. If he wanted an earring, then was it so very dreadful?

And I realised that what really worried me was the mutilation of the perfection of his flesh. He was sixteen, yet he was still my baby, my first-born, complete and unsullied and pure. I didn't want somebody making a hole in his ear. I had never had it done myself. It seemed a shocking violation. As I noisily washed the dishes, I heard the children slam out of the room without helping. Resigned to being the villain of the piece, I turned to clear the table, and saw Matt still sitting there.

'And you could have supported me,' I flared. 'Or if you couldn't, then you should have kept quiet.'

He had the grace to look discomfited, but he still said, defiantly, 'But I think you're wrong. And you run the risk of him doing it anyway.'

'Stefan wouldn't. He likes to have my approval.'

'But he's growing up. He's starting to make his own decisions.'

'Then why did he ask me in the first place?'

Matt spread his hands helplessly. 'Okay, okay. I'm sorry.' He gave me a disarming smile, but I was not to be won. I brusquely handed him a tea towel, and marched out of the kitchen. I felt very much alone, and I didn't like it.

Over the following weeks, Stefan set out to undermine me. He went on and on, so that in the end I became angry.

'Just stop it,' I shouted. 'When you're eighteen, you can do what you like. Until then, you do as I say.'

I didn't like it, falling out with my son. I didn't like his crestfallen face. And I knew, then, that he would win in the end. It was just a question of choosing my moment, of not losing face. His seventeenth birthday was coming up. Perhaps I would surprise him. But until then I clung obstinately to my position.

Natalie, too, was moody and evasive. She had started neglecting her piano practice, and hanging out with her friends. If I asked her what she was doing, she flared up. 'Mum, why must you always be asking me about things? We just play music, and talk. You wouldn't understand.'

And she would flounce off, slamming the door behind her.

I quietly despaired. Matt, when I applied to him for help, professed himself to be ignorant of teenagers. He advocated letting them both have their head. Anything for an easy life. When I told him it wasn't easy, he said that I didn't seem to have much choice.

And then everything changed, for Matt got a job. A proper job, with an oil company, in its laboratories out near Heathrow Airport.

I was inordinately proud of him.

'You were wasted at that garden centre. Will you wear a white coat?'

He threw back his head and laughed. 'Is that so very important to you? Yes, if you want to know. A white coat, instead of a brown one.'

'And it will be more money?'

'Considerably more. And we're going to have a treat, to celebrate.'

I was as excited as a child. 'A treat? What? Where?'

'How about Paris? On Eurostar. We'll travel first class, spend a couple of nights in a hotel, walk under the bridges like proper lovers.'

I did a little dance of sheer happiness. 'Sounds fantastic! I've never been. I shall want to go up the Eiffel Tower. And to the Louvre. Do you think we can leave the children on their own?'

'We'll wait till after Stefan's birthday. I should think they'll be all right.'

I hesitated. 'Do you think we should take them with us?' I didn't want to, but my maternal instinct was still strong.

'No way. This is our treat. We didn't have a holiday last year.'

'True. But I shall feel guilty all the same.'

'We'll bring them presents.'

I was silent, thinking. Then I said, 'And I'll let Stefan have his ear pierced for his birthday.' And I knew that he had won.

We stayed at a little hotel, The Manoir, on the Boulevard St-Germain opposite the Café des Deux Magots; according to the guidebook, once the haunt of Jean-Paul Sartre and Simone de Beauvoir. We went there for coffee, and found it ridiculously overpriced, as was the lunch we ate on the Champs-Élysées, sitting on the pavement in chilly spring sunshine watching smart Parisians parading themselves. But, as Matt said, 'It's only money, after all.'

Then we walked. For two days we walked. Out to Montmartre with its paintings and the Sacré-Coeur, round the Louvre to see the *Mona Lisa*, under the Arc de Triomphe with its eternal memorial flame, along the Left Bank with our arms entwined, stopping to kiss under every bridge. On the last morning, we went up the Eiffel Tower and Matt took my photograph leaning against the parapet with the Sacré-Coeur gleaming whitely in the distance. Then we stood silently, looking at the view, Matt with his arms round me so that I could feel him breathing quietly against my back. I felt very happy.

After a while, I said, 'So – what now?'

'Now,' he said, 'we have to go and catch our train. And when we get back, I think we should get married. Don't you?'

PART FOUR

FOURTEEN

I read Matt's letter out loud in a flat, bleak, final tone, for that was the tone of his words.

'Julia – I can't go through with it. I'm sorry. Forgive me. Matthew.'

'Matthew?' I cried. 'Why did he sign himself Matthew?'

We were sitting round the kitchen table – the children, my parents and myself, on the day I was supposed to have been married. Stefan was holding my hand. Dad had his arm round the back of my chair in a helpless gesture of comfort. My mother was crying quietly, looking pinched and shocked.

'Don't, Nana,' said Natalie, who looked near to tears herself, bewildered and hurting. She was mouthing her pendant, and for once I understood.

Mother said in an upset voice, 'I can't help it, and I'm not going to apologise. We thought, at last, everything was turning out all right.' She sniffed, and blew her nose on an inadequate lace hanky. The sort one takes to weddings, I thought idly, though at least she hadn't turned up in her wedding finery, but wore a sensible tweed skirt and a Viyella blouse. 'But I'm not surprised. He never struck me as very responsible.'

'Mum! That doesn't help.'

'No, Eleanor,' my father said. 'There's no point in running the man down. It won't make Julia feel any better.'

'But what can one say about a man who walks out on a girl on her wedding day? No one treats my daughter like that and gets away with it.'

'So?' asked Dad reasonably. 'What do you intend to do about it?'

She looked at him as if she hated him, but it was Matt she hated. I was touched at her concern, in a distracted, distant way that seemed to have nothing to do with me.

'Well,' I said flatly. 'It was nice while it lasted.'

It had lasted only a week since Paris; time to get a licence, to buy a new pink suit and a pair of wedding rings.

Time for Matt to change his mind.

I sat, stupefied, at the table, while my father sensibly suggested we try to eat something, and went to the fridge where he stood looking in, rather helplessly, until Natalie took pity on him and fished out cheese and tomatoes and cut thick slices of bread. Stefan put the kettle on. My mother sat on, opposite me, powerless to help herself, let alone me. I wondered where Matt was, whether he was eating lunch, whether he was feeling happy, now that he had shed his responsibilities. When I had rung Claire, she had burst into tears and said angrily, 'Well, he'd better not come here, that's all I can say.' But I couldn't be sure. Blood was thicker than water.

And where, after all, could he go? Natalie had said he had taken a bag. I hadn't trusted myself to look into his room, at the many scattered possessions he must have left behind. But in the months we had lived together, his things had spread all over the house. There were motoring magazines on the coffee table, a half-read thriller by the bed. His clothes were in the linen basket, and amongst the pile of ironing on the washing machine, I could see the sleeve of his plaid wool shirt – limp, creased, unbearably empty. He was going to be impossible to forget. From the depths of my anguish, I moaned silently, 'Oh no, not again.' I had been through all this before. I doubted my strength to do it again.

Dad made me a sandwich, and urged me to eat, but I felt

sick at the sight of it and shook my head, pressing my lips together like a rebellious child.

'Well, have some tea at least.'

Stefan put a mug in front of me and I closed my hands round it, shivering. I guessed that I was in shock. I wanted only to crawl into bed and never get out again. The future was a bleak pool that I must swim across, endlessly, with no shore in sight. It was too soon for the empowering vigour of anger; I felt only grief. And humiliation. I had not, after all, been enough. I brought with me too many responsibilities, or that was how I chose to see it. I could not bear the thought that he had never, actually, loved me.

Everyone else was making strenuous efforts to eat. I felt a deep pity for them that I should have inflicted this on them all. This need for silent compassion, and shared rejection, and angry recrimination.

And I burst out, 'I'm so sorry.'

'Sorry?' exclaimed Dad. 'What have you got to be sorry about?'

'All this mess. For letting you down. For being a failure.'

'You're not a failure. Matt's the failure. He's the one who's let you down, let us all down.'

But now the tears would come, flooding hotly down my cheeks and over my fingers as I brushed them away. I put my head on the table and cried with ugly, racking sobs.

I heard Natalie cry, 'Mum!' and then I felt arms round my shoulders. It was my mother.

'Oh Julia. Baby. Let it all out, you'll feel better.'

Something in me responded. It was like it had been when I was a child, fallen from my bike or wailing with earache. The realisation that she was crying too was like a balm, and I sat up and let her rock me, back and forth, against her Viyella'd chest, as if I were a little girl, and nothing, really, could hurt me.

*　　*　　*

291

'Don't you think it would be better if you came back with us tonight?'

Dad was trying to be practical. He had telephoned the hotel where, I had belatedly remembered, we were to spend our wedding night. Now he stood before me, looking weary and rather old in his tweed jacket and woollen tie.

'Do come, Julia. All of you. We can't leave you alone.'

I shook my head. If I left the house, I would still have to come back and face the emptiness. Besides, Matt might call. Or return, to collect his things. I needed to talk to him. I needed explanations.

'Well, we could stay with you.'

'No, Dad. The spare room's full of Matt's stuff. And Mum likes her own bed. And you've nothing with you. I'll be all right.'

They looked doubtful, but they also looked exhausted. They needed to go home, to recoup in privacy.

'You go home,' I urged. 'I'll talk to you tomorrow. I've got the children.'

I looked at Natalie and Stefan and they smiled bravely. What it cost them, I didn't know.

Reluctantly, my parents took their leave. Mother kissed me, her lips dry, her tears and demonstrations over. 'Take care, dear. We'll be thinking of you.'

Dad hugged me, hard and briefly. He sounded choked when he said, 'That's my girl,' and squeezed my hand. I watched them go, noticing for the first time the Porsche-shaped space on the drive. I supposed, numbly, that it was the beginning of a pain that I was going to have to learn to live with. It had been fun, all of it. Now, it was over. And I was going to miss it.

We sat round, the children and I, talking it over.

'How could he do it, Mum? Didn't he like us?'

'I'm sure it had nothing to do with you, Nat. This was

between Matt and me. He just got carried away in Paris, offered something he couldn't give.'

But I was not so sure. If I was honest, I realised that Matt had never really taken any responsibility for the children. In the past, it hadn't mattered. But if he had become my husband, I would have had expectations. Maybe he had expectations of himself, and realised he couldn't meet them.

'I'm sorry,' I said to them. 'I know you liked having Matt around.'

Stefan took my hand in his big strong one. 'We always managed before, we'll manage again. Only, now I suppose everyone will feel sorry for me again.'

I turned to him with a question on my face.

'My friends always feel sorry for me because my father's dead. I hate that. Heaps of them have parents who are divorced, but that's not the same. At least they have fathers, they see them sometimes.'

'So you felt that when I married Matt, you would somehow have gained something? Been the same as everyone else? Oh Stefan, I'm so sorry.'

He shrugged, withdrawing his hand.

'I don't think I would ever have thought of Matt as a father. But he was fun to have around. And I liked the car.' He looked embarrassed at so trite a confession. 'Well, I mean, I liked seeing you go in the car. I felt you deserved it.'

I got up and put some coal on the fire, standing over it for a moment, feeling the welcome warmth on my cheeks. 'Don't apologise,' I said eventually. 'I know you liked the car. We all did. But we have our own car. And you can get a licence now, I'll give you some lessons.'

I turned, but he did not look as delighted as I had expected.

'Matt was going to teach me,' was all he said, flatly. I felt a deep despair, and the first glimmerings of a healthy fury. How dare Matt play fast and loose with my children's feelings? How dare he renege on his promises?

How dare he leave us alone again?

When they had gone to bed, I rang Kate.

'Julia! How are you? I'm so bloody angry.'

'I'm in pieces,' I admitted. 'Can you come round? I know it's late . . .'

'I'm on my way. I'll bring a bottle.'

She arrived in five minutes, clutching a bottle of red wine. Looking at me appraisingly she said, 'You look as if you could do with this. Have you eaten?'

I shook my head.

'Cheese? Biscuits?'

I nodded, and let her go through to the kitchen, sitting passively on the sofa with my hands between my knees, staring at the floor, at a stain on the new cream carpet. I thought idly that I would have to get some carpet shampoo. Sometime, in the trackless space that was the future.

When Kate came back, with the cheeseboard and a tin of biscuits, I realised that I was so hungry that I was beginning to tremble. Gratefully, I helped myself while she poured the wine. I crammed the biscuits into my mouth with a sort of desperate appetite, while a little voice in my head murmured something about comfort eating, and I wondered if, now, I would simply eat and eat, and get fatter and fatter, and realised that if I did, there would be nobody to care.

Kate sat down opposite me, her glass held in pink-tipped fingers. Her silver bangles clanked at her wrist. I was still wearing the old sweatshirt and jeans I had got up in. My pink suit hung untouched in my wardrobe, the hairdresser had been cancelled, my hair was unkempt. I took huge gulps of wine and stared at Kate speechlessly. There was so much to say, and yet nothing.

She took a drink, and wiped her lips with a tissue.

'The bastard,' she said quietly. 'If he couldn't stand the heat, he shouldn't have come into the kitchen.'

I raised a hand to stop her, but let it drop, for I realised that I agreed. We had been going along very nicely before. Why did he have to suggest marriage? I had never asked for it, never put any pressure on him.

In my confusion I asked Kate, 'Why did he bother? Why didn't he just leave things as they were?'

'You tell me. Paris perhaps. Carried away with the magic of the place.'

'Well, why did he have to go? We could have cancelled the wedding. I wouldn't have minded.' I emptied my glass. The wine was already going to my head, making it swim. I took a piece of cheese to steady myself, but as I swallowed, my throat clenched and I knew I was going to cry.

'I'm going to miss him, Kate,' I wailed weakly. 'How am I going to bear it, again?'

She looked at me worriedly. 'You will.' But she sounded far from certain.

'Tell me,' Kate said after a long silence, during which she had stared rather helplessly into the fire while I wept and mopped my eyes. 'Were you in love with him? I mean, was it like David? Only . . .' She hesitated, looking embarrassed. 'Maybe I'm speaking out of turn, only it didn't seem so to me.'

I stared at her, astonished. Deep down a little coil of realisation began to wind its way to the surface, but I said firmly, 'I loved him, Kate. Matt's a very lovable man. I always felt happy with him. Is that so bad?'

'But,' she persisted, '*in love*? There is a difference. I don't have to tell you that.'

I didn't answer. 'Only you see, if you weren't, then this isn't really a tragedy. You could call it a lucky escape.'

So, I thought, she's only trying to make me feel better. But something undeniable was still struggling upwards, something I had been keeping hidden for a long time, something that had always threatened to spoil things, but now might, actually, help.

I put down my empty glass. I felt woozy and foolish, but also clear-headed for the first time that day, maybe for the first time for a long time.

I spoke hesitantly, but with a growing sense of relief.

'You know, you may be right. I'm not in love with him. Not in the starry-eyed, running through fields of poppies, kind of way. I tried to tell myself this didn't matter, at my age. It just felt so good to be loved and wanted – to be part of a couple again. I was sure we could make a go of it. I got carried away with Matt's enthusiasm. And my parents were so pleased . . .' I looked at her, aghast. 'What was I thinking of, Kate?'

She reached across and took my hand. 'I think,' she said, 'you were thinking of yourself. And there's nothing wrong with that. But was it fair to Matt?'

'I thought it was what he wanted.'

'But perhaps, in the end, he guessed?'

I shook my head in bewilderment. 'God, I hope not. But maybe that's why . . .'

She nodded. 'Maybe.'

We stared into each other's eyes for a while, wondering. Then she said, 'Do you feel better now?'

I thought for a bit. Then, 'A little,' I told her. 'But it's not going to stop me missing what we had. We could have gone on like that indefinitely. I don't want to be alone.'

'Nonsense.' She got up, briskly, her bangles jingling as she smoothed her skirt. 'It seems to me you've always managed very well alone. And you've got the children.'

'They're going to miss him terribly.'

'They'll get used to it.'

I walked with her to the door. She turned and kissed me.

'Get some sleep. It will seem better in the morning. Bring the children over to lunch – don't be alone.'

I thought unwillingly of the empty bed, and realised it hadn't been made since Matt had fled it so precipitously

296

that morning. My heart quailed. When Kate had driven off, I gritted my teeth and went up to the bedroom. Without looking, without thinking, I seized the crumpled sheet and pillowcases and stuffed them into the linen basket. I made up the bed with clean linen, setting my pillows in the centre as I had been used to do, tossing the others into what had been Matthew's room. In the light from the landing, I saw the wardrobe door standing open, his clothes, which he had never moved into mine, still hanging there. His CD player stood on David's table. A pair of shoes was discarded by the bed. It was as if he had never left. He would certainly have to come back. Perhaps I could persuade him to stay. We had been good together, too good to waste. I didn't want to be his wife, but I realised as I lay between the chilly sheets that I still wanted to be his lover.

My problems with Natalie really began after that. For the first two days, she was loving and thoughtful, treating me like an invalid, practising the piano without being asked, doing everything she could to please. But on Tuesday night, she said she was going round to her friend Helen's house to do her homework.

I couldn't really object. She had done her bit, and our house wasn't the most cheerful place to be. I let her go, with instructions to be back by ten. When it got to half-past, I was beyond being fidgety, and getting cross. When she finally came in at nearly eleven, I snapped at her angrily, and she flew off the handle in the old familiar way, saying she wasn't a child any more. When I asked her where she'd been she simply said, 'Helen's, I told you,' and slammed up to her room.

On Thursday, it was the same. 'I'm taking my homework to Helen's,' she said after supper.

'Why can't Helen come here?'

'Because they've got the Internet. We look things up.'

'What about your practice?'

'I'll do it in the morning.'

'Well, you'd better be home early. I mean it. If not, you won't be going out at the weekend.'

This time, she was home at ten past ten. She looked flushed, and didn't kiss me good night, merely peering through the door to let me know she was in, then going up to her room. I could hear her moving about for a long time, and longed to go up and talk to her, but I couldn't face her closed face and evasive eyes. Miserably, I went to bed, wishing I had someone to share my worries with. Matt, I realised, would have been no good but at least he could have given me a cuddle.

At work, I had had to explain that I was not, after all, a married woman. I did not say that I had been left in the lurch, rather, that we had changed our minds. It had just been a foolish whim. But Betty said sympathetically, 'It's hit you hard, hasn't it? You look awful.'

She put a motherly hand on my shoulder. 'Men are all the same,' she said. 'I gave up on them long ago.'

Suddenly, I longed to tell her everything. It would have been a soothing balm to confess, not to have to keep up a pretence. But one of the other receptionists came in, a new girl called Sylvie. She was very young. I had no wish to let her in on my secrets. So I just smiled at Betty and said, 'I'm all right.'

'Well, if you want a shoulder to cry on . . . I'm always here.'

I nodded my thanks and returned to my desk where an elderly man was waiting, rheumy eyes watering from the cold wind. I listened sympathetically while he told me about his wife, who was crippled with arthritis and was now having trouble with her eyes. He wondered if Dr Millbank could call after surgery. I suggested that perhaps an optician might be the answer, but he said he couldn't get her to an optician's, it was impossible for her to get into the car. The doctor had always been so kind, he would know what to do. Besides, she was a diabetic. Could that be the cause of the problem? He had read somewhere . . . and he trailed off vaguely, as if his troubles were too much for him to articulate.

I took his name and address, and added it to the list. Watching him walk away, stooped and with a slight limp, I felt a surge of both pity and gratitude, for while talking to him I hadn't been able to think about my own problems at all.

The week dragged by, and on Saturday it was overcast, threatening rain. Undeterred, after breakfast I set out for a walk. I had to get out of the house. I left Natalie grudgingly doing her practice, and Stefan mowing the lawn. Through the suburban streets I wandered, and found myself on the common, and heading for the Old Barnes Cemetery. It had been a favourite walk when the children were small, when David was alive, and after his death I had come there sometimes, to cry. Now the ancient grey stones peering from their smother of ivy and long grass, the crumbling angels and chipped, lichen-clad crosses seemed once more to match my mood of hopelessness. As I walked, peering now and then at faint lettering commemorating long-forgotten dead, the promised rain set in in a steady drizzle, dampening my hair, but I took no notice. I thought of David's grave, guiltily. I had been wrapped up in Matt. It was some months since I had taken flowers. Something now urged me to visit it, but it was not only guilt, it was a longing for comfort. I gave a harsh, tear-choked laugh. What was I thinking of? Running crying to David because I had been let down by another man? The thought was intolerable and I pushed it away. I plodded on, round and round the overgrown paths, under the dark trees, letting my tears join the rain in wetting my cold cheeks. Finally, I looked at my watch and found it was time to be getting back. I retraced my steps, out onto the more cheerful common where people, with collars up against the rain, were walking their dogs, back along the quiet streets with cars parked bumper to bumper because people had no garages, thinking how lucky I was to have a garage, and a drive – and when I got home, there on the drive was the Porsche.

I found the children in the kitchen, making toasted cheese.

'Where is he?' I asked quickly.

'Upstairs,' said Stefan.

'Did he talk to you?'

'He said hello. I think he was embarrassed.'

'I was embarrassed,' confessed Natalie. 'I didn't know whether I was supposed to just ignore him. Or what.'

'It is difficult,' I agreed. 'You must do what you want to do.'

'I wanted to ask if he was staying,' Stefan said, pulling out the grill pan. 'Are you ready to eat?'

'You go ahead.' I took off my damp coat and pushed at my limp, wet hair. 'I'll just find out what's going on.' I gave them a nervous smile and Stefan gave me a thumbs up sign. I felt heartened, and climbed the stairs quite boldly.

I could hear Matt in his room, opening and closing drawers. The door was ajar and I pushed it open, standing silently watching. He was cramming underwear into a holdall, but he had the grace to look miserable as he did so. I felt a rush of misery myself. So he hadn't come back. He had only come to collect his things. I gave a little gasp and he looked round.

'Julia. You're back.'

'Looks like it. Were you hoping to sneak away again, without my seeing you?'

'Don't!'

'Well, for goodness' sake, what do you expect me to say? You could have had the decency to tell me to my face.'

He sagged down onto the bed, his hands clasped loosely between his knees. He looked the picture of dejection, a little boy who knew he had done wrong. Like an idiot, I wanted to touch his shiny hair.

'I know. I hope you can forgive me.'

Daringly, I sat down beside him, on a folded pile of clothes which I had ironed the night before and left there, hoping I knew not what.

'Are you going to explain?' I asked him, trying to keep my voice from trembling.

He looked at me. There was real pain on his face. 'I couldn't do it, Julia. I thought I could. I hoped I could. But I'm just not the settling down kind.'

'Then why . . . ? I mean, we were fine as we were. Why change everything?'

'I thought it was what I wanted. I thought it was what *you* wanted.'

'I never said so. I never put any pressure on you. It was all your idea.'

He nodded. 'I know. But when it came to it – I was scared stiff. The only way out was to run. I'm sorry.'

'And where have you run to?'

'I've been in a hotel. A seedy little dump in Earls Court. Now I've found a flat in Hounslow. Handy for work. So I've come to get my things.'

'And to explain. I hope you came to explain.'

He pushed at his glasses, rubbed his hands together, then set them on his knees. 'I expected you to be here certainly. I wanted to see you.'

He didn't look at me and I reached up to turn his face towards me.

'Did you, Matt? Or did you hope that I would just mysteriously vanish? Not be your responsibility? You never were one for responsibility, were you?'

He shook his head. 'That's what I'm saying.'

We stared at each other miserably. Then, and I couldn't help myself, I said in a small voice, 'But you don't have to go away. Why couldn't it be like it was before?'

He was surprised, as well he might be by so pathetic an expression of need.

'Would you want that?'

I was going to say, 'Yes, yes, anything but this awful loneliness,' but something stopped me. Things had changed between us. A long week had passed, during which I had realised that I wasn't in love with him, and it followed, surely, that I could therefore live without him. If that was so, then what was to be gained by trying to turn back the clock? It was not being honest with myself, let alone Matt.

So I asked instead, 'Do you love me, Matt?'

He paused for a long moment and when he finally spoke I could hardly hear him.

'Speak up. This is important.'

'I said yes, but I suppose not enough. I thought, in Paris, you know, it was all so romantic, you were so lovely, and I thought, this is it at last, it will be all right.'

I waited, letting his words sink in.

'So you really wanted to be married? Or you thought you did?'

'I thought I did. I thought I could be like everybody else. But it's no good. I haven't got what it takes.'

I could have hugged him, but something held me back. 'Oh Matt,' was all I said.

Then he got up wearily and zipped up his holdall.

'I'm afraid I can't take everything in one go. Can you bear me coming back again?'

I shrugged. 'If you have to.' Then I said, despite myself, 'I shall miss you. We all will.'

He had unplugged his CD player and was winding up the flex. 'I suppose we could still see each other,' he said hesitantly.

I opened my hands helplessly. 'What's the point?'

'I was going to teach Stefan to drive. I was looking forward to it.'

'He told me.'

'I still could.'

'No, Matt.'

I was surprised at my firmness. I watched him leave the room, carrying his things.

He said, 'I'll come straight back for the rest. Get it over with.'

'Yes.'

His brown eyes flicked over me without the hint of a smile. Where had all the laughter gone? I was swept with desolation, but all I said was, 'When you've finished, don't forget to leave the key.'

Then I sat very still, hearing him go down the stairs, and the final slam of the door. After a while, I heard the growl of the car, loud at first, and familiar, then fading away down the road. I stood up, feeling my knees weak beneath me, and went slowly down the stairs, hanging on to the banister like an invalid.

FIFTEEN

Some weeks later, Shelley invited us to her wedding. She had kept in touch, and we knew that she had changed her job and was now living and working back in Gloucestershire. She was marrying a farmer, a widower older than herself, with two teenage daughters. I was pleased for her. She would be a good wife.

The wedding was to be in July, and as it was the school holidays I suggested taking a cottage for a week. It would do us good to get away and spend some time together. I felt quite excited, but the children had other ideas.

'Bor-ing,' was Natalie's response, lolling back in her chair and making no attempt to be agreeable. 'What would we do for a week? In the *country*?'

In the face of such a negative reaction, I was nonplussed. 'Well,' I ventured, 'there are always things to do, old houses to visit, walks – there's the Roman villa at Chedworth. And Cheltenham, Cirencester, they're not country.'

'Oh God, Mum, too crass. It all sounds mega-dull. You go, I'll stay here.'

'I'm not leaving you. How about you, Stefan?'

At least he had the grace to look uncomfortable. 'I thought I'd get a job for the summer. Stacking shelves or something. Earn some money. I thought you'd approve of that,' he finished defensively.

'Oh I do. That's a good idea. Well – I guess a holiday's out. We'll just go for the weekend. I take it you can both cope with one night in a hotel in Cheltenham?' I spoke sarcastically, hiding my hurt and disappointment.

'S'pose so.' Natalie looked at me moodily. 'We've got to go, have we?'

'Natalie! You were always so fond of Shelley. Surely you want to wish her well?'

'I do. Only there's bound to be a party, the last weekend of term.'

'Then you'll just have to miss it.' I spoke firmly. Natalie went to quite enough parties, and she usually came home late. I seemed to have no control over her at all. When she came in, she would put her head round the sitting-room door, looking flushed and almost angry, as if expecting trouble. I would remonstrate, threaten sanctions which I felt powerless to impose, and she would stamp off to bed. It was a long time since she had kissed me good night. I felt saddened, and worried. She needed a firm hand. She needed a father. I had begun to miss David all over again.

Now she looked at me sulkily, and her pendant went into her mouth.

'Oh, do stop that. You look like a baby,' I snapped.

She let it drop, and leaped out of the chair. 'Well, you treat me like one! What can you expect?'

I reached out a placatory hand. 'Nat . . .' But she had gone, slamming out of the room in her usual way. I looked at Stefan helplessly.

'What's up with her, Stefan? Why is she so moody? Is there something she isn't telling me? Does she talk to you?'

He shook his head. 'No. But she's in with a pretty wild set. I've seen the girls she hangs around with. That Helen is left pretty much to her own devices. And her parents have pots of money.'

I looked at him thoughtfully. 'She never brings her friends here now. Perhaps she's ashamed of them. Or of us. Just what exactly do they get up to? Half the time she says she's working. Maybe I should be checking up on her. Only that would be admitting I don't trust her.'

'Well – do you?'

It was painful to admit that I didn't; more painful to acknowledge that I didn't know what to do about it.

'You could try keeping her home. I'd back you up.'

I looked at him gratefully, but said doubtfully, 'I fancy if I did that, life wouldn't be worth living.'

'But that's as good as saying she's won, she can do anything she likes. Are you saying that?'

'Of course not!' I felt helpless, and confused. 'If only your father was alive,' I said weakly. 'He'd know what to do. Though she probably wouldn't be behaving like this if he was.' I paused, then voiced a thought that had often been with me during the past weeks.

'Do you think it has anything to do with Matt leaving? She's been so much worse since then.'

He stood up, looking at his watch. 'She's never said much, but she was hurt. She thought he was fond of her. She did take it rather personally.'

I put out a restraining hand as he passed on the way to the door.

'But surely not. It was between me and Matt . . .'

He paused with his hand on the doorknob. 'She quite liked us being a family. Though Matt didn't seem like a father exactly. You wouldn't have got much help from him,' he added perceptively, with a wisdom beyond his years.

A thought occurred to me. 'Do you think she blames me? And that's why she's so angry?'

He shrugged. 'She's never said so.' He looked at his watch again. 'I must go, Mum. I'm meeting Simon.'

'Right. Off you go. And, Stefan – thanks for talking. And if Nat tells you anything, you will let me know, won't you?'

He nodded, and left me alone. Alone, with nobody to help and guide me, nobody to lean on or comfort me. For the first time in ages, I asked David what I should do, but of course there was no answer.

306

I felt a panic of desperation, and blamed myself bitterly for deserting David and defecting to Matt. What had I been thinking of? How could I expect David to help me now? Crazily, I forgot how happy I had been with Matt. I forgot that I had every right to a new life. I simply felt that I had forfeited David's love for nothing. Here I was, forty-two, with nothing to show for it but betrayal and desertion, with problems that were quite beyond me.

To my horror, I found my thumb wandering to my mouth as it hadn't done for years.

Suddenly, with the onset of summer, the house in Cornwall sold, to a retired couple from Birmingham who wanted a holiday home. Part of me was sorry. I would have liked a family living there with children growing up, like David had done. But the agents said the buyers had grandchildren, who would be using the house for holidays, so I had to be content with that.

With the money in the bank, I felt rich and secure. The bank's investment department advised me as to its safe disposal, and for the first time in my life I held stocks and shares. I felt as if I had moved into another league, though I was well aware of the risks involved. For that reason, quite a lot of the money had gone into the building society. I did not intend to lose any of Colin's legacy, which had made such a difference to our lives. But I wanted us to have a treat, to celebrate, and I suggested to the children that we go to the opera.

The suggestion was made tentatively, as Stefan had no interest in serious music, and Natalie was as combative as ever. But to my enormous surprise she seemed quite keen.

'Do you mean Covent Garden?'

'If we can get tickets. *The Marriage of Figaro* is on next month. That should be quite light. I'm a beginner myself, remember.'

Her grudging enthusiasm made her seem quite approachable for a change and I hugged her impetuously. 'It will be fun – going together.'

She didn't respond, but neither did she pull away. Stefan, when I asked him, seemed unimpressed, but willing to go along with the idea. It was ages since we had all been out together. We could have a meal first, really paint the town red. Their exams would be over in a fortnight. I managed to get tickets for three weeks' time. I was shocked at the price, but told myself it was worth it. It was about time we did something as a family, and I began to feel quite excited.

Meanwhile, I had begun to teach Stefan to drive.

I cannot describe my feelings as he took over the wheel for the first time, and eased the car jumpily out from the kerb, taking my life in his hands. I was both nervous, and proud, and even a little in awe at the coolness with which he approached it. My son, my child, my baby – now he was propelling us both down the road, albeit at only twenty miles an hour, but with apparent confidence and safety.

'Turn left,' I told him, and without being told to, he flicked the indicator and turned the wheel.

'Do I change gear?' he asked.

'No. You're still in second. Don't swing out too far from the kerb.'

We rounded the corner. I took him round and round the block, sticking to quiet roads, whose main hazard was the cars parked along the kerbside. Eventually, he eased up into third gear, and began to whistle under his breath.

'How'm I doing? I'm starting to enjoy it.'

'Fine. But don't get overconfident.' I realised that I had been gripping the seat as his speed increased. There was a terribly helpless feeling about putting myself in his hands. Suddenly, from between two parked cars, a pushchair nosed out, followed by a young girl holding a toddler by the hand. Stefan braked sharply and crashed the gears noisily. I spared a passing thought for my gearbox, and glared at the girl. 'I think perhaps we'll make for home now, my nerves have had enough,' I told him apologetically.

He grinned. 'Not very flattering. I thought I was doing rather well.'

'Oh you are. But I think there's only so much I can teach you. It would be better for you to have proper lessons eventually.'

'I'll be earning soon. I can pay for them.'

He was starting work in the new Waitrose which had just opened in Putney, but I told him that he wasn't to spend his earnings; thanks to Gramps I could afford to pay for lessons.

'I feel a bit sad,' he said as he switched off the engine and I sat back, relieved, into my seat. 'About Gramps' house. We'll never go there again.'

'Well, we haven't been for years.'

'No. But it was still there. Still ours. Now it belongs to strangers. It will be as if we were never there.'

I thought of the empty rooms as I had seen them on my last visit. It was true. Houses soon forgot, even if people didn't.

I put my hand on his as it rested on the handbrake. 'I'm glad you feel like that, because I do too. And no one can take away the memories. I knew that house for longer than you did, and it will always be part of my life, just as it will always be part of yours.'

We undid our seatbelts and got out. My legs felt damp as I eased off the seat. I realised I had been sweating with tension. Stefan, on the other hand, seemed as cool as a cucumber, and very pleased with himself.

'Thanks, Mum.' He punched the air, grinning with triumph. 'I can't wait until next time.'

Oh dear, I thought, resolving to make some enquiries at the local driving school.

The crush bar at the Opera House was as crowded as I

remembered it as I queued for our drinks in the interval. Natalie had asked for wine which surprised me, as I didn't think she liked it. I thought perhaps she felt it was a suitable thing to drink, in such surroundings. As I stood at the bar awaiting my turn, I scanned the faces around me. I was the only woman standing there, and I suddenly felt very exposed, and very lonely. Everyone else, it seemed, had a partner to run the gauntlet of the crowds, to jostle for service and make the difficult journey back, carrying the glasses. I realised belatedly that I would need help with that, and turning to call Stefan to my side, found myself looking straight towards a short, fat, flustered little man who was only too familiar. It was Samuel.

I turned away quickly, before he met my eye. Confusedly, I heard the bartender ask for my order, and requested two white wines and a lager. As I paid I imagined Samuel's piggy eyes boring into the back of my head and felt the uncomfortable heat of embarrassment. My ignominious and hurtful departure from the Opera House felt like yesterday and I was sure he had never forgiven me.

I picked up the wine. There was nothing for it but to turn and signal to Stefan to come and get his beer. I spun on my heel, expecting to come face to face with Samuel, but instead found myself staring into the eyes of a tall man with white hair. I turned sideways and saw that Samuel had taken the place beside me at the bar. Clearly he had forgotten me, chose to ignore me, or hadn't seen me. Whatever it was I felt a flood of relief. I caught Stefan's eye and called him into the crush to fetch his glass. I handed Natalie's to her and watched her take a first tentative sip. I expected her to wince and shudder, but she appeared to relish it. Her eyes met mine over the glass and I sensed bravado. She looked very grown up, in a short red dress with a tight skirt, only spoiled from my point of view by her mandatory heavy black boots. She often wore red, in defiance of her hair, which blazed now under the lights of the chandeliers. Stefan, in his first suit, looked incredibly handsome, sipping his beer like a man. Even his earring, glinting in the lights, didn't spoil him. I grudgingly had to admit that it suited him. Turning again to Natalie, I thought how attractive she would look with a pair of earrings swinging at her white neck. It was only a matter of time before she, too, started insisting. It would, perhaps, be a tactical move to forestall her.

'Would you like your ears pierced for your birthday?' I asked her quickly, before I could change my mind.

She looked startled. 'What – you're offering?' she said caustically.

I chose to ignore her tone. 'Yes. You look so grown up. I think it would suit you.'

She looked awkward. Gratitude between us had become so foreign that she was finding it hard to meet me halfway. 'Actually,' she said at last, 'I was going to do it anyway,' which rather spoiled my gesture, and I sipped my wine angrily, conscious that I had achieved nothing.

The bell rang for us to return to our seats and we left our glasses on a crowded table and began to make our way back to the auditorium. In front of us, moving towards the best seats in the stalls, was Samuel, holding the arm of a short fat woman with bleached hair. And I wondered if he was, after all this time, still trying to find somebody to suit. Or if, perhaps, he was already suited. I found myself rather hoping that he was, but at the same time feeling envy.

Shelley looked every inch a bride, and there were a great many inches of her for she had put on weight. Her figure wasn't helped by a dress of many lace flounces with huge puffy sleeves and a revealing low-cut bodice. But her usually impassive face radiated happiness and when we greeted her in the reception line I told her, quite truthfully, that she looked lovely.

Her two stepdaughters were in attendance, dressed in an unflattering green. I hoped they would be good to her. Her husband, Gordon, was a short, kindly-looking man who seemed unable to believe his good fortune. He held Shelley's hand tightly clasped in his as he greeted his guests. I felt reassured; they would surely look after each other.

I had met Shelley's parents before, when they had visited her at the house, and I was pleased to see them again. We chatted for a while, and I lost sight of the children. When we took our places at the long tables, I found that I had been seated between two strangers, while Stefan and Natalie were on another table with a crowd of younger guests. I could see Natalie laughing with another girl with long blonde hair which she kept scooping back with her hand. Reassured that she was happy, I turned to address the lady beside me, who turned out to be Shelley's aunt, and a retired nurse, and the meal passed pleasantly enough, while we dissected the health service and all its failings. The best man made a hesitant speech and read out a few telegrams, toasts were drunk, and the guests began to circulate again.

I made my way towards Stefan, who was deep in conversation with a tall dark girl. He introduced her as Jennifer, a cousin of Shelley's. I asked him to fetch me a soft drink, and looked around for Natalie.

I soon found her. There was a noisy crowd at the bar, and in the centre, as if she were holding court, was my daughter. She was holding a glass of wine, and her face was flushed, her eyes dancing, as she regaled her audience with something which they obviously found very funny. I looked away, feeling confused, and guilty, as if I were spying on her. This was a girl I didn't know. Was this how she was with her friends? If so, why was she so morose and moody with me? Was it my fault? I took my orange juice from Stefan and looked anxiously back at the merry group. Natalie had draped her arm round the shoulders of one of the boys, and seemed to be leaning on him. I didn't like it. And I didn't like the truth which hit me with a sickening thud. Natalie had had too much to drink.

Nor did I like the realisation which swifly followed this; that her flushed cheeks and bright, feverish eyes were all too familiar. It was how she looked when she came in at night when she had been with her friends, ostensibly doing her homework. The casual way in which she handled her glass confirmed it. She was no novice. At fourteen, Natalie was used to drinking.

Stefan said, 'You all right, Mum?' He had been watching me as I watched Natalie.

I looked at him with stricken eyes. 'No. I'm not. And neither is Natalie. She's drunk. What am I going to do?'

He looked across at his sister. 'I agree she looks a bit overexcited. But it is a wedding. They all look pretty merry. It's quite harmless.'

'But I didn't think Natalie liked wine. She's too young. She's making a fool of herself. Who's that she's draped all over? He looks at least twenty.'

Jennifer had been standing beside me all this time, and now she spoke. 'He's my brother, Alan. He's quite harmless.'

I spoke quickly, feeling embarrassed. 'Oh, I'm sure he is. It's not him I'm worried about. I'm going to break it up. I won't be popular, but I think it's time we left.'

I felt Stefan's restraining hand on my arm. 'Leave it, Mum. She won't thank you.'

'I can't help that.' Anger, at myself for being so blind, at Natalie for being so wilful and so stupid, propelled me across the room. As I reached the group Natalie caught my eye with a challenging look. I flinched, but heard myself saying firmly, 'I think it's time we left, Natalie. The party's over now.'

She looked at me angrily. 'No it's not,' she said defiantly. 'We're all going back to Alan's flat. To watch a video.' There

313

was a burst of laughter from the group. I felt horribly out-numbered, and unsure of myself. Desperately, I wondered what David would have done; and then I knew that I had to exert my authority or all was lost.

I shook my head. 'Sorry. I think you've done enough partying. You're coming back to the hotel with me.'

Natalie's mouth gaped open, then closed into a thin, angry line. 'You can't mean it!'

'I can, and I do. Say goodbye to your friends.'

She glowered at me with hatred in her eyes. I had humili ated her and she wasn't going to forgive me. With a studied gesture, she raised her glass and drained it dry, slamming it down on the bar. Then, without speaking, she pushed through the group of silent young people and marched towards the door. I followed her. Stefan caught my arm as I passed.

'Mum? Does that apply to me? Only Jen and I thought we might like to go on somewhere. I'll be back by eleven.'

I stood awkwardly, looking at the two of them. Natalie's fury would know no bounds, but it didn't seem fair to impose the same sanctions.

'Go on then,' I said helplessly. I had been rather counting on him for support, but that was expecting too much. It wasn't his job. As usual, I was on my own. With a rebellious, drunken daughter, who hated me, and no one to tell me I was right.

Natalie spent the evening in her room at the hotel, refusing to speak to me or join me for supper. I ate alone, in a sparsely populated pink and gold dining room, and mourned the evening I had planned for us all. The hotel was sumptuous, it should have been a treat, but it was all wasted on my children. I told myself that it was natural that they should prefer to be with their own age group. The last thing I wanted to be was an obligation, a burden, a responsibility. They must lead their own lives, as I expected to be able to lead mine. But Natalie's drinking was something else. She was risking her health, her education and her reputation. More than that, what did it mean? I decided she must be deeply unhappy, and if that was the case, then I must find out why. But how could I do that now that battle lines had been drawn? Where could I meet my daughter, and talk?

She was silent at breakfast, and on the drive home, which should have been a pleasure through the mellow Cotswold countryside. After a while, I suggested that Stefan took the wheel. He had had several lessons, and needed the practice. He changed places with alacrity, while Natalie glowered in the back. Despite my depression, I was impressed with the progress he had made, and thrilled to be driven, although my feet operated imaginary pedals and I found myself gripping the seat when he speeded up. We changed back again when we reached the motorway and he grinned at me happily.

'I think I'll book my test. I feel I've got the hang of it now.'

'You need lots of practice,' I warned. 'I'll take you out more if you like.'

'It's ridiculous,' he said as we joined the M4. 'We should be taught how to drive on motorways.'

'I quite agree. And how to park in car parks. And drive in the dark. At least I can help you with those two.'

I pulled into the outside lane to overtake an airport coach. 'Did you have a good time last night?' I asked casually. He hadn't said anything but I felt I should take an interest.

'Yes. Jen's got her own car, we went for a drive, and had a pizza.'

'Her own car? How old is she?'

'Eighteen. She's going to Nottingham to read maths.'

'Clever girl.' I pulled back into the centre lane and a sweating Volvo roared past.

'But she's taking a gap year. Going to work on a kibbutz.'

'Really? I'm not sure that that's a good idea. You must get out of the habit of studying.'

'Yes, but it's probably the only time in your life you have the opportunity to just push off.'

I looked sideways at him. He had just started gathering university prospectuses, and was going to read geology. He was studying geography, maths and physics for his A levels, and working really hard. I was already preparing myself for his leaving in a year's time. University, I could cope with. Getting himself jabbed for tropical diseases and pushing off to Thailand with a backpack was quite another thing. 'I hope,' I said quietly, 'that you're not thinking of doing that.'

But he didn't answer, and we drove the rest of the way in silence.

When we got home, Natalie disappeared to her room. In a way it was a relief to be freed of her brooding, resentful presence. Stefan went upstairs to work. I sat at the kitchen table, feeling worried and helpless and guilty. For I had clearly failed in my duty towards Natalie, and now she seemed to have slipped from my control. I knew nothing of her friends, or her friends' parents; I had accepted what she told me without question, I had watched her abandonment of her music almost with complicity, thinking, sadly, that she had just grown out of it.

Now the time had come to take control. Standing up, I realised that I was frightened, frightened of my own daughter, of her anger and her scorn. I wanted us to be friends, I didn't want confrontation, but I had avoided that too long, and where had it got me? The time had come to grasp the nettle.

But as I got to the kitchen door, I heard the front door slam. I ran and wrenched it open, to see Natalie running down the road, her baggy shoulder bag swinging. She had changed her clothes for tight jeans and a red cropped top which showed her pale, thin midriff. Her hair blazed defiance. I went to call her back, but her name froze on my lips. With a sickening lurch of my heart I closed the front door slowly. It was going to be a long, lonely evening, but when she came back I would be waiting for her.

It was nearly midnight when I heard her key in the lock. I sat forward, tensely watching for the sitting-room door to open, for her angry face to appear. But nothing happened. I heard her feet pass down the hall, and up the stairs. She wasn't going to come in. Angrily, I sprang up and opened the door. She was at the top of the stairs when I called.

'Natalie. Aren't you going to say good night?'

'Good night,' she said, without turning round.

Incensed by her insolence, I ran up the stairs and took her shoulder as she entered her room, turning her roughly round to face me.

'That won't do,' I told her. 'We have to talk.'

I thought her eyes looked frightened, and I relented, loosening my hold on her shoulder. We were standing quite close, staring into each other's eyes, and then I smelled her breath.

'Natalie,' I cried accusingly, 'you've been drinking.'

She looked sulky and her hand went to her mouth, then nervously up to touch her hair.

'So what if I have?'

'But you're fourteen years old. Where are you getting it?'

She shrugged. 'Not everyone's as fussy as you. Helen's parents have got a bar. They give us wine sometimes. It doesn't do any harm.'

I looked at her flushed face and bright eyes. 'How much have you had? And what else have you been doing?'

'We surf the Internet. I've told you before. Not that you'd know anything about that.'

I took her shoulders again and propelled her roughly into

her bedroom, closing the door behind me. 'There's no need to be rude.' I pushed her and she subsided onto the bed. I stood over her, trying to feel strong.

'I don't want you going there any more, do you understand? You'll just have to do your homework here. And I want to see that it's done. You've got an important year coming up, with your GCSEs. And what about the piano? Do you want me to get rid of it?'

'No!' She looked anguished.

'Well, let me hear you play it sometimes. I used to be so proud of you.'

She looked mutinous and said nothing. I took a deep breath and sat down beside her on the bed, taking her unresponsive hand in mine.

'I don't want to be cross,' I said, more gently. 'But I'm worried about you. I've been remiss. I don't know what you're doing half the time, where you are.'

'I'm at Helen's.'

'Well, why can't Helen come here sometimes?'

She shrugged. She looked pale, the flush fading from her cheeks and dark rings beneath her eyes. The best place for her was her bed, but I was forced to ask, 'Are you unhappy about something? You can tell me.'

She didn't look at me, but stared across the room at her reflection in the mirror. 'No. Only at you, going on at me.'

'But I have to, don't you see? I care about you. I'm responsible for you. Girls of your age shouldn't be drinking. I don't know what Helen's parents are thinking of. I think I'll give them a ring.'

'Don't!' She spoke sharply, and an expression very like panic crossed her face. 'What will they think? I won't go there any more – okay? Or . . .' and she hesitated, 'if I do, I won't have anything to drink. Okay?'

I looked at her doubtfully. 'Can I trust you? Because if I can't, there'll be no more going out, no more parties.'

'Mum! I've said, haven't I?'

I squeezed her hand and released it. 'Well, get to bed now.' I stood up, feeling sad. I didn't seem to have accomplished much, and the rift between us was as deep and wide as ever.

For several weeks, she kept her word. It was the holidays, and I worried about leaving her every day, but to my relief she had started to play the piano again, and resumed her friendship with Chloe, who came to the house and made lunch and hung around the shops in the West End with her. They went to museums and art galleries, and in the evenings Natalie either went to the cinema or stayed in with me, watching television. I couldn't believe my luck. For her birthday, she had her ears pierced, and I bought her a pair of silver filigree earrings to be kept until such time as she could take the original studs out. She bathed her ears religiously night and morning, and hugged me gratifyingly with pleasure.

Then she told me that Helen was having a birthday party in September. She hadn't been to a party for ages, could she go?

She had been so docile and amenable that I didn't have the heart to refuse. Anyway, I had to trust her sometime.

'Okay,' I said. 'But you know the rules.'

'Surely, just one glass of wine. Everyone will be having it.'

'But it's nonsense. You're all fifteen. You should be drinking Coke.'

'Some of them are older. Helen's brother will be there, he's eighteen.'

I was alarmed. 'I really feel I should give Helen's parents a ring. They should be keeping an eye out for you younger ones.'

She looked at me furiously. 'If you do, I'll never speak to you again. What am I, a baby? No one else's parents make all this fuss.'

'I'm not anyone else's parent, I'm yours. And I care what happens to you.'

'Okay. So I won't get drunk. Okay?' She fiddled with her pendant uncertainly, waiting for my reply. I felt utterly at a loss, but told myself again that I had to begin to trust her.

'All right,' I said eventually. 'You can go. But I'll come and get you at midnight. You're not walking home alone.'

'God! I'll feel like Cinderella!'

'Midnight. And that's later than I'd like. But I'm trying to meet you halfway. Make sure you meet me.'

If I expected her thanks, I was to be disappointed. She turned on her heel and walked away, her big boots clumping, her bare pale legs looking somehow pathetically young.

Claire came round with Zoe, and it was obvious that she had something to say. After the usual pleasantries, she said, 'We saw Matt at the weekend. He's got a girlfriend.'

I wasn't prepared, and the pain sneaked in before I could stop it. My voice wasn't quite steady when I asked, 'Really? Have you met her?'

Now she sounded reluctant, as if she sensed my pain. 'Actually, he brought her to lunch. She's okay. She's twenty-two.'

'Twenty-two! Talk about the sublime to the ridiculous! Do you think it's serious?'

'Oh, you know Matt,' she said, which told me nothing.

'I don't want to know her name,' I said warningly. Somehow, that would make her more real, myself more dispensable. In retrospect, the months with Matt seemed bathed in perpetual sunshine. Since he had gone, everything had been tense and troubled. I longed to go back, yet knew it was impossible; knew, in truth, that it wasn't the answer. But it didn't help to know that he had moved on, and I hadn't.

Tactfully, Claire changed the subject. 'How's things generally? We haven't talked for ages.'

My eyes were on Zoe, who was scribbling pictures at the

320

coffee table. I suddenly remembered Josh, when we had first met him, doing just the same in Claire's bare little house. I had known her a long time. It would be a comfort to talk.

'Well,' I said, 'things have been better. I've been having a bit of bother with Natalie.'

'What sort of trouble?'

'Well, she's been drinking. Can you believe it? She's got in with a girl whose parents seem to have more money than sense, and let them drink at their house.'

'Well, be thankful that's all it is. I see them on the common sometimes, groups of youngsters in the shelters with cans and bottles. Some of them no older than Natalie.'

I stared at her, doubt and suspicion coiling up through my head.

'You've never seen Natalie? I mean, you would have told me?'

She shook her head. 'Of course I would. What are you doing about it? Have you grounded her?'

'It's difficult. I'm out all day. And I've got to trust her. She's stopped going to Helen's. Or so she says. But next week she's going to her party. There will be older boys there. I'd like to speak to the parents, but she gets so angry. And it's hardly fair to single her out. I've got to believe her when she says she'll be sensible. She's got to grow up, I can't be with her all the time.'

Claire reached out to Zoe and pulled her sturdy little body onto her lap. 'They're so much easier at this age,' she said with gratitude, dropping a kiss onto her curls. 'Though I worry about Zoe too. She's having speech therapy now, for her stammer. I would have liked it sorted out before school, but she starts in the mornings next week. I'm frightened the other children will tease her.'

I remembered Natalie's agonies over her hair, and shuddered in sympathy.

'I'm so sorry, Claire. It is a worry. But it will sort itself out, I'm sure it will.'

But she looked drawn and tense as she hugged her child to her as if to protect her from all hurt. And I thought: Children! Why do we have them? The only comfort I could offer was a cup of tea.

On the evening of the party if was pouring with rain.

'I'll drive you round,' I told Natalie, when she came downstairs, dressed in a denim pinafore over a white tee shirt, her boots jutting incongruously below a white broderie anglaise frill. Her gold studs gleamed in her white lobes. Her hair, which she had recently had cut short, made a soft red halo round her pale face. 'You look very pretty,' I added. 'You don't want to get wet.'

'Thanks.' She sounded reluctant, but got into the car without protest. It was a short ride to the large double-fronted house where Helen lived. When we got there I said, tentatively, 'Now would be a good chance to meet Helen's parents. I'll come in with you.'

She darted me a warning look. 'No you won't. I'll look like a kid, being taken to school.'

I sighed. 'Well, how about thanks for the lift? I didn't have to turn out.'

'Thanks.' She had turned away, opening the door.

'I'll see you at twelve. Have a good time.' I longed to tell her to be careful, to be sensible, to be good, but bit my tongue. I watched her walk up the path and ring the bell, and still I waited. The door was opened by a black-clad boy. I could hear music. Natalie disappeared inside, where I couldn't follow her, and the door closed.

I sat all evening listening to the rain, unable to concentrate on anything, wondering what she was doing, willing midnight to come round. And then, just as I was preparing to go and fetch her, there was a knock at the door.

It was a policewoman, telling me that Natalie had been taken to hospital.

SIXTEEN

I ran up to Stefan's room and found him already in bed.

'Nat's in hospital. Please come with me.'

He flung back the covers and grabbed his jeans from the floor.

'What's happened?' He pulled a sweatshirt over his head, brushing his hair flat with his hand.

'Alcohol poisoning. She's having her stomach pumped. Oh Stefan . . .' I stared at him, tears flooding to the surface.

He grabbed my arm. 'Not now, Mum.'

I pulled myself together. 'The police are here. They'll drive us.'

'Then how will we get back?' he said sensibly. 'We'll take our car, I'll drive, you're in no fit state.'

The policewoman was standing in the hall. Suddenly, it occurred to me to wonder why. What had it got to do with the police?

'How come you are involved?' I asked her as I fumbled into some shoes.

'We got called in by some neighbours. The party got a bit rowdy, there were complaints. We arrived at the same time as the ambulance. Luckily, they'd had the sense to call one when your daughter passed out.'

I was bewildered. 'Who called the ambulance? The parents? How on earth did things get so out of hand?' I felt a swift bitter anger at their negligence.

'Oh the parents weren't there. They've gone away for the weekend apparently.'

'What?' I was horrified. 'I'd never have let her go if I'd known. What sort of people are they, for heaven's sake?'

'Come on, Mum.' Stefan was urging me towards the door, the car keys in his hand. I picked up my handbag. The policewoman followed us out, slamming the door behind her. The rain was still coming down in sheets, soaking my hair and face as we ran to the car. The policewoman drove off down the road, leaving us to our nightmare.

We were shown into a cubicle in the casualty department, where Natalie lay like a corpse, her cheeks alabaster, her hair plastered to her forehead. She was still unconscious. There was a drip running into her arm.

I felt very frightened. 'Why is she on a drip?' I asked.

'It's glucose. And fluid. She needs fluids.'

The nurse was clearing away a contraption of tubes and bowls. There was an offensive smell that I didn't want to associate with my daughter. I picked up her limp hand, and found it cold.

'Will she be all right?'

The nurse looked at me tight-lipped, as if she didn't deserve to be.

'They usually are, if we catch them quick enough.'

'Does this happen often?' I asked, appalled at the thought, yet comforted in a way too. Perhaps after all it wasn't so very dreadful? And yet I knew in my heart that it was.

'Far too often. We've got better things to do.'

She gathered up the apparatus and left the cubicle.

'What do we do now?' I called after her in panic.

She turned, looking irritated. 'Wait till she comes round,' she snapped.

I looked helplessly at Stefan who put his arm round my shoulders.

'Sit down, Mum. I'll see if I can find a doctor. Someone a bit more sympathetic.'

He left the cubicle, closing the curtain behind him. I sat

on a hard plastic chair beside the bed and took Natalie's hand again, stroking at her nails which shone like pearls against her white skin. I stared at her unconscious face, willing her eyes to open, her pale lips to move. Someone had removed her boots. They stood beside the bed, huge and ugly. Yet she thought they were wonderful. I gave a strangled sound, a cross between a laugh and a sob, and straightened the blanket which lay over her, which was all I could do to tend her.

'Please wake up,' I murmured, over and over again. It was the nearest thing I could manage to a prayer.

After a while, the curtain was pulled back, and Stefan came back with a young Pakistani doctor.

'I'm sorry to have been so long, Mrs Leathlean. Saturday nights are always very busy.'

'I'm sure they are. I'm so sorry . . .' I nodded apologetically towards the bed. 'But can you tell us a bit more? What can we expect now?'

'Well, we've emptied the contents of her stomach, so now we just have to wait. There's a lot of alcohol in her blood. But I think we caught her quickly. Luckily, someone had the sense to ring for help.'

Sense? What sense had anyone shown in the first place?

'Can she – could she – die?' I asked tremulously.

'It has been known. But as I say, we got to her quickly. She'll have a nasty hangover, and her throat will be sore, but hopefully nothing more serious than that.'

I felt I needed to explain, to excuse myself. 'I really didn't know what was going on,' I said. 'I mean, I thought the parents were there.'

'Yes. Well, we can't be with them all the time, can we? Let's just hope she'll have learned her lesson.'

'Yes.' I spoke meekly, feeling myself to blame. 'Well, thank you for all you've done. What do we do when she comes round?'

'Call a nurse. She can probably go home then, but I'll take another look at her.' He turned to Stefan. 'Why don't you get your mother a cup of tea? There's a machine at the end of the corridor.'

Stefan left, and the doctor turned back to me. 'And her father? What will he have to say about it?'

'She has no father.' I read censure in his eyes and said angrily, 'I'm a widow.'

'I'm sorry. Well, I guess you've got a bit of a problem on your hands. There are people who can help.'

'Thank you. She's not a bad girl. Just misguided.'

A nurse pushed her head through the curtain. 'You're wanted in cubicle three,' she said breathlessly to the doctor.

'If you'll excuse me,' he said, already on his way out.

I sat down wearily beside the bed and looked at my watch. It was a quarter to one. It looked like being a long night. At least I had Stefan with me. I glanced round, suddenly desperate for hot tea. Eventually, he pushed through the curtains and I seized the polystyrene mug gratefully. The scald of the liquid was some comfort. Despite his presence, I felt desperately alone. 'She has no father,' I had said. Perhaps, if she had, this never would have happened.

By half-past two, I was worried.

'Perhaps we should call someone. This seems to be taking a long time, perhaps too long, we don't know what to expect.'

There was rising panic in my voice and Stefan said he would go and get some help. He came back eventually with a nurse who lifted Natalie's eyelids and took her pulse.

'What's happening?' I asked her, fighting down hysteria.

'We can only let things take their course,' was all she said. 'Be patient.'

'But for how long?'

'I don't know, Mrs Leathlean. I'm sorry.'

She left the cubicle and we settled down to wait once more. I looked at Stefan. He was looking pale and strained, but managed a smile. 'It will be all right, Mum, you'll see.'

I tried to believe him, but thought, it should be me comforting him. What sort of a mother am I? And I turned my eyes back to Natalie, feeling a burden of guilt that I could hardly bear.

We sat for another hour, silently preoccupied with our thoughts. And then, quite suddenly, Natalie opened her eyes. One minute, there was nobody there; then, suddenly, there she was, staring at the ceiling with a puzzled frown.

'Nat?' I touched her cheek.

She turned her head slowly, and met my eyes.

'Mum?'

'You're in hospital, darling. But you're all right.' I took both her hands in mine, rubbing them warm.

Her voice was hoarse. 'My throat hurts. What happened?'

'Never mind that now. You passed out, at the party. But you're better now.'

'You got drunk, that's what happened.' Stefan spoke brutally, his relief turning to anger. 'They had to pump your stomach.'

Her eyes widened. 'Is that true?' she asked me in a whisper. 'I don't remember.'

I squeezed her hand. 'I'm afraid so, darling.' I felt it was too soon to show my own anger, my disappointment at her foolishness.

'Can I have a drink of water? I'm so dry.'

'I don't know.' I turned to Stefan, and asked him to fetch a nurse, but it was the doctor who returned with him and he asked, briskly, how she felt.

'I've got a terrible headache,' she told him.

'That's called a hangover,' he said without much sympathy. 'Can you sit up?'

She struggled up into a sitting position. The blanket fell

down, revealing her clothes damp and crumpled. Her hair was stuck to her forehead and her face looked bleak and pained.

'Put your feet to the floor,' said the doctor, and she obediently swung her legs over the side of the bed. Her thin bare feet braced on the floor. 'Now stand up.'

She put her hand on my shoulder, and stood.

'Fine. Well, I guess you'd best get home and get some sleep. Drink plenty of water. And don't let us see you in here again, okay?'

She nodded, like a small obedient child, and watched bemused while he disconnected the drip.

'Thank you, doctor,' I said. There didn't seem to be anything more to say. Natalie was stooping for her boots, fumbling with the laces. Stefan was already standing, eager to be away. I took Natalie's arm and we made our way down the corridor and through the waiting room, where despite the hour, there were still people waiting. One man had blood all over his face. I averted my eyes, anxious to be out of the hospital, back to normality, whatever that was. I opened the car and Natalie crawled into the back seat. 'I'll drive,' I said. I felt quite calm now. Stefan got in beside his sister. As I started the engine, I heard him say, 'You're a bloody little fool. Don't you *ever* do that again.'

At midday, I went into her room carrying a mug of tea. She was still asleep and I put the tea on the bedside table and drew back the curtains. The rain had passed over, it was a sunny day and the sun streamed onto her pillow so that she stirred, stretched and opened her eyes.

'Hello,' I said. 'I've brought you tea. How's the head?'

She shook her head experimentally. 'Better. But I'm so dry.'

'Dehydrated, I expect. Are you hungry?'

'Empty. Not hungry exactly. And my throat's sore.'

'They said it would be. It's from the tube.'

She shuddered, cupping her mug in her hands. Then she met my eyes defensively. 'Well, go on. Lecture me.'

I sat down on the bed, rubbing her feet beneath the duvet.

'I don't want to do that. I'm hoping you've learned your lesson. But I would like to know why. After all I'd said, the promises you made. I'm disappointed in you, Natalie. And worried. About why you behaved like you did.'

She gulped her tea, staring at the sunny window. Her green eyes were very bright in the light. I thought she wasn't going to reply but at last she said, 'I only meant to have one drink. But there was just so much stuff. We were egging each other on to try different things. I had cider, and beer and then somebody opened a bottle of whisky. I didn't like it, but it seemed the thing to do and I was having fun. Then I don't remember anything else.'

She put down her empty mug. 'I'm sorry, Mum.'

'I'm sorry too. I thought you had more sense. You could have died. As it was, you took up the hospital's valuable time. They have better things to do than deal with silly drunken teenagers.'

She winced.

'And they had to call the police, things were getting so rowdy. How do you think I felt when a policewoman arrived on the doorstep? I was terrified; it's what every parent dreads.'

She lowered her eyes, pleating the duvet cover between her fingers.

'What on earth were Helen's parents thinking of, leaving you alone in the house with all that drink? I'm sure they're not going to be very pleased.'

'It wasn't all their drink. People brought bottles.'

There was a silence, and then I felt myself compelled to ask her. 'Natalie, do you ever go drinking anywhere else? On the common, for instance. I know it happens.'

She looked startled. 'How do you know?'

'Never mind. Do you?'

She looked sulky. 'I have done. What difference does it make?'

I was appalled, but not surprised. 'Where do you get the stuff? Surely you can't buy it?'

'Tim gets it. Helen's brother. Or one of his friends. We all hang out together. There's nowhere else to go.'

'Oh Natalie. Is your life so very empty, so pointless that you have to get drunk to amuse yourself?'

She shifted uneasily. 'No. I don't suppose so. It's just fun, that's all. We have a laugh. There are not many laughs at home here.'

I shrank into myself. So it was all my fault.

'Do you miss Matt?' I asked her.

She looked at me warily. 'Sometimes. He was good fun.'

'But you can't make that your excuse. I refuse to be held responsible just because Matt and I parted. It's not fair, Natalie.'

'I'm not making it an excuse. You asked me, that's all.'

I stood up and went to the window. The sunny street was empty, dahlias bloomed in the front gardens, a thrush was sitting in a bush beside my gate singing. I turned to face her neat room, with its tidy bookshelves and absence of clutter. Even last night she had folded her clothes neatly on the chair. Outwardly, her life seemed so organised. How, then, had it spiralled out of control? And what was I to do about it?

'So,' I asked her. 'What happens now? Have you seen sense? Are you going to stop this nonsense? Are you going to be able to? Or should we try and get some help for you? To help you cope with life?'

She looked horrified. 'What, you mean like Alcoholics Anonymous? No way.'

'Well, it's up to you.' I pulled back the duvet. 'Get up now, have a bath and I'll get you something to eat. And we'll try and think what we can do.'

She stood before me, thin and pale, her expression truculent. I wanted to hug her to me, tell her how precious she was, beg her to change her ways. I also wanted to shake her, violently, and make her see sense. Instead, sternly, I stood back and let her go.

Henry Millbank wasn't my doctor, but next day, when I went in to work, he asked me whether everything was all right.

'Why?' I asked in surprise.

'Because you look upset. And you don't look as if you've had much sleep.'

He sounded sympathetic, and faced with his kindness I suddenly found myself subsiding onto the chair in his office and telling him everything. Not just about Natalie, but about Matt having another girlfriend, and how bleak and dreary my life was, and how worrying, and that I didn't know which way to turn. And while I talked I began to cry, and once I started I couldn't stop, but sat and sobbed, rocking back and forth in the chair with my face in my hands.

When I eventually raised my head and scrubbed my eyes with a handkerchief, he was looking at me kindly.

'I'm sorry. Things haven't been easy for you. You're obviously very depressed. I could give you something to help, but it would be better if you saw your own doctor.'

'You mean antidepressants? But how would that solve the problem of Natalie – that won't just go away.'

He sat back and pressed his fingertips together, just as David used to do. It seemed to be the universal gesture of doctors when they were thinking. Finally he asked, 'How does Natalie see the problem? Does she in fact acknowledge that there is one? Is she prepared to be reasonable?'

'You mean has she said she'll stop drinking, give up her friends, stay in in the evening and work? No. Far from it. She brushes it all aside as if there's nothing extraordinary about it at all.'

'And is there no one at all who could speak to her? Someone a bit further removed, whom perhaps she would listen to?'

I pushed the wet handkerchief into my skirt pocket. 'I did wonder about my father. But I didn't really want to worry my parents.'

'I can understand that. But I don't think you have much choice. You need some support here. You must think of yourself for a change.'

I said guiltily, 'I'm afraid that I've been doing too much of that, and that's why Natalie's in this state. And I think she blames me for Matt leaving.'

He gave a dry laugh. 'The perpetual curse of parenthood – guilt. I even felt it when my wife died. As if I could have saved her.'

'But your children didn't go off the rails?'

'No. I was lucky. But they were older, leading their own lives.'

I stood up, conscious suddenly of the time. There would be patients waiting. 'Thank you for listening,' I said.

'Any time. Remember – I know what it's like to be alone.'

I smiled at him gratefully. 'Are you ready for your first appointment?'

He turned to his computer screen. 'Mrs Henderson. Hypochondriac extraordinaire! Yes – wheel her in!'

He gave me a reassuring smile, which suddenly made me feel very much better. I returned to my desk, resolving to ring my father. I would invite us down for the weekend, and ask him to talk to Natalie. Mentally shelving the problem, I took my seat, and over the intercom, called Mrs Henderson in to her appointment.

We arrived at my parents' house in time for lunch on

332

Saturday. My mother was in the garden dead-heading the roses. My father was mowing the lawn. The September sun was mellow and the old brick house glowed; it looked safe and reassuring. Surely, I would find help and succour here.

Mother put down her trug and gave me a dry kiss.

'How are you, dear?' She did not sound overly concerned. Presumably my father had not told her. I had confided in him on the phone, and he had promised to talk to Natalie. I had felt an extraordinary sense of relief, as if matters had been taken out of my hands.

So I kissed my mother back, and told her I was fine. 'How about you?'

'The arthritis isn't so bad. I'm on some new pills.'

'Good.' I gave her a clumsy hug and bent to pick up the trug. 'Have you finished here?'

'All I'm going to do now. Come inside.'

Dad asked Stefan if he would take over the mowing, and the rest of us trooped indoors. I heard Dad invite Natalie to join him in his study, while I stayed in the kitchen to help with the lunch. I felt tense and anxious, all my attention focused on the study, but Mother clearly wanted to talk.

She was tearing lettuce into a bowl while I sliced tomatoes. 'Tell me,' she said, 'do you still miss Matt?'

I was surprised. She was not usually so forthcoming, preferring to let sleeping dogs lie. Since she had asked, I decided to be honest.

'Yes, I'm afraid I do. He was nice to have around. I know you didn't approve of him, but he made me happy.'

'I didn't disapprove of him, only the way he treated you.'

I felt obliged to defend him. 'But he couldn't help himself. Marriage was a silly idea. A mistake. We should have gone on as we were.'

She gave a little snort, turning on the tap to wash the lettuce.

'That wasn't ideal. Not with the children growing up.'

333

I sighed, not knowing what to say. We had been here before; besides, it was all academic now. I wondered what my father was saying to Natalie, and how she was taking it. I hoped it would not make matters worse, that she wouldn't resent his interference. Abstractedly, I assembled the salad in a bowl, and offered to make some dressing. My mother was talking inconsequentially about her bridge partner, who had to go into hospital for some investigative surgery. I listened with half my mind until Stefan came into the kitchen to wash his hands.

'I'm starving,' he said, picking cucumber out of the salad bowl.

I tapped his hand. 'Don't pick,' I admonished him. But I looked at him fondly, full of pride. 'Stefan's taking his driving test next month,' I told my mother, who was counting out knives and forks.

'And then I suppose he'll want a car,' she said, rather sourly. I felt put out. I had expected congratulations.

'Perhaps you can give me one for my eighteenth, Nana?' he said teasingly, but she pursed her lips.

'You youngsters think you can have it all,' she snapped, and went off to lay the table.

I felt peeved and disappointed and Stefan was looking hurt. I put my hand on his shoulder.

'Make allowances,' I said gently, but I didn't know what for.

'Fetch your father, would you?' Mother said when lunch was ready. I went to the study door and tapped tentatively. After a moment, Natalie opened the door. I searched her face anxiously, for tears, for rebellion, for repentance. But her face was expressionless, telling me nothing. I glanced at Dad. He was sitting at his desk, his arms folded, looking quite relaxed. His legs were crossed, his feet encased in shiny brogues. He always had immaculate shoes. He was an immaculate sort of man, and I had confidence in him.

'How did it go?' I asked him when Natalie had left the room.

'Well, she let me have my say. I think she'll see reason, but in her own time. She has her pride, after all.'

'What did you say to her?'

He touched the side of his nose. 'That's between Natalie and me. You asked me to help, and I've done my best. Now just let's see what happens, shall we?'

'That's not easy.'

'Try and trust her,' he said.

He looked kind and wise and I slipped my arm through his as we went through the hall. As he had said, he had done his best. Now I could only wait, and hope.

I watched her anxiously all through September and into October, trying to trust her, not to ask where she went nor who she was with. I wanted to pull down the wall of suspicion and resentment. I wanted us to be friends. She seemed to be working hard, and spent long hours in her room. Sometimes, she played the piano, but she said she didn't want to take any more exams. I was disappointed. I had thought she had real talent but obviously I was mistaken. Ideas of her having a career in music evaporated. When I asked her, tentatively, what she thought she would do, she snapped, 'I've no idea. Just get off my case.'

Another time, when I assiduously forbore to ask her where she'd been, she burst out, 'Aren't you even interested in what I'm doing? You're so self-centred!'

I was deeply hurt, and out of my hurt my voice rose shrill. 'Natalie! I'm just trying to trust you.'

'But you don't, do you?' she flared back.

I took a deep breath. 'You've never actually asked me to. You've never made me any promises. I'm trying to let you have your head, just hoping that you'll see sense.'

Her face closed up and she turned and left the room. I

felt deeply depressed. We seemed to be making no progress whatsoever.

In the middle of October, Stefan took his driving test, and failed.

He had been so confident, and his disappointment cut me to the quick.

'What went wrong?' I exclaimed in disbelief.

'My three-point turn was a disaster. I touched the kerb twice. And I stalled on my hill start. I can't believe how hopeless I was.'

'Well, never mind,' I said bracingly. 'You can take it again.'

He looked at me mournfully, and I was shocked to see tears in his eyes. My great son, actually crying with disappointment. Tears started to my own eyes and I hugged him. 'I'm sorry, love. But these things happen. You can't win them all. Try and put it out of your mind. There are other things to think about. You've got university applications to get off.'

He stepped back and looked at me warily. 'Actually,' he said, and something about his voice made me quail, 'I've been thinking about that, and I think I'm going to put it off for a year. Take some time off after my exams.'

I sat down heavily. It wasn't what I wanted to hear, but I tried to keep my voice even as I asked, 'Is that a good idea?'

He looked at me steadily. 'I think it is. Simon's uncle has got a sheep farm in Australia. We could take off there and work for a while. And I want go up to the Northern Territories to see the Aborigine cave paintings and the rock formations. They're supposed to be fantastic.'

I looked at him, already resigned. 'Is there anything I can say that will stop you?'

He shook his head. 'No, Mum, not really.'

I thought for a while. 'Well, will you do one thing for me? Will you apply and get your place, even if it is deferred for a year? I should like to know that it's all settled.'

He looked doubtful.

'Please, Stefan. I don't ask you for much. Talk it over with your teachers. I'm sure they'll agree.'

He chewed his lip thoughtfully. I knew he wanted to please me, he always did. Finally he said, 'If that's what you want, I'll do it. You've had enough aggro with Nat.'

I smiled gratefully. 'That's not your problem.'

'But I worry about you, Mum. Will you be all right while I'm away?'

I shrugged. 'I shall have to be. I don't want you worrying about me. You've got your own life to lead. But,' I couldn't resist adding, 'you will come back, won't you?'

'Sure thing. I'll be back.' He gave me a crooked, rather embarrassed smile, and went up to his room. Soon, I heard music pounding from behind his closed door. Hip-hop, it was apparently called; a black band called the Fujees. I smiled, but there were tears behind my eyes. I was going to miss that, but I would just have to get used to it.

It was Nurse Betty Marker's fiftieth birthday and we had a little party after evening surgery. The doctors brought the bottles and the rest of us made food. As I was helping myself, I found myself standing next to Dr Millbank.

'How are things going?' he asked. 'Your daughter sorted herself out?'

'Well, there's been no more trouble, if that's what you mean. But we've a long way to go. We still seem to be at loggerheads.'

'Is she still drinking?'

'I've no evidence that she is. But none that she isn't either. But she's getting down to some school work. I went to a parents' evening and her teachers seem quite pleased with her.'

'That's something. If you ever need to talk, remember I'm here.'

'I will.'

Betty came up to me, carrying a plate of food. 'Great idea this, I'm so grateful. I would have been on my own, otherwise.'

'Well, we can't have that.' We sat down on two of the chairs usually reserved for waiting patients and I cleared some magazines and set my glass on a table.

As we ate, Betty said, 'You've been having a bad time recently, haven't you?'

I stopped, my fork halfway to my mouth. 'Can you tell?'

She gave me a warm, intimate smile. 'With you, yes. I can read you like a book.'

I was embarrassed. She went on, 'I think women can see these things where men can't. Are you having trouble at home?'

I hesitated. It was supposed to be a social occasion, but her concern seemed so real that I found myself saying, 'I'm having problems with my daughter. She seems to have got in with bad company.' I couldn't bring myself to tell the whole truth. 'And now my son's decided to up and off to Australia next year. I dread it, I shall miss him so much.'

She put her hand on mine and I found myself looking at it with surprise. It was warm, and unexpectedly strong. Then I looked into her soft, motherly face. It was the sort of face that made one want to unburden oneself.

'And I miss Matt,' I told her in a rush. I had told everyone the decision to cancel the wedding had been mutual, but that needn't stop me missing him. 'And he's found someone else. That's taken a bit of getting used to.'

She raised her plump shoulders. 'Well, what can you expect, with men? I've never bothered with them, myself.'

I looked at her speculatively, wondering. I knew she lived alone, had never married. Her hand was still on mine, and I found myself pulling away, standing up with my empty plate, saying I was going to get some pudding. Helping myself to cheesecake, I found her beside me.

'Come back with me after the party?' she suggested. 'We'll open a bottle. It will be an anticlimax, to go back on my own.'

I hesitated. I didn't really want to, but I knew all about loneliness.

'Okay. Just for a while.'

And then someone called for us to raise our glasses in a toast and we all said, 'To Betty,' and her broad face creased with pleasure, and soon after that, the party was over.

Betty lived in a small flat behind Putney High Street. We walked there through cold November streets, with frost in the air and the sky bright with stars. To my surprise, she put her arm through mine as we walked. I had not thought we were such friends, but put it down to the wine. I had had quite a lot myself, and I felt mellow and relaxed and ever so slightly woozy. I told myself that I would just have one more glass with her, then go home.

But once inside, it was so warm and cosy that I suddenly didn't want to leave too soon. She settled me on a soft pink sofa beside a coal-effect gas fire, and unscrewed a bottle of whisky which she put on a low table with two glasses.

'This is nice,' she said. She turned bright eyes on me. 'I've often wanted to ask you here actually.'

I was surprised. 'Well, why didn't you?'

She looked at me consideringly, then turned and poured the whisky.

'Because I wasn't sure how you'd take it,' she said, handing me a glass.

There was something disturbing about her look. I took an anxious sip from my glass. I am not a whisky drinker, and I shuddered.

'Why not?' I asked her.

'Oh well, you had Matt.'

'Matt's been gone for ages.'

She said nothing, staring into the fire.

'Are you lonely?' I asked her. 'And did you think I might be lonely too?'

She turned round. Her cheeks were flushed and she said, quickly, 'I rather thought you were. And I knew you were unhappy. I thought maybe I could help.'

I didn't know what to say. I took another sip of my drink, then another. The whisky was beginning to go down well. My head felt swimmy and my face was hot. There was something very persuasive about her warm sympathy, her soft motherly figure sitting next to me in the hot little room. I wanted to fall into her arms and cry and cry. I wanted her to say, 'There, there, it will be all right, you're not alone.' Weakly, I closed my eyes, feeling the smart of tears.

Then I felt her hand take my glass gently, and her arm go round my shoulders.

'There, there,' she said, unbelievably. 'You don't need Matt. Or any man. I'm here.'

A warning struggled through my fuddled brain, but she was holding me firmly now and I couldn't get away. What's more, I didn't want to, I wanted to sink into her soft warm flesh and forget everything. Then I heard her murmur, 'You're lovely. I've always thought so.'

And her hand cupped my breast.

I felt a curious melting. Things which had seemed unthinkable now seemed possible, even desirable. With a sense of fatality, I let her kiss me on the lips.

I lay in my bed, feeling sick with shock and disgust. Also, my head ached. I had a hangover. But that was nothing to the shame I felt at what I had let Betty do. More appalling still, I had actually enjoyed it.

I rolled over, shuddering at the thought of her searching hands. In the cold light of day, my feeble surrender, my ultimate complicity, seemed both shocking and unreal. Was I really so lonely, so desperate, so pathetically without resource? And what's more, she had seemed to think that I felt the same as she. Her face had been glowing as she kissed me goodbye. 'I'm very happy,' she had said. 'I hope you are too.' I had stared at her in confusion, then run home through the cold streets as if all the hounds of hell were after me. By the time I reached the house, I was stone-cold sober. I flung myself into a hot bath and scrubbed myself clean. Then I had rolled into bed, and hadn't slept till dawn.

I sat up, putting my hand to my thumping head. The day had to be faced; and the day included Betty. As I stood, nausea rose in my throat and I had to run to the bathroom. I stared at myself in the mirror, weak and trembling. I looked haggard. And Betty had called me lovely. How on earth was I going to extricate myself from this one?

I arrived at the surgery full of dread, hoping in vain to avoid her. Then, suddenly, she was by my desk, her face pathetically eager.

I avoided her eyes. 'Good morning,' I said formally, sitting down.

She glanced round. There was nobody about.

She touched my shoulder. 'Morning, dear. Sleep well?'

She gave me a knowing smile and I felt a coil of embarrassment.

'Not very.' I spoke tersely, shifting under her hand.

'Nor me. Too excited.'

I spun round on my seat. 'Listen, Betty,' I said, but just then the telephone rang, and one of the doctors appeared. When I looked up, she had gone.

Later, she caught me in the kitchen. Quickly, while we were alone, I said, clumsily, 'I'm sorry, Betty, but last night was all a mistake. I hope we can forget all about it.'

She banged the kettle down with a thump. Her eyes when I dared to look were shocked and hurt.

'But I thought . . . well, you know, you seemed to enjoy it.'

I gripped my mug. 'I was drunk. And depressed. I didn't know what I was doing. I'm not like that. You know I'm not. Please – can we forget it? I didn't mean to hurt you.'

'Well, you have.' Her fleshy face seemed to collapse. 'I'd waited so long for you, I thought everything was coming right.'

I looked at her with pity, and incredulity at what she was saying. All this time, and I had never guessed. It sent a cold shiver through me. Gently, I said, 'Well I'm afraid it's not. I'm deeply ashamed at what I did. I never in my wildest dreams . . .' I couldn't go on, I had hurt her enough. I reached out and touched her hand.

She snatched it away. 'Don't.'

There didn't seem to be anything more to say. I wanted to be away, to forget, to pretend it had never happened. But now she reached out her hand. It was broad and capable. I recoiled at the thought of it touching me, I shrank back as she reached out for me, holding my coffee mug between us like a barrier. She withdrew, and turned away.

'Well, it's your loss,' she said, and her voice was bitter.

The following evening the phone rang and Natalie answered it.

'Somebody called Betty,' she said, handing me the receiver.

My heart sank. Natalie had slumped back down in front of the television. I turned my back on her, hunching the receiver.

'Hello. Can you talk?'

'Not really.'

'Was that your daughter?'

'Yes.' Resentment at her intrusion flared above my caution. 'I don't know what you want, but I'm sure I made myself clear yesterday. It was all a mistake. I don't want to be unkind, but if you care for me at all, you'll leave it at that.' I was almost whispering; even if she couldn't hear, Natalie would surely wonder. I spoke more firmly. 'We'll just leave it at that, shall we?' I repeated.

Her voice was tremulous. 'I just thought if we could talk it over . . .'

'No. There's nothing more to discuss.' She said nothing.

'Goodbye,' I said firmly. I replaced the receiver. My hands were trembling.

'What on earth was all that about?' asked Natalie, without taking her eyes from the screen.

'Oh, there's just been some trouble at work. People are taking sides. It will blow over.'

I didn't like lying. But how could I ever tell her the truth?

I wondered how I would cope at work, and felt angry at both Betty and myself for creating an impossible situation. But to my relief, she ignored me, which made it easy, though uncomfortable, for me to ignore her. But then, a week later, a bunch of flowers arrived at the house. The card said, 'Love from Betty. Can we try again?'

I was shaken, my pity for her subsumed in anger. I looked up her number and rang at once, before I had time to think.

When she answered, I said without preamble, 'No, Betty, we can't. Please understand that I'm not interested. I appreciate your caring, but there's nothing you can do for me. This has got to stop.'

There was a long silence, then a small voice said, 'Very well. I'm sorry to have bothered you.' The phone clicked down. With a sense of relief, I felt that I wouldn't be hearing from her again.

I threw the flowers into the dustbin, and tore the card into a thousand pieces.

Soon after that, Betty gave in her notice. I felt an irrational compunction that it was my fault, but there was nothing I could do. Her replacement was a perky brunette with a boyfriend in the army, whom the patients adored.

And I would not disguise my relief. I had got off very lightly, though I felt I didn't deserve it.

SEVENTEEN

That was over six months ago. It is now July, hot and dry. There are hosepipe bans all over the country, but not in London. I can never understand how in London, the water just keeps on flowing. Not that I do much watering. Since Matt left, the garden has fallen back into neglect. There are perennials blooming among the weeds, and Stefan cuts the grass, but that is all.

And Stefan is preparing to go away. He has taken his A levels, and, subject to his grades, he has a place next year at York University to read geology. Now he has his air ticket, paid for with his earnings from the supermarket. He and Simon fly to Perth on the first of August. I am bracing myself for the pain. It already hurts, seeing the new purple backpack sitting in his room, the possessions disappearing into it. I am missing him already.

But he is leaving me a consolation prize. He has a girlfriend, a lively blonde with fluffy hair called Leonie. She is American and her parents have gone back to Minneapolis. She is starting at Camberwell Art School in September, and she is going to live with me. Together, we will wait for Stefan to come home.

Natalie has a boyfriend too. A dark serious boy called Rupert, who plays the flute in the school orchestra. He works hard, so Natalie works too. When they are not working, they go to concerts and recitals, or make their own music together, on the piano and the flute. She doesn't see Helen any more. And we are friends again.

Two months ago, she came with me when I had my ears

345

pierced. It was her idea. She has such fun with her earrings, she persuaded me I would enjoy it too.

So, giggling like children, we held hands while my ears were punched and the tiny studs inserted. Then we went to choose some long silver droplets, which I put away until such time as I could use them.

I wore them for the first time today. I have had my hair cut short and crisp to show them off. I swung my head as I walked into the surgery, feeling them brush my neck. I felt wonderful. I felt like a new person – positive, optimistic even. But I am still Julia.

Still alone.

P.S. Henry Millbank has just telephoned and invited me out. I said I'd think about it. But I think I shall probably go.